The Pegasus Passion

To Kara,

el hope you enjoy
reading my labor
of love. You're such
a great queen.

Loves to You

Victoria James

The Pegasus Passion

The Soul Keepers

Victoria James

authorHOUSE®

AuthorHouse™
1663 Liberty Drive
Bloomington, IN 47403
www.authorhouse.com
Phone: 1-800-839-8640

First published by AuthorHouse   09/17/2011

ISBN: 978-1-4634-3953-8 (sc)

Library of Congress Control Number: 2011913001

Printed in the United States of America

This Book is Dedicated to My Children:

Shalis LeAnn, Gary Leigh, Tarin Barbara, and Collin John

And to My Mother and Father:

Rayola and Gary (in Memoriam) Webb

A Special Thanks to All My "Maven" Friends.

April, 1666

Jillian walked slowly along the shore, her feet sinking slightly into the white sand, leaving delicate prints to be swept away by the next rush of foaming water. The ocean swirled about her bare feet, cooling them with its soft kiss, as a lazy warm breeze drifted from the south and played with the loose strands of her thick golden braid.

She stopped her stroll to gaze at the ocean's blue swells, trimmed with silver laces, as they rolled onto the shore. The swells spread like a blanket of jewels, glistening brilliantly, and then disappearing into the depths of the sand, only to be replaced by yet another dazzling display. Jillian tucked her billowing skirt into the band of her waist so her dress would not be completely wet by the gentle waters.

Overhead, gulls floated upon an invisible cushion. Gracefully, the small flock shifted in unison as their calls echoed above the roar of the ocean. In the distance a horse neighed, calling to someone unknown. Jillian's mind drifted.

She worked her way toward the cliffs that shot skyward out of the beach, creating a barrier between her life and the rest of the world. Life's adventures called to her often and Jillian dreamt of the day she would be old enough to seek them out. She felt as if that day would truly never come, and that she would most likely spend the rest of her days stuck here, trapped by the massive walls.

Shaking herself from her dreams, Jillian again focused on her immediate task. Even though she had been warned by her mother not to stray from home, today was her little sister's birthday and she needed a special gift to mark the occasion. Siriann had been terribly upset that Father had to leave so abruptly last night and Jillian wanted to make her birthday especially nice. She hoped to cheer her up, which could prove to be a difficult task, because her sister often possessed a most horrible disposition.

Jillian made her way along the cliff base as she searched the white sand for its treasures. She had come here many times before to find beautiful shells. She was looking for just the right sizes and colors to match the lovely pink gown that Father had brought back from London for Siriann. The pink gown brought out the rosy color of Siriann's cheeks and the sparking blue of her eyes. She looked so grown up in it. Jillian thought her quite a beautiful sight indeed. A chill ran through Jillian remembering how happy Siriann had been with her dress, and how awful she herself had felt realizing that, once again, Father brought nothing back for her. Jillian continued her search, knowing that none of her disappointment was her little sister's fault. That's just the way Father was.

The particular shells she looked for were not hard to find. She saw them often around the base of the cliffs. Jillian came here when she was troubled and sat upon the largest of the rocks that found its resting place at the bottom of the cliff. She dreamt that the rock came to rest there after a horrible giant pushed it off the cliff edge, hoping to squash an unaware victim. Such was the way of Jillian's active imagination—always danger and intrigue, always a damsel in distress waiting to be rescued by a handsome savior.

This enormous rock was Jillian's safe place. She often sat on her perch high above the beach and watched the ocean, searching the horizon for just a glimpse of a sail from a vessel at sea. She longed to be on those ships, longed to be anywhere but here. Jillian sometimes sat for hours, thinking about how different life was now compared to when she was a small child. She missed her grandfather's estate, and she especially missed Sophie.

Sophie was nurse to her mother when she was a child, and years later she was Jillian's nurse as well. Her mother, Sybil, lived with her father on his estate at the time of Jillian's birth. Sophie had immediately assumed the welcomed task of nursing the newborn babe, forming a bond between them that knew no bounds. Jillian had grown and prospered on the estate as she captivated the entire staff.

Lord, how she missed Sophie. Jillian's heart ached for her, but through the years she came to realize that Sophie was always with her, especially when she came to the rock. She felt Sophie near her, soothing her, telling her everything would be all right. Visits to the safe rock gave Jillian a sense of peace, something she rarely felt since leaving the estate.

Jillian wasn't sure why she was so unhappy, but she knew her father caused her much distress. He was so critical of her and so uncaring. He favored Siriann. Even though her mother tried to make up for his lack of compassion, Jillian knew that for reasons unknown to her, her father never showed her his love. She gave up hope long ago of ever being close to him. His continued dislike of everything she did made it virtually impossible for her to feel any closeness.

She approached the huge stone, and for an instant she thought of climbing onto it to rest and daydream, but instead she turned toward the brush that skirted from beneath it, making her way around, winding between briar bush and the sharp stones that lay upon the beach. Jillian spotted a small opal shell just the right color and shape for Siriann's special gift. She kept her eye on the shell as she headed for the jewel, paying little attention to anything else.

Out of the corner of her eye, Jillian caught a glimpse of something. Movement. Color. As she turned her head to look, she felt her legs catch the underbrush. Falling suddenly, her legs buckled beneath her, entangled in an unknown web. Jillian laughed to herself for being so careless. She knew better than to stop paying attention to the path, because vines and shrubbery grew from between the rocks. Her legs must have caught in some new growth along the path.

Hitting the ground had knocked the wind out of her. She lay motionless, with her eyes closed for a moment, gathering her senses. Suddenly, Jillian felt that something was very wrong. She felt a presence around her and knew that she was not alone. Cautiously, she lifted her head to search for the source of danger that she now felt. Her skin prickled with anticipation as she slowly opened her eyes.

The sight of a black boot, not six inches from her face, instantly blocked her view. A finely etched winged horse was carved in the boot. Jillian's heart pounded wildly. She slowly raised her eyes, wanting to see who was responsible for her fall, and responsible for the fear she now felt.

Before she could see her attacker, Jillian felt blinding pain in the back of her head. Her mind spun wildly with images and sounds of things foreign to her as she struggled to gain some sense of understanding. She heard loud, angry voices above her and felt the touch of someone gently brushing golden strands from her face. She felt the heat of the sun upon her and heard the call of the gulls, as if bidding her farewell. Then she was lifted gently into someone's strong arms. The combined smells of the ocean and leather soothed her nostrils. Jillian knew that she was being lifted onto a horse with her body cradled against a stranger's. Her last

3

thoughts were of the ocean, the beach, her safe rock and the strong arms which held her firmly, yet so very gently against his body.

The sound of someone moaning in the distance stirred Jillian from the black depths of sleep. The pain-filled moan grew closer and louder until it thundered within her head, pounding against her skull. Jillian fought to come back from the shadows, fought for control of her spinning mind. But, then there was darkness.

Sometime later, Jillian woke, her head still pounding out an unbearable rhythm. It took great effort to raise her hand to feel the back of her head from where the pounding came. Each and every small movement caused her great pain. The thick braid that Mother had put in her hair lay flat against her head, matted by a thick sticky mass. Under its protection, Jillian could feel a large goose egg. She silently thanked God that Mother had insisted upon the braid, for surely it had saved her from having her skull crushed.

Her head danced with motion, a gentle sway rocking her. It took her a few moments to realize that the motion was not just the spinning of her head, but the whole room moving. Jillian focused on a small round window at the other side of the room and slowly lifted herself up, trying to steady herself enough to walk toward the opening. She only managed a few steps before she collapsed to the floor. Her head pounded, spinning with pain. Resting for a few minutes, Jillian again mustered all the strength she could to crawl the rest of the way to the window. She pulled herself up over gunnysacks that were stacked against the wall beneath the window and peered out of the tiny opening.

She froze, the scene outside the window instantly terrifying her. Jillian gasped as she realized where she was. The vast ocean surrounded her with its blue depths. On the horizon a tiny sliver of land was barely visible. She watched as it dipped beneath the surface, growing thinner and thinner with each wave. Finally, with one last surge of the ship, it disappeared from sight.

Desperation consumed her as she panicked at the thought of her plight. She sobbed against the glass of the porthole and wished that she could somehow climb through it and swim back to the beach, back to her safe place. Her thoughts overtook her with a nauseating wave, and Jillian doubled over, fighting to overpower the sickness rising in her throat.

"You must get your wits about you," she commanded herself. "Dear God, what am I to do?" Her voice sounded so foreign, as if someone else was speaking.

Jillian heard footsteps above her, and fell silent, her heart pounding in her ears. Sitting firmly on top of the gunnies, her back pressed against the rough surface of the wall beneath the porthole, she looked around the room for some sort of weapon to use for protection.

The room was stacked with sacks and crates, filled she imagined, with supplies. Across the room she could see that there was a large door. She quickly noticed that the door had no handle. How strange that there was no way out for her or any other captive brought to this room. The thought made her shiver.

Jillian's mind turned to her mother, who just that morning, had warned her to stay away from the beach. She often ignored what her mother told her, as did most of the girls her age. Surely, Mother would be looking for her by now, Jillian thought. Someone had to know that she was gone. Perhaps Father was already out searching for her with all the villagers. The thought gave her little comfort. Yes, they would all be looking, wouldn't they?

But then, maybe they assumed that she had simply run away and wouldn't search for her at all. No, that wouldn't happen, Mother knew better. She wasn't the kind of daughter to just take off, and even when she was gone for a long stretch, Mother always knew just where she would be, at her safe rock. Sometimes Mother would climb right up there with Jillian to sit and watch the horizon with her. Mother's expression was vague much of the time as she stared out at the ocean. Jillian often wondered what was in her thoughts as she sat, never saying a word. Then a tear would spill from her mother's eye, and she would say it was time to return home.

Reaching into her skirt pocket, Jillian pulled out an emerald pouch made from velvet cloth and dumped its contents into her trembling hand. A wonderful pendant was among the various shells she had gathered only this morning. She held it up to the porthole to let the sunlight shine upon its surface. Smiling to herself, she clutched the pendant to her heart feeling that somehow all would be well.

Jillian's eyes drifted once again to the view beyond the porthole. Now low in the sky, the sun rode the horizon, giving the room a crimson glow that chilled Jillian to the core. Her nails dug deeply into the fibers of the gunnies as she grasped them tightly in frustration.

The ship gently swayed, back and forth with calming rhythm, and Jillian felt a sense of peace as she watched the sun follow the land and dip beneath the horizon. She was so entranced with the scene that she didn't see the door open slowly behind her.

Careful to not spill its contents, a gentle hand slipped a tray onto the floor inside the door. Slowly, a little man backed out of the room, never taking his eye off the young woman upon the gunnies, and making no sound as the huge wooden door slowly closed.

Hearing the click of the lock behind her, Jillian turned too late to see the intruder. She bolted toward the door, hearing the latch lock firmly in place just before she reached it. Her head spun, and she fell against the door. Her body hit it with such force that she cried out in pain and frustration.

Slumping to the floor, Jillian cried against the wooden roughness. "Please, whoever you are, please let me go." There was no reply. "My grandfather will reward you, I know he will. He loves me dearly and would pay much for my return." Jillian listened again for a response but there was only silence.

Anger swelled within her, realizing that someone beyond the door listened, but did not answer her plea. The thought of this enraged her. Did this person have no heart? She pounded her fists against the door, beating at it violently and spewing every foul curse that she had ever heard at the person beyond. She pounded and pounded until the pain in her hands was more than she could bear.

With the sun setting, the room grew dim before Jillian came to her senses, remembering the tray that had been placed inside the confines of the room. She focused on it, surveying its contents. The tray held a plate of food, and the aroma from it was intoxicating. Jillian wasn't sure what kind of food it was, but her stomach growled in anticipation. Beside the plate was a goblet filled with warm liquid. Jillian lifted it to her parched lips. It was tea, like no tea she had ever tasted. It was deliciously sweet. She remembered that Mother used to make tea like this when she wasn't feeling well. Surely it couldn't hurt to eat and drink just a little. After all, she needed strength for the days to come. Jillian didn't intend to be a passive captive.

The food was much needed and delicious. Flavor exploded in Jillian's mouth with every spoonful. She thought that she had never eaten anything so delectable. It didn't take her long to finish every last morsel on the plate.

The room was completely dark now, making it hard to see if there was anything left, so she felt its surface and was sadly disappointed when she found nothing there. She raised the goblet and emptied the last of the tea into her mouth, then wiped her lips with the back of her hand.

"Ouch!" she exclaimed, at the stinging of her knuckles. "Serves you right, you silly twit. Beat your hands to a pulp, for it did no good at all."

But the pain in her hands didn't seem to mean much at the moment. The pain in her heart was greater than any pain she could ever imagine. Jillian grew weary as she thought of her troubles. Her head spun, and her mind swayed with the rocking of the ship. Drifting into a peaceful sleep, she slowly crumpled against the gunnies, letting the goblet fall to the floor with a soft clang.

The door opened cautiously and the little man, accompanied by two others much larger than he, crept silently into the supply room. The little man had long black hair braided all the way down his back. The braid swung over his shoulder as he bent to peer at Jillian. She opened her eyes, seeing that his were tiny slits sitting upon chubby cheeks. He smiled down at her as the others gathered near.

"She be fine, Cappy. She be good after sleep."

"You had better be right, Ki," growled Terrance, a huge Viking Captain.

The first mate, Gavin, entered the storage room, warily holding the lantern high to light his way. Before him on the cold wooden floor lay the most beautiful woman he had ever seen. Her scent still lingered on his shirt from when he had carried her aboard. He felt the warmth that her body, so close to his, had left on his soul. Her fine features were those of an angel. Her hair spun the color of honey within the long thick braid that hung the length of her gentle curves. She was a vision indeed. He repeated her name in his mind, memorizing its song.

"She be fine, Cappy," Sue Ki, the ship's cook, reassured the Captain again. "She sleep for long time maybe, but be good as new when wake."

"She had better be Ki, or you might just walk the plank," Terrance said without taking his eyes off the sleeping girl. He knelt beside her, and with his massive hands smoothed the hair away from Jillian's peaceful face.

"Oh, but she is a vision of loveliness. She will add a bit of excitement to the Pegasus, don't you think, Gavin?" Terrance waited for the reply, but Gavin was deep in his own thoughts.

"Gavin?" Terrance said, nudging his shoulder.

"Sorry, Sir," Gavin whispered quietly. "But indeed, she is a beautiful woman who cannot be trusted with the likes of us."

Jillian's thoughts were confusing to her. She heard voices above her but did not understand what they were saying. Her mind drifted in and out of the darkness with the swaying of the ship. She tried to understand what was happening to her. She felt the gentle touch once again upon her brow, lending a sense of peace that seeped into her soul.

A slight smile curving the corners of her lips, Jillian sighed to herself, as she closed her eyes to the men above. The three statues encircling the child looked at each other in surprise for she grew even more beautiful with this smile on her face.

"Well, I wonder what that was about?" Captain Terrance asked no one in particular. "We best be getting the lass to her bed. She's been frightened long enough in this old storage room, don't you think, Gavin?"

Gavin cringed with guilt at the Captain's words. He had carried her on board the ship but, in the Captain's great haste to leave, wasn't given orders on where to take the girl. Because she had been kidnapped, Gavin imagined that she would be held for ransom, so he put her where they normally put captives, but was chastised by the Captain when he found out.

"It's time we be getting the wee one to bed. She'll need much rest for her days ahead."

"That's for sure, Cappy. She needs much rest."

Sue Ki motioned to Gavin, giving him the silent order to bring the girl. Gavin was quick to oblige, not minding at all having her once again against his body. His blood quickened as he gently lifted her into his strong arms. The very touch of Jillian against his chest made Gavin ache for the promise of her.

He held her firmly in his arms as they made their way down the narrow corridor. Gavin stopped in front of the door that was used for guests of the Captain's, most of whom were women of a certain nature, but Ki pushed him on to the next cabin, which belonged to Captain Terrance. Gavin's heart sank with the blow of knowing that this woman was to be the Captain's woman and no one else's.

Terrance folded back the coverlet from the feather bed and motioned for Gavin to lay Jillian within its softness. Reluctantly, he released her from his arms slowly letting her body slip from his grasp. Jillian sighed with contentment as she settled into the folds of the silken surface.

"I bring wata and bandage for her hands, Cappy," Sue Ki said as he left the cabin.

Terrance took her fragile hands in his. "She's a fighter. That she is. She took all the skin off her hands fighting for her freedom. An amazing girl. Yes, quite amazing."

Terrance crooned over Jillian as Sue Ki bathed the broken skin and firmly wrapped her hands in the clean white cloths. He knew from experience that she felt no pain from her wounds, for Ki had given her his special potion that brings sleep. One thing that was so special about it was that you knew what was going on around you, but you felt no pain while under its spell. Gavin was given the potion many times when Ki would have to stitch him up after a battle.

"I'll stay with her. You two may go and see about your business," Terrance ordered.

Terrance never took his eyes off Jillian's sweet face. She was here, and she was his, which was all he could think of at this moment. For this time, Jillian belonged to no one other than Terrance McCarthy.

Gavin slowly closed the door as he left the Captain's cabin. His last glimpse of Jillian brought an unexpected shudder. He saw her there, Terrance at her side, cooing his love to her no doubt. It made him chill with the thought of the Captain in her bed. Gavin was confused by his reaction to Jillian. She was beautiful and he'd wanted her from the beginning and felt strongly that she should not be the Captain's.

Captain Terrance had been so mysterious about coming to drop anchor at a simple fishing port the Pegasus had never visited before. He had acquired horses for the men, along with two extras, to ride to a tiny village not far down the shore. His actions completely baffled Gavin but stunned him even more when Terrance inquired about the whereabouts of the House of William, someone Terrance apparently knew.

When they arrived at the cottage, a young girl played in the yard but ran inside as they approached. Terrance dismounted and rapped loudly on the cottage door until finally the door opened.

The lady of the house nearly fainted as she seemed to recognize Terrance, and he caught her to him as he entered, shutting the door behind him. Nervously, the men glanced at each other, afraid to question the Captain about their purpose. A moment later the girl child emerged, looking back thoughtfully at the cottage door as it slammed behind her.

Gavin tethered his mount at the gate and gently approached the child, asking her name. She told him her name was Siriann and that today was her birthday. She was ten years old and smart as a whip.

She told Gavin of her older sister who, at this moment, was gathering shells from beneath the cliff in order to make her a wonderful gift. Siriann pointed toward the white cliffs. Gavin could see the cliffs that shot up from the beach like a great wall of magnificent marble.

"It's supposed to be a secret," she told him as she put her small finger to her lips. "Mother told her not to go today, so Jillian and I took an oath of silence." She smiled brightly up at Gavin. He smiled back to reassure her of his silence.

"She really is quite a good seamstress, you know."

"And of whom might you be speaking?" Gavin knew of course, but the little nymph was so cute that he wanted to keep her talking until Terrance finished with her mother. He didn't want the babe scared out of her wits by the band of strangers at her gate.

"Why Jillian, silly. Jillian is the finest seamstress in the entire village."

"I'll wager she is," Gavin said as the door of the cottage opened abruptly.

Terrance's face was as pale as the cliffs when he emerged from the cottage with the woman clinging to his sleeve.

"Please, Terrance! You must understand. I cannot! I have more now to consider," she said, glancing sadly toward Siriann, with tears welling in her eyes.

Terrance shouted at the woman, "If I can't have you both, then I will certainly have her!" He turned to his men frantically. "Mount up boys, and search the area."

"But Captain, what are we looking for?" one of the men shouted.

"Jillian, my sweet Jillian." Terrance sighed.

The woman screamed woefully, "No, no, Terrance! You cannot! She is but a child!"

Mounting his steed, Terrance whirled his horse to face her. "She will be safe with me, Sybil. You can rest assured." Terrance gave the command to leave and the men followed him, riding swiftly away from the cottage.

Not understanding any of this, Gavin glanced back at the woman as she fell to her knees in the yard, begging Terrance to stop. The child, Siriann, was at her mother's side, frantically trying to soothe her.

He kicked his horse into a faster pace in order to catch up to Terrance's mount. "Who are we searching for, Sir?" Gavin timidly asked, hoping not to anger him.

"Jillian. I am searching for Jillian."

Terrance suddenly realized that he had no idea where to search. He slowed his mount, and a puzzled look crossed his face. How could he be so dense? He didn't even know what she looked like, and yet here he was, frantic to find the poor girl. Of course, Terrance was sure he would recognize her the moment he laid eyes on her. He had to.

"Jillian is there," Gavin pointed toward the cliffs. "She's searching for shells along the cliff."

"How do you know this?" Anxiety sounded in Terrance's frantic voice.

"Back at the cottage, the girl, Siriann, told me of her sister Jillian. She's at the beach near the cliff at this very moment."

With Terrance in the lead, the horses thundered toward the cliffs at breakneck speed.

Laying low with anticipation, Gavin watched Jillian as she approached the base of the cliff where the men waited. With a keen eye, every movement of her body remained vivid in his mind. She carried herself proudly, with her head held high, as she wound her way between the briars. Her skirt was tucked into her waistband, exposing long slender legs. Golden tresses were pulled back into a thick braid that fell over her shoulder. The wind loosened thin strands of gold which curled around her face, causing her features to be goddess-like, surrounded by this halo.

Captain Terrance told the men of his plan to capture the young girl, and they all held fast in their appointed positions, ready to pounce on her if she were not willing to come on her own. Gavin and the men were puzzled but excited by his actions. They trusted Terrance, for he would never lead them to disaster. This was one of those times when no questions were asked.

His heart beat wildly within his chest as the moment came for Gavin to strike. He reached out, quickly clutching both her slim ankles with his hands. She fell gracefully but landed upon the sand rather hard, knocking the breath out of her. Instantly, Gavin felt guilty for what he had done, but felt more so after Jason's deed.

Without warning, Jason, a cruel smile upon his lips, clubbed the poor girl on the back of her head with a piece of driftwood. At that moment, Gavin thought the Captain would surely kill Jason. He only remembered seeing Terrance that angry one time before. The look in Terrance's eyes terrified Gavin as he watched his fist land squarely on Jason's jaw. Captain Terrance threw his fist with all his might and propelled Jason's body through the air ten feet before he came to rest, prone on the sand.

Turning Jillian carefully over onto her back, Gavin laid her head gently on his lap. He smoothed the golden curls away from her features and studied every curve, every line of her beautiful face. Her breath was slow and even. Gavin said a silent prayer thanking God for her survival.

Once assured of her well-being, Terrance gave Gavin the order to carry her to the awaiting horses. Gavin did all of Terrance's lifting for him because his back was stiff from the scarring that never seemed to heal completely. Some of the men helped Jason to his feet and the band made the climb up the steep hillside to where the horses were tethered. They made good time, Gavin's burden being light in his strong arms. He would gladly carry her to the ends of the earth and back if it meant that he could hold her for a little while longer.

Jillian moaned once, and Gavin caught his breath with the thought of her awakening in his arms. He held her close to him the entire time, even in the long boat, hoping never have to let her go.

Once on board the Pegasus, the alarm sounded to get the ship under way immediately. Gavin placed Jillian in the storage room because he knew she could not escape from there. He knew that she would be safe from anyone who might decide to harm her because only Ki and the Captain had a key to the room.

Returning to present thoughts, Gavin sat high above the deck of the Pegasus, scanning the ocean in the moonlight. All seemed well on the ship after the events of the day. Micah's fiddle played a ballad, the tune drifting in the night mist upon the sea. Peacefully, the ship rode the ocean's waves, their sound against the hull bringing solace to his weary mind.

Gavin volunteered to keep watch that night because he wanted to have some time to himself. He had to come to terms with the reality that Jillian was the Captain's woman. He had naught to say about it and thoughts of her haunted his mind with wild fantasies, that somehow, someway, he could make Jillian his own. He longed for Jillian to be his woman, not the Captain's. Deep in Gavin's soul, he felt that Jillian was meant to be his. Anger seeped into his thoughts, anger for his Captain, his friend.

Below deck, in the Captain's cabin, Terrance stood watch over the sleeping child, her angelic face serenely peaceful, cradled in the billowing pillows. He studied her delicately bandaged hands as he held them between his massive claws. She possessed hands of character and strength, hands not unlike those of his mother's and her mother before her. Their memory brought a smile to his unshaven face.

He rubbed the roughness of his chin and then stroked his hand through the mass of unruly red curls that grew wildly around his face. He looked a mess he knew, and mentally he made note to himself that on the morrow he would start life again. It was time to clean up and start to live once more, if not for himself, for her, the one he had longed for for so long.

The sun rose in the east, bringing light to the vast ocean. Having been relieved of his duty, Gavin went below deck after an exhausting night and made his way to the galley for some nourishment. He could hear the crew gathered in the galley for the breaking of the fast. They fell silent when Gavin entered.

Ladling some porridge into his small wooden bowl, Gavin then poured a goblet of tea from the pot that Sue Ki kept filled on the cook stove. Gavin took his place at the long wooden table and began to eat his meal, silence still prevailing.

Micah was the brave one who finally broke the silence. He leaned across the table to Gavin, speaking quietly, cautious not to rouse his anger.

"The men, Sir, are very worried about the Captain, or might I say . . . the Captain's woman." Micah proceeded slowly, eyeing Gavin, who did not lift his eyes.

"They are superstitious fools, scared of the wind they are. Aye. Scared of their own shadow most of the time." He laughed half heartily and then grew quite serious, "Sir, they say it is bad luck for a woman to be on board a pirate ship. They say that she will bring us naught but trouble and pain."

Gavin looked him square in the eye, still not saying a word. Micah could not read his look and took a chance in continuing, for indeed his own feelings were not the same as the men's. He felt no threat from the fragile girl.

"You must beg the Captain to rid the Pegasus of this woman before it is too late, before we fall prey to peril. She bewitched the Captain. He acts not like a man, but like a mouse in her spell."

It was more than Gavin could tolerate. The crazy insults of the men infuriated him. Over the table, he flew at Micah, spilling his meal beneath him. Before Micah could defend himself, Gavin had his throat between his hands, squeezing the life from him. The crewmen pried at Gavin's hands, begging him to cease his attack.

"What goes on here?" Terrance shouted above the pleas of the men. "Release him! Gavin, have you lost your wits?"

The room was still. Gavin gained his senses as he peered into Micah's eyes, now bulging from their sockets, his throat still in his strong grasp.

"Just having a bit of a jest, Captain. No harm done, aye Micah?" Gavin released Micah's throat and slapped him merrily on the back.

"Right, no harm," Micah choked the words forth, and quickly left the galley coughing, with most of the crew in tow.

Terrance poured himself a mug of tea and came to sit next to Gavin at the long table.

"What say you, Gavin? Were you to kill poor Micah or just see how far his eyes would bulge?"

"They think she's a bad omen, Captain. They think she's cast a spell over you and that you have become daft under it." Gavin kept his eyes lowered and did not look at Terrance.

"And what is it that you think, Gavin? Have I lost my mind to her witch's spell?" Terrance waited for the reply, sipping the strong tea, his lips curved in a smile against the mug.

Gavin thought carefully before he spoke. He didn't want the Captain's fury but he had to say something, anything, to get the Captain to make some sense of all this.

"I believe that she must hold you somehow within her spell. Why else would you go beyond reason to bring her aboard the Pegasus? Why would you be so secretive with your plans in bringing her here? Why else would you be so angry with Jason and almost knock his head off his shoulders?" Gavin waited for Terrance to answer his questions, waited for him to make things clear.

"There is much that you do not know Gavin. Much, which I cannot tell you now." Terrance was cut off by Sue Ki yelling down the corridor.

"She wake, Cappy. She wake! Come, come!" He beckoned the Captain to come back to the cabin.

Terrance and Gavin came quickly down the corridor, stopping at the cabin door. Sue Ki motioned for them to be quiet so they would not frighten the poor girl.

"I get wata, Cappy. She need drink now." With that Sue Ki left them to return to the galley.

They entered the room slowly, Terrance going first, as was his right. He walked over to the side of the bed and sat beside Jillian. Her eyes were still closed but she stirred with the movement of him beside her. Trying desperately to open her eyes, Jillian struggled to awaken fully. She sensed the presence of the two and fought for a glimpse of her captors. Blinking her eyes slowly and deliberately, Jillian tried to clear her vision. It was almost impossible to keep her mind focused on even the smallest of tasks, but Jillian willed herself to wake and be strong. A gentle hand took hers in his, and Jillian could hear soft words of comfort.

"There little one. You're safe," he murmured.

She tried to pull away from him, but it was a futile attempt on her part because she was so weak. Again she blinked her eyes, clearing them enough to make out his features.

His head was covered with an unruly thick mass of copper hair. It whirled wildly about his face in a devilish way. His chin was covered with the same red stubble, quite unkempt. His brow held a concerned look as he gazed deeply into her eyes. His eyes had a familiar look to them. She found herself lost in their amber depths.

Sue Ki shuffled back into the room with a goblet of water. "She must sit," he commanded the Captain, who quickly did as Ki said. "She must drink."

A strong arm slipped its way beneath Jillian's shoulders, and she felt herself being gently lifted from the bed and propped up against his body. She felt so weak and dizzy that all she could do was lie against him, using him for support.

Terrance pressed the goblet to Jillian's parched lips and bid her to drink the cool water, which she did. Her mouth had never felt so dry.

"Drink, my love," he cooed. "You must keep your strength," Terrance said, as he lifted the goblet once more.

Jillian feebly sipped the remaining water, letting it soothe her dryness. Its coolness brought her closer to consciousness. She tipped her head back and gazed deeply into Terrance's eyes and he into hers.

"Who are you?" she asked, the words but a whisper from her dry throat. "Where am I? Please tell me." Her words drifted, and then Jillian lost consciousness once more.

Terrance lowered her onto the pillows which enveloped her in softness. He glanced up at Ki with a puzzled look on his face.

"She be fine, Cappy. She needs west now. Good as new afta she sleep mo," Ki reassured him. But Terrance was not so sure.

"How long will she sleep this time, Ki? When will she awaken so that I might speak with her?"

"Three, maybe four hours, Cappy. She be good as new then."

Terrance grumbled to himself while he pulled the coverlet up around Jillian's shoulders, tucking her safely in. Three or four hours was a long time to wait, but he knew he wanted to clean himself up before talking to her. This would be as good a time as any to get the task out of his way. But he didn't want to leave her, not even for a moment, so he stood by her side, contemplating his next move.

Sensing Terrance's dilemma, Gavin stepped forward and put a hand on the older man's shoulder.

"I'll stay with her for awhile, Captain," Gavin said, breaking the silence. "You must be exhausted after staying with her all last night."

"Indeed I am fatigued, and I must get myself cleaned up a bit for when she wakes."

Gavin's heart sank with Terrance's words. Again he was reminded that she was the Captain's woman.

Terrance stood, stretching his weary limbs. "One of Ki's potions will clear my head. That and a nice hot bath," he said, putting his hand on Gavin's shoulder. "Guard her well this day, Gavin, for indeed you are the only one I can trust with such a treasure. All will be clear soon. All of your questions will be answered."

Terrance turned and walked toward the cabin door. "Yes, things will be much clearer and very different from now on." Terrance and Sue Ki left the Captain's quarters and closed the heavy door behind them.

Terrance felt suddenly tired, very tired, as he made his way back to the galley. Sleep had eluded him for quite some time now. No matter how tired he felt, he never fully slept the night through, tossing and turning as frequent nightmares plagued him. Ki had made a potion that would allow Terrance to sleep, but he used it only sparingly.

Terrance entered the galley. Ki, who hurried ahead of him, handed him a mug of hot steamy tea, and Terrance sat at the long table, deep in thought.

"She finally here, Cappy. She where she belong now."

"Yes she's finally here. But for how long?" he asked, not really expecting an answer. How long could he keep her? How long had it been since the beginning? Deep in thought, Terrance sipped the tea Sue Ki gave him. It seemed like only yesterday that he first met Sybil Chandler.

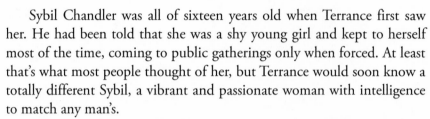

Sybil Chandler was all of sixteen years old when Terrance first saw her. He had been told that she was a shy young girl and kept to herself most of the time, coming to public gatherings only when forced. At least that's what most people thought of her, but Terrance would soon know a totally different Sybil, a vibrant and passionate woman with intelligence to match any man's.

After a long voyage of trading and tax collecting, Admiral Chandler invited Terrance to his home for dinner and conversation. Terrance gladly accepted the invitation, craving a home-cooked meal. The food at sea was lacking in flavor and variety.

Anxious to get to the Admiral's estate, Terrance realized that he had arrived quite early that afternoon. Because the estate was still ahead, he stopped beside the road to let some time pass before entering the grounds. He wanted so much to make a good impression, but it was poor manners to arrive too early for a dinner invitation.

Leading his mount, Terrance walked his horse up the incline beside the road. He found a place beneath a sturdy oak where he could sit comfortably, then tied the bay to a branch that hung close to the ground, allowing the horse to freely graze a small distance.

Resting his back against the tree, Terrance was lost in thought when the sudden thunder of hooves startled him. Alerted by the passing steed, his mount called to the unknown traveler.

Terrance scanned the hillside opposite the road for a glimpse of the horse and rider. His keen eyes caught a flash of a stallion thrusting through the thick foliage along the forest's edge before disappearing into the trees. Terrance saw the shimmer of an emerald satin gown flowing across the sorrel's back and a chill ran through him as he realized the horse's breakneck speed.

Panicked, he quickly mounted the bay, urging the horse toward the place where he last saw the sorrel entering the forest. Terrance raced his mount to its limit through the thick stand of trees, following the faint traces left only moments before. He sensed that the woman must be in terrible danger.

The deeper into the forest Terrance went, the darker the day became. He strained his eyes in search of the sorrel, but he found the steed nowhere in sight. He slowed the bay, patting his neck to calm him, waiting but unsure for what.

Suddenly, just ahead, the sorrel bolted into view, and the chase was on once again. He was behind her now. Her bonnet loosened from her head, allowed chestnut hair to escape and flow freely behind her. The wind blew through the mass of waves as she held her body low against the sorrel, to avoid falling from its broad back. Terrance assumed she indeed held on for dear life because the sorrel was traveling at top speed through the dark woods.

Terrance urged the bay on, finally coming up beside the sorrel. He leaned dangerously sideways to grasp its reins. Just as he had the reins within his hand, Terrance felt the sting from a riding crop smartly upon his cheek.

"Unhand me, you filth!" the woman screamed at Terrance, while hitting him about the shoulders with the crop. But he held the reins firm, never letting go, slowing both mounts.

"You idiot!" puffed the woman, springing agilely from the sorrel's back. "You fool! My father will have your head."

Amused by her actions, Terrance gazed at her in disbelief. She obviously was not in need of a rescue; that was apparent to him now.

Before him stood the most defiantly beautiful young woman he had ever seen. Her breast heaved in anger, her hands clenched into fists at her side as if ready for battle.

Slowly, so as not to frighten her, Terrance eased off his mount. They stood motionless for some time, studying each other.

His rugged, wild appearance startled Sybil. She was tall for a woman, but he stood a good foot taller than she. His square shoulders were broad, giving him an immense, intimidating look. It fascinated and frightened her at the same time. She was intrigued by this man.

Her hair covered most of her face, but Terrance knew that beneath those chestnut tresses, was the face of a goddess. Her body trembled. He wondered if it was from the chase or from something else.

Terrance took a step toward her, but she backed away suddenly. Her hand motioned for him to stop, keeping him at bay. He was puzzled by her actions.

She spoke softly to him, "Please, take the horse and leave. It is what you came for, isn't it?" She again backed a few steps deeper into the forest.

"Wait, miss. I'll not harm you," he said.

"Take the horse and leave. Leave now while you still have a chance."

How odd, he thought, for this beautiful lady to be warning him off away from an unknown danger. He laughed to himself. "I have been through many battles. I have seen much danger. I see no threat here. Aye, no threat to me, that is."

"My father will have your head if you touch me. He doesn't take kindly to strangers harming the one he loves."

Terrance quickly looked over his shoulder and around the forest, "I don't see your father here, at this moment, to save you from the likes of me."

"I'm telling you to take the horse and go, or you will regret it." Again she backed away from him, hoping to make the distance between them quite enough for her to bolt into the forest if he came closer.

Fidgeting with the reins from both horses, Terrance pondered his next move. Instinct taught him to be cautious. Terrance realized that the sun had grown dim in the forest and that he would be late for dinner with the Admiral.

He spoke to her gently from a distance. "So sorry to frighten you, Miss, but I thought you were in need of assistance. My mistake, as I can now see clearly that you are a fine horseman. Or should I say, horsewoman."

Silence fell between them. Terrance led her horse to a nearby bush and tethered it there. "I'll be on my way now, that is if you can mount on your own," he teased as he mounted the bay.

"Of course I can," she spat indignantly. "Don't be foolish. Please, go."

"I trust that you will not be needing my assistance again this day, fair lady." Tipping his head in mock salute, he rode quickly away from her before he changed his mind and fulfilled her worst fears.

Terrance rode swiftly back to the roadway. He never looked back to see if the young lady regained her mount, but he knew without question that she had. Once again, he was on his way to the Admiral's estate. The bay's hooves beat a steady rhythm on the gravel road.

Soon the road turned to cobblestone as he neared the estate's entrance. It was a glorious place, the Admiral's home, with vast land holdings. Servant quarters could be seen in the distance with children playing and scurrying at their mother's command. He passed one small girl dressed in black, with a white apron, and tipped his head in her direction. She immediately ducked behind a hedge as he entered the gardens surrounding the estate.

Terrance had been told by many how Admiral Chandler came to have such a wonderful gift. The estate was a reward from Queen Henrietta herself, a reward for his loyalty to her and for his performance in her bed. It mattered naught to Terrance, for seeing it now he knew it was worth the cost, and felt he may have been tempted himself to pleasure the Queen for a reward as grand as this.

He made his way up the long drive as he took in the sights and smells of the vast gardens that lined it. The fragrance of many varieties of flowers was seductive and it soothed Terrance as he ended his eventful journey. A liveryman appeared before him to hold the bay's reins while Terrance dismounted. He thanked him, and the man led the horse to the stable.

Terrance stood before the mansion in awe of its magnificence. He took the stairs to the entrance easily, two at a time, and his long legs quickly brought him to the huge door of the mansion. Before Terrance could knock, the door creaked open.

"You're late," a pert little woman, most likely the housekeeper, said, bidding him entrance.

"So terribly sorry, milady, but I was waylaid."

"Terrance, my dear boy. You've finally made it here. Come, come, Sophie has our sup prepared. I'm afraid she doesn't like to be kept waiting." The Admiral took Terrance's cloak and gently nudged him toward the dining room, chatting merrily as they went.

The dining room was large, grander than anything Terrance had ever seen. A beautifully jeweled chandelier hung above the long cherry wood dining table. Its light spread a rainbow of colors throughout the room. The table was set with just three fine china plates, two at each end and one on the right hand side, close to the Admiral. No one appeared to take the third place. Terrance wondered at the time whom the setting was for. Nothing was mentioned about its occupant, who was obviously absent from the meal.

A most prim and proper butler served the first course. He stopped at the empty plate, not knowing quite what to do. The Admiral gave him a stern look, and the butler moved quickly away, leaving the setting behind.

"I must say, dear boy, that I was hoping my lovely daughter, Sybil, would join us this evening. I can't quite say what the devil's gotten into her. She went riding earlier and has not returned."

"I hope that no harm has come to her, Sir," Terrance said. "Do you think we should ride out to search for her?"

Just then there was a loud commotion in the foyer. Voices, raised to a shrill pitch, echoed through the mansion. The Admiral's face lit with concern as he flew from the dining room and left Terrance still sitting at his meal.

Terrance sat bewildered at the table, quickly losing his appetite. He thought about what the Admiral had said about his daughter going riding. Of course, this couldn't be the same girl that he had rescued, or rather had chased. No, the Admiral's daughter would never go out unescorted.

Some moments passed before the voices quieted beyond the door. Terrance made out very little of what was said because there were many voices sounding at the same time. But the last thing he did hear were the sobs of a woman and the Admiral comforting her. A few moments later, Admiral Chandler reappeared in the dining room looking frazzled, his graying hair in disarray.

"Forgive me, dear boy," he said, running his fingers through his hair, trying to straighten it a little. "I'm afraid my daughter has had a slight mishap."

Concerned, Terrance rose from his chair. "Is it serious, Sir?"

"No, no, my boy. Nothing that a good night's sleep won't cure." The Admiral motioned for Terrance to sit and again took his own seat. "Seems as though she was attacked while riding by a thief who was trying to steal the sorrel, Blaze, from her. She's had the stallion since he was a colt. I forbade her to ride him at first. A stallion is not a proper mount for a lady. But Sybil fell in love with the horse and just won't give him over. Sit, my boy. Eat."

"Was she injured, Admiral?" Terrance anticipated the very worst.

"No, no. Sybil is a fine horseman, or should I say horsewoman." Terrance smiled, remembering his own words not long before. The Admiral continued, "I can see you appreciate that she can ride. She whipped the poor fellow viciously, causing him to fall from his horse, and was able to get away. We should be able to identify the bloke by the whip marks she says she left across his cheek."

The Admiral eyed Terrance curiously from across the table when he unconsciously touched his cheek. Terrance worried that he may indeed have a mark left from her riding crop. Had she hit him that hard? He could not remember. He composed himself as much as was possible, willing his voice to be steady.

"Did she get a good look at him, Sir?" Terrance waited anxiously.

"No, no. She cannot say just what he looked like, but only that he was riding a dun mare with four white stocking feet."

"You don't say," Terrance said in disbelief.

"You sound surprised, Terrance. Did you spy the man on your way here tonight?"

Terrance chose his words carefully. "No, Admiral. I did not see the man, but I wish that I had. Maybe I could have been of assistance to your poor daughter."

Admiral Chandler reared back with hearty laughter. "Don't you be worrying yourself about that, my boy! My poor daughter, as you put it, has put many a man in his place, which seems to be under the tip of her dainty little riding boots. That includes me."

Both men laughed with the Admiral's words, one with amusement and the other with relief. Terrance began to relax a bit, but still he wondered why she would lie about the horse.

"I must apologize, my boy, but under the circumstances, my daughter has asked to be excused from tonight's sup," he said, his face still rosy from laughter.

"No need to apologize, Admiral. I understand completely."

But of course, he didn't understand at all. The story she told the Admiral was incredible. She may have mistaken him for a thief, but a dun mare? She couldn't have mistaken the bay stallion that he rode so skillfully.

When the meal was finished Terrance and the Admiral retired to the study for a bit of sherry. He felt at ease with the Admiral, and the Admiral with him. The study was filled with many shelves of books that took up two entire walls. A large fireplace with a white marble mantel gave the immense room a cozy feel. Terrance was speechless, standing motionless to survey its wonder.

"It quite takes you off guard, doesn't it?" Admiral Chandler walked to the cabinet to pour the sherry. "Sybil quite likes this room herself. I think she has read every book on these shelves, some of them twice. When she was small, I would find her down here asleep on the davenport, a book still open to the page she was last reading."

He handed Terrance a glass filled with red liquid, motioning him to sit. Admiral Chandler took his place opposite him in one of the two overstuffed chairs near the fireplace.

"It is such a grand room. I spend much of my time here, reading and keeping my ledgers. Sybil is very helpful with the books. That is, when she isn't on the back of that dammed sorrel."

"Sounds like you and your wife, have done a fine job of bringing her up." Terrance complimented.

Admiral Chandler stiffened at Terrance's words, staring into the flames of the fire. Terrance became uneasy with the Admiral's silence and knew he had said something to upset him. He remained quiet to allow the Admiral to gather his thoughts. Terrance didn't want to push him.

"I suppose you really couldn't have known, dear boy. Sybil's mother died shortly after her birth. It's a hard burden to bear, raising a child, especially a girl, but Sophie has quite literally taken the child as her own. Poor Clarice, Sybil's mother, was hardly missed, by her."

"I must apologize, Sir. I had no idea that your dear wife had passed on."

"No need for an apology, Terrance. It was long ago, and long forgotten."

The Admiral downed his glass of sherry. "My marriage to Clarice was arranged when we were both very young. These types of arrangements are quite common, most often made to bring powerful families together to form a strong alliance."

"This marriage was no different from most of them, except that I could never bring myself to tolerate Clarice, much less love her. She possessed a most dispassionate disposition. It was a wonder that Sybil was ever conceived. Once she was, I was never allowed to enter Clarice's bedchambers again. Not until the night she died."

"The birth had been a hard one, and Clarice was barely able to spew the child forth. I heard her screech when she found that the baby was a girl. She screamed for the midwife to take 'it' away."

"I imagined that her actions were due to the shock from so much pain while giving birth. Clarice was of a fragile nature, but she told me that she wanted only to have a boy, my namesake. She didn't want a girl who would surely suffer the same indignation as she herself had. It would be the only child that I would ever conceive with her, and here it was a girl. She swore her hatred for the innocent child and cast us both from her room."

"Clarice took a fever and would not eat or drink after the birth. Having no will to live, she died three days later, without ever having held her babe. Her father blamed me for her death, and we have not had any contact with the old man since the funeral."

"Having no one to nurse the babe, I feared for her survival. That is when we found Sophie, or you might say, that she found us. She appeared from the forest one morning. She explained that she heard word in the village the need for a wet nurse at the estate and tearfully told how, only days before, her own babe had taken ill and died."

"Why, I was appalled by the very thought of a stranger breasting my flesh and blood, but I did not want the babe to starve to death and felt that I had no choice but to let her try and save my little Sybil's life."

"The babe took to her as if it were the way it was meant to be. She suckled until she was quite a chubby, healthy little cherub. She is the light in my life."

The Admiral shifted in his chair, swirling the sherry thoughtfully within the snifter. There was a moment of silence. Terrance needed that time to take in all of what he had just been told, and the Admiral began again.

"In spite of it all, Sybil has grown to be a very lovely young lady, quick witted and intelligent. It will soon be time for her to wed. I shall miss her sorely."

Terrance felt the Admiral's gaze directed toward him, and he raised his eyes to meet it. He knew by the way the older man smiled what the Admiral wanted him to do. It shocked and excited Terrance at the same time. The Admiral wanted him to court his daughter. Although no words were spoken of it, Terrance felt sure that that was precisely the Admiral's plan.

The conversation shifted to the end of the week when there would be a ball at the Admiral's estate. It was Sybil's début and the Admiral requested his presence. Many suitors would be there, and Admiral Stephan Chandler wanted Terrance to be one of them.

The night grew late. It was hard to end the evening, but Terrance knew he should be heading back to the city. He sensed the Admiral was a very lonely man who craved the companionship of someone young and vital. Terrance wondered why the Admiral had chosen him to be the one he confided in so intimately, yet felt great honor by it.

"I will see you at the ball then, my boy," Admiral Chandler said as they neared the entranceway.

Terrance cringed at his words, "I'm not certain about it, Admiral." Terrance hadn't attended many formal affairs and with the revelations this evening, he wasn't sure if it was a good idea to attend this one.

"Terrance, my boy. I'm convinced that you must attend. Now don't force me to make that an order."

"No, Sir. Yes, Sir. I guess I can manage to come if you insist."

"And I most certainly do insist, my boy. Now have a safe ride back to the city. There's a chill in the air. You're lucky to have a full moon above to light your way."

Standing at the top of the stair's entrance Terrance pulled his collar up around his neck to keep the rush of cool air from creeping in. "Yes, it's a beautiful ride back to the city, especially on a clear night such as this."

The moon, now at its fullest, lit the way to the stable, giving the world around Terrance a blue hew. The color seeped through even the warmest cloak and chilled the bones.

"I'll call for the liveryman," the Admiral said looking out into the stillness.

"No need, I quite enjoy fetching my own mount. It's quite a treat indeed after being so long at sea."

Terrance bid the Admiral good night and walked to the stable in silent thought of the turn of the evening's events. He wondered if Sybil knew of her father's plans for her nuptials and if she had agreed to them.

The stable was black except for a small light from a lantern that hung next to the doorway. It did little to illuminate within. Terrance hesitated for only a moment, letting his eyes adjust to the darkness before going farther. The sounds of the horses settling for the night gave him a sense of peace. He strolled from one stall to the next, patting each occupant playfully in his search for the bay.

He stopped short when he came to the stall that held the sorrel. Blaze, the Admiral had called him. Quite a fitting name indeed for his color flickered through the forest like that of a flame bursting into brightness. He was a fine and powerful horse for such a lovely young woman. Remembering now; the chestnut hair, the glimmer of emerald, the heaving of her breast as she stood defiantly before him, Terrance's blood quickened with the thought of her.

He reached out his hand to stroke the sorrel's nose, tracing the pattern of white that striped down its length. The stallion nuzzled against Terrance's strong hand, seeking a hidden treat.

"Sorry to disappoint you, my fine friend, but I haven't a grain to give."

"Nor a brain to use."

He stood fast, the tip of her dagger pressed firmly into his back, catching him off guard.

"So we meet again, sweet lady," he said, not moving.

"Meet again!" she laughed angrily. "I don't believe you could call what you did an introduction, but more of an abduction."

Terrance shifted slightly, reaching forward to brush a strand of straw from the sorrel's neck, paying no heed to the dagger's point.

"For sure, milady. If I had wanted to take you then, I most certainly would have."

He relaxed his stance, feeling now that there was little danger of being wounded by the woman's knife.

Sybil sensed his assumption and it angered her. How could he take her so lightly? He didn't even know who she was. She could maim him for life with her dagger, having always made it a point to keep the edge razor sharp.

"Don't be so sure that you are in no danger here," she said as she added more pressure to the dagger at Terrance's ribs. "I could stab you claiming self-defense."

Feeling the dagger's point painfully piercing the skin under his clothes, Terrance's patience with her grew steadily thinner, but his curiosity kept him still. How far would she carry this game of deception? How far would she be willing to go to prove her abilities?

Again, his thoughts made him more aware of Sybil than he wanted to be. Her scent filled his nostrils with the slightest hint of rose, like those in the gardens that lined the cobblestone drive. It was a scent like no other woman. Most of his previous experiences were with women who reeked of heavy musk and lavender, a most putrid combination.

He remembered the fragrance from the flowers that had filled his senses earlier. Her scent overwhelmed him. The need to see, to touch, to feel this woman under his caress, shook him. Terrance, suddenly aroused at the thought of taking her now, in the stable, became very uneasy. He must use caution with her. She was the Admiral's daughter.

Trying to be serious, to not anger her further, Terrance chose his words carefully. "So, what will you do with me, Miss?"

Contemplating that she may have taken on more than she could handle, Sybil said nothing, but still held the dagger firmly in place. What would she do? Why had she ventured to the stable knowing that he would come here? She had watched until he'd entered, then crept up behind him, unaware of what she would do next. He excited her and piqued her curiosity, this Viking warrior she had heard her father talk so mightily about. "A better man cannot be found to stand beside you in battle or in marriage," he had told her. "He suits you and you him. You'll have a long life together."

Sybil wanted to kill this stupid man. Hadn't he let a mere woman best him? Stand beside her? That was a jest at best.

Breaking the silence, Terrance spoke. "What's the matter, Miss? Has the tyrant lost her whip?"

He felt her hand relax in frustration at his words and seized his opportunity. Turning suddenly, Terrance's strong arm came down painfully across Sybil's, knocking the dagger easily from her grasp. She cried out as Terrance whirled toward her wrapping one arm tightly around her waist holding her back firmly pressed against his chest. He quickly covered Sybil's mouth with his free hand, hoping that no one had heard her cry.

Sybil's body arched away from his as she fought to free herself, but Terrance merely stood in place, holding her tight. She was no match for his strength and size. Sybil kicked and struggled against Terrance for as long as she could, which seemed to her to be a very long time, but she soon gave up the fight in complete exhaustion. Terrance held her tightly, letting her feet dangle beneath her like a rag doll's. Sybil came to realize the strength with which he held her. Firm, yet gentle arms enveloped her in warmth.

Feeling this, she froze in his grasp. Her only movement was the rapid rise and fall of her chest as she fought for breath beneath his hand.

Terrance gazed over her shoulder eyeing silken skin that rose and fell with each intake of air. The sight was almost his undoing, and he struggled for control of his body, his need becoming evident.

"If I take my hand away," he whispered softly against her ear, "do you promise not to scream?"

She nodded in agreement. Terrance slowly removed his hand but still held it ready to return if need be.

"We don't need to have the estate awakened to such a scene, now do we?" He waited watching for a sign that she would bolt. "After all, one would surely wonder what the Admiral's daughter was doing out so late, and in the stable of all places. Was she here to meet her lover? Or does she prefer the company of horses?"

"Better the company of horses than the company of a horse's ass such as you!"

With those words Sybil's futile struggles resumed, making Terrance grow weary with her attempt. He caught her flailing arms easily with his strong hands, and in one motion turned her to face him, whipping them mercilessly behind her back. Their eyes met intimately for the first time. The power of this moment captivated them, holding each frozen like a silent statue against the other's body.

Her beauty held Terrance spellbound. The color of her eyes matched the emerald of the gown she had worn earlier. Her thick lashes encircled jewels with lushness that made their green deeper than the forest. Her crimson lips reminded him once again of the red roses along the drive. Her scent drugged him, seduced him, and invited his tender kiss.

He studied her fine features, the arch of her brow flowing gently onto high cheekbones now brightened in color by her struggle. The curve of her delicate chin gave way to the silken length of her neck, her shoulders, and her breast. Chestnut hair, its ringlets framing the perfect portrait, gave her fair skin a glowing perfection. Terrance held her gently now against him, completely entranced in her wonder. Would he ever be able to let this woman out of his embrace?

Sybil was caught completely off guard by him and his sudden gentleness. Never before, had she been held in such a manner. He excited her beyond anything she had ever dreamt about. Since the first moment she caught sight of him riding along the road, she had longed to feel his powerful arms around her.

This was the man her father had chosen for her to marry, the man who would be the father of her children. He was the man she knew she was destined to cherish for the rest of her life.

Her father had described Terrance as, "a fiery haired devil", a man to have at your side in battle and in life. The Admiral spoke of no better fighting man than Terrance McCarthy. But nothing had prepared Sybil for the raw strength of this giant.

Even when she faked not having control of her horse, his strength and skill had saved her. Although she hadn't needed saving, his swift gallantry had made her swoon with desire. Ashamed of her actions, Sybil couldn't bear to see him at dinner. She had waited in the forest until she was sure that the meal had started without her, and then made up her incredible story. Oh, but Father would throttle her if only he knew what she had done.

Sybil was lost in the depths of his amber eyes, their richness softening as he looked upon her face. His skin, tanned from the many days at sea, was smoothed by a fresh shave and looked as soft as satin. His fiery hair, indeed more copper-colored, softened with gold from the sun, turned his eyes deeper in contrast. His nose, an acceptable size for a man so big, accentuated the fullness of his lips, inviting Sybil's gaze. Her lips parted slightly with the need for their touch.

"Sybil," Terrance sighed.

The sound, her name upon his lips, made Sybil's heart leap, and she went limp in his arms. Terrance released her arms and gently cupped her face in his hands. With great caution, Terrance bent forward, kissing Sybil softly, and she returned his gentleness with the same, running her fingers tenderly through his copper hair. This kiss lasted only a moment, but spoke of a love that both hoped would last forever . . .

Chapter 6

Gavin removed the leather belt that bound his sword around his waist and laid it quietly beside the chair near the head of the Captain's bed. He never took his eyes off Jillian and was careful not to disturb her with his movements. Gavin tugged at his blouse loosening it slightly and sat on the edge of the chair.

Once assured that Jillian wasn't disturbed, Gavin began the chore of removing his boots. Black leather covered Gavin's legs tightly to his knees and after unfastening them, he slipped his boots off, placing them next to his sword.

Satisfied that he could finally relax, Gavin settled into the plush chair beside the bed and sighed deeply. To be so near this beautiful creature was pure torture for him. He tried his best to ignore her beauty and after some time was able to close his weary eyes. Sleep did not come easily; his mind filled with thoughts of Jillian, the woman who belonged to his Captain. She would not be his. Only in his mind could he possess her. He tried not to think or feel, but as he drifted into sleep, he saw her there.

Frozen with fear in the huge feather bed, Jillian's heart raced. She had listened as the men had left the room, hoping that they all would go, but one had remained. She had peered through her lashes, watching him, hoping that he wouldn't know that she was awake. Then, he had started to take off his clothes. In fear of what might happen to her, she had closed her eyes tightly. Her mind had searched through the haze for an escape as she listened to the soft sounds of his boots slipping to the floor and then the sigh that said her time had come. But, there had been no movement toward the bed. Jillian waited a moment more before opening her eyes to see where he was.

He lay slumped in the chair, his head back against the plush cushion behind him. His long muscular legs stretched out before him, crossed at the ankles. Covering them were pants made of black leather, so tight and form fitting that Jillian could see hard muscles bulging beneath the thick material. His white blouse, tucked at the waist, lay open exposing his chest and stomach. Almost completely hairless, golden skin rippled tightly to his waist.

Jillian studied his handsome face, the likes of which she had never seen. His brow formed a worried stance above his deep-set eyes, making Jillian wonder what he might be thinking. His skin was deeply tanned, and his hair lightened, almost white against his bronze skin. He looked more a god to Jillian than a mere man, but indeed he was a man. Jillian smiled to herself, thinking of the foolish village boys who tried to capture her interest. Now this man captured more than her interest; he captured her.

Suddenly, Jillian realized that this was the man who had carried her so gently in his arms. He was the one whose scent of leather still lingered in her mind. He was the stranger who had taken her away from everything she ever knew. Oddly enough, knowing this, she felt no threat from him. She somehow knew he would not harm her. He stood guard over her, protecting her. Relaxing, Jillian felt a sense of peace fill her and once again the effect of the tea began to take her mind. She drifted into darkness. However this time, she was not alone.

She felt their hands all over her body, hands that relentlessly probed and touch her. Jillian struggled to be free from their grasp, but the hands held her, pushing her from one to the other. Sheer terror rose within her. She tried to scream and fight the hands, but there was only silence. They held her tightly, pulling her down among them. Jillian fought, kicking and scratching, but they only laughed at her efforts. She gained no ground against the strong hands that held her. She tried to cry out and scream for help, but no sound would come.

"Please! Please!" her mind screamed with terror. "Please, help me!" A soft whimper escaped her trembling lips.

"It's alright, Jillian. You're safe," a strange but gentle voice called to her. "You're safe, little one."

Suddenly, hands disappeared, and Jillian was sitting on her rock on the beach. In the distance a sail from a ship beckoned her. Brilliant light was everywhere and she heard the voice. She slowly stood her arms outstretched, ready for his embrace.

"You're safe, little one. I am here."

Jillian opened her eyes and gazed up into his. Gavin could see the blankness within them; their depth frightened him. Wasn't she awake?

Her eyes were open, but he knew she could not see. He repeated his words to her. "You're safe. I am here."

Slowly, Jillian's eyes softened. He watched as she gained awareness, coming back from an unknown place. She had made her way through the darkness upon hearing his words. Emptiness filled her, an emptiness that was with her for a very long time.

Gavin comforted her, his soothing words giving her peace. "You're safe. You were having a bad dream." He smoothed the golden strands away from her face. "Have no fear. I will not harm you. All of this must seem like a nightmare to you. For that I am truly sorry."

Jillian said nothing. His eyes held her gently, their blue soothing her. She thought of her rock and how the blue ocean gave her peace. It was the same blue she gazed into now.

Tears welled in her eyes as Jillian fought for control of her emotions, of the despair and turmoil of her life. For the first time, the fear and pain of her abduction began to seep in. She could not control the pain. She could not control her life or her tears. She cried softly against Gavin's shoulder, her arms clinging unconsciously to him. Jillian nuzzled her face against the bareness of his chest, the feel of him bringing new sensations to her body. She wanted him close. She wanted his body touching hers, protecting her. She had an overwhelming feeling that she could never get close enough. She pulled him closer, not wanting to release him.

He held her gently, letting her shed the pain and fear of uncertainty. With every tear that fell from her swollen eyes and with every shudder of her frail body, his heart wrenched. He knew he could not take what he had caused away but could only hold and comfort her. He stroked the small of her back softly.

"There, there, little one. You have no reason to be so frightened. The Captain has his reasons for bringing you here."

"The Captain? But why? Why am I here? Why have I been taken from my home?" Jillian's sobs quieted as she gathered her wits about her, looking around the room. "Where am I?" she asked, pushing herself away from him.

The room was large, with two portholes on one wall. The sun shone brightly through them, telling Jillian that it was daytime. A large armoire stood beside the cabin door, and another stood between the portholes. They were made of fine cherry wood and were a perfect match for the large chest that was at the foot of the bed. Two chaise lounges were placed at intervals against the wall, taking up the unused space between the portholes. In the center of the room was the biggest bathing tub Jillian had ever seen. It was deep black porcelain with fine paintings along its rim. The back of the tub was higher than the front, and deep enough to immerse one's entire body comfortably. The tub stood on four claw feet, holding it a good six inches of the floor, giving it an even bigger appearance. For an instant, she longed to be in that tub, to cleanse and forget.

Gavin's eyes followed hers, realizing her amazement at the tub. When the Captain bought it, only a few weeks before, the crew had thought the man was crazy. Still, no one had used the thing, not even Terrance.

"It's grand, isn't it? The Captain had it brought in from Paris not long ago."

Jillian again became aware of his closeness. Her thoughts of the tub made her feel exposed to him. Did he sense her thoughts? Did he know her feelings and her needs? Her heart leapt when she realized how tightly she clung to him. Jillian pushed away. Gavin let her move from him, releasing her gently.

"Please don't be afraid, Jillian. The Captain is a fine and gentle man. He is no threat to you."

"This is all his, isn't it? The armoire? The chaises? The bathing tub? Everything in this room is his. Am I also his? Nothing but a possession? Nothing to him but another one of his rewards for being the Captain?"

Jillian's eyes pleaded with Gavin to tell her it wasn't so, but he could not deny it to her. No more than he could deny it to himself. As hard as it was for him to face, so must she know that she was brought here for the Captain, for his pleasure and no one else's.

"He has laid claim to you." Gavin lowered his eyes from hers, feeling ashamed of his part in this. Never before had he felt such cowardice.

Backing away from Gavin, Jillian held one of the large pillows to her, hugging it for comfort. She rocked back and forth upon the bed, staring blankly at the cabin door.

"He has no right. No one has that right," she said.

Gavin could not bear to look at Jillian. He also questioned Terrance's rights. Jillian was truly innocent in all of this, and Gavin couldn't imagine what Terrance's reasons were. Yet it mattered not, for Gavin was loyal to his Captain and would uphold his wishes, even if it meant holding Jillian captive.

"He will not hurt you. You must believe this. He is very kind and is fair with women," he said, trying to comfort her.

"Fair with women. You are a fool. Is it fair that he has taken me without warning? Is it fair that my family will suffer with no knowledge of my plight?"

Gavin's heart tore with her words. He painfully brought his eyes to hers, holding back the words that his heart pleaded to say.

"No, it isn't fair but he is my Captain."

Confused and frustrated, Jillian felt helpless. The look of pain in his beautiful eyes only made her feelings more intense. Suddenly, she wanted to be free from this place, away from him and his confusing words, away from this man and her overwhelming feeling of wanting him. She threw the pillow at Gavin, catching him off guard and bolted from the bed. Gavin dove after her, but she eluded his grasp and ran for the door. The instant she reached it, Gavin was upon her. Their bodies hit the door forcefully. He held her there with his muscular arms caging her from both sides and his body pressed tightly against her back.

"You cannot escape, Jillian," his voice whispered warmly on the tender skin of her neck. "We are at sea. Where do you think you could go?" With his arms encircling her, Gavin turned Jillian to face him. "I'm sorry. There is no escape for you."

"You could help me," she pleaded. "I have to get away. I am not a possession but a human being with feelings and a family to think of."

"I cannot. I have sworn to keep you safe, and this I will do. But to help you escape would be to let you go, and that I will never do."

With his words, Jillian's eyes closed in defeat. Gavin gently caressed her cheek with his fingertip wiping a tear away. Timidly his finger touched the fullness of her lips, tracing their edges. Her lips parted slightly, her motion inviting his gaze.

Jillian's breath caught with his touch. His gentle arms were holding her so near. The smell of leather and of him reminded her of before, when she had thought she was dreaming. Was this the man she sensed so close? The one who carried her against his body? The one who filled the emptiness that she felt? She opened her eyes to his and saw only kind, gentle thoughts behind them.

"It was you? You are the one who carried me here."

"Yes, love. It was I who carried you here."

Before Jillian could protest, Gavin gently lifted her and turned to take her back to the bed. She wished for an instant that he would take her to the bed and lay there with her, wrapping her tightly in his arms. Jillian felt as if she would burst. She felt cherished being cradled in his arms and wrapped her delicate arms around his neck. Then, without giving it a thought, she kissed his cheek.

Gavin stopped next to the bed, surprised by her actions, her trusting way. He fought to maintain control, the wanting in him becoming potent. His body grew taut, reacting to her trust. How could she trust him after his part in her abduction? Why did he want her so badly, knowing full well that she wasn't his for the taking?

"You are not mine to have," he stated flatly, as he lowered Jillian to the bed.

For all the emotions that swelled within him, not one showed in his voice. But he knew that his eyes could not deceive her, for she gazed knowingly into them, as if into his very soul. A smile crossed her lips. She could see the pain in his eyes as he struggled for composure. His thoughts showed in them with such intensity that she looked away in fear of it.

She pondered their situation but could see no just end. If she were to escape and return, the world she once knew was gone. The peaceful fishing village, the long walks on the beach, the innocence she once wished herself rid of was a thing of the past. If she returned to her home, the people of the village would most assuredly brand her a tarnished woman, even if she were not. She could not bring herself to shame her family in such a way. Jillian considered this and realized that options did not exist for her.

"What is your name?" she asked softly, gazing into his blue eyes, seeing his true feelings within them.

"Gavin," he answered, a smile curving his smooth lips.

Jillian's gaze met his lips, and she longed to touch, to feel their smoothness against her own.

"Gavin," Jillian repeated breathlessly. "Gavin," she sighed, bringing his head down to hers.

Just then the cabin door flung open, banging loudly against the wall behind it. Jillian screamed at the sight of the red haired devil who flew into the room, sword raised.

"Unhand her," Terrance growled. "I trusted you with her and this is what you do?"

The massive man came forward threateningly. Gavin swiftly turned placing Jillian upon the bed, and in the same motion lunged toward his sword. He grasped the hilt within his hand and turned to face his attacker, readying himself for battle. Before Gavin could stop her, Jillian leapt from the bed, placing herself between the advancing warriors. She raised her hands for both to halt, knowing that her small form would be no barrier to stop the raging men.

"Jillian, no!" Gavin commanded from behind her.

But she stayed him with her hand. Neither man moved but only stared at the fragile girl standing between them. Her eyes were alight with the flame of her passion. She looked from one to the other as if making a choice between them. At seeing this, Gavin's face paled beyond his hair. What would her choice be? Did she even know that she had no choice in the matter, that indeed the Captain made all the choices here on board the Pegasus?

"Why am I here?" she asked fearfully, yet holding her chin up in defiance.

Terrance ignored her words and looked straight into Gavin's eyes. Both men stood in silent threat of the other. "If you have harmed her in any way, you will regret it!" he said, venomously, making Jillian's knees quake beneath her skirt.

"He did not harm me, but only sought to aid me. When I failed an attempt to escape, my legs became too weak to stand, and Gavin caught me before I fell to the floor," she lied.

Terrance looked down at Jillian sternly, the look in her eyes taking him by surprise. He saw there not a child but a woman of sixteen years, a woman of feelings and charm. She stood bravely before him defending Gavin. His heart swelled with pride at this sight. She was such a tiny thing, yet here she stood protecting Gavin from a madman's wrath.

In his divine plan of revenge, he hadn't given Jillian's feelings a thought. His need to punish those responsible for the wicked twists in his life had blinded Terrance to the pain he might cause in hers. He regretted the decision to bring her without her consent, but what choice did he have? After Jason had practically crushed her skull with his blow, Terrance had told himself he didn't have a choice.

Gavin slowly inched his way to stand at Jillian's side. He put his strong arm out protectively in front of her, to shield her from Terrance. Looking at the two of them, Terrance could plainly see that something had happened to them while Gavin kept watch. The bond that Terrance had hoped would form was now apparent. His heart gladdened with the thought that the two most important people in his life were somehow coming to love each other. He smiled, and Gavin and Jillian stood in confusion before him.

Jillian timidly eyed Terrance from head to foot, gasping when she focused upon his boots.

"It was you!" she exclaimed, pointing to the boots. "I remember the boots, the Pegasus!" Jillian raised her face to him.

"You are the Captain?" she swallowed convulsively, thinking to herself that he couldn't possibly be the one who had claimed her for his own. He was so big, so powerful, so threatening. How could she ever fight to be free from this devil? Would she ever have a chance of escaping him?

"I planned to have this conversation in a more private setting," Terrance said, glaring at Gavin.

It was plain that he wanted to be left alone with Jillian but Gavin was not ready to give in. Not yet. He held his ground.

"Gavin. You know, I will not harm her," Terrance reassured him.

Gavin knew the Captain to be the kindest of all men. He had never given him reason to doubt his word. That is, until now. Gavin wasn't sure of anything anymore. Terrance had never kidnapped anyone before and this made Gavin question his sanity. But his instincts told him to trust Terrance for now.

Catching Jillian's gaze one last time, Gavin stepped forward. She read many things in his eyes.

"You will be safe!" he commanded her.

She reached out to touch his sleeve to stop him, but hesitated, letting him slip away from her. He walked to the cabin door hesitating, as if he wanted to say something, but instead, he opened the door, leaving them alone.

The heavy door slammed behind him. A bone-chilling tremble overwhelmed Jillian with his parting. She did not understand her own intentions. She had to talk to the Captain alone. She had to find out why he had kidnapped her. He was the only one to whom she could plead for release.

Jillian kept her eyes fixed on the cabin door as if she expected to see Gavin return at any minute to protect her from the Captain. But the door did not open, and he did not return to her.

"There, now little one, there is no reason to be so frightened." Terrance reassured her. The sound of his voice brought a tremble through Jillian's body. Seeing this, he took the comforter from the bed and wrapped it around her shoulders. "There are many things for us to talk about." Terrance motioned for her to sit in one of the chaises. Jillian forced her attention away from the door and took the seat he offered. Nervously, she sat, waiting for him to speak.

Cautiously, he began to speak, keeping his eyes lowered. He wanted her to take in his words very slowly so that when he finished, she would not feel threatened by him in any way.

"You may not know me little one, but I know you. I was a good friend of your mother's a long time ago."

Terrance told the story of his first meeting with Sybil. How he'd thought to rescue her from danger when her horse ran away with her.

"Aye, but she was a fine horsewoman after all, and did not need my assistance with Blaze."

Jillian's head snapped up in recognition of the name of her mother's prized stallion. She knew him well, having ridden him several times at her grandfather's estate when she was very young. She listened to him with more interest now, her curiosity showing. Terrance was glad to see Jillian's familiarity with the horse. It was a start, he thought to himself.

"Sybil made up a story to cover for her tardiness and disheveled state. Her story kept her father's suspicions from falling on me. Later that same evening, she confronted me in the stable, holding me at bay with a knife which I easily relieved her of."

Terrance smiled to himself at the memory of what happened afterwards. "It did not take long for both of us to fall desperately in love. I now realize it happened for me the very first time I laid eyes upon your mother. Sybil was a most astonishing woman. So kind and gentle, when not in the possession of a knife that is," he teased laughingly.

"We spent every day together that fall, planning the rest of our lives. We intended to be married by the Christmas season."

His face and manner suddenly changed. He became tense and angry. Jillian was very aware of his emotions, and the realization alarmed her. He was so huge and threatening and now, very angry. Jillian only wanted to be away from him and his ship.

"I don't see what this has to do with me, Captain. That was a long time ago."

"Aye, it was, Jillian. But it has everything to do with you. If only you will hear me out, you will know."

Taking a deep breath, Terrance began again. "I wanted to spend so much time with Sybil that I sorely neglected my duties as far as the ship was concerned. A 'dear' friend of mine took over most of my responsibilities to allow me time with my beloved. I did not suspect the disgrace that he planned in my absence."

"He did a good job of convincing Sybil's father of 'my' guilt when it was discovered that funds and supplies were missing from the ship. They were my duties, and yet I had blindly signed the accounts, trusting him."

Terrance shifted to face Jillian directly. "We were at our favorite place deep in the forest. We had just made love when we heard the first sounds of thundering hooves upon the forest floor. Sybil quickly wrapped herself in the blanket on which we had laid. I barely had time to pull on my trousers when the riders were upon us. I was knocked to the ground by the crashing mounts around us. I remember Sybil screaming as the riders beat and kicked me, holding my body pinned beneath them. One of the men, an officer, held Sybil's face, forcing her to watch while the others brought me near death."

Jillian clutched the coverlet tightly around her. His story chilled her to the bone. If indeed she did believe him, she wondered why her mother had never mentioned the incident. And then she realized that Sybil would never have told her of this sort of disgrace.

"The officer holding Sybil told her that I was a traitor and had stolen from the King's navy. He told her that this would be the last time she would ever lay eyes upon me and to take a good look. By that time I was a bloody mess and only half conscious. I was never allowed a last word with her, never allowed to explain my innocence. That was the last time we saw each other."

"I don't understand, Captain. My mother never mentioned you or any of this to me. Have you, by chance, mistaken me for someone else?"

"This is not a mistake Jillian. What has been the mistake is that I have waited this long to come back to claim what is rightfully mine."

"And you think that I am rightfully yours? A reward for something that happened before I was even born?" Jillian's voice began to rise. "You are wrong, sir. You have no claim on me or my mother. All of what you tell me has nothing to do with me. You are wrong in what you do here, Captain."

"Aye, but I do have a claim to you, Jillian. I have more claim to you than the man you call father does. I told your mother so, when I came to take you both with me, but she would not come, knowing that she would have to leave the other child with William. When she refused me, I told her that I would find you and give you the choice to come with me."

Terrance saw Jillian's panic. "Things didn't go as I had planned," he quickly explained. "When you were hit so viciously, and I saw all the blood, I felt that I could not leave you there. You had to come with us. I never dreamt that you were not told the truth and that this would be such a shock to you."

Jillian couldn't stand it any longer. She leapt from the chair, screaming hysterically, clamping both hands over her ears, hoping to silence his words.

"No! I don't want to hear any more. Leave me alone! Please, no more!" Tears fell from her eyes. She shut them, wishing to block his image.

Her tears melted Terrance's resolve, but he had to finish. He had to tell Jillian everything, to get the truth out once and for all. Terrance pulled Jillian to him to comfort her. She tried to resist, but he wouldn't let her out of his arms. His huge hand delicately caressed the softness of her hair. He began to hum a lullaby.

Hearing it, Jillian sobs quieted. She listened to the sound of his voice, so sweet and gentle for such a fierce man. She suddenly realized that she knew the tune he hummed.

"The lullaby you hum, where did you hear it? What is it called?" she asked timidly.

Terrance ended the song softly. "It doesn't have a real name."

"My mother used to sing it to me when I was little. It was our song and no one else's. Did she teach it to you during your time together?"

Her question was innocent enough, but the memories brought back by her asking, hit Terrance full force. His eyes began to tear.

"Nay, I sang the song to your mother during our time together. She promised to sing it to our babes when the time came."

Silent, Jillian's mind raced with his words. She couldn't believe what the Captain was saying to her was the truth. William was her father. She knew that. There could be no way for this to be true.

"You are a crazy old man. I don't know why you are doing this to me, but you are wrong. William is my father."

Terrance went to the armoire and took out a piece of parchment. "Before you judge me, you must read this. It will lend truth to what I have said. One final thing will prove my story. I sent Sybil a token of my love once I became the Captain of the Pegasus. I had to let her know somehow, that one day I would return. So I sent her a pendant, the exact duplicate of this one."

He pulled a pendant out from beneath his shirt, holding it before Jillian's eyes.

"I'm not certain if your mother would have shown you the pendant, but she has one. I know she received it while still living on the estate. I sent it with a note stating only, *Upon a winged horse I ride to someday make you mine once more.* That is all. I didn't sign the note for fear that William might find it."

The pendant dangled before Jillian. Dizziness threatened to overwhelm her as she pulled out the emerald sewing pouch from her skirt pocket. She slowly opened the pouch, her eyes wide, as if she were frightened of something within. Her fingers shook as she timidly reached inside and brought out her own pendant, the exact match to the one Terrance held.

Reality struck Jillian. She felt as if her life had suddenly ended and she knew that everyone and everything she had ever known was now nothing but a lie.

Seeing for himself that Jillian had the pendant told Terrance more than he could bear. Sybil must have given it to her to keep, for indeed it was a gift from her father. He could say no more to her now. Putting the parchment within her hand, he silently left the cabin, tears finally finding their release.

With the pendant in one hand and the parchment in the other, Jillian walked back to the bed and sat down. Her heart pounded wildly within her ears. She sat motionless for a long while, absorbing all that he had said. The pendant in her grasp felt as if it beat with a pulse of its own. Its heat embedded into the softness of her palm by the strength with which she held it. It somehow gave her the courage she needed to face what must surely be the final proof; the parchment, which she held in her other hand.

Wiping tears from her eyes, Jillian looked closely at the yellowed paper. She could tell by its condition that the paper had been read repeatedly. She assumed its edges were worn by years of Terrance reading the message it held. She was very careful not to tear it as she unfolded the message.

Examining it closely, Jillian saw that it was a letter written to Terrance. The date: August 1650. "Shortly after I was born." she murmured. Jillian thought about ripping the letter up but knew in her heart that she had to find out the truth. She took a deep breath, summoning courage, and then began to read.

August 1650

Dearest Terrance,

I hope this letter finds you well. I felt compelled to write because after all this time Mistress Sybil still loves you and mourns your loss. Her father sent her away shortly after your disgrace. She was crushed when you were branded a thief and banished from the mainland. Sybil never believed what they said about you but knew only that she would never see you again.

William loves her, Terrance. He took your child as his own and is by Sybil's side supporting her in every way. Sybil was persuaded by his persistence to marry him. She did not want to disgrace her father anymore than she already had. I believe she has grown to love him Terrance. He is a fine father to Jillian.

Sincerely,
Sophia

Stunned by the contents of the letter, Jillian sat motionless on the bed. No screaming, no crying, no tears would come forth. There was nothing but emptiness. She felt alone, abandoned. Jillian had relied on her mother, whom she trusted without question, to be honest. Now, suddenly, there was no one she could trust. It was incredible. She thought of all the lies that had been told to her over the years. Her whole life was nothing but one big lie.

Something inside of her stirred as things started to make sense. If all this were true, and the letter was legitimate, it would explain many things that had happened over the years. It would explain her father being so harsh with her and the many times that she had been punished severely for things of minor consequence.

Many times Sybil had tried to come to her defense. Later, Jillian had heard them fighting into the night over the beatings that William gave her as punishment. Jillian often had little or no memory of the beatings but the next day there would always be bruises on her body, "as a reminder," he would say. William never apologized to her or her mother after a punishment. He called them 'lessons'. Mother would cry and tell Jillian how sorry she was for her treatment and that someday a brave knight on a winged horse would come and take her to a safe place.

After a time, Jillian noticed that her mother had bruises on her arms, and one time she spied several on her back. When she asked her about them, her mother would only smile and say that she had learned a good lesson. It all made sense now. All this time, she had blamed herself for being the cause of her mother's lessons, and now she knew why. For indeed she was the reason her father was so angry. Jillian was a constant reminder of someone before him in Sybil's life, someone before him in Sybil's heart.

Feelings of betrayal swept blackness into Jillian's soul. Her heart cried out for relief from the confines of her tightening chest. She lay on the bed, curling into a ball. Tears of frustration poured in waves from her eyes. She crumpled the letter in her hand and held the pendant to her heart as if she were trying to hold on to one last shred of herself. The words that Terrance had said came back to her and she repeated them in her mind.

"Upon a winged horse I ride, to someday make you mine once more."

*   *   *   *   *

He listened to her soft cries from beyond the cabin door, an evil smile curling his lips as he relished in the sounds of her misery . . .

Sue Ki watched Terrance leave the cabin and climb the ladder leading to the deck. He hurried back to the galley to fetch some tea for Jillian. Sue Ki knew that she would be in a terrible condition after hearing all that Terrance had told her. Ki knew the poor girl's world was completely destroyed by this truth.

He brewed a special green tea from his homeland, and prepared a tray of biscuits to go with it. Sue Ki wanted to talk to Jillian himself, for he knew Terrance better and longer than anyone. He also knew that it was very important for Jillian to stay here with Terrance for a while, to get to know him for the kind and gentle person he was.

Sue Ki left the galley carrying the tray he had prepared for Jillian. As he approached the Captain's cabin he caught a glimpse of someone leaving the corridor. Ki never gave the figure a second thought. There were many crewmen on board the Pegasus who may come below deck at any time. He tapped lightly at the door and waited for her to bid him in. No answer came, so Sue Ki knocked once more.

"Go away, leave me be," Jillian sobbed.

Sue Ki was not deterred by her words. He slowly opened the cabin door and crept in holding the tray. By the state she was in, he could see that Jillian was completely devastated by what Terrance had told her. She lay upon the bed with her face buried in her hands. Her whole body shook as she cried uncontrollably. The sounds of her crying tore at Ki's heart and he knew her despair. Terrance, for all his kind ways, had totally destroyed this child's world. He felt that given the chance, Jillian would come to love her father. Terrance needed this chance to get to know her also. She must know the whole truth before she could ever understand why he took the actions that he did. He sat the tray on the nightstand next to the bed and waited. Jillian sobs finally subsided and she lifted her swollen eyes to see who it was.

"I said to leave me alone." Her voice sounded so angry, yet defeated. "I need time to think."

"I know, missy. You confused now, but I tell you things that Cappy not tell you." He smiled a wide smile and sat beside her on the bed.

Jillian wasn't sure that she could bear to hear any more. Her life was a shambles now, since hearing the Captain's revelations. How could she hear anymore words that might destroy her? But there was no stopping the words from the little man.

"Know Cappy for long time," he began, and then in his own broken English, he told the tale of how he met Terrance McCarthy.

His captors had put Terrance on the first ship that left port the same day he and Sybil were separated. He was thrown in the hold and bound to the wall with his arms raised full length above his head. They fed him once a day, nothing but bread crust, usually stale or moldy, and very little water to drink. Terrance was allowed on deck only once each week. That was when the crew had their fun degrading him in every way imaginable. They threw buckets of seawater on him, to "bathe" him. After a while, the salt from the water began to dry and crack Terrance's skin, leaving open, festering sores on most of his body.

Sue Ki was the ship's cook. He had been forced into service after being caught by the Captain stealing food at one of the ports where the ship docked. Ki was the only one of the crew who took pity on Terrance and tried to help him.

"No matter the crime, no man should be treated as Cappy was treated," he told Jillian. But no matter what they did to him, Terrance held his head high. Most of the time, it only got him more of the same but Terrance never let them destroy his dignity.

After some months passed, the men lost interest in torturing him and left him alone. Some of the crew even started to respect Terrance for his defiance. However Captain Morris never lost his disdain for this captive who was forced upon him and he demanded that the crew continue his penance.

A few years passed and how Terrance survived, Sue Ki often wondered, but he was determined to live and return to his beloved. Captain Morris made those years as miserable as he possibly could for Terrance. Several times Sue Ki would plead with the Captain for the flogging to stop. Terrance's back became so dense with scars and open wounds that he could barely flex his muscles. They were frozen in place by the countless hours his arms had been chained above his head. Nevertheless, the beatings and whippings never stopped. As soon as Ki would succeed in getting

Terrance's back to heal, the Captain would be on him again, opening his tender skin.

Such was the day that, by fate alone, Terrance would gain freedom from his prison ship. Captain Morris was in a most foul mood from the beginning of the day. He decided that this would be the last day he would deal with Terrance McCarthy. He had never wanted the burden of this prisoner, but had taken him out on the very day of his arrest as a favor to the Admiral. The Admiral had wanted him as far away from his young daughter as possible, and the sooner the better. Young William Garret had brought the man aboard relaying the orders from the Admiral.

"He is to suffer for his crimes. Suffer until the day he dies," the young officer told him.

Therefore, they made him suffer, day after day. The Captain frequently left it to the crew as entertainment on their long journeys. However, the time had come to put an end to this captive's arrogance. It was time to put an end to his life.

He ordered Terrance be brought onto the deck and secured to the mast. The day was especially hot, the ocean air thick with heat. Two of the crewman dragged him up the ladder, and shoved him to the deck before Captain Morris.

"Stand, you swine," the Captain shouted down to Terrance. "I have grown weary of your ugly presence. Today will be your last, for today you walk the plank. But first, a final lesson must be taught."

Terrance lifted his face, squinting into the bright sunlight. "It would be my pleasure to depart from your presence, dear Captain," he sneered, "the sooner the better."

A large fist caught Terrance under the chin and sent him flying across the deck. The angry crew were instantly upon him, kicking and beating him with their fists. Terrance tried to fight back with all his strength, but being out numbered and having little strength left, soon he lay still with blood flowing from his face and ears. Terrance gasped for breath as he held his ribs, knowing that several were almost certainly broken. The men circled him while waiting for the final order.

The Captain shouted for the men to bind Terrance to the mast. They did so easily. With his face pressed hard against the splintered surface, the crew bound him to the mast with strips of wet leather. The Captain kept a supply of the straps soaking near the mast for just such occasions.

"Funny thing with leather, once it begins to dry, it shrinks up nice and tight." Captain Morris laughed evilly as he watched the men bind Terrance. "I don't suppose you realize what that means will happen to you, do you my wretched friend? I've waited a long time to rid myself of your ugly face, Terrance McCarthy. At long last my task is at an end."

The leather straps bound Terrance's hands and feet, stretching them painfully around the mast. Several thick strips were wrapped tightly around the mast at his waist and neck, forcing his body to absorb the small splinters that jabbed painfully into his flesh as his body molded to the mast. Eyes shut against the pain, Terrance waited for his final sleep.

The sun hung high in the sky above the water. The temperature of the air above the ocean soared. Sue Ki had never remembered a hotter day; it was truly the perfect day for what the Captain had in mind. The leather strips began to dry in the heat, painfully squeezing the life from Terrance's limbs. Terrance no longer had any feeling in his hands and feet, their skin gray from the lack of blood flow. He knew it would not be much longer before death, and his thoughts went to Sybil one last time.

Sue Ki made his way quietly to the mast, a bucket of water in his hand.

"I not let him die, Missy," he told Jillian, shaking his head. "He a good man. He not die that day."

Sue Ki lifted the dipper of water to Terrance's parched lips spilling it into his gasping mouth. He instinctively began to swallow the cool liquid.

"You not die today. No, you not die," he whispered to Terrance. His squinty eyes searched wildly for an instant hoping that no one had noticed him. He carefully lifted the dipper once more only to have it knocked from his hands by an angry crewman.

"What goes on here? The traitor is to have no water," the crewman shouted at Sue Ki. Some of the others stopped their labors to see what the commotion was. The little man stood fiercely in front of Terrance, protecting him from the gathering mob. With his hands raised, posing in ancient defense, a shrill cry escaped his lips, and some of the crewman backed cautiously away from the dragon man.

"So, we have ourselves another traitor," a sailor shouted over his shoulder to the others. "What should we do with him, boys?"

"String him up, like the other."

"Aye, string him up."

"Let them hang together."

The men's shouts fueled the tension of the throng. They hovered over the defiant Chinaman, ready to take him. Still, Sue Ki held a defensive stance in front of the now unconscious Terrance.

The silence was broken by the blast of a cannon in the distance. The men stood frozen in place for a second, but chaos quickly erupted as they realized their ship was being fired upon. Hastily, the men returned to their posts preparing to return fire, but it was too late. The pirate ship had already placed several clean shots just below the water line and the war ship was fast taking on water.

Pirates boarded the ship, fighting their way through the ship's crew. One by one, the men perished in the battle. The crewmen were no match for the pirates' swift swords, and it wasn't long before the men lay sprawled upon the bloodied deck.

The pirate Captain fought his way aboard the ship shouting at his men "Take what you can mates, and be quick. Leave no survivors."

His attention was immediately drawn to a battle at the ship's center near the mast. Sue Ki fought his attackers with cunning skill learned in the orient. His tiny body hurled the larger opponents one by one in every direction. The Captain stopped short of him to observe and admire the little man. Even the Captain's most skilled men were no match for this black dragon. His kicks were quick, never missing their mark, and he used the men's own bodies against them. It was plain to see that the little man had no competition from his crew.

The last man stood ready for his turn at the little man, but the Captain took hold of his arm to stop him.

"Hold on mate. Let's not be too hard on the man."

The pirate Captain smiled at his own jest. He could certainly tell that the little man would have no trouble with this last opponent and himself, without so much as breaking a sweat.

The Captain and the wounded pirate crew gathered around the Chinese man who obviously protected the man strapped to the mast, the latter looking as though he were dead. All eyes focused on Sue Ki, who held his ground with arms raised in readiness.

A call rang out over the ship, alerting the Captain to the danger of the ship sinking. Still, no movement came from the pirates or the little man.

"Come with us. Join my ship. We need your skill in fighting without weapons. You could train my men." The Captain motioned to the men to ease back. "You haven't much time to decide, little man. Come or perish with the rest of your shipmates."

The Captain turned to his men and gave the order to abandon ship. The men swiftly made their way to the side rail, and with ease, swung on ropes across the distance between the two ships. The Captain turned to see Sue Ki cutting Terrance down from the mast.

"Leave him. He is of no use to us!" the Captain ordered.

"You want me, we take him too," Sue Ki said, easing Terrance to the deck.

"Good God, man! Look at him. The devil won't last the night."

Sue Ki and the Captain both hesitated. Terrance was a horrible sight. The leather had cut through his wrists and ankles, leaving muscle to dry in the sun. He bled badly from the wounds, the straps releasing the blood to flow freely. His back, already carved from repeated floggings, bled crimson on the deck.

Terrance sensed what Sue Ki was trying to do, and with what he thought would be his last breath, pleaded with Sue Ki to go.

"Leave, my friend. Your task is at an end. I am ready to go. Please, save yourself." Another warning shot rang out. "Go, Ki." Terrance smiled and shut his eyes one last time.

Sue Ki gave the Captain a look of warning and then heaved Terrance's brittle body off the deck and onto his back. He quickly made his way toward the side rail. The Captain shook his head at the determination of the little man, and then helped him get Terrance aboard the pirate ship. As they boarded the ship, Morris's vessel upended and sank beneath the cool waters of the ocean.

Sue Ki watched, with Terrance still across his back, as the ship sank from sight. He muttered a few words in his native tongue and spit into the foaming swirl of water left by the sinking.

"Take him below, dragon man. Care for him. If he makes it, he will have only you to thank."

Sue Ki made his way to their new home below deck. Little did he know that this was the beginning their of new lives.

Above the deck of the ship flew the pirate flag, a black flag waving above the ocean, a winged horse gracing its surface. The ship's name—The Pegasus.

"He very sick for long time. I fix him. But some things not fix so good," Sue Ki said as he handed Jillian another cup of tea.

She sat on the bed fascinated by the little man and his story.

"He still have big scar on his back and in his heart. He only wanted your mama all this time. He made big plans to bring her and you here, but she no leave. She not believe Cappy about what her man done. Cappy love her for long time. Now she no love him. He hurt very bad."

Jillian listened calmly, wondering how her life could have been such an awful lie. She believed Sue Ki and Terrance. She now wondered how she could have been so naïve to think that she was just a plain, ordinary girl with an uneventful life, despite the fact that all the while she felt that there was something out there, something was missing. Jillian never dreamt that the "something" was her identity. The true Jillian had hidden in the darkness, just beyond reach of the real world.

Sophie had taught her to distance herself from pain and sorrow when she was just a small child. Sometimes Jillian had a hard time coming back from that world tucked away inside, but, as she grew older, she learned to control the urge to disappear there. The long walks on the beach were her salvation after leaving Grandfather's estate. It was the only time Jillian truly found any peace without having to hide in the darkness.

Watching the horizon of the ocean helped her keep her wits about her. Had she been looking to the distance for the answers to her unhappiness? Was this the winged horse of which mother spoke? She felt as if she knew the answer to that now. Maybe, in her heart, she had known for a long time that things were just not the way they were supposed to be.

Oh, how she longed to be on her beach once more. She closed her eyes with the memory of her home, of her family, and of all that she ever knew to be hers. It was all gone now; everything real and secure in her life was now more of a dream than the nightmare she had been through the last few hours.

She opened her eyes looking into the face of the small, gentle man. Concern and love glowed in his features. She wished things were different; she wished this hadn't ever happened.

Her thoughts were desperate but she could not help it. She couldn't go back and she wasn't sure she could stay here amongst strangers. It all became a blur to her. There were too many things happening too fast. She needed time to think, time to sort through this confusion in her life.

Sensing her state of mind, Sue Ki knew she needed to be left alone for awhile. He took the china cup from Jillian's trembling hand and put it back on the tray.

"You be good, missy. You rest and think for awhile," he soothed, as he eased her back softly to lie upon the plush bed. "Things be better with the sun in sky."

He nestled Jillian tenderly with the coverlet, and without a sound, left the room. She needed time to think, to heal her heart and mind. Sue Ki slowly closed the cabin door and made his way back to the galley with the tray. Things would be better with the sun, he reassured himself. Yes, things would be much better tomorrow.

Not being able to sleep, Jillian grew weary of staying in the cabin and decided to try the door. She discovered that it was not locked and made her way up to the deck of the Pegasus, wanting more than anything just to look out across the ocean. She hoped to catch a glimpse of a shoreline in the distance. Jillian saw no crewman as she emerged from the hatchway, the deck deserted for the night. A misty breeze greeted and refreshed her, lending her a sense of peace as she walked carefully to the ship's railing.

He watched her in silence as she seemed to glide across the deck in the moonlight, her shoulders held proudly against the night breeze. The pale glow of her soft features called to him high upon his perch. High above the deck, he watched like a bird of prey readying itself for the chase. His heart pounded rapidly within his ears as he secretly fantasized about her impending doom. Yes, it wouldn't be long now before she would be his and then he would send her to her end at the bottom of the ocean. The thought of it all gave rapid rise to his body. He could wait no longer to make his move. He must do it now while the others sleep soundly in their hammocks.

The Pegasus swayed with the rolling of the ocean waters, dipping into them, riding upward on their smooth lengths, splashing into the next swell, and then beginning the gentle ride once more. The sound of the water washing against the ship soothed Jillian, calming her. She felt as if she belonged here, as if she had always been here upon the ocean. Jillian loosened the thick braid still in her hair. It had only been hours since she was a simple girl living near the beach. Her life had changed so quickly. She wondered if that same girl had ever really existed. She would never be the same, she thought, as she stroked her finger through the masses of gold, slowing carefully over the goose egg at the back of her head.

Maybe this was indeed her destiny, the destiny that she had fantasized about so many times as a young girl. All the hours she had spent dreaming, high on the safe rock, about the day she would be free to find her own life, were now given new meaning. She had spent most of those days dreaming of a life she knew would never be her own. A life of adventure was not something that young girls were allowed to have, but now that had changed. For now, Jillian had little choice but to stay with Terrance and try to make a life upon the Pegasus. Somehow, the thought didn't frighten her in the least.

The sun was just beginning to light the sky; shades of gold and silver flowed across the water's surface, inching its way toward the Pegasus. She thought to herself that Sue Ki had been right; indeed she felt better with the rising of the sun. It was the start of a new day and a new life for her.

A smile crossed her face as he silently crept up behind her. Jillian felt something brush the folds of her skirt but before she could turn, a strong arm encircled her waist pinning one arm to her side and grasping the other firmly. She cried out, only to have her mouth covered by his pungent hand.

"You didn't think I would be back for you love? I only waited for the Captain to have his fill before I got what I wanted from his slut."

His breath was hot against her neck as he held her painfully against his body. Her feeble struggles were of no use against his great strength now fueled by the feel of her beneath his hold. His lips traced the length of her shoulder, his tongue licking the soft flesh at the base of her neck. Jillian fought to be free from his grasp but knew that she was no match for him. She searched frantically for an escape, knowing that if she could keep her wits about her, maybe she could save herself from him. She willed her body to be still, to stand calmly under his touch.

Her struggles ceased. Her body was motionless except for the rapid rise and fall of her breast. She willed her breathing to slow and began to take longer, deeper breaths. Jillian prayed that this would give her the chance she needed to break free. Her sudden stillness most certainly caught him off guard. He had fantasized about her fight to be free and the many things he would do to her while forcing her to let him have his way. Now, she was motionless in his arms. He wondered, did she want him to make love to her? What a fool this young girl must be to think that he was capable of gentleness.

"So you want it, do you now? Then you can have what you ask for, slut," he threatened.

He turned Jillian to face him, still holding her firmly about the waist. Their eyes met and she pulled away from him in shock. He was strikingly handsome, nothing like what she may have expected her attacker to look. His hair was black as a raven's, his eyes even blacker. Something in them made Jillian feel as if she were looking at the devil himself. She felt his gaze penetrate her soul with ease, making her shiver against him.

"What exactly am I asking for?" Her voice shook with fear while her mind raced for an escape. "Who are you?"

"My name is Jason. I am the one responsible for that lump on your head. If it were not for me, that idiot Gavin would have botched the whole thing and the Captain wouldn't have his bitch for the voyage."

Jillian's anger flared. She wasn't sure if it was the insult to her or to Gavin that made her so angry but she knew she couldn't take another second of this repulsive man holding her in such a way. Suddenly feeling strong and sure, she knew she was not about to let him get away with his actions.

"Unhand me, you brainless jackass! I'll have your head for this!"

As soon as the words escaped her lips, Jillian realized that she had misjudged him. He wasn't easily put off and pulled her closer, his face just inches from hers.

"So, you'll be needing a teaching, you stinking bitch. Fine by me. Always did like them uppity sluts."

Without thinking, Jillian brought her hand, claws bared, painfully across his cheek, leaving a bloody trail from her sharp nails. He released her; amazed that she had the stupidity to attack him. It was more than he ever hoped for. Now she deserved anything that he did to her. His eyes flashed with the thought, his lips curling into an evil grin.

"You little she-devil. You'll pay dearly for that," he said, wiping the blood from his cheek.

His blood glistened, crimson, on his fingers. Jason brought them to his face, inches from Jillian's eyes and, with purpose, licked each finger slowly, cleaning his blood from them. Jillian sucked in her breath, holding it in terror of the sight before her. A scream lurched within her lungs as she bit into the back of her hand. No sound came from her; there was only silence upon the deck. It seemed the whole world held its breath watching the evil scene before it.

Jillian took a few steps back away from this deadly being, but Jason matched her steps, knowing she had nowhere to run. She dared not take her eyes from him, trying to anticipate his next move. With her next step, Jillian knew that she was backed against a stack of kegs near the railing.

She was cornered, with no way out of her predicament, no way out of this awful nightmare. She watched as he came nearer, his knowing smile piercing her soul.

Suddenly he lunged, hurling himself toward her, but she ducked his attack by throwing herself upon the deck and then scrambling away from him on her hands and knees. He was quickly upon her. His hands caught the hem of her skirt, and with a strong tug, ripped it from her waist, leaving only her chemise to protect her from his invasion. Jillian turned and tried to kick him away with all her might, but he easily held her bare legs, pinning them beneath him as he covered her with his body. She could feel the hardness of his loins pressing painfully against her and she knew that all was lost.

"Please, don't do this. Please, just let me go. I won't tell the Captain," she begged.

"Do you think I give a damn about your Captain? Silly girl. Do you think he'll be coming by to rescue you?"

Jason laughed a low, deep laugh. His evil smile frightened Jillian to her very soul. There was blackness beyond description within his eyes. She was no match for this dark creature.

His mouth was all over her, nipping and sucking painfully at her flesh. His hands grabbed at her legs, their nails raking and digging into her softness. He grasped her legs, prying them apart at the knees, his body lifting slightly to allow him full view of her. His eyes lit with satisfaction. She was even more delicious than he had expected; the taste of her flesh upon his lips brought him closer to his peak. He laughed with the anticipation of himself fully within her as he stole the last breath of life from her sweet lips. He ripped open what was left of Jillian's bodice, the chemise underneath tearing with it, then sunk his teeth deeply into the tender flesh of her breast, sucking her life's blood into his mouth as he drank from her.

The pain seared through Jillian. A scream escaped her lips as she began to fight with everything she had to rid her body of this invader. She scratched and kicked, bucking her tiny form. The movement beneath his hardness only made him want her more. He raised his eyes to hers and she read his intentions in them. Jillian saw her life blood upon his lips. A tiny droplet dripped from one corner as his mouth curled into an evil smile.

"Your life tastes sweet upon my lips, your body so warm beneath my touch. I shall enjoy holding my shaft within you when your body shudders with its last breath. Your body, your life, your soul, all mine."

His mouth covered hers once more, his tongue probing within. Jillian tasted her own warm blood. Her stomach churned, nauseated by its tang. It sickened her, for she knew that he meant what he said; she was indeed doomed. She pushed against him with all her strength, gasping for air beneath his suffocating probe. The darkness came, surrounding her in its embrace, protecting her from pain, from him.

Somewhere, from beyond the darkness, Jillian heard a voice. Jason's hold on her loosened slightly, but his lips remained firmly against hers.

"Jason! Release her!" Gavin ordered, running toward them.

Jason lifted his lips slightly from hers, whispering against them, "I'll finish with you later, slut."

As Jason lifted his head to look at Gavin, a boot caught him under the chin, sending him flying backward, away from Jillian. Gavin was upon him with vengeance; the two men attacked each other with brutal force, equal to none.

Jillian backed against the kegs, curling herself tightly inward as if to become invisible to the battling men. She wrapped her arms around her legs, cradling them, fighting the shuddering of her body. Her world swirled around her. She caught only incoherent glimpses of the battle raging above her.

The two fought their way across the deck, spilling kegs of ale and stacks of supplies. To set him off balance, Jason threw everything he could in front of Gavin, but Gavin advanced with purpose, wanting nothing more than to kill Jason for what he had just witnessed.

The noise of the battle brought most of the ship's crew above deck to see what was causing it. Sue Ki, one of the first on deck, immediately spotted Jillian's cowering form by the railing. He went to her, fear pounding within his heart. Jillian didn't move, only clutched herself tighter as he approached, as if he were going to strike her. She was in a horrible state, her legs covered with deep gouges, blood flowing from her chest. Brushing her hair back from the side of her face, he gasped at the sight of her neck covered with teeth marks seeping blood. She shied from his touch but her eyes flicked around the deck as if she had lost something.

The crewmen gathered around Gavin and Jason, now at the far end of the deck, rooting on their fight. Sue Ki knew that he must get Jillian below before the Captain and the others saw her. All hell would break loose if they became aware of her state. Gently, he picked her up from the deck and made his way toward the stairwell, hoping not to be seen. Micah, the last of the crew to come from below, stopped short as the little man brushed past him. The sight of the girl held tightly in Sue Ki's arms stunned him. She was in an awful state; her face was covered with bruises, her lips swollen and bloodied. Seeing the teeth marks upon her neck and shoulders, Micah knew that Jason had attacked the girl. For a moment, he watched the two men viciously beating each other, hoping that Gavin would come out the victor. Then Micah turned and followed Sue Ki down the stairwell.

Terrance watched the two pummel each other, neither man giving in to the weariness that they both were beginning to show. He wondered what had set them off. Something terrible must have happened to make them act with such hatred. Terrance usually let his men settle their own disputes, and after seeing Jason's display of violence toward Jillian yesterday, Terrance wasn't certain that he wanted to stop Gavin, but he relented.

"Hold them men. I've seen enough of this foolishness."

With Terrance's order, several crewmen subdued Gavin and Jason, pulling them apart. In spite of the men holding him, Gavin lunged at Jason, but was not able to free himself.

"Enough, Gavin," Terrance ordered. "What is this about?"

Before Gavin could speak, Jason hurried to tell his side of the story, for he knew very well how the Captain favored Gavin. For many years he had watched Gavin weasel his way into the Captain's confidence.

"I was on watch, sir," Jason spoke between breaths. "I saw the girl strolling along the deck. Then, from out of the darkness, Gavin jumped her. He was all over her, Captain. I tried to stop him."

"That's a lie! It was you who attacked Jillian." Gavin again lunged at Jason but the men held tight.

Terrance's anger soared; his face became crimson as he realized that Jillian may have been harmed. Never could he believe that Gavin would attack her. After what had happened at the beach, with Jason striking her, he knew that Jason was lying. Giving Jason a look of disdain, Terrance turned to Gavin for the truth. With calm control, Gavin looked at Terrance squarely and told him what he knew to be the truth.

"I came on deck, Captain. It was Jason, sir. He held her down under his body. She fought him for all she was worth. He was doing such awful things to her . . . just awful," Gavin glared at Jason, daring him to deny it.

"He lies, Captain! He wanted the slut for himself. He wasn't willing to share her."

Terrance fought for control; he wanted nothing more than to tear Jason's head from his body and throw it into the ocean.

"You are evil, Jason. A more vile man, I have never known. Take him below and chain him like the animal that he is," Terrance ordered.

Suddenly, Jason broke free of the men who held him, grabbing one of their knives, and lunged into Gavin. Because the men were holding him, Gavin was unable to stop Jason's attack. The knife sunk deep into Gavin's side before the crewmen were able to pull the men apart. Gavin went limp in the hold of the men, the dagger embedded in his flesh. His life's blood staining his side.

"He's a cowardly dog, Captain. He deserves to die!" Jason yelled, lunging once more toward Gavin, but this time the men were ready and held him fast. Gavin sunk to his knees in pain, grasping the handle of the dagger. The crewmen tried to help him, but were only able to ease his way to the deck. Terrance was instantly at his side, laying Gavin's head in his lap.

"I saved her Captain. She is alright, isn't she?"

Terrance's heart filled with pain for Gavin. His eyes searched the Pegasus for Jillian, but he could see her nowhere. "Aye, Gavin. You saved the lass," he reassured him.

Jason fought the men holding him, cursing them as they dragged him toward the stairwell. "You'll pay for this! All of you will pay dearly. No one treats me this way and lives to tell about it. You're doomed. Every one of you, doomed!"

"Shut him up!" Terrance yelled at his men.

Cy, a large man with only one good eye, hit Jason squarely in the chin with his fist, knocking him unconscious. Then threw him over his shoulder and disappeared into the stairwell.

"Someone find Ki. Quickly!" Terrance bellowed, looking into Gavin's face and seeing the small boy he had rescued so long ago.

Terrance yelled for Sue Ki as the men carried Gavin to his quarters below deck. Where was that little man when Terrance needed him? As they passed the Captain's cabin, Sue Ki and Micah quietly emerged from it. Micah's face paled when his eyes met the Captain's. Terrance realized that Jillian must be inside. Sue Ki put his hands up to stop Terrance before he could enter.

"She be fine, Cappy. She one strong girl." Terrance pushed past Ki, almost knocking him down. He had to see Jillian for himself.

A wave of sickness came over Terrance when his eyes fell upon Jillian's still form on the bed. He approached her with caution; the pallor of her skin frightened him. He thought that he had never seen anyone closer to death than Jillian was at this moment.

Jillian's eyes were open but Terrance could see no life within their depths. Her lips were swollen with bruises that trailed oddly down the side of her neck. Although, the black silk robe was wrapped tightly around her, Terrance sensed there was more and loosened it, exposing to his eyes only, the hideous bite marks leading down to her breast. There upon her silken flesh, blood oozed from the openings his teeth had left in her creamy skin. Anger in seeing her pain escaped him. Fists clenched in frustration, Terrance's mighty roar was heard by everyone on board.

"Father, where is Gavin?" Jillian asked, her voice but a whisper.

"Jillian. My sweet Jillian," Terrance cried, taking her hand in his, and realizing that she called him father. "I'm so sorry. I shouldn't have brought you here. I didn't keep you safe."

"Father, Gavin saved me. I must see him." She began to push herself from the bed.

"You must rest, Jillian. Sue Ki will see to Gavin."

"No, he needs me. I must go to him now." Jillian pushed past Terrance, stumbling to the cabin floor.

Terrance lifted her, lending support as she continued to the entryway. "Which one is his?"

"It is there," Terrance said, as he pointed to the door Sue Ki and Micah entered.

"Then, that is where I must be also."

Ki struggled to remove the britches from Gavin's clammy form. Without a thought Jillian began the duty of helping Ki with Gavin. The leather pants slipped from Gavin's legs and Sue Ki quickly covered him with warm blankets. He began to cleanse the wound with clean cloths, washing the blood from his skin. Jillian stood behind Ki, taking care to study his every move. The little man was quick and sure in his ministrations. Gavin never winced or made motion from the pain that Jillian knew he must be feeling.

The flow of blood lessened, and once the wound was clean, Ki gave Jillian a cloth to hold against it. He prepared a potion for Gavin to drink. Jillian watched him as he carefully allowed four drops from the small vile to fall into a cup of warm tea. He looked at Jillian and then at Gavin and after a moment of thought, added another four drops to the tea.

"He a big boy, must not wake. Must not move," he told her. He finished the potion by adding a rather large spoonful of sugar, a precious commodity on any ship. With hurried steps, Ki returned to Gavin's side.

"I hold him up. You make him drink. Must drink all or will not sleep deep." Ki instructed.

He lifted Gavin's shoulders, holding his head so that he could drink. Jillian cooed to him holding the cup to his lips.

"Gavin. Gavin, my love. You must drink this," Jillian told him gently. He struggled to wake, his eyes rolling back in their sockets.

"Gavin, please. Please drink the tea."

A small amount of tea spilled into Gavin's mouth, wetting it. "Too sweet," he whispered. "Too sweet. Ki always . . . puts . . . much . . . sugar."

His words faded and Gavin drank the tea slowly. Jillian knew that time was against them; his breaths were little more than gasps now. Whatever Sue Ki was going to do, he must hurry if they were to save Gavin's life. Ki lowered Gavin back to the bed.

"He sleep for long time, missy. We must hurry, sew him up."

Jillian watched as Ki prepared for the surgery. He laid his tools on a cloth on the night table. Carefully he threaded a thin needle, holding it up to the light, and placed it upon the cloth. He opened a bottle, removing the cork with his teeth. With a small piece of cloth, he dabbed a dark liquid around Gavin's wound. Once satisfied with his work, he then dipped the needle into the same liquid. The wound, a deep gash in Gavin's side above his hip, still oozed. Ki slid his finger inside the wound opening it even more. He peered through the opened skin into Gavin's body, giving it a thorough examination.

"He cut deep inside. Must sew deep inside. You hold, I sew."

Jillian shook her head no. She couldn't do it. She stepped back from him, her eyes wide.

"Then I hold, you sew."

Sue Ki knew that Jillian was frightened. He also knew that he could call one of the crew in to help him, but Jillian needed to be the one to help. She needed to be the one to save Gavin.

"You hold, I sew," he said once again.

Jillian agreed and stepped forward. Ki showed her how to put two of the tools at either side of the cut and pull the skin gently apart. This allowed Ki to slip the needle deep into Gavin's wound and stitch the flesh within.

It was amazing to watch the little man work. He worked quietly and efficiently, tying off each knot and then cutting it close to the stitch. Jillian watched, studying his every move. Soon, Ki finished stitching inside the wound and was ready to stitch the outer flesh of Gavin's side. He took the tools from Jillian and eased the skin together. Holding it tightly, Sue Ki stitched with fine precision to close the wound one stitch at a time.

Sue Ki had put six stitches in when he suddenly stopped and turned to Jillian. "You put stitch in. You must learn." He pushed the needle toward her.

"I don't know how to sew a man's skin," she told him, fighting back nausea. "I cannot."

"You sew clothes? You sew necklace? You sew skin," he assured her, as he placed the needle in her hand. "I show you."

Jillian took a deep breath, then with a remarkably steady hand, pushed the needle into Gavin's skin. Sue Ki guided her first stitch carefully, his hand holding hers gently. She did just as Sue Ki had, spacing the first stitch exactly the same distance as his. Once the skin was brought together, he showed her how to tie a knot that would hold until the healing was complete.

Once Jillian had put five more stitches into Gavin's skin, their work was finally done. Jillian felt as if she had held her breath the entire time she worked, and let out a sigh of relief as the last stitch was cut. Sue Ki gathered up his tools and cleared away the bloodied clothes, leaving Jillian gazing tenderly at Gavin.

*   *   *   *   *

"It isn't good, mates. Gavin is in a sorry state. He's lost a lot of blood. But if the lass has any witch's power, he will live, for she is at his side," Cy said as he poured himself some ale from the keg mounted in the corner of the galley, and sat at the table with the men. "She's a strong one, that she is. She's covered with bruises and scratches from that animal, but still has the strength to tend to Gavin in his time of need."

Micah agreed, "He'll not die as long as she is near him, for she holds his heart in her hands and must be strong."

The men sat in silence, each of them calming their fears for Gavin. A melody drifted into the galley from the corridor, its sweet notes caressing their minds. It filled the air around the men, enveloping them within its warmth. Sounds of love emanated from the melody, a song of passion's sweetness like no other echoed through the Pegasus. The men, like stone statues, sat mesmerized by it. It was Jillian's song they heard, Jillian's song for Gavin.

She felt Gavin's forehead and found him very cool to the touch. His face was beaded in sweat, his color pale. Concerned, Jillian caressed his cheek, studying him.

"Sue Ki, something is wrong!" Jillian shouted. Ki stopped what he was doing and came back to the bedside. "He is cool to the touch, yet he sweats," Jillian said, her face pale with fear.

Ki knew immediately what was wrong and what must be done. He took several blankets brought in by the men and put them over Gavin, tucking them in around him.

"Blankets too cold. I get more." He rushed from the room leaving Jillian to tend to Gavin.

Sweat beaded on Gavin's brow. Jillian took a damp cloth and swabbed the moisture away. Gavin's chin began to tremble, his teeth chattering together. Jillian put her arms around his shoulders hoping to give him her warmth. Sue Ki rushed into the cabin, his bundle toppling onto the foot of the bed.

"Take old blanket off," he ordered her. "Must walm him velly fast."

Careful not to disturb his wound, Jillian stood and pulled the damp blankets off Gavin's naked form. As soon as she lifted them, Sue Ki covered him with several layers of warmed blankets from the galley. Gavin's teeth chattered, and even though he should have gained warmth from the blankets, he seemed to be freezing beneath them. His whole body began to tremble, quaking from the mysterious cold.

Jillian lay her body across his hoping to stop the shuddering. The fear of losing him to this cold caused a panic in Jillian and she cried out to him, "Gavin, you must hold on. Please!"

"You hold him, missy. Stitch so new, must not move. I get more walm blankets, you hold him tight."

Jillian didn't need to be told to hold Gavin; she clung to him with all her strength. He shuddered under her, almost throwing her from the bed. She maneuvered her body more fully onto his so that she lay fully on top of him being very careful to keep her weight from his side. The fragile stitches, she knew, must remain intact. Very slowly, warmth seeped from her to him, filling his body with much needed heat.

It seemed like hours before the quaking stopped and his body calmed beneath hers. His breaths slowed to a normal rhythm; Jillian knew that he slept peacefully beneath her. Fatigue crept into her body as she laid her cheek against his chest, sighing with relief that he was out of danger. She closed her eyes, humming to him once more, but was soon swept into sleep by the warmth radiating under her.

Sue Ki entered the cabin, his arms loaded with more warming blankets from the galley. The crew had stripped their cots clean in order to find enough bedding for Gavin. Ki took his time getting the blankets warm, knowing the coldness would soon subside, and that Gavin would be out of danger. He wasn't surprised to find that Gavin indeed, had calmed and now seemed very warm beneath Jillian. Ki smiled to himself. The little princess instinctively knew what to do in a crisis. She would be a very good pupil for Ki; he was anxious to have a student to whom he could teach his healing skills. For now, she was sound asleep on top of Gavin, with her head resting on his chest and her arms encircling his broad shoulders. She looked so tiny lying on her perch, a fragile guardian of such a giant.

Ki gently put a layer of blankets over top of the sleeping pair. Jillian smiled and snuggled into their warmth. He put his hand against Gavin's forehead and felt that he was once again warm and dry to the touch. Sue Ki knew he was out of danger and must rest; Jillian too needed rest.

The galley went silent when Sue Ki entered. The men huddled together, ceasing their discussion upon his arrival. He eyed them sharply, then threw the blankets he carried into a huge boiling pot that he had prepared earlier. Ki stirred the blankets into the water as if to make a giant stew of them. The men watched, waiting for his report. Ki was never one to keep secrets and after the last time he came from Gavin's cabin, the men were more than anxious to hear what he had to say.

By the time Sue Ki had finished the last details of Jillian's fight to save Gavin, the men sat in silence. Their thoughts ranged from disbelief to envy. Not one man uttered a word but only watched as Sue Ki went about his duties in the galley leaving them to interpret his story in their own way. Each of them formed a picture in their minds of Jillian making intricate stitches in Gavin's flesh, of Jillian humming a song that brought strength to their dear friend, of Jillian's tiny form sleeping atop Gavin in sheer exhaustion from her own ordeal.

The men felt a closeness to her that knew no bounds. Their eyes met each other's in a silent vow to protect and love this fragile life that had so suddenly appeared in theirs. Her position on the Pegasus was still a mystery to them. She was bound to them, yet each man felt, from deep within, that they were also her guardians, entrusted by her deeds to keep her safe from harm, even if that harm were the Captain himself.

Jillian stirred beneath the warm layers of blankets, her eyes blinking away the sleep that she had so needed. She was immediately aware of Gavin cradled beneath her body, her arms enveloping his. Raising her head, careful not to disturb him, she searched his face for signs that he too had awakened. After a few moments of watching him, she knew that he was still deep within the drugged sleep from Sue Ki's potion.

A blush came over her, warming her entire body, as she shifted slightly and felt his length beneath her. The blankets between them suddenly felt thin as parchment. She sensed every rise and fall from his even breaths. The tensing of his broad chest aroused a sensation deep within her like nothing she had ever felt. She rested her cheek against him once more, taking in the feel of him and the smell of his maleness. Her fingers traced the hollow of his throat and there she felt the pulsing of his heart, strong and true, her own matching every beat.

She searched her mind for some rhyme or reason for the feelings that welled deep within her soul. The strength of them overpowered her senses. She wondered how she could feel this way about him so soon, and then, in the same thought, wondered how she could ever have lived before knowing him.

She took his essence into her and with his every breath, his soul settled deeper into her own. These overwhelming emotions brought tears to her eyes. Tears danced on her delicate lashes and gently traced a path onto Gavin's flesh, pooling beneath her cheek.

"I love you, Gavin," she whispered.

Jillian's words drifted into the darkness of his mind. He knew that she was near; he knew that she loved him. This knowledge gave him strength.

Jillian felt that he was aware of her, this thought making her suddenly realize the advantage she was taking of him. Guiltily, she eased her body off his, careful not to disturb his wound. Her face flushed and she questioned her behavior. How could she be so brazen as to lay on him when he no longer needed her for warmth? The shuddering of his body had ceased long ago. But even now, Jillian could hardly tear herself away from him. She felt emptiness surrounding her, touching her, where his body had been. She hugged herself for warmth, attempting to fill the void her leaving created.

A noise at the cabin door brought Jillian's attention away from Gavin. There in the doorway stood Terrance, his face aglow with admiration for the strength that he saw in his daughter. Even though her wounds were significant, she would not be persuaded to rest. She had insisted on administering to Gavin who had saved her life. Terrance had given in to her pleas to administer to him alongside Sue Ki.

"Thank you," Jillian whispered to Terrance. "Thank you for letting me help him. Gavin saved my life."

"You're welcome Jillian. I'm quite certain that Gavin is grateful also," he chuckled. "Now, I believe our little princess needs to have some royal treatment. Come, Jillian, I have a surprise for you."

He led her from the cabin, his face lit with secrets. Jillian eyed him and wondered what he could possibly be up to. After all the events that had taken place since she had arrived on the Pegasus, she didn't think that there was anything else that could surprise her.

As they stopped outside the Captain's cabin, Jillian's look questioned Terrance. Sue Ki hurried down the corridor behind them. Terrance waited for him to arrive before revealing his secret.

"Now, shut your eyes, Jillian. Don't peek," he said, watching to make sure she didn't open her eyes too soon. Reaching behind him, Terrance shoved the door, letting it creak open.

"Please, what is it?" she asked, becoming nervous. "If truth be told, I don't like surprises."

"You'll love this one, Jillian." He gently pulled her into the cabin. Jillian knew Sue Ki was close behind them as they made their way into the room. Terrance moved to stand behind her.

"You may open your eyes now." Terrance said, anxiously.

Jillian drew her breath in sharply. The sight before her pleased her immensely. On the bed lay the most wonderful gown Jillian had ever seen. She timidly approached the bed as if she were frightened to get near. Emerald silk shimmered in the light from the lanterns, illuminating its flowing lengths. The gown wasn't adorned with ruffles or lace, but swept floor-length with clean, formfitting lines. The sleeves puffed at the shoulders, becoming tight above the elbow and snugly flowing to the wrists. The skirt was full at its hem and draped the width of the bed.

"It's magnificent." she said

"It's yours," Terrance laughed.

Jillian blinked away tears.

Micah's cough broke the silence. "Buckets coming through," he announced, pushing his way into the cabin, followed by Cy.

Both were carrying buckets filled with steaming water. Jillian watched as they poured the contents into the huge tub at the room's center. They smiled cleverly at her as they passed her, leaving to retrieve more.

"A bath. How did you know?" she asked but then caught herself. Of course he knew. Gavin's blood still stained her hands. She looked at them, remembering the needle, the blood. Oh, so much blood.

"I have to see Gavin first," she said starting to leave suddenly with the urge to see him.

Terrance stopped her. Placing his hands on her shoulders, he looked into her eyes to see the determination within.

"Aye, we'll go see to Gavin. Then it's time to see to you, Jillian. You need caring too." Terrance said, leading her back to Gavin's cabin.

Gavin lay sleeping peacefully in just the same way that he was when Jillian had left him. His face was now soft and serene, showing no signs of pain. Jillian reassured herself by feeling his forehead. Again, the fire leapt with her touch and her heart pounded. He felt so good under her caress; his skin called to her for attention. She wanted to stay and hold him longer, but Terrance ushered her back to his cabin where her bath lay ready.

Sue Ki awaited her return, standing near the tub with blankets folded over one arm and a bottle of sapphire liquid in his free hand. Jillian questioned Terrance silently, and held onto his arm, keeping him from leaving.

Patting her hand to reassure her, Terrance eased away. "Let Ki work his magic, Jillian. Let him soothe your weary body and mind. Don't be afraid." He gently lifted her hand to his lips placing a soft kiss upon it. Terrance smiled at her, and then shut the door behind him as he left the cabin, leaving Jillian alone with Sue Ki.

She stood in place, arms wrapped around her for protection. Ki never moved toward her, wanting only to gain her trust in him. Jillian looked at the tub as if trying to decide if she really wanted to bathe or not.

"I take good care of you. I take pain away for you. Let me help you," Sue Ki said.

His voice soothed her fears; his gentleness was sincere. She wanted to trust him, and somehow, she did trust him. She remembered the care he had taken with her after Jason's attack. He had stripped away the remains of her tattered dress, then put the robe around her battered body, and not once did she feel a threat from him. Jillian felt no such threat now.

Seeing Jillian relax, Sue Ki smiled to himself for now he could go to work healing her a little at a time. He helped her out of the robe, turning his back while she climbed into the tub. The sensation of the warm water seeped through Jillian, leaving her breathless, her apprehension dissolving into the depths of the water, and the pain of her battle disintegrating with it.

Lost in the release with which the water gifted her, Jillian paid little attention to Sue Ki. She took pleasure in the water, bathing away her troubled thoughts in the soothing warmth. Sue Ki added the azure liquid to the water. The scent of this oil surrounded Jillian and she breathed it in deeply, absorbing its fragrance.

"It's jasmine," he said, answering her unspoken question. "Cappy got it just for you."

She smiled a knowing smile, and said, "Remind me to thank him again for all these wonderful gifts."

"Cappy knows. You don't need to say words. He knows."

Sue Ki went to work bathing Jillian, who allowed him to do so, relishing the care with which he took. He gently washed her hands and arms, his touch causing flashes of pain where the scratches broke the surface of her fragile flesh. He soaped the cloth and massaged her feet with its soft texture to remove the splatters of blood left from her ordeal.

Jillian relaxed against the back of the great tub, feeling as if at any time she may drift to sleep. Sue Ki shook her arm, bringing her back to consciousness, then handed her the cloth so that she could finish cleansing the rest of her body. He left her for a moment to retrieve another bottle from the tray and returned to help her wash her hair, its long lengths floating across the water's surface.

Once her bath was complete, Sue Ki helped Jillian out of the tub, wrapping her in a soft blanket. He slowly dried her tender skin and then wrapped her hair, letting the cloth absorb the moisture from it. She let him guide her to the bed and followed his instructions to lie upon it face down. Ki pulled the blanket down to expose her back, and then rubbed the jasmine oil into her skin, massaging away the last bit of tenderness. He did the same with Jillian's legs, applying salve to medicate the scratches.

She began to feel her skin tingle with the heat from the oil. Its healing magic took away her will to stay conscious and she drifted into a deep peaceful sleep. Sue Ki smiled with satisfaction. She was healing and would wake a whole new being. He rolled her over onto her back and massaged the oil into her arms. The marks down her delicate neck and breast swelled with color. Sue Ki took great care applying the extra salve to them, and then wrapped her battered body snuggly in the feathered comforter.

She slept through the night in a deep, peaceful sleep. No nightmares plagued her; no fear entered her thoughts. She was at peace. At long last she had found herself.

Misgivings   *Chapter 13*

When Jillian woke the next morning, her body felt fortified despite what her mind knew she had been through. Sun crept through the portholes, casting brilliant circles of light upon the polished floor; the details of its grain stood out vividly under the light's embrace. Within the beams, minute specks of dust danced a carefree rhythm. She held out her cupped hands as if to catch the tiny fragments.

Everything in the room had changed somehow. Colors, shapes, and sizes of the cabin's contents were enhanced by the light of a new day and a new life. Jillian examined everything, from the grain of the cherry wood armoire to the finely embroidered fabric of the luxurious chaises. She ran her hand down the sleek black surface of the porcelain tub, its coolness inviting her touch. One at a time, she studied the miniature paintings on the rim with her fingertips. Each painting depicted a scene from a far away land; the intricate details fascinated her.

The emerald gown given to her the previous night by Terrance lay on the foot of the huge Captain's bed. She picked it up and held it to her dreamily, feeling it against her bare skin. Swaying to the rhythm of her heart, Jillian danced a slow cadence around the room, the gown swirling softly around her smooth legs. She was anxious to feel its silkiness covering her body.

Without further thought, Jillian lifted the gown over her head, smoothing it down to fit her petite form. She could not have hoped for a more perfect fit. It felt wonderful on her. Indeed, she felt as if she was a princess in a fairytale world and she cherished every moment of it. A knock upon the door nudged Jillian back from her dream world.

"Who is there?" she asked softly.

Terrance's voice came from beyond the door and she smiled as she made her way to open it, "It is I, Jillian. May I come . . . ?"

He stopped short as the door opened and Jillian came into view. A more beautiful woman he had never seen. His mouth agape, he stood captivated before her.

Finding his tongue, Terrance was humbled. "My darling girl, you must permit me to introduce you to my crew," he said bowing to her.

"That would please me greatly," she said, taking his offered hand.

He held her delicate hand within his, gently pulling her into the companionway. "I must introduce the men before I decide to lock you away in the cabin to keep you safe from harm."

"I could not be safer than I am right now with you. There is one matter to discuss before we go above," she said, stopping him.

"What could that be, little one?"

Expecting to hear that Jillian wanted to see Gavin to make sure of his progress, Terrance was surprised at her answer. "It concerns the man who attacked me. I believe his name is Jason," she said, choking out his name.

Terrance's anger flared just hearing his name. The man was a lecher, a rapist. "Don't be concerned with that devil," he spat. "He will not live long enough to harm you again."

"No! You must not kill him because of me. I couldn't live with myself knowing that I was the reason for someone's death."

"You? Responsible for him? Don't be absurd, Jillian. The man deserves to die. It's not any fault of yours."

Clutching Terrance's hands together within her own, Jillian held them to her breast pleadingly. "Please, Terrance, promise me that you will not kill him, but leave him at the first port in which we dock. Please? For me?"

Seeing that this seemed to mean a great deal to Jillian, Terrance surrendered. "Aye, it will be as you wish. We will leave him on the mainland at our first stop. Aye, but you have a way that melts a man's soul; I just hope I don't end up regretting my weakness." Wrapping her arm in his, they walked to the ladder leading to the deck. Jillian stopped him there.

"Thank you," Jillian said, kissing Terrance's hand.

Having gone up the ladder first, Terrance emerged from the stairwell onto the deck. It was a beautiful day to be upon the ocean; the vivid blue sky was dappled with white clouds of softness suspended within it. The ocean reflected the azure color, deepening with its own. Terrance loved the sea and was growing to love the beautiful girl now emerging from the stairwell.

The ship's crew cheered as Jillian appeared and stood blushing before them. They gathered around, each welcoming her, some with fond looks and others with warm hugs. All thanked her for saving Gavin's life and for bringing joy back to the Captain's heart.

Jillian returned their kind words with her own, as she thanked them for accepting her and promised to eventually remember all their names. There were so many that by the time they had all greeted her, she was truly overwhelmed. Each man returned to his post and Terrance led Jillian around the deck, giving her a grand tour. He pointed out the riggings of the massive sails, the crow's nest at the top of the center mast, and the man within it.

A thought flashed through Jillian's mind; was this where Jason had been when she came to the deck? The thought of him watching from high above gave Jillian reason to tremble. Terrance noticed the shudder running through her and pulled her gently against his side. Feeling his strength, Jillian knew that she no longer had to fear Jason, for soon he would be gone and she would be safe. They stood for a time in silence overlooking the Pegasus, watching the crew skillfully sail the mighty boat over the vast waters.

"She's a marvelous vessel. I hope I can become a part of her crew."

"You already are, my dear. Didn't you see the looks of appreciation upon the men's faces? They have accepted you as one of their own. It's as it should have been long before now."

A sudden sadness came over Terrance's face. Jillian knew he was thinking of her mother and all the years that had been wasted because of one man's greed.

Hearing a familiar cough behind them alerted Terrance to Micah's presence. "Aye, Micah. You must do something about that cough," Terrance teased.

"Sue Ki told me to come up and give you word of Gavin," Micah's voice broke with high pitched tones of excitement. "He's awake, Captain! Awake and very hungry."

"Aye, that's a good sign for a man. Hunger is the first thing that returns when the healing starts. Let's go below and welcome him back from the dead, shall we?" he suggested, offering his arm to Jillian.

Jillian knew her face was absolutely glowing from the rush that she felt in hearing that Gavin had awakened from his ordeal. She couldn't wait to speak to him and thank him for saving her from Jason. She wanted to tell him she was the Captain's daughter.

Her legs were weak beneath her as they made their way toward Gavin's cabin. Many of the crewmen were gathered at his door welcoming him back. His laughter could be heard as the crew teased him about being a lazy sod laying in bed for no good reason. She listened as they approached realizing that she was hearing his laughter for the first time. The sound was sweet music to her ears.

As she and Terrance neared the cabin, the men grew quiet, turning to her in reverence, parting to give her a clear pathway into Gavin's room. Their eyes met and everyone felt the magnetic pull between them. Slowly, Jillian made her way to stand at the foot of Gavin's bed. Smiling, Terrance came to her side, wrapping his arm tightly around her slender waist.

Upon seeing this exchange of affection, Gavin's expression became grim. He remembered her voice; he remembered her body pressed to his and her words of love. Words filled with promises that he could now see she had no intention of keeping. He felt like such a fool to think that she would leave the Captain's bed for his. Anger took over Gavin's senses as the reality of what he thought he saw hit home. Jillian was nothing but the Captain's whore after all.

Puzzled by Gavin's silence and the sudden fierce look in his eyes, Jillian looked up at her father, questioning Gavin's behavior. Terrance too, wondered at Gavin's anger and sensed Jillian's fear. He gave her a loving squeeze, reassuring her.

It was the last straw, Gavin thought. To see Jillian before him dressed so beautifully and then to have the Captain hold her in such a way was more than he could handle. He spoke in anger, not thinking of the consequences of his words.

"I was such a fool. To think I risked my life to save you when you most likely wanted what Jason was about to give you."

"Gavin, what are you saying?" Terrance demanded, fighting the urge to strangle him.

"What I am saying Captain, is that I should not have saved this whore from Jason, but perhaps saved him from her instead, for she is a cruel hearted slut."

The words tore Jillian to shreds; pain filled her breast, choking her. Unable to look at his anger, she turned her back to him. Terrance tried to catch Jillian to him, but she broke free and ran from the cabin, not looking at any of the crewman, running down the corridor to the Captain's cabin, completely devastated by Gavin's angry words. Once inside the cabin, Jillian threw herself upon the bed, a tormented cry escaping her lips.

The men in Gavin's cabin shuddered as they heard the sweet girl's cry. It echoed through the hull of the ship, bringing an eerie silence to its depths. The men stared at Gavin in disgust. In unison they turned their backs to him, leaving Gavin alone with Terrance.

Standing at the foot of the bed, Terrance tried to contain his anger before speaking; reasoning in his mind why Gavin would want to hurt Jillian so. He suddenly realized that Gavin was not aware that Jillian was his daughter, but that did not excuse his insult to her.

Waiting tensely for Terrance to speak, Gavin could see that what he had said had not only hurt Jillian, but had wounded Terrance to the core. He was sorry as soon as the vile words had escaped his angry lips. But the look of love that passed between Terrance and Jillian was more than Gavin could bear. Gavin had lashed out, wanting to hurt Jillian, not giving a thought to anything else.

"You don't know what you've done, Gavin." Terrance's voice was steady, "I believe the girl loves you deeply." He held up his hand to Gavin, demanding silence, "Let me have my say, before you get yourself in any deeper. She, Jillian, loves you. I have seen it in her eyes and know it in my heart. She is my life, Gavin. My blood."

Gavin's head jerked up at his words, bringing his eyes to meet Terrance's. There were tears there, and Gavin felt a sudden jolt of guilt.

"What have I done, Captain? Who is she to you?" Gavin asked.

Terrance sighed, "Jillian is my daughter."

The words pounded in Gavin's head. Terrance's daughter? Not the Captain's whore? Oh, how he wished he could take back his angry words. What he had said sickened him. Gavin felt remorse for the impact his words had on Jillian. How could he ever make it up to her? How could he make it up to the Captain?

"Terrance, I am very sorry. I thought . . . oh, you know what I thought. I don't understand any of this. You never told me you had a daughter. You kidnapped her? My God, what have we done?" Gavin asked.

"I couldn't tell you, Gavin. I couldn't tell anyone until I knew what Jillian wanted to do. I told her how this came to be. She believes me and wants to stay. That is, until now. I'm not sure what she'll do, but I must go to her and try to make things right."

Terrance turned on his heel and was out of the cabin before Gavin could say anything more. Gavin wondered how he could right the wrong his words had caused. Somehow, he would make Jillian see that she must remain here, even if it meant that he would stay away from her.

Later, Terrance sat on the bed cradling Jillian, cooing softly to her. She had cried for hours in his arms, but now only hiccupped softly. Terrance smiled to himself, for it was the same thing his own sister used to do when she would cry. If she had cried terribly hard, the hiccups would sometimes last for days. He remembered how he used to tease her unmercifully, most of the time causing her to laugh and forget why she had cried, until the hiccups went away.

This was different; this was his daughter lying in his arms and with every sob, his heart tore within his chest. During her crying, Terrance explained that Gavin was mistaken and very sorry for his behavior, but nothing seemed to help Jillian. He knew that she was not only crying over Gavin's words but also over her own plight. Gavin's assumption about Jillian had made Terrance realize that people may think ill of Jillian, branding her a tarnished woman. They would assume this because she was such a young girl on board a ship full of men. He felt regret in bringing her here, destroying in the eyes of her people, her innocence.

"I can take you back, if that is what you wish," he said, smoothing a curl from Jillian's brow.

Jillian slowly opened her eyes, capturing his gaze in their amber depths. "You don't want me to stay? You want me to leave? But, I can't possibly go back." She sat up, straightening the folds of her skirt. "You heard what Gavin said. I know he didn't mean it, but he only said the words that many would be thinking if I were to return home. No one would believe for a moment that I would be untouched on board a pirate ship. And after what Jason did to me, my . . . fa, I mean William, would make me pay dearly and probably marry me off to some fat, old croon."

"Jillian, my love, I am sorry to have destroyed you so. I only wish there was some way to make things right."

"You have not destroyed me. Things will smooth out between Gavin and me. I intend to set him straight very soon. I just want him to wallow in his own self-pity for a time. Sophie used to tell me if you leave someone alone with their thoughts for a time, they become punishment enough."

"Aye, but you are a wise young woman, Jillian. God help us all. You have captured every heart upon the ship."

"My heart has somehow always been here, where it belongs. I'm so sorry to have lost myself, crying like I did. It's just that in hearing Gavin's words, reflecting what I already knew, I felt the doors to my old life suddenly close. Mostly, I wept for the loss of Mother and Siriann."

Suddenly, the ship lurched beneath them and Jillian fell forward against Terrance who caught her to him, swearing under his breath.

"What is it? The ocean is suddenly so rough." Jillian said, holding onto him.

"There must be a storm blowing above. I have to see to my men, Jillian." He pulled away from her, settling her back upon the bed. "You stay here. Promise me. Don't leave the cabin no matter what happens."

"But!" she protested.

"No matter what, Jillian," Terrance commanded.

Seeing her nod, Terrance turned and left the cabin, closing the door behind him. Jillian steadied herself as the ship dipped and rose with the fierceness of the rising storm.

Moments later, above the roar of the storm, Jillian heard someone knocking at the cabin door. She tried to reach it, steadying herself by holding the bedpost, but quickly decided that making the distance to the door could only bring her injury.

"Who's there?" she called out. She could hear a muffled voice from beyond the door but couldn't distinguish what was said. "You may come in, I can't make my way to the door." she yelled.

The cabin door flung open and Micah fell to the floor at her feet. Jillian reached down to help him up, but when she did, another lurch from the ship sent her sprawling on top of him. Micah caught her and the two held onto each other, trying not to make matters worse. Jillian began to laugh. This must be what being drunk feels like, she thought.

"Miss Jillian. I'm so sorry. I'm so clumsy. I just . . . just came to secure the cabin," a frazzled Micah gasped in explanation.

Jillian couldn't help but laugh at poor Micah. He stuttered and stammered his apologies while all the time rolling around the cabin floor with her in his arms. They were face-to-face, and she saw the total embarrassment in his eyes. His face was flushed with color, only making her laugh all the more.

"Micah, Micah. You are such a tease. I didn't know you cared," she chuckled teasingly.

By this time she felt terribly giddy, giggling at her own joke. Micah stopped his stammering long enough to study her face and saw that she was teasing him. Again he felt his face flush, realizing that he held her so tightly in his arms. He reached up and grasped the bed's frame, steadying them so that Jillian was able to pull herself off him and climb onto the bed. She couldn't stop laughing and rolled on the bed joyously.

"I'm sorry, Micah, but you looked so utterly mortified with me lying across you. I hope I didn't hurt you when I fell. I didn't mean to, of course."

"Certainly not, you weigh but a feather. No man in his right mind would blink an eye at having you on . . . . oh, you know what I mean."

"Yes, Micah. I know what your intentions were. Now, just tell me how I may help you secure the room, that is if we are able to stay on our feet long enough to do so."

"No need, miss. I just need to make sure the lantern is out and placed where it can't tip over. Fire, you understand, can mean a disaster on a ship," he said, as he extinguished the lantern.

"Yes, I'm sure it would. I never realized so much time had passed; it's dark already," she shouted above the wail of the storm.

"That's due to the squall, miss. The sea gets mighty black when there's a big one like this. A gale comes on quickly and then leaves just as fast. Strange things, these storms at sea."

"Does this happen often, Micah?" She held on once more to the bedpost, staring through the darkness at his silhouette.

"Not often, miss. But as you can see, once is more than enough on a voyage such as this."

Micah made his way to the free swinging door, catching it just before it hit him. "Best stay in your bed for the night, miss. It looks like it could be a long one. You'll be safe as long as you stay put."

Micah shut the door firmly behind him. Jillian was alone again, but this time the room felt terribly dark and vacant. All Jillian could do was curl up inside the warm bed and ride the storm out. This she did, careful to brace herself so as not to fall off the bed again. The memory of Micah's red face made Jillian smile. He was such a gentleman, probably not much older than herself, and horribly bashful. Yet, she sensed that he was very aware of her feelings. He made her feel welcome. He was the one who had helped Sue Ki with her after Jason's attack, not once making her feel self-conscious about it. Micah had seen the damage that Jason had inflicted on her body, but never gave a look or spoke a word to make her feel uncomfortable in his presence.

Down the corridor, the Pegasus rocked and swayed with the waves of the storm. Gavin ached to be above at the helm, fighting the rush of water with the rest of the men. Sue Ki had given the men strict orders that if he came on deck, to take him back to his cabin immediately. Gavin knew that no man in his right mind would go against the "Little Dragon Man", as he had called Sue Ki since the first day they met. There was no use attempting an escape to the deck, but maybe he would be able to make it to Jillian's room without being caught.

Gavin slowly eased his legs to the edge of the bed clinging to it to steady himself. The motion of the ship did not help his plight. Between being dizzy and the dancing of the vessel upon the waves, it was even more difficult for Gavin to get his legs beneath him. But, he was determined to see Jillian. If only he hadn't lost so much blood, if only he hadn't said those angry words, and if only he hadn't fallen in love with Jillian. He had taken a lengthy chastising from Sue Ki after Terrance had left his cabin. Sue Ki had told him of Jillian's help with the fight for his life, and how the men had been taken with her gentleness.

"You lucky one of the them not slit your throat or maybe cut out your tongue and give it to her on a platter," Sue Ki had admonished.

Gavin felt he could go no lower than he'd already gone and even if he had to grovel at her feet, begging her to stay, he would. He would do anything to keep her here, for Terrance, he told himself.

Holding his side firmly under his arm, Gavin heaved his body from the bed. Swaying with the rhythm of the ship, Gavin made his way slowly from his cabin holding onto anything he passed. Feeling the pull of the tiny stitches in his side, he imagined her delicate hands sewing his open flesh and winced. How could he have doubted her? She was indeed a wonder, one minute a frightened girl, the next a confident healer. But, the most amazing aspect of Jillian was her beauty. When he had first glimpsed her on the beach, she was beautiful. When the lantern light played upon her delicate face lying so serene within the pillow, she was even more wondrous. When the men parted and she walked into his cabin wearing that shimmering emerald gown, her golden hair cascading in curls to her waist, Gavin was at a loss for words to describe her beauty. His envy had reflected in each man's face in the room, and he again felt the pain of jealousy he'd felt then. He regretted letting his jealous thoughts lead his tongue to her ruin, all because of her beauty and his need to possess it. Gavin never wanted to hurt her again and had to tell her so.

Fighting to stay upright, sweat poured from Gavin's brow by the time he reached Jillian's door. His side throbbed; his head spun. Leaning with his forehead against the door for support, Gavin knocked, then waited to hear her voice beyond.

Inside the cabin, the violence of the storm threw the ship as if it were a feather upon the wind. The roaring waves and wind combined rang within Jillian's head. She held a pillow over her ears to block out the sound, and huddling in the covers, shivered even though she wasn't cold. Suddenly, the door burst open, slamming against the wall, startling her.

"Micah, is that you?" she asked into the darkness, trying to focus her eyes. "Is anyone there?"

A low moan came from the foot of the bed. Jillian carefully crawled to its edge, peering at the body lying on the floor. Another moan escaped the intruder's lips.

"Gavin, my God. How? You shouldn't be out of your bed!" Jillian quickly made her way to the floor near Gavin's head, touching his face gently to make sure that it was him. "How did you get all the way to this cabin?"

"Jillian . . . I had to," he managed to stammer.

"No Gavin, don't talk now," Jillian said, placing his head upon her lap. "You mustn't use up what strength you have left. Your words are needless."

"But I have . . . to tell you. I have . . . to make things right." Wincing with pain, Gavin raised his hand to her lips. She held it there with her own. "You have to listen to me. You can't leave Terrance because . . . of me. I will keep my distance . . . if that is what you wish . . . but please stay with Terrance. It is very important to him . . . that you stay."

"What about you, Gavin? Do you also want me to stay?" Jillian held her breath waiting for his answer.

"I would like more than anything in the world for you to stay . . . . But I know I have wounded you deeply . . . I would do anything if you could only forgive my angry words and stay here with us."

"You would do anything?" Jillian asked.

"Yes, Jillian. Just tell me what you want me to do. Just tell me what would keep you here."

Jillian hesitated. He didn't know that she had already decided to stay, and she didn't want to use him for her own personal gain.

"I will stay, Gavin." Jillian smiled at the look of surprise on his face. "Yes, I'll stay."

"I thought that I would never see a more beautiful woman than you this morning when you came to my cabin. But, I see something different now, a beauty radiating from within you." He gently pulled Jillian to him, their lips grazing lightly. "Thank you," he murmured, shutting his eyes.

They rode the storm out together. There, upon the cabin floor with Jillian cradling Gavin's head in her lap and humming a fairy lullaby of love. This is how Micah found them after the storm had passed, Gavin sleeping peacefully in Jillian's warm embrace. She stroked his brow, humming softly. The scene tugged at Micah's heart; he silently wished he was the one who lay in her arms.

The storm had calmed; night had fallen and the ship was surrounded in blackness. Micah had come below to relight the lanterns in the corridors and see to Jillian. He hadn't been able to take his mind off her during the storm, knowing that she was below, frightened and alone. He was somewhat relieved to see that Gavin was with her.

Sensing his presence at the door, Jillian put her finger to her lips and whispered "He's asleep. I don't want to wake him just yet."

"How did he get here?" Micah whispered. "How long have you been here like this?"

"He arrived shortly after you came to check the lantern. At first I thought it was you returning. As you can see, he fell in the same spot that you did." Her smile lit the room as she teased him.

"Aye, but I was not as helpless as Gavin. It didn't take you long then to overpower him."

They both laughed softly. Jillian liked Micah and wanted to become good friends with him.

"Micah, might you find some help? I think that Gavin would be more comfortable back in his own bed."

"I'm not so sure about that, Miss Jillian. He looks to be very content right where he is."

"Yes, he does look as though he has no intention of going anywhere, but if truth were known, it is I who must move. I'm afraid that my legs have fallen painfully asleep under me."

"Oh, my lord, Miss Jillian," he said with concern. "I'll get you some help directly." He rose quickly, striding toward the cabin door.

"Micah" she called, stopping him. "It would please me if you would call me Jillian."

Turning to her with a wide grin on his boyish face, Micah answered, "It would be my honor . . . Jillian."

Micah's face beamed as he entered the galley, collecting Cy and several other men to help him with Gavin. He noticed that the men's faces also lit with smiles as they entered the Captain's quarters. Micah soon came to realize that he wasn't the only one taken with Jillian.

Carefully, the men lifted Gavin from Jillian's lap and carried him out of the room; not waking him. Micah waited until they were gone to help Jillian. He did not want the others to see that she was in pain from too many hours sitting with her legs tucked underneath her.

"I can't thank you enough, Micah, for all your help, not only with Gavin just now, but also before." He extended his hand to her. Her eyes deepened as she took it and squeezed it firmly. "I'll never forget your kindness" she said, gently.

Micah lifted her slowly from the floor, allowing her enough time to get some circulation back into her legs. Jillian held onto him for a time, steadying her legs beneath her.

"No need to thank me, Jillian," Micah whispered softly.

"Micah, you will always hold a special place in my heart. You are truly a loyal friend."

He stood tall and proud, mesmerized. Her face was lit with such warmth and caring. He made a silent vow to always be there to help and protect her if need be.

"I feel as if I have known you all my life," she said, looking into his eyes, "As if we were meant to be like brother and sister. I do hope you feel the same for me."

Micah glanced away from her, gathering his thoughts. If only she felt more than brotherly love for him. If only she could fall in love with him. Regretfully, Micah would not burden her with his own selfish needs. He would accept what she offered and be honored by it.

"Aye, I feel it too, as though we were meant to be family. You fill my heart, sister dear. I vow to keep you safe from those who would harm you."

His eyes met hers once more; a knowing gaze between them brought back memories of Jason. Jillian's hand unconsciously went to her breast where he had so savagely bitten her tender flesh. Seeing fear return to her eyes, Micah took her trembling hand in his and held it to his chest.

"He will never touch you again, not as long as I am alive," he vowed. "Not as long as I am able to protect you."

"Thank you, Micah. I know that you will keep your word. You are such a dear friend."

He kissed Jillian's hand and wrapped it under his arm. "Let's go see if Gavin is comfortable for the night. I'm sure it would ease your mind to know that he is."

"Thank you again, Micah."

They walked together to Gavin's cabin. Stopping at the door, Micah bid Jillian good night and gave her a soft brotherly kiss on her forehead. Jillian watched Micah until he entered the galley then slowly pushed the door open, hoping to not wake Gavin. Once inside, she could see that he was deep in sleep and likely to remain that way for the rest of the night. She tucked the coverlet up around his neck, then kissed his lips gently to bid him goodnight.

"Sleep well, my love."

Discoveries   *Chapter 15*

The next few days passed swiftly for Jillian. She kept herself busy tending to Gavin's needs and helping Sue Ki in the galley. Delighted to have such a willing student Sue Ki was determined to teach Jillian everything he knew about healing. They had several men who came to the galley for treatment. Sue Ki soon noticed that some of the injuries were not serious enough to need his attention and tried to hurry them back to their work. But, Jillian didn't seem to mind wrapping a finger or plucking out a sliver. Ki laughed to himself at their obviousness; they beamed with delight at her gentle touch and words of comfort. For each of them, Jillian gave compassion as well as reassurances for a quick recovery.

Jillian loved the ocean and the Pegasus. She loved to be on deck watching the men handle the ship so skillfully, and often sat at the helm to absorb everything they did. Today was no exception; it was a glorious day to be above enjoying the Pegasus.

Cy called down to her from the crow's nest, high above the deck. Jillian craned her neck to see him and waved in greeting back to him. Terrance stood at the helm navigating the ship over the vast waters. Jillian watched him with envy. Handling the ship with ease, Terrance stood tall above the deck like a god, his hair gleaming in the sun, the copper turning gold under its glare. Powerful arms held the wheel steady; Jillian marveled at his skill and strength.

"How do you know that we are heading in the right direction?" she asked, now standing at his side. "There are no land marks to guide you."

Terrance smiled down at Jillian. She was curious concerning everything about the Pegasus, asking questions of all the men, including him. He watched her with great pride, knowing that she wanted to learn everything there was to know about his ship. The men told Terrance how quick a study she was and how she had learned their every move. They all took a certain pride in being the one to teach her a skill and beamed when she thanked them with a gentle hug or friendly kiss on the cheek. Terrance himself, felt the same warmth when she was near, as she was now, asking another question, seeking even more knowledge of the ship's functions.

"The sun and the stars are our guide," he answered. "The sun rises in the east and rests in the west. That is how we find our direction. At night, we follow the stars, finding the North Star and guiding ourselves with it."

"Would you like to take the helm for a time?" he asked, and at once was rewarded with her excited smile.

"Are you not afraid that I would get us off course?"

"You will do fine, Jillian. We are in the open sea. It is quite simple to correct our route if anything should happen. Come, take the wheel. I have many things that await my attention, and it would please me greatly to have your help."

Timidly, Jillian stepped to the wheel, grasping it in her small, strong hands. Once Terrance released it, she was amazed at the strength it took for her to hold the ship on a steady course.

"See, it's as if you were born to captain a ship. You have a great talent for so many things, Jillian. I am proud to be your father."

"And I am proud to be your daughter."

He hugged her to him, standing at her side. The crew below noticed and smiled at the joyful scene. Truly, Jillian had brought the Captain back to life. It had been a long time since he looked so content and filled with happiness as he had since Jillian was brought to them.

Leaving Jillian at the wheel, Terrance went below to check on Sue Ki and Gavin. Ki had ordered Gavin to stay in bed for six days and Terrance knew that he was becoming terribly restless. Even Jillian commented on how short his tolerance was. Of course, Terrance recognized this as a sign of Gavin's recovery, but Jillian had kept her distance from him today due to his rather foul mood.

As Terrance entered the companionway, Sue Ki backed out of Gavin's room, holding a tray of food. Gavin yelled from within the cabin, his voice raised in frustration. "I want some solid food. Not that mushy mess you call food. Give me meat and ale before I come to the galley and get it myself!" With that, a mug flew past Sue Ki's head, crashing against the wall behind him.

"You one bad boy, Gavinson. You not eat, you not leave bed. You one bad boy." Ki turned toward Terrance in the corridor, smiling a broad smile. "He better, Cappy. He get up now. You tell him."

Sue Ki swung back around and quickly went to the galley, giggling all the way. Terrance watched the little man. Ki had been his friend, his healer and his soul mate for many years. A wiser and more stubborn man, Terrance had never known. Ki had a way about him that made everything work in one direction, as if it were meant to be. Things went smoothly when Ki was in command.

"So, you're tired of being in that bed, aye?" Terrance asked entering the cabin.

"Ki intends to starve me. If I stay here much longer I'll be nothing but skin and bones."

"Well, we can't have that, can we? Come, I'll help you escape the little dragon," Terrance said, helping Gavin stand and put on his pants.

He could tell by Gavin's slow pace that his side still bothered him more than he would like to admit. He winced as Terrance fastened the waist of his britches, holding his breath with the pain. "Aye. Are you sure that you want to be doing this so soon Gavin? There's time enough for you to rest before the ship will be needing another pair of strong hands."

"Aye, Captain. I cannot tolerate this cabin for another minute. I've already scared Jillian off today with my foul temper and long to apologize. I must go to her."

"Somehow, I don't think that our fair Jillian will be pleased to see you on deck so soon, but I don't blame you for not wanting to stay below any longer."

The pair made their way slowly down the corridor. The deck and Jillian awaited Gavin, whose head grew light with each step. The anticipation of seeing her in the light of day made Gavin's heart pound. He longed to see her golden tresses waving in the sunlight.

As they neared the stairwell, a shrill scream echoed from above. Terrance's heart leapt with its sound. Something terrible must have happened to Jillian. He raced up the steps, leaving Gavin to climb them unassisted. Gavin wasted no time in taking the steps, for the sound of Jillian's cry erased any pain that he may have been feeling.

Terrance's eyes flew to the helm, where he had left Jillian only minutes before. At the helm stood Micah; there was no sign of Jillian. He looked at his crew who stood gazing above them, pleasure written on their faces. Both he and Gavin's eyes followed their gaze. Both gasped at the sight high above the deck.

There, in the crow's nest was Jillian with Cy at her side, showing her how to use the eyeglass. The crow's nest seemed to lurch more than usual with the motion of the ship and Terrance felt immediate fear for her. Gavin had a similar reaction to Jillian's predicament, but also felt jealous seeing Cy's arms around her, steadying her so that she could hold the glass to her eye.

"Dear God, what is she doing?" Gavin asked, breaking the silence. "She'll be killed."

"Don't you be worrying about her, dear boy. I've come to know that she has a mind of her own and a will to match."

They watched as Jillian surveyed the vast ocean a moment longer and then handed the glass back to Cy. She looked down at the deck and saw Terrance and Gavin. They stood together, their mouths hanging partially open, staring up at her.

"Oh no, it's my father and Gavin," she said, bringing Cy's attention to the deck below. "They don't look too pleased with me."

"Aye, I would say you are correct, missy. I told you they wouldn't be happy with you climbing up here on your own," Cy said, smiling.

"It probably didn't help crying out when my foot slipped . . . I suppose I'll just have to deal with them," she said. "They both have barks worse than their bites, you know."

"Let's hope that you are right, missy. It's not a good day to walk the plank."

Jillian waved to the men below. "I'll be down shortly, Father!" she shouted, and then turned to Cy, a sly smile upon her lips. "Cy, if you don't mind could you show me the fastest way down to the deck? I don't think my father or Gavin will have much patience watching me make my way slowly down the rigging."

With their hearts in their throats, Terrance and Gavin watched as Jillian climbed out of the crow's nest with Cy at her side. Cy skillfully maneuvered around Jillian. He grasped her around her tiny waist with one strong arm, and held a hook in his free hand.

"Hold onto my neck as tight as you can, Jillian. I'll have you down before you can blink an eye."

Jillian did as he said, and seeing his intentions, she held her breath, trusting that they would make it to the deck unharmed.

"Are you ready, Jillian?" he asked, leaning back away from the hook.

She nodded, her face lit with excitement. Then with a light thrust, Cy and Jillian were airborne, gliding their way to the deck below. It only took a matter of seconds for them to reach the deck and the ride down sent Jillian's stomach reeling. It was a wonderful feeling, so totally new to her, and Jillian felt a rush that made her heart pound wildly.

They landed on the deck smoothly just a few feet in front of Terrance and Gavin. The two stood in place, their mouths still gaping open. She laughed with the thrill of the ride and also at the two faces before her, looking so ridiculous.

"Captain, Gavin, please. If you don't close your mouths, you'll surely catch brine flies."

Terrance was first to recover from the shock of seeing Jillian in so much danger. He couldn't believe that she could be so foolish and that Cy would encourage her outrageousness. The relief he felt from seeing her safely before him died, and was replaced with sudden anger.

"Cy, how could you do such a foolish thing, taking Jillian to the crow's nest? She may have been killed!"

Jillian immediately came to Cy's defense; she wouldn't allow anyone to be blamed for her actions. "Wait!" she said, stopping Terrance from advancing on Cy. "He is not to blame. I climbed to the crow's nest on my own. He had nothing to do with my being there."

"Why, Jillian? You could have been killed. We heard you scream. Were you hurt?" Terrance's anger shifted back to concern for her.

"No Father, I wasn't injured. I only slipped when I reached the nest. Cy was there to assist me."

"Thank God, you weren't hurt. It was foolish to do such a thing. Don't ever do that again Jillian. I don't think this poor old man could take another shock like that."

"I'm very sorry if I startled you. I'll try to keep my curiosity on the deck from now on."

"See that you do," Terrance said, pulling her into his arms and hugging her so tightly that she protested that if she hadn't injured herself, he would surely break a few of her ribs.

Jillian's gaze went to Gavin, who stood watching the two, a smirk of satisfaction on his face. He was amazed at the ease in which Jillian handled her father. She had him wrapped around her little finger. Gavin could see that Terrance could never stay angry with Jillian for very long and he couldn't either. She was an exquisite example of her gender. She knew how to get what she wanted but never used that talent to do harm to those she loved. God help anyone who had the courage to cross her.

"As for you, Gavin," Jillian started, her attention now focused on him. "What are you doing out of bed not yet even healed? You should be back in bed where you belong."

"Back now," he said, holding up his hands to stop her advance. "I'll not spend another minute in my cabin. I need to see the ocean in order to heal. I need to breathe fresh air."

"Ki said it was time for him to be up and about, Jillian," Terrance said, coming to Gavin's defense.

"Very well. Sit with me for a time, for your face is as white as paste."

"Yes, from being scared senseless by a beautiful young pirate maiden." His smirk mocked her.

Jillian smiled up at him as she led him slowly to the railing, sitting him on one of the casks stacked nearby. Terrance watched the two, thinking to himself that Gavin certainly had his hands full.

The afternoon passed swiftly. Jillian and Gavin sat together talking the entire time. Gavin answered all of Jillian's questions to the best of his ability. She inquired about everything, from the color of the ocean, to the workings of the sails. He showed her several knots that the sailors used to tie the riggings securely, each one having a distinct purpose. He watched her expressions as he taught her, marveling at the wisdom behind her amber eyes and the skillful way in which her hands followed his every direction. She learned everything so quickly, as if she had waited all her life to be taught.

Jillian enjoyed spending time with Gavin. He had so much patience with her when she tried to tie the knots the way that he showed her. She wanted to learn more about the Pegasus, about its crew, and especially about Gavin. She was drawn to him and was beginning to have even deeper feelings for him. But, there were moments when he seemed to be so distant from her since the night of the storm. Something had changed between them and Jillian was not sure what it was. She remembered seeing his nakedness and feeling his body under hers, and then holding Gavin until the storm passed. Thinking about what they had previously shared sent a wave of warmth through Jillian, making her stomach spin. She turned away from Gavin, pretending to spy something of importance in the distance.

Sensing the change in Jillian, Gavin wondered if her feelings were the same as his own. It was all he could do to keep his thoughts from wandering when being so near to her. He wanted to take her into his arms but feared that it would be too much too soon for Jillian. The memory of her fighting off Jason kept Gavin from making any unwanted advances toward Jillian. Jason's assault had wounded her. Her change in mood was testimony to how affected she was by Jason's attack.

"Jillian, is something wrong?" Gavin asked, putting his hands carefully on her shoulders.

Her breath caught with his touch. He seemed to know her every thought. Did he know how much his presence affected her? Did he know how much more she wanted from him? She felt so ashamed of herself for having such lustful thoughts of Gavin. He had seen her disgrace. He had witnessed what Jason did to her. Would she ever be worthy of him?

"No, Gavin, nothing is wrong . . . no, everything is wrong! I don't understand what is happening to me, Gavin. I'm so ashamed," She cried, tears welling in her eyes.

"Jillian, what is it? Did I say something to upset you?" He pulled her close to him, trying to comfort her.

"No, Gavin, it isn't you. It's me."

Gavin turned Jillian to him. "Will you tell me Jillian?" He studied her, trying to read her thoughts.

"I have feelings for you Gavin, but after what Jason did . . . . I'm not sure what to think. I'm not sure what to feel."

"Oh, sweet Jillian. Do you know how much I want to take you in my arms? Do you know what it does to me being so close to you? I only keep my distance so that I will not scare you away. I would never do anything to hurt you. It matters not what he did to you. You are not to blame." Gavin pulled her to him and Jillian clung to him with all her might. The past few days had been filled with emotion for both of them. "You cannot let what Jason did destroy you, Jillian. He is an evil man. You are innocent in all of this. You should not feel disgraced by his actions. You are as innocent and beautiful in my eyes as the first time I saw you walking on the beach. I knew then that I wanted you, more than I have ever wanted anything in my life. That has not changed."

"Is this true, Gavin?"

"You have my word and my heart, sweet Jillian."

Placing her hand lovingly against his cheek, Jillian studied his handsome features. The blue of his eyes deepened with her touch, fluttering shut at her embrace. Sliding her other hand around his neck, she pulled him to her, their lips meeting in a gentle kiss.

Breaking the moment for Gavin and Jillian, the men of the Pegasus cheered at the sight. Jillian blushed with the knowledge of having an audience for their tender moment. Gavin played along with the men's jest and took a deep bow, as if just completing the best performance of his life. They all joined in hearty laughter, each of them enjoying the joyous moment of passion between Jillian and Gavin.

In the hold, the cheers of the crew scorched Jason's ears. He loathed the sound and hated more the source of it. He had had plenty of time to plot the demise of the little wench, Jillian. The thought of having her in his power made him hard. Oh, how he would enjoy making her scream with pleasure under his body. He would enjoy her struggles against his need. He would enjoy making her watch as he killed the men responsible for his being shackled like an animal. Yes, she would pay and her payment would last as long as Jason wanted it to. He would make sure that he was satisfied before releasing her through death. For that would be her only escape from him.

"Ship ahoy, ship ahoy," came Cy's call from high in the crow's nest. "On the horizon, starboard, Captain."

Terrance held the eyeglass to his eye bringing the ship into view. A merchant ship from France or maybe Spain, he thought. She sat low in the water, lumbering toward her destiny. He watched as the ship raised its flag having seen the Pegasus. Contemplating whether or not to seize her, Terrance remembered Jillian. Could he take the chance of putting her in danger? His dilemma was answered for him when Cy called out again from above.

"Land ho! Captain, land ho!" The coast came into view through the eyeglass and Terrance gave no further thought to the merchant ship. He didn't even stop to see what flag she flew before making the decision to dock as planned.

Like so many other times, the crew made ready to dock the Pegasus. The unloading of the supplies would not take long. Terrance allowed the men to go ashore for a few hours in order to satisfy their need to feel the earth beneath them and to have a pint or two at the local pub.

As they neared the dock, a crowd gathered. Jillian came from below to stand beside her father, watching him skillfully bring the ship alongside the wooden dock. The Pegasus eased to a stop where the village's people stood. A cheer rose from the crowd as the crew lowered the plank to rest at their feet. Several men raced aboard the ship and joined the ship's crew in unloading the supplies.

"Do you always get this warm a welcome when you dock?" Jillian asked.

"When it's the difference between your family eating or starving? I guess they are always glad to see us," Terrance replied.

"I don't understand. The difference between them eating or starving?"

"Jillian, there is much that I need to tell you. But right now I have to get those supplies off the ship and make ready to sail if needed." Terrance turned toward the men. "You men there, secure the hold and put a sentinel in the crow's nest as soon as you're through with the supplies."

"Aye, Captain," they called back to him, then hastily continued their work.

Turning back to Jillian, Terrance hugged her, reassuring her of their safety. "We cannot be caught in port with our sails down now, can we?" He smiled down at her but could see that she was even more puzzled by his words.

"You are a pirate?" Her eyes widened when he didn't deny it. "How stupid of me not to realize it before, but I never even considered what it was you did with the Pegasus. Now I see why you had to be so secretive when coming to get Mother and me. You couldn't take the chance of getting caught."

"Now. Jillian, it isn't what you think."

"You mean you are not pirates?" she asked, watching the men carry heavy sacks from below.

"Aye, I guess you could say that we are pirates, but not the kind that you may think. You see Jillian; we do raid other ships, but take only what they can spare. Once we have enough booty in our hold, we bring it to ports such as this and give it to the poor, unfortunate peasants who are burdened with heavy taxes. Most of them can't afford to feed their own but are still made to give the better portion of what they raise to the Royals."

"Yes, that doesn't seem fair. They should be able to feed their own families first . . . . Have people been killed? Did anyone lose their life because of your . . . uh . . . activities?" She waited for his answer.

"Aye, my sweet. Men have died on both sides, each side fighting for what they believe to be right. I have lost three men. They gave their lives gladly for the chance to see their own village supplied."

"Meaning your men are from the ports that you supply?"

"Aye, Jillian. They volunteer to be my crew in order to secure shipment for their people. It didn't start that way, but that is how it is now."

"How did it start?"

Terrance walked Jillian to the railing while contemplating how much he should tell her. He watched the villagers shuffle back and forth between the dock and the ship smiling at the memory of how it all began.

"When I first came to be the Captain of the Pegasus, she was indeed a pirate vessel. The former Captain was a wise leader of his men. Keeping them from being captured by Charles's navy was something he did with cunning. He attacked the ship that I was indentured to, but with Sue Ki's insistence, I was rescued from it before it sank. The Captain was skillful with his choice of ships to raid. For many years he never made a bad choice, with the exception of once, and it cost him his life, along with the lives of many other men on board. With the Captain gone, the men took it upon themselves to follow me, declaring that I would be their next Captain. I felt such honor from their loyalty that I swore I would make the Pegasus into a fine trading ship, so that the naval warships would no longer hunt us. As fate would have it, this was not meant to be, for the Pegasus was well known for her pirating. To prove that we were no longer murderers and thieves, we started giving away the goods that we took. I didn't realize at the time just how much those supplies would be needed by the villages. I suppose you could say that we are like the legendary Robin Hood, only the ocean is our forest."

"If what you say is true, then you are hunted by Charles II's navy. Is that not so?"

"Aye, we've had our battles with the King, but the Pegasus is a swift vessel. We are always able to outmaneuver them. Or, at least we have been able to so far."

Jillian's mind raced with his revelation. Her thoughts were not what she had expected them to be. She wasn't so afraid of the Pegasus being a pirate vessel as she was afraid that the Royal Navy might catch them. William was now an admiral in the Navy. He had command of his own ship whenever he felt the need. Jillian remembered his swift departure the night before she was taken from the beach. She wondered about a connection between the two incidents.

Was he out there somewhere, waiting to capture Terrance and take her back? She realized that she did not want to return to her former life. She wanted to stay on the Pegasus with Terrance and Gavin. The thought of going back made her shudder.

Terrance saw her tremble and felt that it was with revulsion for him and his way of life but he could not change that now. Jillian would have to accept that this was the way things were aboard the Pegasus. Too many people were dependent on him and the booty the Pegasus provided.

"Is there a chance that you could be caught?" she asked, not waiting for his answer. "William is out there somewhere. He was called away the night before you came. He took all of his gear for sailing. He could be looking for us as we speak." Jillian jumped to her feet in alarm. "Call the men back. We have to leave now."

"Jillian calm yourself. I have men keeping watch. Besides the people of the village keep watch at the mouth of the bay. They will send a signal should a ship appear. There is no need for alarm. You are safe from him."

Terrance held her to him, feeling her tremble. *What did he do to you, child? What did he do to make you so frightened of him?* He held her until her trembling stopped and then lifted her chin.

"Are you having second thoughts about staying with us, Jillian? Because if you are, I can take you anywhere you would like to go. All you have to do is tell me where you want to go."

"Anywhere I want?" He nodded, hoping that she wouldn't ask to be taken back. "I would like to go ashore." The look on Terrance's face told her that he had misunderstood her. "No, Father. Not to stay. Just to purchase a few essentials."

"Aye, but of course, Jillian," Terrance said, very relieved. "Anything that your heart desires."

"Let's find Gavin and Ki and go ashore. I'm sure that Sue Ki needs to pick up some herbs and supplies for the galley, and Gavin can go to the shops with you and me. That will be a first for both of us."

They laughed together as they made their way down the plank to the dock. The harbor was bustling with activity. The people stuffed supplies into carts and wagons, then hurried away from the dock with their booty. Some stopped long enough to thank Terrance and wave a fond farewell, blessing him and his next voyage.

Suddenly, Jillian tugged her father's arm, stopping him.

"What is it, Jillian? What troubles you so?"

Her eyes shifted back to the ship, fear welled in their depths. "There is one more thing I must ask of you."

"Tell me, what is causing you such distress?"

She swallowed hard; knowing even the mention of his name could suddenly sicken her. "It's Jason. Promise me, when we leave this port, he will not sail with us. He frightens me, terribly."

Terrance saw the fear in her eyes and felt it in his heart. She was an innocent. Even asking him to rid the Pegasus of Jason had taken a lot of courage. He scolded himself for not taking care of the evil man before this.

"There, there, Jillian. You have no reason to be frightened. He cannot harm you again. Indeed we will leave him here when we go. I should have made him walk the plank before this."

"Oh, no. It's not that I want him dead. It's just that I don't want him near me, or the people that I love. Leaving him here will take care of my fears. Thank you," she said, kissing his cheek.

Terrance put a protective arm around Jillian and together they walked down the wharf in search of Gavin and Sue Ki. They soon found both and were off to the village. Jillian took in every detail of the small settlement, marveling at the various goods displayed in the shop windows. Terrance enjoyed watching her tug at Gavin's sleeve, dragging him from one window to the next. A smile never left Gavin's face even though Terrance knew that he would rather be doing anything other than going to these shops.

Jillian came to an abrupt stop at a window with men's clothes on display, stopping Gavin with a tug on his sleeve. Jillian giggled with excitement at the thought of purchasing a pair of men's leggings.

"You can't be serious, Jillian!" Gavin exclaimed, once he realized that Jillian was looking at the clothes for herself. "They don't even sell leggings to respectable women."

"We'll just see about that, Gavin," Jillian said smartly, as she pushed the shop door open.

The young man working in the store, who looked to be about sixteen or seventeen, lit up with excitement when Jillian walked in. Gavin couldn't believe how the lad fell all over himself to help her with her purchase. Again, jealous feelings raised their ugly heads within Gavin. Would it never end, he thought, this constant ache for her?

The three men stood back and watched as Jillian sorted through the various styles and colors of britches. Only in the last few years had shops such as this one appeared. In the past, it was customary to fashion clothing from fine materials purchased in stores, and finished products made by unknown seamstresses were not available.

Jillian finally decided on a pair quite similar to those that Gavin wore. They were made of black brushed leather. She held them proudly before her.

"What do you think?" Jillian asked.

Putting his finger to his nose, as if he were contemplating the secrets of the earth, Terrance eyed the pants she held. "Aye, looks as though they will be hearty enough to last you a great while. That is if you don't ruin them with one of your little adventures, like yesterday."

"Oh, I promise to be very careful with them. Now I must get a blouse and belt to be complete."

Having finished her choices, the young man gleamed when Terrance handed him the coins for the clothes. The shop saw very little business; the villagers did not have any money for store-bought clothing. His father would surely be pleased to see that he had taken in so much today. Best of all, he was able to help a beautiful girl with her purchase. She had the face of an angel. He was careful not to let his adoration show because the three men with her were obviously very protective of this young woman, especially the one with fair hair who kept looking at him as though he were going to kill him at any minute.

This must be her love, the clerk thought to himself. He didn't blame him at all for being wary of the attention given to the lass. For if she were his, he would never let her out of his sight. He watched her leave the store, her face alight with a satisfied smile. Feeling a dull ache within his breast, he wondered if this wouldn't be the last time he saw this beautiful creature.

A Proper Seat  Chapter 17

The sun was high in the mid-day sky when Jillian's stomach let her know that it was time for some nourishment. She watched the two giants who walked silently beside her. How could they go for such a long time without a meal, she wondered. None of them had eaten since dawn and Jillian was starting to feel the effects of an empty stomach.

"Do you think that it would be possible for us to get a hot meal somewhere?" Jillian asked clutching her stomach as it growled loudly.

Terrance laughed heartily. "Aye, my sweet, we could all use a good meal. I remember a small tavern near the wharf that serves a tasty meal," Terrance said, guiding them in that direction.

The outside of the tavern was old and rundown and in desperate need of repair but the inside looked as though it had just had a fresh scrub. This set Jillian's mind at ease.

As soon as they were seated, Jillian was surprised by the arrival of three large bowls of stew, placed carefully in front of them. Jillian politely thanked the tavern maid, Meggie, thinking that there would surely be no way for her to finish that amount of food. Meggie waited around a little longer than was necessary and Jillian noticed that she waited on Gavin's every word, a gleam of hope in her eye. She felt a sense of pride knowing that Gavin was so admired, for he was a handsome man.

Jillian made eye contact with the girl and a sudden feeling of dread came over Jillian. She sensed impending doom surrounding the girl, something so horrible and tragic that Jillian had to look away for fear of seeing anything more. It was as if the girl was encircled by a cloud of black so obvious that Jillian wondered if Terrance and Gavin were aware of it as much as she was. This wasn't the first time something like this had happened, but it had been a long while. Jillian focused on the meal, not letting her thoughts stray from the bowl in front of her.

Gavin watched Jillian as she steadily ate the stew. At first she looked a little intimidated by the amount in the bowl, but he knew that her stomach had won out as she ate the stew, matching him spoon for spoon. Everything about her fascinated him, from the way she brought the large spoon in her small hand up to her lips, to the way her lips caressed the spoon's smooth surface. Her every movement caught his attention and breath, for he had never experienced a presence such as hers. From the first moment he laid eyes on her, Gavin knew his life would not be the same and it hadn't. He remembered her slender legs, exposed by her skirt being tucked up around her waist, their movement making blood race through his veins. He remembered touching the hair that curled around her beautiful face while he held her close to him, the fair coils so silken within his fingers.

Their eyes met across the table and Jillian lowered her gaze slowly, hoping that her feelings were not showing in her eyes, as much as Gavin's were showing in his.

Terrance watched the two with fascination. Love was blooming before his eyes and he knew there would be no way to stop it. He thought of Sybil, which sent his heart racing, wondering if she would have approved had she come with him. Terrance still loved Sybil with all his heart. Did Sybil feel the same way about him?

A shout from the street brought all three up from their seats. Terrance hastily went to the doorway to see what all the commotion was about. As he got there the clanging of a bell rang above the shouts. Terrance suddenly whirled about.

"Gavin take Jillian to the ship!" he shouted. "They've sounded the warning. Waste no time. Go to the ship, now!" Terrance was out the door before Jillian or Gavin had a chance to speak.

Gavin grabbed Jillian's purchase and pulled her from the tavern, emerging onto the busy street along with several other crewmembers who were also taking their meal there. Jillian searched for Terrance, but found not a trace, as Gavin guided their speedy flight.

"Gavin, wait. Please! What about Sue Ki? What if he doesn't hear the alarm?" Jillian panicked at the thought of leaving Ki behind.

Gavin stopped, turning back to Jillian, a wide grin on his face. "No need to worry about Sue Ki. I'm sure that's where the Captain is. He won't leave Ki behind."

Feeling reassured, Jillian followed Gavin with her head down, watching her feet as they flew over the cobblestone walk. Their pace being so fast, it was inevitable that they would run headlong into someone. That someone turned out to be the young clerk from the dry goods store. Their bodies crashed together knocking all three to the ground. Jillian hardly had a chance to get her wits about her when she realized that Gavin, who was straddling the poor man, had him by the throat and was choking the very life out of him.

"Gavin! No!" she screamed, trying to wedge herself between them. "Gavin, please. It wasn't his fault!" Her pleads didn't seem to penetrate Gavin's resolve; he continued choking the poor clerk. Jillian had to do something to pull Gavin's attention away from the gasping boy.

Before Gavin knew what was happening, Jillian's lips were pressed fiercely against his. She held his head firmly to hers, and didn't let go. The kiss started as a plea for a life but once Gavin released the clerk and brought his arms around Jillian, it developed into a searching embrace. Gavin's once firm lips softened, opening to her. Jillian gasped with delight, letting her own groan unconsciously escape with his probe.

Beneath them, the clerk choked and wheezed air back into his starved lungs. He was sure that the young lady wasn't aware that her bottom was planted firmly upon his chest. It should have made it even harder for him to breathe but Jillian's slight weight caused him no discomfort at all. In fact, once he was breathing evenly again, he and quite a few other interested bystanders watched as the young couple finished their all-consuming embrace.

Jillian felt a hot blush from the tips of her toes to the top of her head. Her stomach knotted and churned with longing for Gavin. Gavin felt the same longing, but pulled away from her. Without a word, he stood, taking Jillian with him. Then, he held out his hand to the poor unfortunate clerk, still lying on the ground.

The clerk looked from Gavin's hand to Jillian and back again. Would it be safe to take it? Or would the man kill him if he were to get up? His answer came with a reassuring smile from Jillian. He took Gavin's offered hand and was abruptly hauled from the dirt as if he were weightless.

"So sorry, old chap, but when it comes to the safety of my fair lady, sometimes I just get a little carried away," Gavin said trying in earnest to smile at the young man while dusting him off.

"No apologies needed, Sir. I should have watched where I was going."

"Nonsense, it wasn't your fault. Not at all," Jillian smiled, taking his hand, which he jerked back from her as if being burned, then looked at Gavin to see if he would once again be attacked.

Holding his emotions in check for the time being, Gavin extended his hand. "I'm Gavin and this sweet creature is Jillian," he said, introducing them. Jillian took the clerk's other hand in her own.

"And what is your name? Come now, surely you have one?" she asked.

The clerk shook his head, clearing away the remnants of his fall. One hand held the fist of a very threatening pirate devil; the other held the delicate hand of the fairest maiden he had ever seen. Ever since she had left the store, his thoughts had strayed to her. When the warning bell sounded, he had come out of his shop in hopes of seeing her return to the ship, and ran squarely into her and her companion.

"The name's Shelby. Ryan Shelby."

"Gavin! Jillian! I told you to get to the ship!" Terrance's voice thundered above the noise of the streets. Without further comment, Terrance grabbed Jillian's arm and swept her from them, racing down the wharf with Sue Ki just a step behind, cursing in a language no one but he could understand.

Ryan and Gavin stood watching as Terrance, with Jillian in tow, made his way up the gangplank and onto the deck. Gavin smiled a sly smile, then gave Ryan a mock salute and ran for the dock as the ship started to pull away. At the very last minute, Gavin heaved his body through the air and landed safely on the deck of the Pegasus, then turned to wave a curt goodbye to Ryan.

All Ryan could do was watch in astonishment as the ship left the harbor. He shook his head with relief that he was still alive after such an experience. Some of the town's people gave him knowing smiles as they passed by, once again getting about their business.

One of the town's more lively characters, Old Pete, slapped Ryan on the back, almost knocking him again to the ground. "How's it feel to have a bonny woman like that placing her dainty behind on your chest? Aye, boy?"

Ryan didn't answer, but only smiled to himself, going back inside the shop. Surely he would never have another exciting day such as this as long as he lived. He wondered if he had detained them any longer if the ship would have left Jillian and Gavin behind. One could only hope for such a prospect as that. The two could surely cause tongues to wag in a town like this.

On the ship, the excitement of their hurried departure kept the men busy. An explosion from a ship in the distance thundered across the bay. Jillian watched as another flare from a cannon fired in their direction. The first cannon ball landed safely away from the stern of the ship as it pulled away from the dock. Remembering the second flare from the ship's cannon, Jillian's heart raced in anticipation. Where would it land?

It seemed like a long time passed before the second ball showed itself, splashing further away than the first. Several more blasts rang out, but the Pegasus was too swift for the heavy warship. They were at a safe distance now, leaving the dock behind, and heading southward.

From below, Jillian heard yelling and angry voices. Cy, Micah and several crewmen emerged from the stairwell, dragging Jason. He fought them every step, shouting vile threats. His eyes met Jillian's as they approached. Standing her ground, Jillian didn't back away or show any fear as they passed. Evil emanated from this man. Jillian suddenly remembered the same sense of evil that she had felt earlier at the tavern, and Meggie's face came to mind. Fear for the girl surged through Jillian and she knew that Jason had something to do with it. They neared the railing as Terrance came to Jillian's side.

"He won't hurt you ever again, princess. He owes his life to you, for you have spared him."

"Know this Jason," Terrance spoke in forbidding tones, "your life has been spared because Jillian didn't want it taken. You will not be so blessed again. Heave him over," Terrance commanded.

As the men lifted him over the railing, Jason shouted a final threat. "You may not have taken my life Captain, but there will come a time when you wish that you had. Farewell, my sweet," he called, as the men released him over the side. "We will meet again."

Chills racked Jillian's body; she trembled with their intensity. "He frightens me even more than he did before."

Pulling her to him, Terrance could feel the fear quaking through her delicate frame. He knew her feelings were warranted, for the man was pure evil.

"He's gone now, Jillian. He won't harm you again." Terrance tried to listen to his own words of comfort, for Jason was not an easy person to forget. Terrance could only hope that what he told Jillian would ring true, and they would never meet up with Jason again.

The Pegasus breached the point of the bay and headed into the open sea. The warship, trying futilely to block their escape, was now unable to keep up with the sleek vessel and fell steadily behind. The Pegasus flew over the open sea, becoming only a mirage in the distance, before disappearing into the silver horizon.

William cursed the pirate ship as his mighty warship fell further behind. They had come so close, but William knew that if they were to catch up with the Pegasus, he must have a better plan than chasing her down in the open sea. No one had been able to get near her for years. William was sure that the villagers were helping the pirates by alerting them to the warship's presence.

While thinking of a way to out maneuver the pirates, it suddenly occurred to William that if they had information from the town's people, they might find out where and when the ship docked. He remembered seeing someone thrown over the side of the ship before they reached the open sea. If he hadn't drowned while swimming back to the dock, perhaps they could go back and find this man. Yes, the man could certainly be of use.

He ordered the warship to turn about and head back to the bay. William hoped that the man was still alive and could offer him information before he would end his life. Being a pirate was a crime in itself, but being a pirate who gave the plunder to the villagers was every officer's nightmare. For ten years, William had searched for and followed this particular ship. Only once had he seen the colors it flew—a Pegasus. The winged horse stood pale upon the black flag. Its emblem was unmistakable; no other vessel flew this flag.

William watched the sun set on the ocean's horizon. The water was lit with glorious shades of lavender and pink. Just for a second, he remembered the pink of Siriann's new dress and winced with the desire to be home with his wife and daughter.

Shaking his head in disgust, William made his way below. They would never reach the bay before daylight and he questioned his reasons for turning back. Ten years was too long to be after a pirate ship that had a Captain with no name. No peasant ever gave him a clue as to who the Captain was, only that they referred to him as a Devil from the Heavens. A devil indeed; William was determined that this would be the final chase.

The man in the bay would help him with information, even if he had to torture him until he got what he wanted. It occurred to him that this man was likely not on the best of terms with the Captain. After all, he had been thrown overboard. Maybe things weren't as bad as he thought. William smiled to himself as he entered the galley.

*   *   *   *   *

Sometime toward evening, Jason hauled himself up the side of the dock and landed exhausted upon it. The swim had almost done him in, but he wasn't ready to die. That would be too easy. Jason wanted to live so that someday he would be able to make Terrance pay for what he had done. Terrance and that slut of his would pay with their lives.

What he needed now was food and ale. Being in this port before, he knew just where to go, the tavern near the wharf . . . .

In the village, the townsfolk watched as a wet and bedraggled man pulled himself onto the dock. Warily, they tore their eyes from him as he passed by and made his way to the tavern. Ryan Shelby watched from the dry goods store as the man passed. An eerie feeling of dread followed his gaze. The man was trouble; he felt it in his bones. No good would come of his being here, no good, at all, he thought, thanking God that he was not one to frequent the tavern up the street.

Jason entered the tavern, flinging the door open hard enough that it banged loudly against the wall. All eyes focused on him and he returned their stares with an evil warning. He made his way toward one of the tables, calling for the tavern maid to bring him some ale. Meggie gave the barkeep a pleading look, but was met with an angry nod in Jason's direction. Her employer wasn't concerned with her fears; his only thought was of the pounds that the man may spend once he had enough to drink. She timidly took a mug of ale to Jason's table and plunked it down in front of him, then hurried away. Jason smiled to himself at her frightened ploy. "All in good time, slut, all in good time," he murmured.

The Dance

Chapter 18

Jillian stood at the railing, sighing with relief as the last flicker of the warship dipped beneath the horizon. Just before dark it had turned back when they realized that they were no match for the speed of the Pegasus. She should feel safe, but after all of today's adventures, Jillian felt uneasy about her future. A life of running wasn't exactly what she'd dreamt of. The thought of never being able to be at ease while in port gave Jillian a good reason to reconsider her decision to stay with her father. But, she couldn't leave, not now. Not after the way Gavin had made her feel when they kissed. She wanted Gavin. Thinking of leaving him made her feel worse than thinking of a life of running. Why did it have to be so complicated?

"Jillian, could you join me for a moment?" Terrance asked, taking her hand and leading her to a seat upon a keg. "I would like to talk."

"What is it?" Jillian asked.

"I know that you and Gavin are very fond of each other and believe me I heartily approve." His face softened as he watched Jillian blush. "I'm just not certain that I have done my best for you. I mean to say . . . I'm not sure that this is the life for you after all."

Jillian watched Terrance with mixed emotions as he explained all the reasons for her not to stay. His eyes filled with emotion as he spoke of her safety aboard the Pegasus. The fear of losing her during a battle was more than he could bear. His fears were not unfounded, as Jillian had seen earlier today. Hadn't she just been asking herself the very same questions?

"You see child, I want more than anything to have you here with me but the danger I would be putting you in . . . I just don't know how I can sacrifice your safety so selfishly.

Rising, Jillian walked to the railing, watching the foaming waves caress the ship's bow. The sea mist sprayed her with every plunge of the hull against the ocean's power. All her life, she had watched the ocean from its shore, longing for the chance to seek adventure. All her life, some part of her had been here upon the sea. It gave her comfort and strength. The waters power calmed her and made everything bad in her life disappear. She breathed in the salty mist, feeling her longing ebb. It felt right to be here. Even with danger lurking everywhere, it just felt right. For once in her life Jillian felt free, her heavy burden lifted. For once in her life, she could make her own decisions about her future. She wouldn't go back. She didn't want to.

Jillian spoke softly to Terrance, "I know you have my safety in mind. But what about my heart?" She slowly turned to him.

"But!"

"No, hear me out. I want to stay here with you and Gavin. The two of you are all that I have now. Please don't take me back. Let me stay."

"Oh, Jillian. The Devil will have my soul for what I've done but I cannot leave you again," Terrance said with relief. "I will not leave you with William. It will be a dangerous life, but we'll be together."

"Thank you," she said, hugging him tightly.

"A celebration is in order," Terrance announced loudly, motioning to Micah who often played his fiddle for a few of the men. "Micah, a song for Jillian."

Micah fetched his fiddle, which was always close at hand, and walked toward Jillian playing as he came, his eyes alight with mischief. The fiddle's tune danced in the air, a cheerful melody, lifting the heads of the crewmen. They gathered as Micah drew Jillian to the center of the deck playing the fiddle teasingly around her. He danced in front of her and then ducked behind making her spin in time to the lively music. Cy swung down from the mast, pulled a harmonica from his pocket, and began his own version of Micah's melody. Soon, the men encircled them and all joined in, clapping and cheering to the song's rhythm.

Feeling the joy of the occasion, Jillian began to dance to the fiddle's song. Her long golden tresses, falling freely around her shoulders, bounced with the rhythm of her dance. Her skirts swirled around her legs as she wove and spun between the men. Terrance stood in silent fascination, watching his beautiful daughter charm the salty crew.

Giving up his fiddle, Micah handed it to Old Joe, who carried on with the song, and took Jillian's hand, bowing deeply to her.

"May I have this dance, young miss?" Micah asked.

"Why certainly," she said, curtseying before him.

He held her outstretched hand in his and timidly placed the other at her waist. Jillian looked him squarely in the eye, and gave him a smile of encouragement, placing her hand on his shoulder. They moved slowly at first, each getting used to the movement of the other. Micah counted silently to himself and kept careful watch on his feet, trying not to step on Jillian's toes.

Old Joe fiddled for the couple, quickening the pace gradually as they became more accustomed to each other. The crew clapped and cheered with the merriment of the dance. One by one, they took turns dancing with Jillian. Micah resumed his playing, again dancing around Jillian and her partners as they twirled across the deck. Even Terrance took a turn dancing a lively jig with Jillian. The sight was another first for the crew, for they'd never seen the Captain dance and enjoy himself so.

Below, Gavin heard the music and the men keeping time. He finished helping Sue Ki with a heavy steaming pot, then went above to see the festivities. When he emerged from the stairwell he stopped, taking in the scene. All eyes were on her. How could it be otherwise? The sight of her was something that no man could resist, certainly not Gavin. She danced in and out of the men, spinning her body beyond their reach and then stepping close again, teasing each into thinking it was his turn to dance. It gave the impression of dancing not just with one, but with all at the same time. The men laughed heartily at each other when one would think it was his turn. They were like a bunch of young boys waiting for a prize, each hoping that he would be the one to claim it.

Suddenly, Gavin felt an uncanny sense of family with Terrance, the crew, and Jillian. All of the people important to him were here, and they all had a mutual sense of belonging, to the Pegasus and to each other. Gavin couldn't possibly resent their feelings toward someone like Jillian. She never asked for anything, but got love and respect from every man on board. He saw in their expressions that each one would take Jillian under his wing and protect her with his life. He wondered if she knew how many of these lovesick puppies would die for her. Gavin hoped that the day would never come when Jillian was in enough danger that they would have to give their lives for her protection.

From across the deck, their eyes met. For a moment Jillian waited, reading Gavin's expression. From the distance between them, she saw that there wasn't anger or resentment in his eyes, but only a softening of his heart. All eyes followed Jillian's. Micah stopped playing, waiting, as everyone was, for Gavin's reaction to their antics. He walked slowly toward her, the men parting for him. Her heart pounded wildly as he came within inches of her, the closeness making her stomach tighten and her legs wobble beneath her.

Gavin bowed before her and then held her gently, readying for the music to resume. Micah coughed, his usual signal for getting the men's attention, then began to play. This time the fiddle played with softness and love. Gavin led Jillian in its melody, their eyes never leaving each other's. Their bodies swayed in unison, the music setting the pace for the simplest of love making, the dance of their souls joining.

The setting sun glowed brilliantly on the horizon, illuminating the lover's dance. Their embrace continued, oblivious to the impending darkness of the sky. Gavin and Jillian saw nothing beyond each other. Even the fiddle's smooth melody drifted away from them. Both were so in tune with the other that nothing penetrated their world.

Jillian became more aware than ever of Gavin. She absorbed every detail of him. His essence filled her senses. The soft touch of his hand at her waist sent flames up her spine settling in the roots of her hair that stood on end. The sensation intensified when Gavin's grip tightened with the circling of the dance. Her body trembled with excitement when he drew her even closer.

Jillian wasn't the only one who felt the heat. Gavin fought to keep his emotions masked. The way she made him feel was something that he was having more and more difficulty hiding. Never before had a woman affected him this way. There was something about just having her near that sent his pulse racing and his heart aching.

Their eyes locked in a deep, probing gaze. Gavin could see Jillian's thoughts and knew that she too fought for control. He had the strongest urge to pull her to him and kiss her until she could resist no longer. He focused on her lips as Jillian drew her bottom lip between her teeth, holding it firmly in anticipation.

Gavin stopped dancing, holding Jillian as if suspended in time. Micah stopped his playing and he and the rest of the crew stood in silent watch. Even Terrance waited in silent anticipation.

Jillian's heart pounded against the walls of her breast. Her eyes never left Gavin's. She felt the strength leaving her limbs and felt exhausted by the strain of keeping herself from Gavin. What was he doing to her? Why couldn't she think clearly when he touched her? Why didn't he just kiss her?

Gavin drew her slowly to him until their bodies touched firmly against each other. Her delicate hand was still locked in his and he brought it to his lips placing a light kiss upon her fingers. Jillian caressed his cheek gently with her fingertips and then stroked his bottom lip; causing him to sigh helplessly.

"Oh Jillian, what you do to me." Gavin spoke in soft, raspy whispers.

Jillian's face lit with a curious smile. "I feel the same. What are we to do?"

Gavin paused, glancing around at the crew who still stood in silence taking in the moment.

"Jillian, will you consent to be my wife? In the presence of these trusted friends, please say that you will."

A great flood of emotions came suddenly over Jillian. She felt like swooning, like dancing, like shouting to the world of her love for Gavin. She was caught off guard by his open proposal but knew exactly what her answer would be. Jillian looked around at the salty, bedraggled group of onlookers. Their faces were lit with shameless anticipation and smiles of encouragement, except for Micah. Over Gavin's shoulder their eyes met for the briefest of moments. Jillian knew at that second, that Gavin wasn't the only man on board who loved her. It pained Jillian to come to this realization; she didn't want to see Micah hurt.

Micah watched the soft wisps of Jillian's hair blow across her loving face. He could see her true feelings in her tearing eyes. He wanted to do what was right for her. He had to let her know that he would support her decision. A nod of his head gave her the relief she sought, and she mouthed a silent thank you to him, then drew her gaze back to Gavin, who waited for her answer.

"Up until a few weeks ago, I felt that the only people in the world who truly loved me were my mother, my grandfather and Sophie. Now I know that my longing to be on the sea was a premonition and that I truly did have a destiny somewhere else. I know that this life is where I am meant to be as I know that I have found my future with you, Gavin. I couldn't go on if it weren't for the love I have found here with you, with all of you," she said, motioning toward the crew and Terrance. "I want nothing more than to stay with you all. I want nothing more than to become your wife, Gavin."

He pulled her closer to him, their lips meeting in a passionate and searching kiss. Her lips opened to his and his tongue did a lover's dance upon hers. His body felt wonderful against hers. She felt every hard ripple of him as his arms enveloped her, making her feel cherished and safe.

Gavin felt every curve of her softness pressed firmly against him. He molded her to him feeling that he could never get close enough. Gavin realized how well they fit together, as if they had been formed exclusively for each other. It was a wonderful revelation and Gavin knew that it was meant to be. By all the Gods, Jillian was here for a reason, and that reason was him.

The cheering and merriment of the men broke the embrace. Terrance tore Jillian from Gavin's arms and hugged her tightly.

"Are you certain, princess?" he whispered into her ear.

"Oh yes, Father. Very certain," she answered, still blushing from the rush of the moment. Terrance crushed her against him, lifting her in his embrace, and danced around the deck with her in his arms.

At the same time, Gavin was swept into the arms of the crewmen, who congratulated him with vigorous handshakes and hearty slaps on the back, which almost sent him flying onto the deck. Micah took up his fiddle once more and the men danced in a frenzy of merriment. A teasing game of hide-and-seek began between the men and the unsuspecting couple. Jillian was pulled from one embrace to another. Each time she came close to Gavin, another crewman would hug her, and Gavin would disappear into the throng. Soon she joined in the game and laughed at Gavin when he realized that she was part of their ploy.

So she wanted to play, he thought. Suddenly, Gavin pulled his sword and shouted, "Steal my woman, will you?" The men made room around him, keeping Jillian safely hidden behind them. "Looks as though I'm going to have to fight to rescue her from you blokes." He advanced toward them menacingly. "Which one of you goes first? Come on, I'm ready."

"Gavin, wait!" Jillian yelled. "It was all in jest," she pleaded, but was ignored.

"I will be the first, my friend," Cy said, stepping forward. "It will be my pleasure to be rewarded with her gentle kiss once I rescue her from your callous embrace." With that, Cy lunged at Gavin, who pivoted out of harm's way.

Jillian couldn't believe her eyes. The two men were fighting over her. She went to Terrance, pulling on his sleeve, pleading, "Make them stop, Father. They'll kill each other."

"No harm will come to them, Jillian. They are just a couple of young bulls who need to perform for a beautiful prize." His eyes crinkled with amusement. "They show off for you, my sweet. Neither will hurt the other. They are best of companions."

"Is that so?" she said smartly, now understanding and becoming somewhat irritated. "We shall see who is pleased by the show."

Terrance glanced sideways at Jillian, a look of mischief in her eyes. He smiled to himself. She certainly was a surprise and he knew by her look that Gavin had another thing coming if he thought she could be so easily amused.

The mock battle between the two began to wane. Cy seemed to get the upper hand on Gavin, who more and more frequently rolled out of the way of his sword thrusts. Finally, Cy had Gavin pinned to the deck, his sword tip at his throat.

"Aye, seems as though I have won the fair maiden."

"Aye, aye, you have indeed!" came the shouts of the men.

"Where is my prize?" Cy asked.

"Here, here is your prize, my brave warrior," Jillian said, stepping out from the men to offer herself to Cy. "I am but a woman who must abide by the whims of strong men," she said seductively. "You have won me fairly, my brave knight."

"But, but wait," muttered Gavin in protest.

"Do not talk, prisoner. The woman is right. I have won her. She is mine." Cy said, still holding the sword to Gavin's throat.

"But Jillian, you are supposed to plead for my life," Gavin complained. "This is not the way it's supposed to end."

"Oh, but I must reward him as was promised. After all, you are a man of your word, Gavin, and you lost the battle." She stepped up to Cy, then brought his head to hers planting a kiss on his surprised lips.

"Now if the game is over, I would appreciate having my soon to be husband in one piece. If you would be so kind Cy, as not to run him through."

Cy looked down at Gavin contemplating. "I am not certain Jillian. That kiss was very nice. Maybe I should run him through and claim you for myself."

A second of fright overtook Jillian. She suddenly knew what it felt like to use her power as a woman for whom men would fight. It was frightening to think that harm could actually come from a game such as this.

"Don't hurt him, Cy. Please," she whispered, in all seriousness.

"Now don't you worry, princess. I got my prize and you shall have yours for a game well played." Cy put his sword down, then reached down and hauled Gavin to his feet. "I couldn't have beaten him had he not let me, Jillian. None of us can," he said, slapping Gavin on the back. "He's all yours, Jillian. If you still want him, of course."

Jillian ran to Gavin, hugging him tightly. "You crazy fool. Don't ever play such a dangerous game again," she said softly, just to him. "Don't frighten me like that. I love you too much to lose you."

"And I love you. God knows that I would fight to the death to keep what is mine. Don't ever forget that."

Cy, Micah, Terrance and the rest of the crew watched Gavin and Jillian walk arm in arm to the upper deck. They stood at the railing watching the last streaks of color from the sunset disappear on the horizon, their forms silhouetted against the sky. The Pegasus sailed on in serene silence; the cool mist of the sea filled the air.

Sybil watched the sun settle on the horizon, displaying a wonderful portrait of color over the ocean. The water reflected the picture, adding to the extravaganza. She was perched high upon the giant rock where Jillian had sat so many times through the years. She visualized Jillian upon the deck of a mighty pirate ship, a winged horse flying above it. Did she watch the same setting sun? Was she happy? How she longed to be with Jillian and Terrance, to live a life full of love and happiness.

Her thoughts were of her daughter and the life she must now be leading. Sybil hoped that Jillian had accepted her plight and would take her time getting to know her real father. She knew Terrance would be more than gentle with Jillian, for she remembered his gentleness with her. Sybil could see by the look in his eyes, the day that he had come to her, that he had not changed over the years.

She remembered opening the cottage door and seeing his loving face, the sight startling her so fully that she almost fainted, sagging into his strong arms. Terrance had whisked her up and carried her to a chair where he had seated himself, with her upon his lap. Sybil had laid her head against his shoulder, studying his gentle face, and collecting her thoughts.

The changes were slight but Sybil had noticed every one. His image was so finely entombed in her memory that she saw every new line in his smooth skin. She saw that he had spent many long days in the sun; for his color reflected bronze against his lightened hair, which flew in wild disarray. His scent had emanated softly to her senses, and the memory of holding him at knifepoint in her father's stable had drifted into her mind. She smiled at the memory of herself as a young stubborn girl who had just been chased down on horseback by the man her father had chosen for her to marry.

No words could describe the emotions that Sybil felt, disbelief, sorrow, regret, and most of all, love. She hadn't been able to stop the tears from coming, sitting enveloped in Terrance's arms. All the years of holding her emotions inside, all the years of pretending to love an unlovable man, had come rushing to her at once. She had buried her face in Terrance's shoulder and sobbed uncontrollably.

Sitting with Sybil upon his lap, cradled against him, was all that Terrance could think to do at the time. No words came to mind. Just sitting and holding her seemed to suffice. So with his eyes closed, he had held her, allowing Sybil time to adjust to the fact that he was alive and well and holding her while she sobbed against his shoulder. When her sobs had subsided, Terrance had waited for her to speak, knowing that she would have much to say given time. Her voice, when she found it, was nothing more than a whisper against his ear.

"Is it really you, Terrance? Or am I dreaming?" Sybil had asked, turning his face to hers.

"I am real, my love. This is not a dream. I've come back for you, as I promised." Terrance had lifted the pendant from his neck and held it for Sybil to see. "The Pegasus promise. Upon a winged horse we'll ride."

His words still rang in her ears while Sybil watched the last flickers of color from the sunset. She'd had so many regrets since that day when Terrance came to her. She had asked herself over and over, why, why hadn't she gone with him? She could have taken Siriann and just disappeared. William would never have known where to look. They would have had a wonderful life together. Didn't she deserve a better life?

Sybil made up her mind to tell William, when he returned from his latest expedition, that she was leaving him. If it took the rest of her life, Sybil would find Terrance and pledge herself to him.

The light of day was all but gone as Sybil carefully climbed down from her perch and made her way down the darkened beach toward home. She didn't want to go back to the cottage that she had shared with William all these years. There were too many painful memories there. But Sybil knew that she would have to stay until his return, for only then could she finally leave him.

The cottage looked dark and eerie as Sybil approached it. Shortly after Jillian's disappearance, Siriann had been sent to stay with her grandfather and Sophie at the estate. Sybil told Siriann that Jillian had gone to an aunt's home up the coast for a visit. She had explained that her aunt was very ill and that Jillian would be a great help to the old woman. Siriann had never questioned her about Jillian, but did ask repeatedly about the men who had come to the cottage that same day. Sybil told her that they were associates of her father's and were looking for him, but Siriann didn't quite believe the story. She had continued to question Sybil until she suggested that Siriann go visit her grandfather, which she jumped at the chance to do.

Now, Sybil was alone at the cottage, giving her time to think and plan what she would do once William returned. If only she knew how long William would be gone, Sybil could better plan a strategy for how to approach him with her leaving. Upon entering the dark cottage, Sybil lit a lantern, and then began lighting a fire in the small fireplace. The cottage was small but comfortable. However, Sybil had always felt a chill in her bones while living there with William. A blazing fire would not warm what gave Sybil this feeling.

Try as she may, Sybil never felt her heart warm with love for him. At first, she thought that she loved William but within a short time realized that she only felt gratitude for his generosity in marrying her. He had saved her from a life of being an unwed mother, to be scorned by her family and friends. He had saved her from shame, yet shamed her himself every chance that he got, reminding her how much he had given up in becoming the father to a traitor's bastard.

With the knowledge that Terrance had brought to her, Sybil could see him for the man that he was. A greedy, status hungry leach, were now the kindest words she could think of to describe William. She had been such a fool to trust him with her life, as well as the life of the beautiful child that she and Terrance had created with their love.

A loud knock at the door brought Sybil's thoughts back to the task at hand and she placed a pot on the hook above the fire to let the stew within it heat. Another urgent knock sounded at the cottage door before Sybil could reach it.

"One minute," she called, as she approached the door. Without thinking, Sybil unlocked the door, opening it. There before her, stood the drunken figure of Richard Dinkin. Before she could shut the door in his face, he planted his foot, stopping it.

"Now don't be so hasty, missy." His words slurred. "Just came to see if I could be of service to you." He belched under his breath, swaying on his feet.

Sybil waved her hand in front of her face, trying to rid the air of his drunken breath.

"You are drunk, Mr. Dinkin. I suggest that you go home to your wife and let her take care of you," she said, as she tried to push him back out the door.

"I already took care of her for tonight. She won't be needing my services for a time. I have enough to go around if you're as lonely as you look."

His smug smile sickened Sybil and she quite suddenly felt sorry for his poor wife Martha. She held her ground against the door with him on the other side, but her strength was beginning to wane. Sybil looked around the cottage for something to use in defense against his insistence. She spotted the broom near the hearth.

Suddenly letting go, Sybil bolted to the fireplace as Richard fell to the floor inside the door. Before he could gather his senses, Sybil, broom in hand, advanced toward him. "Now, I'm asking you nicely to leave. Don't make me use this broom on you, Mr. Dinkin," she threatened, trying to look menacing, but he only smiled at her from the floor.

"You're one beautiful lady when you get your dander up, Sybil. We could have a fine time if only you didn't act so high and mighty."

"High and mighty! You come knocking on my door while my husband is out to sea and you call me high and mighty." Sybil's anger took over her senses. She began hitting him with the broom, forcing him to cower toward the open doorway. "Get your high and mighty carcass out of my house Mr. Dinkin, and don't come back!"

"Ouch! I know you want me, Sybil. I'll just visit another time."

"Out! Out!" Sybil exclaimed, hitting him on his behind as he crawled out the door. "And don't come back," she yelled, slamming the door and locking it as fast as she possibly could.

Leaning with her back against the door, Sybil waited breathlessly until she heard the slamming of the gate and knew that he was gone. The strength fled her legs and she crumbled to the floor crying into her hands. Her life had to change. She didn't want to be a victim any longer. Sybil was tired of being used and abused, tired of living a lie. In desperation, she called out to the one person who could give her strength to go on, the only person who had ever believed in her, giving her the courage to believe in herself.

"Terrance! Terrance McCarthy, please come back!!!"

Meggie straightened her tired shoulders stretching the muscles of her aching back. The night before had seemed never-ending and she arrived home close to dawn. The tavern nightlife was as unpredictable as the weather and she had learned to expect the unexpected from customers. But, yesterday was beyond anything that Meggie could ever have imagined.

It started with the beautiful Adonis who came to feast with a gorgeous young woman and redheaded devil of a man. The excitement of their departure had all but brought every last soul to the streets to watch. She laughed remembering poor high-minded Ryan Shelby with the seat of the woman planted upon his chest. What a scene it caused!

She thought of the dark man who oozed from the depths of the ocean. Meggie had spent the remainder of the night fighting off his relentless advances. Her employer was of no help, for all he cared about was the money that the man might spend, and would not come to her rescue. She shuddered thinking about his unwanted promises of evil passion.

As she wrapped her shawl tightly around her shoulders, Meggie said a silent prayer that he would be gone when she arrived at the tavern. To her relief last eve, he had passed out at one of the tables before the night was through, thus saving her from another battle with his hands.

She made her way to work through the streets that bustled with the business of the day. Old Pete called out a greeting to her from across the busy street. The old dear was quite a character and a good friend indeed. Friends were something Meggie didn't have a lot of these days. Ever since she went to work at the tavern most of the town's folk acted as if she no longer existed. This hurt Meggie deeply, for she grew up here and didn't deserve to be treated this way. After all, she only began to work at the tavern to help support the family after her father died. If she were given the opportunity, Meggie would have gone away to school or gotten married like most of the other girls of the village.

Arriving at the tavern, Meggie took one last look up at the beautiful blue sky; for it would be the last time she saw it this day. Her shifts at the tavern rarely gave Meggie a chance to take a break from the stuffiness inside. The tavern door was unlocked and Meggie pushed it open entering into the darkness.

"Aye, it's time you got here. I've been waiting for you so I could go out for supplies." the tavern keeper said, sounding very agitated.

"But I'm not late, sir. You said to come in at noon."

"I know what I told you girl, but that scoundrel is still passed out over there," he pointed to the figure lying under the table, "and I can't lock up and leave him inside now, can I?"

Meggie's stomach churned, spying the menacing man still in the tavern. Her heart sunk knowing that she would have to deal with him again.

Toby Finch, the tavern owner, was a short pudgy man, his face marred by pox, and most of his teeth missing. He repulsed Meggie, but he didn't frighten her the way that this handsome dark haired man did. There was something eating the stranger's soul and his presence sent chills down Meggie's spine.

"Don't leave me here with him. He frightens me."

"Don't be daft Meggie. The man's out. He won't be waking for a few more hours," Toby told her, heading to the door. "I won't be long. You can fetch the ale while I'm gone. That will keep you in the back, out of harm's way," he said, disappearing out the door.

Meggie stood in the tavern's center, contemplating walking out and quitting this terrible job. But, remembering the responsibility of her family brought her to her senses. She quickly went to the storage room, trying not to think of the man out front. She removed her shawl, hanging it on a hook near the doorway and proceeded to get to work stocking the heavy kegs of ale.

Some time later, Meggie stopped her labors, straightening her shoulders, once more trying to stop the aching of her lower back. It seemed as though Toby always went for supplies when it came time to do the heavy work at the tavern. Meggie found it harder and harder to lift the massive kegs on top of each other.

The door behind Meggie creaked open, and with a keg in her arms, she turned with a forced smile on her face, expecting to see Toby. Dark eyes surveyed her form as if she stood naked before them. The intruder licked his lips, anticipating her flavor, and smiled seeing the fear that stole the smile from her.

Never taking her eyes away from his, Meggie stepped back from Jason, dropping the heavy keg to the floor. She pleaded with him silently as he reached behind, closing the storeroom door. He took her shawl from the hook and wrapped it tightly in his hands, forming a narrow length that stretched between them. Her eyes widened, realizing that he meant to take her life. Meggie said a silent prayer, asking God to take care of her family, then crossed herself, hoping to ward off her advancing attacker. She hoped that she would not die in vain and that this evil man would be caught and punished for what he was about to do to her.

. . . .

The warship docked just after dawn, with William shouting orders and hurrying his men as much as possible. He was anxious to search the town for the man from the Pegasus. It was high noon by the time they settled the ship's business and the search could begin. William hoped that the man was still here and that the townsfolk would willingly turn him over to them. It would be his only chance to outwit the Pegasus Captain, and he wasn't about to let anything spoil this for him. He told the men to search throughout the village. He and a few men headed for the nearby tavern.

The tavern seemed empty when William and his men entered. He ordered the back rooms searched then went to stand at the door to watch the street for any sign from the others that they had found the man. While standing there, a rather fat man waddled down the walk toward the tavern, carrying a crate. When he saw William standing there in his Navy uniform his face lit with anger. Toby never cared for any man in uniform. To him, all men in uniform were nothing but a bunch of pumped up fools doing the King's business and making trouble wherever they went.

"What's your purpose?" Toby asked with distain in his voice. "Are ye here to spend my time or to spend your coin?"

"Mayhap, some of both," William told him, as he stood to the side, allowing the rotund man to enter the tavern. "We are in search of a man, a man thrown from the pirate ship that escaped us only by a narrow margin, last eve."

124

"A narrow margin, ye say," Toby said, grinning wickedly. "I hear tell that the ship left your warship in the spray off its bow."

William grabbed Toby by the front of his shirt, pulling his face close to his. The crate fell from his arms spilling the contents to the floor. His eyes bulging with anger, William glared into Toby's bloodshot sockets. "Is the man here or isn't he? Don't waste our time with your idiotic chatter."

"Aye, the one you seek was here all last night. But, as you can see, he is no longer," Toby said, looking toward the booth where the man had passed out.

Shoving Toby aside, William searched the booths but found no trace of him. William turned again to Toby, who was picking up the spilled contents of the crate.

"Did anyone else see the man? Mayhap the barmaid or the housekeeper?" he demanded, from above Toby.

"Oh aye, the barmaid indeed. He took quite a liking to that one. Was all over the poor lass the whole night long. She was quite relieved to have him pass out before her shift was over. Sleeping men spend no coin ye know."

"Where is the girl now? Is she at work yet today?" William asked, helping Toby stand with the crate in his arms.

"Oh aye, she is in the back stocking the kegs," Toby grunted, motioning to the storage room as he placed the crate on the bar. "Go and ask her for yourself. I'll allow her a small break. But if it's more than talking that ye be wanting, that will cost ye. If she be letting you, I mean."

William said nothing in response to the vulgar man's words. The only thing he wanted to do was find that man and set out in pursuit of the Pegasus. Toby laughed at William as he brushed passed him heading to the storage room. The Royal Navy's men had not changed a bit and probably never would. All of them were so full of themselves. "What they needed was a good jolt to bring them low." Toby muttered under his breath.

The narrow hallway was dark and cramped but thankfully not very long. William felt a cold uneasiness come over him as he approached the door. Reaching it, his hand hesitated before turning the knob to open it.

The heavy door creaked as William opened it. The room was lit with nothing more than a candle on the verge of extinguishing itself. It took a moment for his eyes to focus. When they did, the horror that William witnessed attacked his senses, forcing a cry from his throat, bringing his men scrambling. Compelling himself to breathe, William fought the bile that rose from his stomach in a choking wave. The gasps of his men, who were not as seasoned as himself, reverberated in the deathly stillness of the cramped space.

The man's head rose slowly. Black pools, filled with unearthly darkness, penetrated each of the onlookers. Fear filled them, surrounded them, holding them in a trance-like state. They could only watch as blood trickled down the chin of this unknown entity. Each of them knew that the flesh clasped between his teeth was that of the unfortunate victim, lying legs spread, on the storeroom floor. The corners of Jason's mouth curved in a lurid, mocking smile, knowing from their stunned faces that the scene before the men sickened them to the core.

William wanted to scream, to stop what he was seeing. But even when he closed his eyes, the horrible scene didn't disappear. It had embedded itself in his mind, making him feel even sicker with the knowledge that he would never be able to forget what he was witness to. William opened his eyes as the man, in an animal-like motion, tilted back his head, then with one precise movement, flipped the mass of flesh to the back of his mouth, swallowing it whole.

"Seize him!" William screamed, but not a soul moved toward the man. "Seize him, I say!" Again, the men stood in shock and fear. Bringing them out of their trance, William grabbed one of them, then another, shoving them toward the man. Timidly, they drew quivering swords, pointing them at the man's chest.

"On your feet." said one of the officers, his voice less than a squeak. To their amazement, the man put his hands in the air and stood. "Get some rope and bind him. Tightly! Make certain that he can't free himself." The officer's meaning was understood.

"Take him to the ship," William said, trying to sound calm. "Secure him in the hold. I'll follow you shortly."

Jason took one last look at the unconscious girl on the floor. He felt no remorse, no guilt. After all, if she hadn't fought him, he wouldn't have gone to such extremes. But she had fought him and he did what he had to do to keep her still.

Holding him at a safe distance, William's men led Jason from the room as William knelt beside the poor, mangled girl. A shawl had been used to gag her. Her skirt was raised to her waist, exposing her most intimate places. A length of cord, cut from netting that hung from the wall, bound each wrist separately to each ankle. The awkwardly spread position of her legs, gave William full view of a gaping hole in her inner thigh. Blood spilled from the cavernous wound and pooled on the floor beneath her.

Tearing a strip of cloth from the hem of her skirt, William folded it into a bandage. Gently, he covered the wound and then brought her legs together to hold the dressing in place. Toby walked in at that moment.

"Dear God! What has happened to the lass? What did your man do to her?"

"He is not my man. I don't know why this happened, but I do know that this man is more evil than any man I have ever seen. When she is well enough to hear it, tell her that I will personally see that this man is executed for what he has done this day."

He cut the cord from her ankles, then removed the shawl from her mouth and listened for the sound of her breathing. In his heart William knew that no matter what, this poor girl was doomed. Wounds such as this would surely never heal. The girl was destined to get a gangrenous infection and perish.

"Here, take this and make her comfortable. Tell her that I am truly sorry," he said, handing Toby several pounds. "I hope that she doesn't suffer long."

There was nothing else he could say. No other words were spoken between them. William left the tavern to return to his ship and the search for the Pegasus, an evil cargo stored securely below.

Meggie's Warning   Chapter 21

Jillian awoke with a start, leaping from the warm confines of the soft coverlet. Her heart pounded wildly, marking her state of alarm. Her dream was so vivid, yet so confusing. Jillian stared blankly around the room, knowing that she was safe but feeling as if she were being watched. She thought about the dream and the dark eyes that pierced her thoughts. Those eyes belonged to Jason. They watched, they waited, they pried.

Swallowing hard, Jillian closed her eyes and concentrated on clearing her mind of the dread that filled her. But as she did, she vividly saw the tavern girl, Meggie. Jillian watched the scene play in her mind. Meggie floated before her as if being carried on a moonlit breeze. Her white gown, illuminated by a heavenly light, whirled around her. Jillian felt no fear in seeing Meggie before her. She felt no fear when Meggie reached out and took her hand.

"Beware," Meggie told Jillian softly. "The one he wants is you. The one he wants is you." Her voice trailed into the shadows, as did her image, and then she was gone.

Jillian opened her eyes once more, assuring herself that she was still within the safe confines of her room. Oddly enough, Jillian felt some relief at seeing Meggie. She felt reassured that the girl was out of danger. Why else would she have had such a pleasant image of her? But then, remembering her words, a chill went through her. "The one he wants is you." What could she have meant by that? Could she be referring to Jason who had haunted her dreams so?

Shaking her head to clear her thoughts, Jillian tried to remove the image and the dream from her mind. She obviously was in no danger now. The warship had turned away, heading back to the small portside village, and Jason had been thrown overboard. The only danger she could be in at this time was from her father. She was sure to be in much trouble for keeping the crew, and especially Gavin, up until the wee hours of the night enjoying their tales and the camaraderie that they all shared. The tales spun for Jillian, wove delicately for her sake, made Jillian feel more a part of the crew and the Pegasus.

A firm knock at the door brought Jillian out of her thoughts. She bounced from the bed, quickly pulling a dressing gown over her before opening the cabin door. Before her stood Gavin, his blue eyes mischievously lit.

"It's about time that you were up and about," Gavin muttered. "You've nearly slept the day away. Imagine loafing when there is much to do."

"Whatever do you mean, Gavin?" Jillian asked innocently. But then the thought struck her. "Oh! Oh, no! What time is it Gavin?" she asked, as she hurried back into the cabin, leaving Gavin standing arrogantly at the door.

"Past midday, I imagine," he answered, grinning as he watched Jillian search the armoire for her leather britches. "Never have paid much attention to the exact hour. I get up with the sun and sleep when the urge befits me. Of course, I don't think I have ever slept past the noon hour," he said, dodging the pillow that Jillian halfheartedly threw in his direction.

"Why didn't someone wake me, Gavin?" she asked, now finding the britches.

Without much thought to Gavin, who still stood in the doorway, Jillian pulled the black leggings on underneath her nightgown. Then, as she prepared to remove it, Jillian remembered the man whose eyes were transfixed on her.

"If you would be so kind, Gavin. I need just a wee bit of privacy." The blush of her cheeks and the softness in her voice reminded Gavin of how truly innocent Jillian really was.

"Oh, of course. If you insist, my sweet," he said, shutting the door. "I'll wait for you in the corridor."

It was all that Gavin could do to close the door, blocking the image of Jillian from his view. Leaning his forehead against the door, Gavin let out the breath that he must have been holding in anticipation of Jillian removing her gown. He felt certain that she would have, if only she hadn't remembered him in the doorway. Gavin didn't know if he felt relief or aggravation at being denied the sight of her enticing curves. All he knew was that he would be hard pressed to keep his hands off Jillian until they could be lawfully married.

Inside the cabin, Jillian privately chastised herself for her scandalous actions. Imagine, undressing before Gavin in her haste to be with the crew. How could she be so stupid, so brazen? Then, she remembered his astonished look; he was just as taken aback as she. But also, she caught sight of the hunger in his features that she'd noticed when he didn't think she was looking. It was the same hunger that she frequently felt for him.

She pulled her nightgown over her head, and reached for her blouse. Looking down at the swell of her breast, Jillian grimaced in disgust at the scar, the shape of teeth that still marred her perfect flesh. Would it ever go away? Not only the physical remnants of her ordeal, but the vivid memories of the vicious man that Jason was. With time, she thought, her mind would heal and so would her body, time that would be spent on the Pegasus, with security and love surrounding her. That would be the healing factor that Jillian needed.

Hurriedly, she tucked the blouse in at her waist, and then braided the masses of her hair. Gavin was still waiting for her when she emerged from the cabin, a vision. The leather pants clung to hers curves with precise definition. Her every movement gave Gavin reason to send her back into the cabin to change into something other than the tight fitting leggings. Her long, shapely legs seemed even longer than he remembered from that first day on the beach. Their strong and graceful shape continued all the way up to the gentle swell of her hips. Her backside was well defined by the britches. Gavin could see and imagine the feel of her tight muscled bottom molded within his hands. The blouse tucked in so neatly, gave even more emphasis to the smallness of her waist and the fullness of her bosom. He held his breath and stared in disbelief as she turned before him, asking for his opinion of her new attire. But her words were lost to him.

Giving a low groan of longing, Gavin captured Jillian to him, his arms locked strongly around her. Surprised but willing, Jillian returned his embrace with her own, feeling the hardness of his need against her. His lips claimed her fiercely with the motions of his urgent longing. She joined him in his need and instinctively pressed her hips against his, inviting another primal groan from Gavin. His hands roamed her body, exploring, caressing, and igniting every inch of her flesh. She felt as though she wore nothing, nothing that could protect her from the flames that licked beneath Gavin's fingers. The intensity of their heat deepened, consuming them both.

Unconsciously, her hands swept over Gavin's back, grasping, searching, and searing the flesh that they touched. She pulled him closer, opening her lips to his probing tongue. A moan escaped her, as she circled his tongue with her own, joining in the playful dance. Jillian responded to Gavin so completely that it took every ounce of his strength to pull his mouth from hers. His body trembled, his mind swam with the emotions that her touch caused, and feelings that were foreign to Gavin welled painfully in the depths of his breast. He felt as if his heart was going to burst with their intensity.

Placing gentle kisses on Jillian's cheek, Gavin tried to calm their pace. The throbbing of his loins against hers was maddening. He wanted her desperately, but knew that now was not the time to take what she so innocently offered.

Feeling Gavin's retreat, Jillian painstakingly slowed her movements. She clung to him, breathing hard, praying that the burning sensation that kindled deep within her would subside until another time. There would be another time when they would no longer have to control the passions that one touch from the other brought.

"Oh, Gavin," she sighed, her mouth close to his ear. "What your touch does to me has no description. I feel as if I am consumed by the heat of you."

"I feel it too, my love." Gavin shuddered. "The slightest touch, the slightest whisper from those glorious lips of yours sets my body on a course all its own. It's pure torture to resist taking you."

"Then why resist?" Jillian asked, a pleading look in her eyes. Gavin silenced her next words, placing a finger on her passion swollen lips.

"No, my lovely. Don't tempt me further." Pain filled, he continued, "our time will come." Gaining some control, Gavin stepped back from her, holding her at arm's length. "Now, there are things that need doing. The crew is awaiting the arrival of their favorite pupil."

Stepping back from him, Jillian straightened herself, taking a few minutes to gain her composure. She stifled the urge to giggle, for her heart was light with the knowledge of Gavin's longing. Still flush with passion, Gavin gave her a boyish grin while running his hands through his hair to straighten it.

"Let's not keep them waiting," Gavin said, motioning to the ladder leading to the deck. "Your life as a pirate begins."

Smiling, she took his offered arm and they walked to the ladder, Jillian ascending first. Gavin closed his eyes as her tiny waist, firm, rounded buttocks and slender legs passed within inches of him. "God, give me strength," he pleaded under his breath.

"Are you coming?" her question from the top of the ladder brought his eyes to hers. "Or are you going to nap the day away?" she teased.

"You are one to talk," he quipped, reaching the deck in three giant strides.

He noticed as she turned and walked away from him that she wore no shoes. Of course, the slippers that matched the gown which Terrance had purchased for her were not fit for the beautiful pirate that sashayed before the crew. He would have to remedy that.

. . . .

The days passed in splendor for Jillian. She could not imagine being any happier than she was this last month on the Pegasus. The crew taught her many things about sailing this mighty vessel. For that, and her happiness, Jillian was eternally grateful. The Pegasus filled her life. The crew was everything to her—friends, brothers, protectors. Terrance treated her with respect and pride but most of all relished in being the father of such a wonderful child. He tried to make up for each bad moment spent with William. Jillian was blessed with a kind and gentle father.

Gavin was, by far, the greatest inspiration in her life. She watched him interact with the men and her father. Never faltering in purpose, Gavin had a way about him that made one feel good just being near him. She wasn't the only one who felt this way, for she could see by the actions of the men how they enjoyed his presence and companionship. Strength and purpose emanated from him and he was in her thoughts every waking hour.

Gavin, also, found it hard to keep his thoughts from Jillian. During the day, while performing the simplest task, his thoughts would wander to her. He would search her out, just to make sure she was safe and happy, to find that she was glad that he did. Stolen moments behind stacks of supplies, and brief embraces while passing in the lower corridors, kept Gavin's mind and body focused on the day when she would be his wife.

The nights were the hardest. On the Pegasus it was an evening ritual for the crew to gather above deck for a time of dance and song. Gavin found it increasingly hard to share Jillian with the others, but knew that when the last song floated across the ocean's surface, it would be his time to lay claim to Jillian's hand. They danced the last together each night, and then took an uninterrupted stroll on the deck. The crew became invisible to them. This was the hardest time for Gavin, for this meant the end to another day of being with Jillian, something that he cherished above anything he ever loved in his life.

Such a night was coming to an end. Gavin watched as Terrance led Jillian in their last dance. He handled her with kid gloves, taking pains not to step on her tiny feet while they danced. Suddenly, Terrance held Jillian away from him, a look of disbelief on his face. "You can't be serious. I won't have it," he said sternly.

The music stopped, the smiles faded. There was silence and all eyes were on Terrance and Jillian.

"You don't mean that, Father. This is a pirate ship. How can we not?"

"Because I command this ship. That's how," his voice bellowed

"But . . ." Jillian stammered.

"Not another word! That's final!" he warned.

"Now, now. What's all this?" Gavin asked, easing between the two. "You aren't having an argument, are you?"

"I know you are doing this for me, Father," she said holding her ground, "but the families in port are depending on us. We must take a ship. And soon."

Gavin swung around to meet Jillian's stare. "You can't be serious Jillian. It is too dangerous with you . . ." Gavin stopped, seeing her determination rise with his words.

"So, you are of the same mind as my father then?" she stood silent, waiting for his answer as did everyone else. "I cannot believe that your families have found other means of support while the lot of you have taken a holiday." Her statement rang true with the men reminding them of their obligations to their loved ones.

"You are right, little one," Cy called from his perch above the deck. "It is time that we get back to what we do best."

Jillian smiled up at his silhouette against the full moon. "Thank you," she called to him. "Does anyone else feel the same?" she asked, anxiously pleading with the pirates. It was Micah who came to her rescue.

"I know my sis and my mum were hoping to have a winter cloak to warm them. I promised," he said, lowering his eyes from Terrance's menacing gaze.

Some of the others then joined in with the same sentiments. It was the consensus of the crew that it was time to take a ship and return to port with the booty. Their families depended on them.

Terrance felt cornered. For the past week he had been trying to decide what to do about the families awaiting the Pegasus. He knew the dependency of these people and his crew. But this was not the life he wanted for Jillian. It was dangerous to pirate a vessel. One could never know how well armed the other was. Terrance depended on the skill and cunning of his crew to keep themselves and the Pegasus in one piece when pilfering a ship. It was different with Jillian here. He dared not risk her life.

His answer came from Sue Ki. The little man seemed to appear from nowhere. "I give lesson. She will fight and protect herself." Terrance could see Sue Ki swell with pride at the thought of teaching Jillian.

"It is dangerous, Jillian. Are you certain this is what you want?" he asked. "Once you participate you will be a pirate, no less than the rest of us."

"I am by being a part of this ship aren't I?" she asked, in protest.

Completely speechless, the men, especially Gavin, couldn't believe that the Captain would even consider what she said.

If he could keep Jillian safe, Terrance couldn't think of an excuse not to take a ship. "We shall see what tomorrow brings," was the only thing he could think to say at the moment.

Jillian lit with excitement at Terrance's words. Gavin's brow bunched in a frown directed at Terrance. How could he give in so quickly to her? How could he put her into so much danger? Gavin vowed to himself that he would stay close to Jillian if a ship came into view. He would protect her.

Gavin wasn't the only man making that silent vow. Each of the crewmen felt the same. She had stuck up for them and their families. It was her way. They would not let her suffer for it.

. . . .

It wasn't long after that evening that a ship was spotted on the horizon. Terrance gave the order for the Pegasus to come about as soon as Cy, standing with Jillian in the crow's nest, identified the ship as a merchant vessel sitting low in the water. This only meant one thing; she was loaded with supplies. The plunder would be plentiful for all. Terrance knew how much the men needed this ship. The men burst into action as soon as the order was given, each of them secretly dreaming of the treasures that would be secured for their loved ones.

Gavin called to Jillian to come down from the crow's nest. His only thought was keeping her near him and safe from the dangers that would certainly come with the approaching battle. Jillian heard Gavin, but stayed in her perch far above the deck, watching the merchant ship coming closer. From below, a cannonball thundered toward the vessel, landing squarely in its path. You could hear the men on the ship shouting with fright and see them scrambling about the deck. Feeling a pang of guilt, Jillian remembered how it felt to be threatened in such a way.

A shout rang out from the merchant ship as the Pegasus came alongside her. Suddenly, as though from nowhere, men swung from the rigging across the space between the vessels. She screamed with terror, thinking that the Pegasus was caught off guard by these ruffians, but the sound lodged in her throat when she saw the crew, swords raised, awaiting their foes' landing. The clanging of metal against metal rang below her. Jillian gasped and clung to the crow's nest tightly with every reverberation.

Below, Gavin held his own against the intruders. He realized that these men must have been hired to guard the vessel from attacks, staying hidden until a pirate ship was close, then taking advantage of the element of surprise to try to overtake their foes. How clever of them, he thought.

In a split second, between defending himself from the attacking men, Gavin glanced briefly at the crow's nest. Jillian was still there and for once he was glad for her defiance of him, for there was at this moment, not a safer place on the Pegasus. Although Gavin could see that his men were gaining on the intruders, the fighting continued.

Terrance fought at the helm, keeping the Pegasus from ramming into the merchant ship. He only wanted to get the booty on board the ship, not to sink it, which would not be hard to do, being the Pegasus was a larger vessel. The crewmen were fighting with all their might to gain an advantage over the inferior ship's guards. Terrance knew that it was only a matter of time before they were taken down by his men. Even Sue Ki came from below to join in the battle. Terrance smiled to himself while he watched bigger and stronger men fly through the air away from the little dragon.

Patting Jillian's hand for reassurance, Cy climbed from their perch to join his men below. Jillian watched him nimbly descend the rigging, bringing himself quickly to the deck. Not far from Cy was Micah, who fought valiantly against a large man wearing a turban. The man's mighty blows came quickly, one after the other, staggering Micah backward, his sword raised as a shield against each strike. The turbaned man pressed on, forcing Micah to the deck, taking advantage of the difference in their sizes.

Jillian's heart leapt, for it seemed that Micah would not last much longer under this kind of punishment. She searched the deck below for Gavin. Her eyes found him with ease and she was reassured that he was well, but not within helping distance of Micah. She had to think of something.

Micah's arm crumpled under the last stunning blow from the huge man's powerful sword, his own sword flying out of reach. Instantly, the foe's blade caressed Micah's neck, the tip lifting his chin for sacrifice. Micah swallowed bravely, then closed his eyes, thinking this would be his last breath. The intruder raised his sword, aiming for his final blow . . .

Above the shouts from the carnage on the ship, there was a shrill cry that pierced the violence. The turbaned man stood suspended in time, his sword still held above his head. In the next instant, he was knocked to the deck, barely missing Micah who rolled quickly away. The turbaned man didn't move, didn't groan. Micah found his sword quickly, and scrambled to his feet beside the silent form of the prone man. Jillian's arms were suddenly around Micah, comforting and reassuring him. Still, Micah held his sword toward the lifeless form, watching for any sign of movement.

"Are you hurt, Micah?" Jillian's voice finally broke through his shock. "Micah, please say that he didn't maim you. Micah?" she pleaded.

"I cannot believe it, princess. It was the most incredible thing I have ever seen a woman do," Cy said, coming toward Micah and Jillian. "One minute she is safe," he said, pointing to the crow's nest, "the next she is on the deck fighting along with the men! It is incredible!"

Micah turned to Jillian with puzzled eyes. "What just happened here?" he asked, gazing down into the depths of her amber eyes.

Before she could answer, Gavin tore Jillian from Micah's arms. He held her, clutching her to him. She made no resistance to his embrace.

Within seconds, many more of the ship's crew stood around Gavin and Jillian, slapping each other on the back and taunting Micah. It took

Gavin awhile before he could let Jillian loose from his fierce hold. When he did, he could see that Jillian was not herself. The amber of her eyes deepened into endless vats, her face ashen and drawn.

Alarmed, Gavin shook Jillian's shoulders. "Jillian, come back. Jillian!" he yelled, panicking. "Come back!"

Her eyes cleared suddenly and she looked into Gavin's panic-stricken face. "Gavin, what is it? Are you hurt?" she asked, dazed, bringing her hand up to gently cup his face.

"No, but you are," he said, pointing out the blood that dripped from Jillian's arm. "You must have caught his sword when you knocked him down."

"Who are you talking about, Gavin? Who did I knock down?"

Following Gavin's eyes, Jillian saw the huge man with the turban lying face down on the deck's surface. Cy checked his neck for a pulse. Finding none, he gave her a knowing nod.

"He can't be dead. Cy, tell me he isn't," she pleaded.

"Sorry," he said, shaking his head. "If he were alive, Micah would not be, and that would be even worse than this. You see, his neck is broken."

Jillian stared in disbelief. His neck was broken? Because she had knocked him down? How could this be possible? The sudden rush of her returning memory made Jillian sway against Gavin. Her eyes darted to the crow's nest, and then to the man sprawled on the deck. She had killed him!

All of a sudden, her stomach churned, Jillian escaped from Gavin's arms and ran to the ship's railing. The contents of her stomach flew over the ship's bow and into the ocean below. Terrance was quickly at her side, holding her. The crew shuddered collectively, watching Jillian. Killing a man was nothing that she would take in stride, nothing that she would ever want to lament. Killing a man was serious, and Jillian was just beginning to know the full extent of being a pirate.

When Jillian regained her composure, Terrance took her below, for he knew all too well what she was feeling. The sickness that enters your soul once you have taken another's life can be a devastating thing. Terrance knew that Jillian needed to be with someone who understood.

"Ki, come quickly," Terrance yelled entering her cabin. But he didn't have to yell, for the little man was on his heels, ready to work his magic.

Terrance laid Jillian upon the bed, and then, at Ki's bidding, hastily went to the galley to heat water for Jillian's bath. Sue Ki would use his magic to pull the awful memories from her mind. She would heal, that Terrance was sure of. His lips quirked into a smile, thinking of his little spitfire flying through the air, flinging herself from the crow's nest to save the life of a friend. He would have to remember to chastise Cy once more for showing Jillian the quick descent that made it possible for her to do so.

Sometime later, Sue Ki quietly shut the door of Jillian's cabin to find both Terrance and Gavin in the companionway, anxiously waiting for word of Jillian's condition.

"She be fine, Cappy. She rest now."

Terrance knew he should feel relieved but Sue Ki wasn't telling everything he knew. Terrance could see it in his eyes. Something else was wrong. Very wrong.

Gavin, why don't you go sit with Jillian?" Terrance suggested. "I'm sure that she would like some company even if she is asleep." Gladly, Gavin quietly entered the room to make sure that she was indeed safe.

"I think you have something to tell me, old man," Terrance said, leading Sue Ki into the galley.

Jillian lay still as stone upon the bed. Her hair, combed smooth, was spread upon the pillows to dry. An emerald dressing gown lay loosely upon her body. Gavin lifted her hand to his lips, holding it there, caressing its surface. He gently touched the wrappings around her slender arm remembering the gash that the sword left. He came so close to losing her today. The thought made him wince and tears welled in his eyes.

Through the chaos on deck, Gavin had watched in amazement, as Jillian climbed out of the crow's nest and grasped the hook left behind by Cy. She had flung herself toward the deck, screaming at the top of her lungs at the man, who in Gavin's estimation, was about to behead Micah. The man froze, Jillian kicked out as she passed over him, snapping his muscular neck. Gavin heard the snap over and over in his mind as he watched the huge man fall to the deck. Jillian had landed on her feet not far from Micah, then flung herself at him, making sure that he wasn't harmed. All the while, Jillian never showed a care for her own safety. She was incredible, as Cy said, incredibly brave and incredibly beautiful. She was so many things rolled up into one tiny, wondrous creature and Gavin was more than thankful that she wasn't more seriously hurt.

Awakening, Jillian felt the soft brush of Gavin's warm lips on the back of her hand but kept her eyes closed. Even when she felt the moistness of his tears, Jillian could not open her eyes. How could she face him after what happened? A man's death was on her hands, and a man's life was in her hands. It was too much. Try as she may Jillian could not hold back the flow of tears from beneath her eyelids.

Gavin looked up when he heard a strangled cry escape her lips. Tears streamed down her face, mingling with the soft curls surrounding it. He gently climbed beside Jillian on the bed, holding her fragility in his protective arms, and kissed away the tears from her swollen eyes. Gently rocking her, Gavin began to hum the lullaby that she had used to ease his thoughts not so long ago. He caressed and held her until the flow of tears subsided and she was calmed.

"You're safe, Jillian." he cooed, lovingly. "You're safe here with me."

His words helped Jillian face the regret that she felt for the lives that were lost in the battle. How many lives were lost?

"Our men. Did anyone else . . . ?" Jillian struggled to finish the sentence. "How many others perished?" she asked, lifting her eyes to his, studying his face for an answer.

"No. No lives were lost on our part." he soothed, his words giving her some relief.

"I could not bare it if I was not only responsible for the death of an unknown, but also, the death of one of our cherished companions."

"But you are not responsible for anyone's death Jillian. You must believe this," he said, shaking her. "If anything, we should thank you for saving Micah's life."

Pulling away from him, Jillian sat at the edge of the bed, her gaze slipping off into the distance. Gavin knelt behind her on the bed knowing her distress. He ached to pull her to him but waited, giving her time to sort through the torment in her mind.

"Sue Ki says that we are all in charge of our own destiny, that the man I killed today lived his life here, and is now free to start a new life in another place. It is a rebirth of sorts. Death is an opening door that leads down a different path." She hesitated, "I feel the same about being here. It is a rebirth for me; a doorway has been opened to a new life and I must be strong enough to accept that things are forever changed. You, Gavin are my strength. If I am to make my own destiny, I will make my own decisions about what I desire my life to be."

Timidly, Gavin asked, his voice breaking into fragments of his once strong self, "What is it that you desire most, my love?" He waited in silent anticipation of her answer.

"What I desire most Gavin, is you," Jillian said, rising from the bed.

Gavin watched, as without turning, Jillian unfastened her gown and slid it off her shoulders. His breath caught and his heart raced, making him lightheaded with anticipation. Jillian let her arms drop to her sides, giving the gown the final release it needed to complete the path to the cabin floor. She stood, gathering strength to go on with the journey on which she was embarking. Frozen in place, Gavin used every ounce of his being to keep from taking her into his arms. Golden tresses streamed down her shoulders and back, settling into a v-shape at the fullness of her hips. Her petite, muscular buttocks and slender legs were everything that the leather pants had promised them to be.

As if this view was not torture enough, Jillian slowly turned to face Gavin. He paled with the sight of her delicate beauty. The amber depths of her eyes beckoned to him but he remained unmoving, cast in the spell of this moment. Her bottom lip quivered and she caught its fullness between her teeth, the gesture making Gavin want even more to feel its ripeness with his own. His gaze graced her body tenderly, taking in the fullness of her breasts that peaked through the golden ringlets encircling their silky surface, then lower, to the gentle curve of her waist. The silken curls that covered her womanhood gave promise to the treasures that lay hidden within their golden folds. Gavin closed his eyes, for his body screamed out for Jillian's touch. She saw his agony and knew its source, for she too longed to touch, to kiss, and to take pleasure in Gavin's body as well.

With Sue Ki's ministrations, Jillian was released from the pain and torture of all that was her life before, and she now realized how short life might be. She knew she must seek what she desired before the opportunity was taken from her. In this, she knew that Gavin was the fulfillment that would complete the opening of the door to her future.

"Come to me now, Gavin," Jillian beckoned, holding out her hand to him.

Gavin rose slowly, stepping off the bed to stand before Jillian. The heat of her body, so close to his was pure agony, but Gavin held himself in check. This would have to be Jillian's choice for he did not want to push her into something, something that she may regret for the rest of her life.

Timidly, Jillian reached for Gavin, undoing the buttons of his blouse. Her hands trembled as she pulled the cloth from beneath his belt. In a slow, torturous motion, Jillian slid her hands unsteadily beneath the blouse and pushed it off his muscular shoulders, allowing it to fall to the floor. Tilting his head back, Gavin's breath caught with her provocative movements. The feel of her caressing hands against his naked skin sent waves of excitement through his body.

Jillian hands explored every detail, every curve of Gavin's well-defined chest, then slowly made their way to the fastenings of his leggings. His stomach sucked in as her fingers touched the sensitive skin so close to his throbbing core. One by one, the fastenings came loose. Jillian smoothed the fabric down over Gavin's buttocks, leaving a fiery trail that continued to the floor, where the leggings pooled at his ankles. He stepped quickly out of them and his boots.

Passion was thick in the air as they stood in their natural state before one another. Spreading both palms on Gavin's chest, Jillian felt his strength and the warmth of the being beneath her caress. Seeing tenderness in his eyes, and feeling the power beneath his breast, gave Jillian courage. It felt natural; it felt wonderful to be here with Gavin. It was their beginning.

"You are so beautiful," she said softly. Cupping his cheek, Jillian brought his lips to hers, kissing them sweetly. "Make love to me, sweet Gavin," She said against his lips.

With a low groan, Gavin brought her into his arms, kissing her gently on the forehead, eyelids, and then her mouth. Jillian returned his passion with her own, wrapping her arms tightly around him. The feel of his skin against her own was a sweet reward for the many hours of sleepless anticipation that both had endured until now.

Gavin lifted Jillian into his arms, laying her gently upon the bed. He lowered the lantern's light then joined her there, bringing the coverlet over them. Their bodies met in a heated embrace, every nerve inflamed, every sense aroused to a point never before attained. Jillian yearned for even the slightest touch of Gavin's hand upon her and he didn't disappoint her.

He explored her body slowly, keeping his own desire at bay. Knowing that this would be her first time, Gavin wanted to give Jillian the full pleasure she deserved. Kisses tasted the sweetness of her jasmine-scented skin. Slowly, with deliberate and tender caresses, his lips trailed down her neck, then to the soft swell of each breast. Jillian arched into his lip's caress as he took each budded nipple into his mouth, his hands capturing the soft mounds fondly. Flames shot through her body with the impact of his touch. A tightening, deep within, forced a moan from her lips that rewarded Gavin's efforts. While teasing her breast with his lips and tongue, his hands, resumed the sweet descent to other parts of Jillian's sensitive body, igniting a fiery trail. She gasped with delight as every part of her screamed for his touch. She wanted more than his hands could give. She felt an urgent need to feel Gavin deep within her. An aching like no other came from deep inside her womb, screaming to be released.

In her need, Jillian pulled Gavin to her with a strength that came from somewhere unknown. Her legs wrapped around him, her arms clung to him in powerful urgency. Then Gavin touched the core of her desire and she cried out with the intensity of it. He covered her lips with his own, stifling her cries of pleasure, as he brought her closer to exploding with sensations not yet known to her. His hands began a rhythm of their own, and Jillian's body responded to their pace, arching against their probe. As the pace quickened, she struggled for breath with the growing intensity, whispering his name between each gasp.

Seeing her respond to him so fully, Gavin could wait no longer. The innocence of her body's awakening aroused him far beyond anything he had ever experienced. In this, Jillian trusted him to be her teacher. In time, he knew he would teach her the marvel of giving pleasure to him. But for now, it would be for her. Gavin wanted Jillian to savor his love-making beyond anything else.

Feeling her moistness growing, Gavin knew that her body was preparing to receive him. But feeling momentarily uncertain, Gavin stilled.

"Are you certain?" he asked breathlessly, waiting for her answer.

"You don't have to ask me that, Gavin," she whispered against his neck.

"There will be no going back." Rising up slightly, he studied her features, alive with pleasure.

"There is no going back," she gasped, pulling him fiercely to her. "Make love to me Gavin."

Her body arched against him, meeting him, begging his manhood to enter her and force the barrier of her virginity to give, the tearing of the membrane forgotten in the frenzy of their desire. Their bodies, each seeking release from the all-consuming flames of passion, thrust in unison against each other with rapid longing.

Jillian could feel him within her, his smooth member touching her womb, intensifying her urgent quest. She cried out for release from this sweet torture and was answered by her body's sudden shuddering. Sensual spasms burst from the depths of her womb, radiating through her.

Gavin felt her release, felt her body's rhythmic clinching and was lost in the knowledge of the pleasure that she experienced. He took intense pleasure in this and added it to his final efforts, joining her, climaxing their love-making together.

* * * * *

Light filtered through the porthole, marking the forthcoming sunrise, illuminating the strikingly handsome features of Gavin's sleeping face. He slept peacefully beside her with one arm wrapped protectively around her waist. She nestled her cheek against his chest, feeling the smoothness of skin over hard muscle. His essence engulfed her. She smiled to herself with the memories of their lovemaking.

He had taken her only once, and then bathed the remnants of his love and her virginity from their bodies. Afterward, they lay in each other's arms, sharing another kind of love-making—laughing, talking, feeling—and for long hours they did nothing but communicate through touch. Jillian felt she knew every detail, every facet of Gavin's body and life, and she loved him all the more for sharing this with her. Their first night together was indeed wondrous, and they found companionship in each other as well as love.

Although Gavin slept soundly, Jillian felt sensations beginning to awaken within her as she remembered their night of love. The steady beat of his heart beneath her ear seemed to pulse through her. Her breasts throbbed, longing for the fiery touch of his mouth upon them. Again, she felt the tightening of her very core, the feeling giving her courage.

Biting her lower lip, Jillian lightly stroked his chest with the tips of her fingers. With each stroke, the muscles beneath her cheek tightened as her fingers circled the tiny buds of his breast, massaging them into erectness. He groaned, and then moved ever so slightly, settling once more into feigned slumber. Seeing him relax, Jillian began her loving exploration once more.

Moving above him, Jillian placed light kisses on the smooth skin of his shoulders, then continued until every inch of his upper body had been pleasured by her touch. His skin tasted of ocean and leather and she remembered her first thoughts of the man who carried her, who calmed her fears, who loved, and had made love to her the night before. This man had awakened the woman within, the woman who would now return the pleasure that he had so gently given her.

Gavin's body screamed with sensation under her touch. Again, he held himself in check. Jillian's sweet discovery of his body was something new and unusual for Gavin. It heightened his arousal with intense sensations. He remained silent enjoying her exploration.

The light in the cabin, now brightening with the dawn, highlighted the small patch of blonde curls in the valley at the center of Gavin's well-defined chest. Jillian's eyes followed the golden-haired path that led downward to disappear beneath the coverlet at his waist. She traced this golden trail with the back of her hand, his muscles recoiling with her light touch. Before she could go any further, Gavin lurched upward, grabbing her wrist and capturing her within his arms.

"What sweet torture you awaken me with. How much must I endure?" he whispered into her ear, the question bringing a smile to both.

"Oh, but you must endure much more than this, if I am to truly know the ways of men," she said, laughing coyly.

"Don't let me stop you from discovering the ways of men," he beckoned, lying once more before her.

"Oh, I will discover your secrets, Gavin, and more," she teased, her eyes alight with mischief, as she pulled the coverlet off him, his arousal obvious.

Jillian eased herself upright above him, straddling his strong body at the waist. Gavin's hands massaged their way up her thighs in a rhythmic journey. Jillian joined in this rhythm, allowing her hips to settle upon his swollen passion, her womanhood sliding against the length of his arousal. He cupped her breasts, raising his lips to them, tasting their sweet nectar. Jillian threw her head backward and arched into his lip's caress, letting him drink the fullness of her desire. Golden tresses cascaded down her back, tickling his muscular thighs, adding to the delicious sensations aroused in him.

She moved slightly above him, held him, and then raised his rigid member to enter her. With no hesitation, Jillian eased herself down the length of him, whimpering with the sensations his entrance caused. Their joining sent waves of fire throughout their anxious bodies and the tempo of their desire began in earnest. Their skin gleamed with the moisture of this rhythmic ride, which accelerated into a heated frenzy of wanting. Together, they rode the fire storm, until at last, their senses exploded into bursts of light that radiated throughout their very souls.

Afterwards, they lay exhausted in each other's arms; each deep in thought of the complexity that their love-making added to their lives.

Jillian wondered what her father would do to them. Terrance must know what took place inside her cabin last night, yet, she had no regrets. She only worried how she could face him and how she could look him in the eye and not feel guilty about what she and Gavin had done. Surely, Terrance knew what it was like to love someone so very passionately. Then, Jillian thought of her mother and how she and Terrance had been lovers torn apart by a wicked twist of fate. She would rely on Terrance's compassion for her and Gavin's plight, and on his love for her as the child of a passion that he had shared once with her mother.

Gavin was also lost in thought, knowing what Terrance would think and what he would do to Gavin for taking Jillian before a marriage ceremony was performed. Terrance was protective of Jillian. Would he challenge Gavin to a duel? Would he make him walk the plank? Or, would he forbid Gavin to ever see Jillian again? Gavin could not bear to lose Jillian. He would rather die than be denied her gentle love. With great resolve, Gavin set his mind that he would fight to the death before giving Jillian up.

Without a word, Gavin swung out of the bed and began to dress. "It's time, my love," he stated flatly to Jillian. She knew his meaning and followed him from the bed.

"We'll face him together," she said, pulling on her chemise, then the emerald gown her father had given her. After straightening her tangled hair, Jillian took Gavin's offered hand and sighed with determination. "It's time," Jillian told him. Gavin opened the cabin door and they walked through it into the corridor to face Terrance's wrath together.

Gavin climbed the ladder ahead of Jillian, hoping to take the brunt of Terrance and the crew's rage. Jillian watched him disappear through the opening above her. He didn't turn back to aid her ascent. Feeling a moment of abandonment, Jillian wanted to call him back to her. She wanted more than anything to escape this task and go back to her cabin, but deep in her heart she knew this was not to be. She would have to face her father. Indeed, she had made her own destiny by following the desires of her heart.

Gulping down the rising bile from her stomach that threatened her resolve, it took all the courage she could muster for Jillian to place her hands firmly on the ladder's railing and take that first step. A shadow fell over her in the stairwell. Startled by the sudden darkness, Jillian stopped to see who it was blocking her ascent.

"Sue Ki!" Terrance roared above her. "Prepare her, and be quick about it."

He said nothing else, only stared down at her. His features were hard to determine, for the dawn's light made him a silhouette against its brightness. Jillian felt a sudden tugging from behind her. It was Sue Ki.

"Come, missy. You hear Cappy. You must hurry," he pleaded, tugging on Jillian's arm.

Sensing impending danger, an unexpected chill ran through Jillian. Pain shot through her chest as if something were torn from within it, leaving a gaping hole and an emptiness that could not be filled. Her hand shot out to her father, but he turned away and didn't see her reach out to him. Stunned but quickly taking action, Sue Ki loosened the hold that Jillian had on the railing, catching her limp body as she fell into his arms. He carried her unconscious form easily to her cabin, kicking the door shut behind them.

Spiraling down into the darkness, Jillian saw a faint light appear. The vision became clear. Meggie, the tavern maid who had served them while in port, lay dying of fever. Gathered around her death bed were several small wide-eyed children and a graying, kind-faced, woman. Jillian thought this must be Meggie's mother. The children sobbed into their hands, their sorrowful spasms raking their tiny forms. Cradling Meggie's hand against her cheek, the older woman cooed to Meggie of her love for her.

Behind her family were Old Pete and Ryan Shelby, their eyes also filled with sorrow and angst for the suffering of their friend, Meggie. Ryan came to kneel beside her bed taking her other hand in his and bringing it to his lips.

"Sleep, dear friend." he said, tears escaping from his eyes. "Your pain will soon be over, sleep now in peace."

Meggie opened her eyes, looking over the top of Ryan's head, as if seeing someone else standing behind him. She reached for that person and Jillian took her hand, holding its fragility within her own. Meggie smiled into her eyes and Jillian could feel the warmth of that smile emanating from her.

Meggie spoke softly, without pain, without regret, for she knew that her time was near and that she had to warn Jillian before it was too late. Her voice was but a whisper, but the words resounded in Jillian's head. "The one he wants is you. He called me by your name. He called me "Jillian".

Her life fled the agony of her body, and in that instant, Jillian felt as if she absorbed that very life. It sat her upright on the bed, sending Sue Ki tumbling back from her. He watched as her body appeared to expand with an inner light. He saw great strength within her expression but also fear of what had just occurred. It lasted only seconds, and when the entity had settled into her soul, Jillian opened her eyes to an awareness of life that she hadn't possessed before. She saw things that she hadn't seen before and knew what awaited her on deck. She was anxious for it. She wanted it more than anything and was thankful for a father who knew her need.

Saying not a word, Sue Ki concentrated on the task at hand, helping her bathe and dress in finery taken from the merchant ship. He knew that she had just had an experience beyond this world. He had heard about it many times back in his homeland, but only in the secret ceremonies and rituals of his people. For Jillian to possess this power was something of a mystery to Sue Ki. But possess it, she did. He wondered silently if she had any inkling of what it actually meant.

Above deck, the Pegasus was gaily decorated with bursts of color. Bolts of fine silk and satin draped the rigging giving the ship a look of celebration. It was a rainbow spectacular befitting the occasion. The deck was freshly scrubbed. It glistened with the reflection of the morning sun. The deck wasn't the only thing with a fresh scrub, for the crew, clean-shaven, hair combed and dressed in magnificent attire, stood at attention when Jillian emerged from the stairwell. Micah came quickly to her side, extending his arm to her, his face beaming with excitement.

"Thank you for saving my life, Jillian" he said earnestly. "It would be my pleasure to escort you to your intended, who awaits your arrival," he said motioning toward the helm where her father and Gavin stood.

"I'm glad to see you unharmed," Jillian said, taking his arm, then allowing him to lead her past the rows of crewmen to the upper deck.

Gavin watched her approach. She seemed to glide over the surface of the deck, her eyes never leaving his. She wore a gown of honeyed silk that shimmered in the sunlight like a thousand glistening diamonds. The billowing skirt tightened at her narrow waist, accentuating her smooth form and continued upward until just below her breasts which blossomed above it. The low-cut bodice enhanced the look, allowing just the swell of her supple breasts to show. Her bare shoulders and arms, the color of translucent ivory, looked as if made from the finest porcelain. It was an elegant gown, but not nearly as regal as the beautiful woman wearing it. Her hair cascaded in tiny curls around her face. Its golden shade, highlighted by the sun, sparkled in the sunlight, giving richness to her crowning glory. But Jillian's most remarkable feature had to be her eyes, which now seemed lighter in color than before. Gavin sensed a change in Jillian, an awakening of some kind. Her eyes reflected the light and the knowledge that this renewal had brought. He smiled deeply at her as she came to stand beside him; his handsome features alight with the joy of this day.

Emerging from the stairwell, Gavin had been dreading the day and the responsibility of facing Terrance. He was stunned by what greeted him there. Terrance and the crew, faces beaming, had embraced him, giving him words of congratulations and encouragement. In all his kind wisdom, Terrance had already announced to the crew that this would be Gavin and Jillian's wedding day. The dread that Gavin had been feeling fled him, and was replaced by exhilaration. The day couldn't be more perfect, the time so right for a wedding to take place. He knew that he couldn't be happier than at this very moment.

Jillian was heady, intoxicated by Gavin's handsome form. He was male perfection itself and he was soon to be her husband. He wore black knee-length boots with black leather pants tucked neatly into their tops. The pants hugged his muscular length in a way that she remembered was not too tight when removing them. He wore a freshly laundered white linen blouse tucked in at his waist. It clung to the broad expanse of his lean chest and shoulders. As was his signature, a few of the top buttons were left unfastened, allowing muscular ripples and sun-bleached chest hair to show. His blonde hair gleamed with transient light from the sun lending pleasing contrast to the healthy glow of his skin. Sea blue eyes glistened with a shimmering of moisture drawn from the magnificence of this moment. Gavin was manly, handsome, and powerful to Jillian. Her heart raced within her breast with her wanting of him.

She felt honored by her position as his wife and privately vowed to always uphold that honor. Never would she disgrace this sanction between them.

He took her hand in his, treating it as if it were the most precious, fragile thing ever held within his powerful grasp. As large and as strong as his hands were, Jillian knew that they could also be so very gentle, performing the most delicate movements when making love. Looking at his hands, Jillian remembered their feel upon her breast and sighed contently with that memory. She squeezed his hand lightly and he returned the gesture in kind.

"Soon," she told herself. "Soon the words will be spoken."

They stood before Terrance in loving splendor. He knew he had made the right decision by having the ceremony now, after hearing their love-making through the cabin door last night. Never, would he permit Jillian or Gavin to face the humiliation of love unsanctified, never would he allow his sweet daughter to be abandoned in that love. Terrance knew that terrible twists in life could indeed lead to the instant loss of the one you love. The best thing for all was to complete their union and let their life together begin. As Captain of the Pegasus, Terrance would be the one to perform the ceremony, and this pleased him beyond words. To witness Gavin and Jillian's love was something sacred to Terrance. It was time to begin.

Terrance spoke the words necessary to unite Gavin and Jillian, but they went unnoticed by them. The only thing they heard was the beating of their own hearts. The only thing they felt was that same throbbing, pulsing between them by the joining of their hands. Gavin was just as spellbound as Jillian, and it wasn't until cheers went up from all the crew as Gavin and Jillian sealed their pact with a passionate kiss, that the world around them entered their private sanctuary.

Before the kiss ended, Micah began playing a merry jig on the fiddle. Then the crew took turns with both Jillian and Gavin, kissing, hugging and dancing with them in congratulations. The celebration lasted throughout the day. The only time it quieted was during their sunset dinner, but as soon as the meal ended, the celebration began again in earnest.

By the time midnight arrived, most of the crewmen were lying sporadically, passed out upon the deck. Having to keep watch that night, Cy and two others, who were conservative in their drinking, were the only ones joining Gavin, Jillian and Terrance in their ability to stand. The exhausted couple bid good night to the others and walked with Terrance to the companionway.

"Good night, sir," Gavin said, proudly. "Thank you for today."

"There is one last matter that needs our attention." He spoke to Jillian, taking her hand in his.

"What is that, Father?" she asked, wondering what they could have possibly forgotten.

"Under the circumstances, there was no time to get a gift for you." He paused smiling at both blushing faces. "I think I have the very thing you need."

Terrance withdrew a chain from his pocket. From it dangled a pendant, the same one that Jillian's mother had given to her so long ago—a Pegasus. "It has always been my thought that your mother and I would be the ones to wear these matching pendants, but it is not to be. I want you to have mine, Gavin," Terrance said, placing the chain over Gavin's head. "By taking my daughter as your wife, you have become lawfully, my son. I have always felt it, but now it is official."

Gavin was speechless, as was Jillian.

"It's time you got to it then," Terrance said, slapping Gavin on the back. "Being her husband I mean." He kissed Jillian lightly on the forehead.

"Good night, Father," Jillian said emotionally.

"Good night, Jillian."

Turning toward the helm, Terrance wiped a tear from his cheek, thinking of Sybil. He wondered if she would be happy about this union between their daughter and his son.

For Jillian and Gavin, the night was filled with love, laughter, tears and happiness. They made love playfully and then fiercely. Their passions ran high with the sensations of being together. They were secure, content and confident that these feelings would never diminish. The night was intense and tranquil at the same time, and between their love-making they stopped to rest and talk and laugh, and to tell each other everything that was important. It was close to dawn before the torrent of love-making calmed and they lay in each other's arms exhausted by the night's passion.

Guiltily, Jillian lay still contemplating whether to tell Gavin about the vision that she had. She had told him all else, but she held this back, feeling frightened of his reaction. The vision was so real, and perhaps evil. Meggie's face and words, vivid in her mind, made her body shudder suddenly.

Feeling her tremble, Gavin came over her. "What is it, my love? What frightens you so?"

"It's nothing," Jillian lied. How could she possibly tell him that she had somehow left this cabin and gone to the sick bed of a woman that she only saw once? How could she tell him that Meggie was somehow entwined in their life?

"Tell me what troubles you so. You look as though you have seen a ghost." His voice softened with concern. "Tell me Jillian, what causes you so much fear?"

"It's only that we are so happy. I suppose I just don't ever want this to end. I don't want to lose you Gavin."

"You will never lose me, Jillian. For our love is something that will last forever. I will be with you always. "This," he said, kissing the swell of her breast, "will never end."

Shivers of heat, radiated from the taut bud as Gavin suckled. Jillian soon forgot the vision and the fear that it brought her. Gavin was all she needed and her body responded to him with uninhibited desire. After a full night of such intense love-making, Jillian felt that it would be impossible to respond again to him so fully, but respond she did. Gavin moaned softly, lost in the feel of her gentle but urgent hands upon his length. The simplest touch from her sent his body spiraling to the brink of his control. With his own hands he bid her to join him, binding them into that same euphoria that enveloped them in a world of ecstasy. They were each lost in the embrace of the other and the love that they were now free to experience.

Unexpected Sight

The warship hung menacingly on the morning horizon, barely visible against the glare of the dawning sun. A feeling of dread filled the air as Terrance shaded his eyes against the brightness. This was not the first time Terrance had seen the ship and he knew it would not be the last. The warship had dogged the Pegasus since their last day in port when they came close to being captured by it. Since then, it was as if the ship knew their every move, and Terrance had caught glimpses of it on the horizon many times.

He gave orders to anyone in the crow's nest to report the sightings directly to him and not call them out to the crewmen. This kept Jillian and Gavin, who had not been taking up his post since the wedding, from knowing that the warship was close. This was easy to do, for they were so completely consumed by one another, that neither paid much attention to the happenings on the ship. Terrance smiled to himself, remembering what it was like to love someone that intensely. He remembered what it was like to be lost in a world of your own making, but he also remembered what it was like to be so caught up in that world that you were blind to anything beyond. It was very dangerous to take life and people for granted. You never knew when, because of your blindness, your life could be devastated. Terrance knew this first hand.

Being careful, with Jillian on board, Terrance had managed to keep the ship at bay by changing direction in the middle of the night.

The days passed smoothly without incident. Beyond the knowledge of the warship, Terrance felt as if life could be no better. Their hull was full from the few ships they had taken. Terrance thanked God during these raids that the supply ships had given up without a fight. For this, Terrance left them with some supplies; enough to make their voyage worthwhile and enough to make it worth the pirate's taking. Because there had been no more confrontations like the first one they'd had with Jillian on board, Terrance felt that she understood the workings of the Pegasus. They never sunk an adversary, never took any lives unless necessary, and never left a ship without cargo. It was a code that Terrance swore to uphold.

It was time that the Pegasus docked to offload their booty. Terrance was reluctant to do this with the warship so close. The men were uneasy knowing how heavy with goods the Pegasus was and that dependent families waited for them. Terrance had devised a plan with Cy and Micah, and tonight they would carry it out.

Gavin appeared on deck, his hair freshly combed, looking dapper, and beaming. Terrance shook his head as the happy young man approached. Happiness was contagious these days and Terrance held himself from laughing out loud at the joyful face of his son.

"So, I see that you were finally able to pull yourself away from that lovely young bride of yours."

Gavin cleared his throat and examined his boots while his face returned to its normal color.

"Is it that obvious, sir?"

"You could say that, Gavin. I have never seen you happier," Terrance said.

"I don't think I have ever been this happy. But there is just one thing, sir." Gavin's boyish face became serious.

"What would that be? I didn't think anything could spoil that smile of yours."

"When were you going to tell me about the warship?" Gavin asked.

Surprised and taken aback by Gavin's unexpected question, Terrance stared at him in silence. He should have known better than to think that Gavin would not notice the warship. He'd probably seen it on the horizon just as Terrance had. Shaking his head, Terrance grinned at his own ignorance.

"I should have known that you are not one to be so easily fooled, are you Gavin?" Terrance asked, feeling as if he had betrayed Gavin in the worst way.

"I know your reasons, Captain. And I appreciate you trying to protect Jillian and myself but I have the responsibility of making decisions about our future and would like the opportunity to do so."

Gavin hadn't wanted to sound quite so direct but it angered him that his old friend had kept something like this from him. The ship was in danger and it was Gavin's right to help with its defense.

Reading Gavin's expression, Terrance knew that it was a mistake to keep the plan from him. From the beginning, many years ago, the boy had been incredibly perceptive of things around him. He was not easily fooled. Terrance remembered Sue Ki trying to dose him with some sort of potion for Gavin's ills by putting the liquid into sweet tasting drinks, but always, Gavin knew Ki's intentions and would not take it until forced.

"I suppose I should tell you of our plan." He hesitated. "Does Jillian know?" Terrance asked.

"No, I don't think she does. Although she's seen a ship on the horizon, I don't think she knows it's the same one each time."

"I'm relieved; I don't want her worrying. I have a plan as to how to get our supplies to the people without docking in port. I thought to use Micah and Cy, but would be pleased if you would consider the task."

Gavin felt reassured that Terrance hadn't lost confidence in him. He may be a married man but he still knew his duty to the Pegasus and her crew. After the warship had appeared several times Gavin waited for Terrance to come to him and consult with him on a plan but Terrance hadn't and Gavin started to think that maybe he no longer wanted him to participate in the adventure of protecting the Pegasus.

"I would be honored. It has been much too long since I had a quest."

"Aye, I would say, maybe, since last night?" Terrance laughed, slapping Gavin on the back lovingly.

"Every night is an adventure with Jillian by your side."

Both men laughed as they walked across the deck to Micah and Cy who stood, anxiously, waiting for Terrance to finalize their plan. In her cabin, Jillian remained lazily in the comfort of the huge feather bed that she had recently became very fond of. She thought about the long hours spent here in Gavin's arms and hugged his pillow tightly to her breast inhaling his scent that lingered upon it.

"Will I ever get enough?" she asked herself. Life with Gavin was adventurous, alluring, and enthralling. It held Jillian, enslaving her mind and body with the fascination of him and their hours together. He was everything to her.

When she thought about her life before that fateful day on the beach, she realized that much of it seemed a mystery to her. The more she tried to recall her childhood, the more she realized that she could not remember a great part of it. She felt that it was better that these lost memories were left tucked away, for deep inside, Jillian knew that they would only bring heartache if she were to remember.

When searching for answers from her childhood, one person did come to her mind—Sophie. Jillian recalled visions of Sophie, the light of a fire, or maybe candles nearby, reflecting off her kind face as she stroked Jillian's forehead, soothing her fears. Jillian looked into Sophie's eyes and saw things, but was not able to remember what. She only knew that Sophie was the key to the memories locked within her, and when times were at their worst, Jillian would think of Sophie and life would be better for her.

So much time had passed since she last thought of Sophie. Now, her life with Gavin and her father made her feel safe and secure. She didn't want to look back and try to unlock something that was better left forgotten. Jillian wanted nothing more than to forget her past and concentrate only on her future.

That evening Gavin strolled on the deck with Jillian. The sun sank, dipping below the blue ocean's horizon. To Jillian, its color tonight seemed to be cold and forbidding. The Pegasus sailed close to the coastline, and Jillian considered this odd; never before had they come so close to shore without actually docking at some small village port.

"I have something to tell you, my love," Gavin said, facing Jillian.

"There is something wrong Gavin, isn't there?" she asked, looking toward the now darkening water.

"Not wrong, in truth," he paused, letting her prepare for his words. "It's that I must leave you for a few days to go ashore and arrange for the disposition of our supplies. Families are depending on us. They need us."

"And I need you. Can't anyone else go? Does it have to be you, Gavin?" she pleaded with him.

He couldn't lie to her. "It doesn't have to be me, Jillian. It must be me. I cannot sit idle and let others take on what I used to do for the Captain."

"I'll go to my father and ask him to send someone else," she said, her tone threatening. "He won't refuse me."

"No, your father would not refuse you." He hesitated. "But, I do this for both of us Jillian. We can survive a few days apart and be better for it. You are strong and independent. I know that when we are together again," he added, "our love will be stronger because of it."

"Oh, Gavin," Jillian said in resignation. "Come back to me safely."

"My love, I will come back and I will spend the next days in bed making it up to you."

His lips lowered to hers. "Before I go, I will fill you with so much of me that you will want for not until then," he assured her, grinning.

"Promise?" she sighed.

"I promise," Gavin said, picking her up and carrying her in his arms toward the stairwell.

Later that night, the Pegasus slipped silently near the shore. Shrouded by a fog bank, two men slipped off the side of the ship and swam unnoticed to the beach. The ship didn't stop, but slowed to a pace that made it possible for them to go, then just as silently as it came, the Pegasus sailed for the open sea once more.

Jillian stood at the railing searching for sight of Gavin in the shadowed water below, the memory of Gavin dipping beneath the fog etched in her mind. Her heart raced, pounding within the tight confines of her chest, with his leaving. Closing her eyes, she concentrated all her strength upon Gavin's plight, willing him to reach the shore safely. She envisioned the water parting with each stroke of his strong arms. She heard the surf pounding against the shore not too far ahead of him. He looked to his side to make certain Cy was near and saw the waves in the water caused by his swift strokes. Feeling reassured, Gavin pressed on, coming into the roaring surf off shore. Once in the shallower waters, Gavin and Cy were both able to get their feet beneath them and walk up the sandy shore. Gavin turned suddenly, finding Jillian's eyes, a smile coming to his face. Startled by the feeling of being on the shore with Gavin, Jillian's eyes flew open and she gulped for air.

"Jillian. Are you ill?" Terrance's voice broke the stillness.

Catching her breath, Jillian reassured him that she was fine. "I was just holding my breath until Gavin was safely ashore."

Terrance eyed her warily. "I'm sure he has made it by now, my sweet," he said, taking her hand in his.

"Yes, he reached the shore," Jillian reiterated. "I'm certain of it."

The next day and evening went achingly slow. Jillian found herself wandering aimlessly around the Pegasus. The crew and Terrance left her to her thoughts most of the time, knowing that she pined for Gavin, and not knowing what they could say to reassure her. At dinner, she had no appetite and refused to eat most of the meal that Sue Ki had prepared for her.

Ki eyed her curiously, knowing that she had the power to bring herself out of this stupor. He contemplated talking to her about what had happened that morning in her cabin, but reconsidered. Power could be frightening to someone who didn't understand it. Sue Ki was not certain that Jillian was even aware of what had happened that day, let alone had the knowledge to control her power.

"You must not die when Gavin is gone, little flower," he said in earnest.

His words struck her as odd. She looked at him as if seeing someone she didn't know anymore.

"Why do you say that, Sue Ki?" Her angry voice gave him a start.

"Ah, so you do have fight left, missy. I thought you were nothing without Gavison. Now I see that you are." His face brightened with her sudden fury.

"It's just that I don't know who I am, or how I would live without Gavin."

"I see. You feel you have no identity of your own, perhaps?"

"I never have."

"Only you know the reason," he said, smiling. "One has to decide for themselves who they are. It not depend on others."

"Mayhap it's time to discover who I am. Thank you, Sue Ki," she said, placing a soft kiss on his forehead, then leaving him to go to her cabin.

Sue Ki stood, watching Jillian until she entered the stairwell. He had a plan, a plan that would give Jillian the opportunity to test herself against all odds, a chance to let her see the strength that he saw within her. It would take some doing, but Sue Ki was on a determined path.

The next morning everything went according to Ki's plan. Even though Terrance had predicted an incoming storm, he played along with Ki's scheme. Terrance would do anything to bring back the radiance to Jillian's face. He stayed in his hammock, complaining of the rot, and warding off his crew. Soon, Jillian came to his sick bed. She felt his head for signs of fever and found him warmer to the touch than he should be. She insisted on staying with Terrance in case he needed anything, and until he felt better. But Terrance would have none of it, asking Jillian instead to help with the running of the ship in the absence of Gavin and Cy.

"There is only Micah and he has never been on his own. He'll need your help. You can come below and inform me of any problems that may arise."

Sweat beaded around his lips and Terrance without doubt felt that he might heave at any moment. When Jillian consented to be his eyes and ears for the day, Terrance breathed a sigh of relief. Once she left his side, he immediately ripped the covers back, flinging the bed warmer across the cabin. The trick Sue Ki came up with had worked, and Terrance actually felt as if he were going to be sick. He was glad to be rid of the extra heat that had been hidden from Jillian.

Above, Jillian informed Micah of Terrance's condition, advising him that he would not be able to come on deck at least for a while. Seeing his stricken face, Jillian promised to help Micah if he needed her.

Nimbly, Jillian climbed the rigging to the crow's nest. She relieved Corky, one of the crewmen, of his duty so that he could go below to breakfast. Corky got his name because when he was in water, be it lake, ocean, or bath, he bobbed like a cork. Gavin told her many stories of him falling over board, only to bob to the surface and wait for the ship to turn. Jillian watched Corky descend the rigging, and then put the glass to her eye, searching the ocean's surface.

It was a rather gray, overcast day. Off in the distance Jillian could see tiny flashes of lightening beneath blackened clouds. She checked the ship's course, deciding that they were not heading into danger, for the storm seemed to be moving in the opposite direction of the Pegasus. Settling back against the mast, Jillian let the breeze free her hair, feeling the coolness against her face. It was refreshing, alive, and brought with its crispness the smell of air renewed by the washing of the storm in the distance.

After an hour's time, Jillian felt a shift in the Pegasus, as if Micah had changed the ship's course. Fearfully, she scanned the ocean. The storm circled near them, the sea grew silent, and the pounding of her heart was the only sound that she could hear. The wind left her sails and the Pegasus came to a standstill, directly in line with the approaching storm.

The Pegasus seemed to be moving slowly toward the storm, as if it were sucking them into the very core of its darkness. Pulling the ropes with all their strength, the men frantic to lower the sails, climbed the rigging to set them free. From where she was, Jillian helped the men and once the sails were below her, she fearfully climbed down the rigging.

"Micah, what is it?" she asked, clutching his sleeve in the darkened silence.

"Nothing good," Micah answered, bracing himself against the wheel.

No sooner had his words been spoken than the first torrent from the storm came in the form of blackening rain. Before Jillian could seek cover for herself, she was soaked by the downpour. When Micah ordered her to go below Jillian remained on deck, helping the crew secure the casks and boxes of supplies upon it, giving no thought to her state.

Within minutes, the sky darkened even more. Bursts of lightening flashed and thundered at the same time, vibrating the ship. Then, without warning, the ocean rose mightily beneath the Pegasus pitching it into the air, then catching it upon the next rolling wave.

Below, Terrance was awakened from his slumber to be pitched out of his hammock and onto the floor. Terror shot through him, knowing a white squall when he felt it. Barefoot, Terrance headed to the upper deck to guide the ship through the violent storm. It was all he could do to stay on his feet. Terrance made his way through the blinding rain, by feel, finding Micah and Jillian at the helm, clinging to the wheel.

"Why wasn't I called?" he shouted angrily to Micah.

"It hit so suddenly, Captain," Micah yelled above the roar of the storm. "I thought we were skirting her when, without warning, we were right in the middle of it."

A wave washed over them, knocking Jillian to her knees. Terrance helped her up, holding her tightly to his side. He wanted to send her below to safety, but the rain and wind were almost too much for even him to fight. He knew that Jillian couldn't make it below without help and he couldn't spare a man to assist her. The three clung to the wheel and each other, riding out the storm together.

A deafening roar washed over them as they steered the Pegasus head-long into the waves, trying to keep from being capsized. In terror, Jillian watched as the ocean lifted before them, as if to swallow their miniature vessel. The waves, thirty to forty feet high, loomed above them, and then plummeted to the deck, sweeping its length. The men tied themselves to the mast and anything else they felt was secure enough to hold them. With each lightening flash Jillian could see their drenched forms, as each wave washed away from them. The men showed little sign of life and Jillian feared that they'd drowned in the constant dousing from the ocean. She tried not to think, only clung tightly to her father's waist, wrapping her arms through his corded belt.

A clap of thunder exploded above them, striking the crow's nest. Jillian watched the crow's nest fall heavily to the side of the deck, knocking loose supplies secured there. A scream ripped from her, seeing two of the crewmen knocked from the deck into the churning water. A third, Corky, clung to the remnants of the railing that flapped against the ship's side.

Micah charged to his aid through the crashing waves. Jillian blinked in disbelief as Micah hung over the side, trying to reach Corky. Another wave washed over them. When the water cleared, Jillian was grateful to see them again, but still, their plight was treacherous.

Jillian loosened her hold on her father. "No!" His command was apparent, but Jillian felt strong against the storm's power and knew that she needed to help Micah save Corky. Terrance was not able to stop her, for fear of losing all if he let go of the wheel. Clinging to whatever she could, Jillian made her way to Micah. He hung from the ship; a rope secured to the mast tied around his wrist. His other hand held on tightly to Corky, who dangled above the ocean like a limp doll suspended on a string. Corky was unconscious and no help to Micah with his rescue.

"The rope! Jillian!" Micah shouted above the ocean's roar.

Jillian saw a rope tied to the mast and knew what she must do. Turning toward the mast, Jillian grasped the rope just as a wash of water enveloped her. She held her breath for what seemed like an eternity before the water subsided, then fastened the free end of the rope around her waist and pulled on it to make sure that it was secured to the mast. With the next wave, Jillian allowed herself to be swept over the side. She heard both Terrance and Micah yell for her as the ocean surged up to greet her.

The Pegasus plunged into the water, taking Jillian beneath it, and then lifted her from its depths as the ship's hull rose. Once she surfaced, Jillian could see Corky's feet dangling not far above her. Just above Corky, Micah gasped in pain from the death grip with which he held the motionless man. Pulling herself up the rope tied around her waist, Jillian came alongside Corky and wrapped her legs around him. She then brought the length of rope around him, using a slip knot she'd learned from Gavin. Not having any way to bring it over his head, Jillian doubled the knot, slipping her arm through its end to secure it. Reaching up to Micah's hand, Jillian bid him to let go of Corky. "Pull us up," she beckoned. But Micah could not bring himself to release the pair, for surely they would plunge into the ocean and be lost forever. Jillian concentrated all her strength on holding Corky, then jerked Corky's arm, freeing Micah's hold.

Jillian screamed, as the weight of Corky and herself upon the rope, snapped the bones of her arm, the sound thundering in her ears. As she and her burden swung above the water, the rope dug deeply into the flesh between the severed bones. White hot pain shot through her with every movement, rendering her helpless to it.

Micah sprang into action, pulling the rope with all his strength, bringing Jillian and Corky up to deck level. Jillian was barely able to hold the railing with her free arm while Micah lifted Corky onto the deck. The rope had strangled Jillian's arm in a death hold of its own, cutting deeply into her delicate flesh. It was all she could do to pull herself over the railing and land unconscious upon the deck.

The next thing Jillian remembered was being placed upon her bed in the cabin, the ship still pitching with the fierceness of the storm. Sue Ki was at her side, giving her something to drink, something so nauseatingly sweet that her stomach lurched as the liquid reached it. She remembered this sweet concoction, but not quite this strong, from a time before and smiled to herself, knowing that the pain would soon be gone. Indeed within minutes, it disappeared and she allowed the darkness from the drug to overtake her senses, bringing her painless sleep.

The hurricane had taken its toll on the warship. Surveying the damage being repaired by his crew, William could only hope that the Pegasus was likewise delayed. The warship had given up five men to the storm along with many supplies that they could not afford to lose. The most devastating damage was to the ship's rudder, it having been partially severed by the force of the waves. This meant going in to the nearest dock for lengthy repairs.

William was furious. They had been so close to catching the Pegasus just a few days ago and now to have the storm spoil his pursuit was more than he could take. With mounting tension caused by their prisoner in the hold, the warship's crew was constantly at odds with each other.

The slow voyage into port would give the men time to calm before satisfying their needs with the locals. They deserved that much for having to deal with Jason. The man put fear into even the saltiest sailor on the warship and keeping him immobilized with chains had not calmed their fears. William couldn't blame the men, for he felt a quake of dread rush through him every time he had to speak to Jason about the Pegasus. Surprisingly enough, Jason was very cooperative in tracking the ship; it was as if he wanted to find her even more than William. He knew the Captain's habits and destinations, and even though the Pegasus changed course sporadically, Jason could always tell within hours where the ship was headed. William wished that he was not encumbered with the lumbering warship; if he had a sleeker vessel he would have been able to overtake the Pegasus by now. With this new delay, William knew that he would not be catching up with the pirates anytime soon. Patience, he told himself, my triumph will come.

He made his way to the hold below to advise Jason of their predicament and to see if he had any views on where the Pegasus might be headed next. As he slipped into the corridor that led to the prisoner's cell, William could hear the sound of pummeling flesh. He quickly rushed the last steps toward the door.

"You bastard! I'll teach you a lesson!" Johansson, the old cook, shouted, giving Jason a swift kick to his ribs, air hissing from between his clenched teeth.

Jason lay on the floor, curled into a protective ball, his lips bloodied and one eye swollen. This wasn't anything that William hadn't seen before, and he made no move to stop the man from registering several more blows to Jason's body. It had become commonplace; Jason would provoke the men purposely, and in return they beat him. The man seemed to thrive on pain, not only the pain of others, but also his own. The old cook spat on Jason then turned to leave coming up short when seeing William standing at the door.

"What was it this time, Johansson?" William asked dryly.

"The fiend bit my ankle, sir. Clean through my boot, drawing blood," he explained, pointing to his boot. "I thought he was asleep. Got too close I suppose."

"Aye, I suppose that next time you'll be a little more careful," William said, grinning at the old man.

"Next time, I'll bring him nothing but a bone boiled clean from the stew. He can chew on that," he said, drawing himself up to salute William, then leaving the cell.

"There won't be a next time," Jason said, a wicked smile darkening his face.

Ignoring the remark, William sat on a stool near the doorway, it being placed a safe distance from the prisoner and with easy access to escape. William felt more comfortable knowing that the door was nearer to him than was the prisoner.

"As you might have presumed, the storm got the best of our ship. We must put in for repairs." Feeling a little more confident, he went on, "Do you have any idea where the Pegasus might be headed?"

Jason knew of many places that the ship could secret for repairs, but licking the blood from his lips, he suddenly felt no need to tell William anything. It was obvious to Jason that there was nothing in this for him. No deals were made, no promises of release. At this time, Jason knew he had the upper hand and was going to press the point until William relented and granted him freedom.

"Perhaps we should talk of other things such as," he paused, seeing the furry in William's eyes, "such as, my reward for helping you capture this notorious pirate Captain."

"And what do you want, Jason?" William asked, feeling sweat bead on his upper lip.

"I haven't told you much about the Pegasus or her crew," he paused, watching William's interest suddenly pique. "There is a man, the first mate; I want the sole pleasure of taking his life."

Loathing of the first mate was apparent, but for now he would keep Jason pacified thinking that his request would be granted when the time came.

"I'm sure that can be arranged."

"One other thing," Jason added.

"And what would it be this time?" William asked, letting his anger show.

"There is a girl, Jillian." William shot Jason a wary look as he continued. "The Captain's woman. She was mine. He took her from me. I want her as part of my spoils from the ship. For this, I will make the pickings easy."

"Are you saying that you know where the ship is headed?" William anxiously waited for Jason's answer.

"The Pegasus has taken three ships since last in port. She is loaded and sitting low in the water, slowing her. This is the only reason we were able to come as close as we did to her. But, she must put in and relieve herself of some of the supplies. I know which port." Jason grinned in triumph, for William became visibly excited by his words.

"Which one? Tell me! Which one?" William insisted.

"Not so fast. First, release my bonds!" He demanded.

"No, I," William hesitated, "I will not allow you to run about the ship. You are a danger to my men. I will, however, relent to a stout chain at your ankle, if no more instances such as today's occur."

Jason gave it a moment of thought. "It's agreed."

"Very well. I will have my men come and release the bulk of your bindings. We'll talk later of our destination," he said, turning toward the door. "One other thing . . . what is the pirate Captain's name?"

Jason smiled, "All in good time."

Wincing with pain, Jillian swore as she tried to dress herself. Getting her pants up was nearly more than she could manage with the awkward splint on her arm, but eventually she succeeded. Beads of sweat appeared on her forehead and upper lip with the effort of putting her blouse over the bulky bandage, but Jillian was more determined than ever to be out of the cabin today. She closed her eyes, ignoring the throbbing of her arm, and pulled the blouse into position, sucking in her breath with the pain of her actions.

Stopping for a moment, Jillian took deep, even breaths willing the pain to be gone and after a moment it seemed to be slightly better. Struggling with the opposite sleeve, Jillian put her uninjured arm through it and pulled the blouse on completely. Just then, there was a knock at the door. Jillian hurriedly tried to fasten the buttons before Sue Ki or her father came in and forced her back into bed.

The door creaked open and Micah peeked around it, looking at the bed. When he didn't see her there, he searched the room for Jillian, timidly calling out to her. He spied Jillian's movements behind the dressing partition, and put down the tray he carried on the dressing table near the bed.

"Can I be of help, Jillian?" he asked, not looking toward the partition for fear of finding her in an awkward position.

"Yes, Micah. You can," she said, coming out from behind the screen. "I can't seem to manage all these buttons."

"Jillian!" Micah shouted, rushing to her. "You shouldn't be out of bed or attempting to get dressed!"

"Yes, I know. Sue Ki has beaten that into my head for three days now," she said with much determination. "But we meet with Gavin and the villagers tonight and I won't do that lying flat."

Her face was pallid, lacking any of the natural glow that she once had; her hair was a mass of tangles that looked as though it would take hours of combing to straighten out. But to Micah, no matter what her condition, she was the most beautiful woman he had ever seen. Her heroics saved not only Corky's life, but his also. They all respected this little bundle of chaos. She was a marvel to them. Each man had his own version of how she saved lives without regard for her own. Now here she stood, with her pain evident, and still she would not be perceived as being weakened by it.

"The buttons, Micah. Will you help me or not?" she insisted.

"You ask much, little sister," he said, taking the top button in his shaking grasp. "But the risk of punishment from the Captain is worth the price to make you happy."

"Oh, Micah. I'm sorry," she said, placing her hand on his, stopping him. "I never considered my father's wrath coming down on you. This would make you my accomplice."

"Indeed, but never you mind. It will be my pleasure." Micah fastened each button with care, as not to touch anything but the material of her blouse. Jillian stood as still as a statue, knowing the difficult position that she had put him in. Although they had come to an understanding about their relationship, Jillian also knew the desires of men and was careful with all the crew, so as not to put them in awkward circumstances. This one however, could not be avoided, for she knew that Sue Ki and Terrance would never have helped her dress.

"There, all finished." Micah stepped back from Jillian, letting out his breath. "Don't even consider asking me to tuck it in for you," he warned, smiling sheepishly.

"This will be fine. Now, if you will just tie this sling at the back of my neck, I shall be ready." She handed the ends of it to him and then helped him move her hair to the side so he could tie them together.

"I hope to show my father that I am healed enough to join the celebration tonight. I don't want Gavin to panic when he sees that I have had an accident."

"Accident! You can't be serious, Jillian," Micah said, struggling with the knot. "What you did was no accident."

"Maybe you're right, Micah, but somehow I don't think Gavin will be happy about it; no matter how I explain it to him."

"I know your meaning. I wasn't too pleased at the time, myself." Micah finished the knot, then gave her shoulders a squeeze.

"Now don't get all sentimental on me, Micah," she warned. "I'll need you to be my right arm today." She laughed, holding up her injured arm. "I sincerely mean it."

"Dear Lord, but you are a precocious minx."

"And what would you do without me?"

"I'd be dead," he stated honestly. His words hit Jillian hard, making her think about the life she had taken in defense of him.

"But you are not dead and I am glad of that." She smiled. "Who else would help me with my buttons?"

"Aye, I'm sure someone would volunteer to aid you," he laughed.

When they emerged on deck, the crew gave nods of admiration and welcome. Terrance was not as welcoming. As they approached him, he shot daggers at Micah, who cringed with every step, bracing himself for the brunt of Terrance's wrath. Seeing her father's furry, Jillian quickly came to Micah's defense.

"I'm feeling much better, Father. Micah was kind enough to help me."

"I suppose anything I would have to say regarding this wouldn't make any difference to you?"

"Certainly, Father. Everything you have to say makes a difference to me," she answered, her voice having a lilt of sweetness to it.

"Don't use those feminine traits of yours." He looked sharply at Micah who shrunk under his gaze. "It won't work on me."

"Oh, I wouldn't dare try and sway your judgment, Father," she said, now batting her eyes at him shamelessly.

Terrance and Jillian both laughed heartily while Micah broke out in sweaty relief from the stress of being Terrance's target.

"Now, suppose you take me for a short walk in the sun. I've withered away from the lack of it."

"It would be my pleasure," Terrance said, relinquishing the helm to Micah, who was relieved to have them stroll away.

Jillian spent a short time on deck, wanting to save most of her energy for later. After a time, Terrance escorted Jillian to her cabin, summoning Sue Ki to help her bathe and prepare for the trip to shore later that night.

Jillian slept for a few hours after her bath, then began the painful chore of dressing for the night's festivities. The crew prepared the ship and themselves for the midnight rendezvous with their friends and families.

They readied the supplies so as to get them unloaded quickly, freeing them to join in the feast and celebration. Spirits were high with the expectation of the long awaited activities. Terrance had been glad his plan was a success. The crew needed to see their families, something that was sure to lift their spirits.

On shore the villagers, mostly woman and children, gathered, bringing food to cook for their men from the Pegasus. Gavin helped the women carry their supplies to the beach, making many trips to the wagons that waited at the top of the ridge above the beach. They chatted gaily as they laid quilts over the sand and spread the feast upon them. Some of the women erected makeshift shelters, intending to have some privacy while spending the night with their loved ones.

Merrily, Cy helped a young maiden place her wares near a pit where an ox carcass roasted over an open fire. The fragrance of the meat made Gavin's mouth water but the thought of having Jillian back in his arms made him crave more than just a hearty meal.

Thoughts of her never left his mind during the time that he was ashore. Every minute of the day since swimming to shore was spent in contemplation of this night. Gavin had made arrangements with the villagers to meet the Pegasus far up the coast on a deserted beach. The townsfolk had housed him and Cy these past five days, being careful not to let word leak about their whereabouts. For this, Gavin was grateful. It was here that they had waited out the storm that raged a few nights ago.

The last two nights were spent with the family of Corky Ruggles, a man who was notorious for his clumsiness. Gavin remembered Jillian's laughter when he told her how Corky would bob to the surface and just float there, waiting for his rescue. His wife was a short, plump little woman who controlled their children with a wooden spoon. Now older, the two boys took her ribbing with laughter, giving her a swirl and a tight hug, stopping her paddling. She wore a white cap on her head, but a few black strands escaped its confines around her face. The boys' hair was the color of their mother's while Corky's was blonde with a touch of gray in the mix.

Hearing gay laughter, Gavin watched as Cy chased the flirting girl past him almost knocking the parcels that he carried from his hands. It was good to see his old friend acting lighthearted, for Cy deserved to have a love of his own. At this moment, Gavin felt envious of his friend. Lord how he ached for Jillian's company. Tonight could not come soon enough for him.

Finally, the hour was at hand and the signal had been given. The long boat rowed slowly toward shore, lurching forward in the waves. Jillian's heart raced with the anticipation of seeing Gavin again. Her broken arm throbbed with every beat, but Jillian blocked the pain from her mind. She concentrated on one thing—having Gavin's arms around her.

The shore was dotted with flickers of torchlight being carried by anxious loved ones. As they came closer, Jillian searched beneath the lights for a glimpse of Gavin. The boat hull struck the sand, propelling her forward, and then several men pulled it farther onto the beach. Jillian was lifted from the boat by a crewman and placed on the dry sand. She thanked him, smoothing her skirt around her legs.

A feeling came over her as she stood in the darkness. Jillian knew Gavin was there even before she raised her eyes to meet his. They stood facing each other, cast in a lover's spell, feeling the presence of the other completing their world.

Gavin approached slowly, watching her, enjoying his last moments of anticipation. Biting her lower lip, Jillian raised her hand to cup his cheek. He leaned his face into her hand, closing his eyes to her touch. To have her touching him again was almost too much to bear. Gavin raised her into his arms, cradling her against his broad chest. His mouth came down hungrily on hers and Jillian met his famished lips with her own. They devoured each other's mouths, claiming one another, seeking and finding fulfillment. Forgetting about her injured arm and the splint, Jillian's arms went around Gavin's neck, pulling him even closer.

Startled by the feel of the splint against his shoulder, Gavin held Jillian away from him. He slowly lowered her to the sand, a questioning look in his eyes. Jillian covered his lips with her trembling fingers, waylaying his questions. All through the day she had rehearsed her speech explaining the cause of her injury, but no matter how hard she tried, Jillian could not come up with an explanation that would convince Gavin that she had not put her life in danger.

Not taking his eyes from hers, Gavin caught her hand in his and brought it away from his lips, placing it over his heart. He could tell by the frightened look in her eyes that she had been through a terrible ordeal. Then he remembered the hurricane of only a few days ago and his heart leapt in his breast. He suddenly realized that she must have been injured during the storm and he was not there to protect her. Many emotions raged through Gavin, and his face reflected them. Where were the men who would die to protect her? Where were they when she had needed them the most? His eyes teared with the thought of losing her.

Jillian watched his face change from fear to anger and back again. She felt his heart race under her palm and knew that his thoughts were in turmoil. She lifted her fingertips to his temple, knowing that his pain and anger were caused by her. If only she could ease him; if only she could say something that would take this pain from him, something that wouldn't make him angry with her. She found no words.

"My pain is my own, sweet Jillian. The pain of loving you, the pain of losing you is mine alone. I am not angry with you, Jillian."

Gavin's words startled her. She eyed him. How did he know her thoughts?

Before Jillian had a chance to speak, they were whisked away by several of the crewmen and townsfolk heading toward the camp. Gavin held Jillian to him, supporting her as if she were a fragile bird with a broken wing. The sensations of having him protect and care for her took over her thoughts. The question of how he had known what she was thinking was lost in the joy and revelry of the celebration.

The night was filled with magic and surprise. Each crewman brought his family over to meet Jillian. She shook the hands of each spouse, lavishing compliments upon them for the strength of their men. The children curtsied and bowed before her as if they were street urchins at a lady's feet, wanting nothing more than to just be near her. Jillian took great pleasure in the children, bending down to be at eye level with them, whispering secrets into their ears that made them giggle and blush.

Corky took great pride in introducing Jillian to his wife, Corrine, and two black-haired boys, Ned and Randy. She gave Corky a wary look as he told his wife that he owed his life to this slip of a girl. Corky caught her look and closed his mouth, hurrying the family on their way.

"What was all that about?" Gavin asked.

"I'll explain later." Her expression told him that he wouldn't be happy.

"Later, then. But that is not the only thing that you will do later."

"Why Gavin, you are a fiend," Jillian laughed, pushing him playfully.

The night went on and on. Jillian could not remember ever having so much fun. They danced, they sang, the men shared tales of life at sea, and the women of life waiting for their loved one's return. They sat before the campfire, faces glowing, illuminated by the flames that danced low in the fire pit. Gavin sat behind Jillian, his legs enveloping her protectively, his arms wrapped around her. She leaned against his hard chest, the feel of him giving support to her tiring body. Her fingers traced patterns over his hand and up the length of his muscular arm. His skin under her fingertips felt wonderful. It was in this envelope of strength that Jillian wanted to stay for the rest of her life.

Soon Corky stood before the fire, begging the attention of all. Standing in the firelight, his stature was exaggerated because he was holding himself up so proudly before the crowd, as if what he had to say was of utmost importance. The audience grew quiet and Corky began to speak.

"I have a tale to tell, a tale of a beautiful pirate whose strengths outmatched even her beauty, a tale of a princess, surrounded by rotting pirates who were shaken to the core by her presence."

Jillian felt Gavin tense behind her. She grasped his hand in hers and squeezed it. He squeezed hers back and pulled her even closer to him, showing all present his possession of her.

Corky continued looking directly at Jillian. "A tale of the bravest lass a man could ever come to know." Her look pleaded with him to stop but he ignored her. "It was a dark, stormy day. The princess was in her perch, high above the deck of her ship. The mighty ocean gave a sudden shift and the princess, in all her wisdom, knew that the ship was in peril. The men climbed the rigging, releasing the sails, so as not to have the ship blown into oblivion. She helped them and only when she knew that they needed her no more did she climb down to safety herself. A young, healthy lad was at the helm, being the Captain had been indisposed that day with the rot." The audience laughed and then Corky continued, "The princess went to the lad as dark descended upon the ship. The ocean grew still. It struck fear into the hearts of even the most salted sailors, for they knew only too well the calm before the storm."

Gavin shifted uneasily behind Jillian. The scene that came to mind curdled his stomach, bringing the rancid taste of bile to his throat. He'd imagined that Jillian had injured her arm being tossed about in her cabin. Never had he thought that there was even the slightest chance that she would have been on deck when the hurricane struck. Anger raised its ugly head within him. Jillian sensed his reaction and held him firmly, digging her nails into his hand while Corky continued.

"Without warning, before the lad could get the princess below to safety," he added, looking directly at Gavin, "the storm rose up before the ship and plunged its wrath upon her. The mighty Captain came from below, making his way through the dark of the storm. Once at the helm, alongside the princess and the lad, the Captain took control of the helm and all three, wrapped together, clung to the wheel, guiding the ship into the massive waves."

Corky took a drink of ale, letting it settle in his stomach before he continued. The audience was silent. Only their expressions, at full attention, bid him to continue.

"The storm was fierce. It was as if the devil's fury had been unleashed upon the ship. Lightening thundered even before the flashes were seen, vibrating the oceans swirling water. The men strapped themselves down to anything they could find, hoping to make it through the storm without being washed over the side. Then, all at once, a powerful blast ripped the crow's nest from the mast, sending it plunging to the deck. It crashed downward, taking part of the rigging with it, and would not be swayed to miss a stack of supplies bound for the crew's loved ones." Corky looked around at the mesmerized faces, smiling. "The nest exploded into the supplies, sending them over the side. Three men, who were strapped to the kegs went over the side with them. The only survivor stands before you." Corrine gasped, holding her hand to her breast. The crowd shifted in their seats, uncomfortably murmuring to each other.

Gavin understood at last the reason for this grand play; Corky was telling Jillian's story. He was telling Gavin what she, herself, was afraid to say. Gavin knew that this tale explained why Jillian had her arm in a sling and he wasn't certain that he wanted to hear the rest. Gavin looked more closely at Corky, who stood facing him, tears welling in the old man's eyes.

Though his throat was constricted, Corky fought to gain control and continue. "By some miracle, I managed to catch what was left of the ship's rail before I was lost. Within moments, the lad was at the side bidding me to take his hand, but the waves washed over us time after time, blasting me against the stern. The lad grasped my hand just before the surging of the ship ripped the railing from it. I banged hard against the ship and was knocked unconscious." Corky stopped talking. His part of the story had ended, for he knew only from being told by the other crewmen what had happened next.

Corrine flew to Corky's side, hugging him to her. All the women held their men even tighter to them; the children's eyes were wide and frightened. Jillian suddenly felt the need to end this. She rose from Gavin's arms before he could stop her.

"That was a good story indeed, Corky. We are all so glad that you were saved." She turned to Gavin. "Now I think it is time that we all rest, for dawn will be here soon enough and we must return to the Pegasus." She held out her hand to Gavin, but he didn't take it. He wanted to hear the rest of the tale and so did everyone else. The villagers bid Corky to continue.

"Aye, but I cannot complete the tale for I was not there to see it, only to hear about it later. Alas, I was unconscious."

"Then someone must tell us. Finish the tale, what of the princess?" the people begged.

It was Micah who rose from the sand. It was Micah who came to stand in front of Jillian. "No Micah, you saved him. That is all they need to know." Jillian's voice was soft, only a whisper just for him.

"There is someone else who needs to know the truth. Go to him now and he will understand." Micah pressed her to sit once more and Gavin held his hand out, drawing her down into his protection.

"I will understand," Gavin whispered into her ear as Micah continued.

"I left the Captain and the princess to help Corky, catching him just as he was knocked unconscious. Although, now that I reflect upon it, I should have let him go, for we all know how well he bobs." Laughter erupted once more. "But as fate would have it, I could not let him go. The storm thundered on and soon my hold on Corky began to pain me. After all, he is no small boy, and being unconscious, he was no help to me whatsoever." Jeers and laughter again lightened the tale. "Through the drenching rain she appeared. At first I thought that she was an illusion, a ghost, an angel," his voice softened. "But it was her, the princess. There was a glow about her, some kind of inner strength, its light bringing sight to the darkness. She was at my side, giving me strength in my task. I bid her to hold onto a rope that was tied to the mast, for I didn't want to have her washed over the side with the others. She grasped the rope just in time, for a mountain of water washed over us. I thought we were lost. It seemed like an eternity before the water receded, but when it did, she was there, tying the length of rope around her small waist."

Micah turned to Jillian and Gavin, looking steadily at Gavin. His voice was strong with the conviction that Gavin must understand that Jillian did what she had to do to save all of their lives. Jillian's head dropped to her hands as Micah continued and Gavin tensed behind her.

"With the next wave, the princess threw herself over the side." The sound of indrawn breath echoed through the villagers. "The length of rope held the princess suspended just under Corky's feet. She gathered her strength and climbed the rope until she was even with him. I watched as the princess wrapped her long legs around Corky's rotund body. But that is not the last. Jil—I mean the princess, wrapped the rope around Corky bringing the loop around to double before her. With nothing else to secure the loop, the princess put her arm through it. She bid me to let go of Corky, but I couldn't bring myself to do it. I didn't trust in her plan, and for that I am sorry. It was because of my lack of trust that she made the decision to jerk Corky's hand free from my grasp."

Jillian's body shuddered at the memory of her arm breaking. She remembered thinking at the time that the sound was thunder, and not until the pain settled in did she realize that it was her arm snapping that made the explosion in her ears. Most of the story Jillian remembered but from here things were a blur. She didn't look up when Micah continued.

"It took a moment, for I was in shock at the actions of the princess, but once my hand was free, I realized that I had both strong arms to pull the two up to the deck. She clung fiercely to Corky. The storm blew them to and fro but soon I had them up. The princess made me bring Corky over the edge first. I could see that she was in pain, but never had I seen a woman so strong, so brave. She pulled herself over onto the deck and collapsed upon it. It was only then that I saw what my deed had cost her. Her arm nearly doubled back to her elbow, broken and bleeding."

Micah hung his head in shame before the people who sat in silence, not knowing what to say. Jillian stood to address them.

"People do the things they must. Mothers nurse the sick, giving no thought to their own safety, for when they are needed they heed no one. Men fight side by side for causes only known to the Nobles but just like mothers, they heed no warning for they are needed. What Micah did was a brave and honorable thing. He fought for Corky's life without fear for his own. It would have been easy to let him go, but he was needed. He saved Corky's life as well as mine, for had he not been there to pull us up, we would both have perished."

"It sounds to me as though it was a shared effort," Gavin said, rising behind Jillian. "We are all glad that Corky, the lad and the princess survived the hurricane," he said, placing his hands on Jillian's shoulders. "And now, I think it is time that we return to the ship. The rest of you return at dawn's first light," he said to the men.

"Aye, Gavin," the men responded, watching the two make their way to the boats at the water's edge.

Behind them, Cy stood before the fire, a tale of his own to tell.

"And now a story about a lovely princess who swings from the rigging to save poor pirates from being beheaded." Cy's hearty laughter echoed over the beach and out to the dinghy that Gavin rowed steadily toward the Pegasus.

"Sounds as though its Cy's turn to entertain the villagers," he laughed.

"Heaven forbid that it will be about a princess," Jillian sighed.

"Oh, I would say he will tell of the princess and her handsome pirate lover who has come to cherish her even more, if that were possible." Gavin's voice betrayed the light amusement of his last words by crackling.

"Oh, it is possible, for I feel it too," Jillian said, gazing through the darkness at Gavin's silhouette. "I am overcome by the love that swells within my breast each time you are near, my handsome pirate. I missed you so much, Gavin."

"And I missed you, Jillian. There was not a moment that you were not on my mind and in my heart during our days apart."

He stopped rowing and leaned toward her. His fingertips traced the smooth line of her cheek, then continued across the fullness of her lips which parted slightly with his touch. He felt the intake of her breath as his fingers entwined through the curls at the base of her neck and pulled her lips to his. The feather-light touch of her lips made his heart thunder within his breast, which rose and fell rapidly with the quickening of his breath. God, he wanted her.

Jillian could hardly contain the ecstasy that filled her the minute his fingers found her in the darkness. Their touch sent her pulse racing and her body quivered with unspent desire. She held her breath as he drew her near, eager for the feel of his mouth on hers. Their lips met ever so slightly at first, just barely brushing but the passion that thrust itself into their slight meeting stormed Jillian's senses.

Bringing her uninjured arm forward, Jillian pressed her palm against Gavin's chest. His heart raced beneath her hand and Jillian felt her own match his rapid pace as she pressed her lips more fully against his. The searing kiss, as brief as it was, brought an urgent message to both of them.

"We must go aboard the Pegasus before the tide carries us back to shore," she whispered breathlessly against Gavin's lips.

"I expect we would make quite a sight for the villagers," he said, leaning his forehead against hers. "But I don't think I can make it until we are on the Pegasus. I want you so badly," he whispered, his face showing the pain it took to not take Jillian at this very moment.

"And I you," she said, gaining some control of herself. "Don't forget that you owe me two days."

"Two days!" he exclaimed, his lips curling with the thought of Jillian, all his for two days. "But your arm, Jillian. How are we to manage without bringing you pain?"

"Aye, there are ways. Just hurry, Gavin. I cannot wait much longer." She smiled devilishly as she settled back against the front of the dinghy.

"Nor can I, my pirate princess. Nor can I," Gavin sighed, as his urgent tugs on the oars sent the dinghy speeding toward their promised paradise.

Desertion  Chapter 27

Jillian made her way up the stairwell, emerging onto the deck of the Pegasus. Around her the active crew took no notice of her arrival. Jillian sighed to herself with a feeling of belonging. It had been three months now since she came to the Pegasus, three months of adventure and happiness. She hugged herself, feeling completely content with her new life. Her fingers traced the small scar on her arm where the sword had pierced her skin while rescuing Micah from the turbaned sailor. Another scar was freshly healed, where her own bones had broken through her delicate skin while they snapped when helping Corky. Jillian smiled to herself, remembering the incidents which seemed so long ago but were just mere weeks prior.

She searched the deck for signs of her father and Gavin and found them near the mizzenmast in deep conversation. This was not the first time Jillian had seen them whispering to each other as if they had some big secret. Each time she approached them about what they were discussing both men made up stories about what it was and quickly changed the subject.

Jillian watched them and realized that they weren't, as of yet, aware of her being near. Maybe this time she could find out what was so important and why they wouldn't tell her. She ducked behind some crates near the stairwell, then slowly made her way behind them, as to get closer without being seen.

As she approached, she overheard Gavin's raised voice saying that he wouldn't go along with it. His words stopped Jillian in her tracks. "She isn't dim-witted, Captain. She will know that she is being fooled," Gavin protested.

"Then we will come right out and tell her Gavin," Terrance reasoned. "But it must be done tonight and no later."

"What must be done tonight?" Jillian asked, emerging from behind the crates. "What is it that has you two at each other every time I turn my back?"

Startled, Gavin and Terrance both jumped at the sound of Jillian's voice. Terrance's face brightened as it always did when Jillian was near, but Gavin's expression gave Jillian reason to doubt her father's cheer.

"Aye, Jillian my sweet." Terrance greeted her, ignoring her question. "We were wondering when you would finish with Su Ki and grace us with your presence."

"Don't attempt to sweet talk me again Father. Something is amiss and I want to know what it is."

Gavin gave Terrance a weary look and turned away, leaving Terrance and Jillian to themselves. He didn't agree with what Terrance was up to and could not face Jillian and pretend that he did. This plan was the Captain's and even though he had to go along with it, he wouldn't be a part of convincing Jillian.

Jillian watched Gavin leave and sensed his discontent with Terrance. Something was going on and Gavin apparently didn't agree with Terrance; that much was evident.

"What is it, Father? What has come between the men I love?" Jillian asked, still watching Gavin until he disappeared down the stairwell.

"Come with me, Jillian, I have something to tell you," he said, leading her toward the stairwell.

Terrance said not a word until they were in his cabin and the door was shut. Jillian watched his expression change as he bid her to sit.

"You are troubled, Father."

"Aye, my girl. I cannot fool you. There is something that I need your cooperation with in order to resolve the situation." He settled into the chair opposite hers, then leaned forward, grasping her small hands in his. "I ask that you obey me in all that I say, Jillian. It is for your safety and the survival of our crew that I ask this of you."

"Of course, Father," she answered, seeing he was completely serious.

"Then I must tell you that I will be putting you and Gavin ashore this night."

"What? You aren't serious, Father. Putting us ashore? You mean, deserting us!" She jerked her hands loose from his and stood abruptly before him.

"We are not deserting you, Jillian. We need a few days to . . . ." He couldn't finish.

"To what? To get as far away as possible?"

"Yes. No! I mean . . . Lord this is the hardest thing I've ever had to do." Terrance lowered his head into his hands.

"Next to kidnapping me, I suppose leaving me when I have just come to find my place in life would be a little difficult to do."

"You don't understand, Jillian. I will not be leaving you forever, but just for a short time, until something that I should have finished a long time ago is taken care of."

"What is it, Father? What is so important, so dangerous, that you cannot have me with you?" Suddenly, Jillian could see in his eyes that her words had hit upon the very reason for Terrance not wanting her with him. He was planning something so dangerous that he feared the Pegasus may not return and he didn't want her to perish along with them. "Father you can't do it," she pleaded. "Whatever it is can be avoided somehow can't it?"

"You don't understand, Jillian. We have been avoiding this for months now. It is time to stop running. If we don't, we will forever be looking over our shoulders, never able to stay in one place more than a few hours."

"You're speaking of the warship, aren't you, Father?"

His face softened. Gavin was right. Jillian was not easily fooled and she sensed his every thought. She knew that he was going to confront the warship. She knew the danger involved, for if they were unsuccessful in this undertaking, it would surely mean capture or death. But, she also had to know that he couldn't involve her in this. The thought of her being captured and branded a pirate, a traitor, was reason enough to put her ashore. Terrance could not fathom Jillian being killed during the battle. He had no choice. Jillian must not be on the Pegasus when it came time to do battle with the warship.

"Aye, I'm speaking of the warship. Gavin warned me that you couldn't be easily fooled" he said, straightening his shoulders. "It has been following us since we put down our anchor in the bay. I have a plan to bring her out into the open and attack while her sails are down. I cannot take the chance of you being injured, Jillian. I won't."

"Don't do it, Father. We can sail faster and farther than the warship and stay away until she gives up looking for us. We could . . ."

Terrance stopped her words, taking her into his arms tightly. "No, Jillian. We cannot run forever. I believe that this Captain will follow us until one of us is dead. I have to face him now before your life is ruined. It's time to turn and fight."

"But Father, who? Who, would be so determined to catch a single pirate ship that he would pursue us forever?"

"I'm not sure who the Captain is," he lied, "only that he is very clever and has come close to doing us harm once before. I won't let that happen again and put you in more danger."

"I won't leave you, Father. I won't."

"Aye, you will, Jillian. You must," he said, holding her at arms length and shaking her gently in order to make his point. "I cannot take the chance with you here. You could distract the men. You could be hurt."

"I could help," she pleaded.

"Not this time, Jillian. I am sorry. Not this time . . . . Gavin will be with you to keep you safe until I can return."

"Doing this will leave you without your first mate."

"Aye, and Gavin would agree with you, but there is no other way, little one. I can't leave you all alone either. This is the only way. Don't you see?"

"Yes, I see, Father. I understand, but I don't necessarily agree with you. It's just that I've come to love you and the Pegasus."

"And Gavin?"

"Yes, and Gavin even more. I can't bear to watch the people that I love go off to fight a battle from which they may never return. How can you ask me to?"

"I'm asking you to do this for me, Jillian. Let me win this one last battle for you, for all of us, so that you may be safe. Let me ensure that you and Gavin can give me the grandchildren that I thought I would never have."

Jillian blushed at the thought. A grandchild, a child, a soul carved from the images of his parents and grandparents. Jillian tried to imagine such a child, forged from the love between Gavin and herself.

"Yes, Father, it would be wonderful to have a child, but only if you are here to be his grandfather. What if you are not successful?"

"I will be. I want to give you the freedom that you need to start that little family, Jillian. You can't do that while constantly on the run."

Remembering what she had overheard Gavin say earlier, Jillian asked, "Father, what about Gavin? I overheard him say that he wouldn't go along with it. He doesn't agree with you, does he?"

"He agrees that I must turn and fight. He doesn't agree that he should be left behind. He's a fighter, a brave man."

"Yes, he is. I can see why he doesn't want to be left behind. I don't care for that notion myself, but we will do this for you, Father. Promise me that you will return."

"I will return, Jillian. I promise."

Terrance hugged Jillian to him so that she didn't see the doubt in his eyes. The battle would be fierce. Men may lose their lives, but this was something Terrance had to do for Jillian and for himself.

That evening, just before darkness descended, the Pegasus made her way silently through a craggy opening in a rugged cliff shoreline. Beyond the cliffs lay a hidden, secluded lagoon, deep enough for the Pegasus to weigh anchor. The crew handled the ship skillfully, avoiding the rocks that jutted from the cliff's surface. One miscalculation and the ship could be ripped from stem to stern by the sharp rocks. Just as many times before, Gavin's expert handling of the Pegasus had brought them safely into the lagoon.

Micah and Cy loaded the trunks of supplies and clothing, that Jillian had hurriedly packed, into the dinghy that waited alongside the Pegasus. They waited as their friend's bid the Pegasus and the crew farewell. It was a solemn time onboard the ship. Losing both Jillian and Gavin was a worry to all, yet each man understood the circumstances of their departure. Not one man on the Pegasus wanted to see Jillian in danger, on this ship or on land, and therefore they had no choice but to leave Gavin to protect her until they could return.

Giving Terrance a stern look, Gavin shook his hand; bidding him goodbye, then descended the rope ladder to the dinghy below. Terrance turned to take Jillian, who cried softly, in his arms to reassure her of their return. "Aye, little one," Terrance said, with a strangled voice. "You mustn't cry. The time will pass quickly, you will see."

"If only I could be sure that you will return, Father," Jillian choked.

Terrance didn't answer Jillian with assurances, for he had doubts himself whether he would be returning. "Take heed, sweet Jillian," he said, bringing her chin up and looking into her eyes. "Think of this as a holiday for you and Gavin. You haven't had much time alone since you were married."

"I am not certain that Gavin or I want time alone under these circumstances, Father. Our time together will mean nothing unless we know that you and the Pegasus are safe."

"It's time, Jillian," Terrance said, leading her to the ladder. "Until we meet again, little one."

"Until then, Father," Jillian said, wrapping her arms around his waist. "Be safe. I love you."

"As I love you, my sweet child."

She made the difficult climb down the ladder using what little strength she had to leave the Pegasus. Jillian felt completely drained when she stepped into the dinghy and the protective embrace of the man she loved. Her world had changed so drastically in only a few hours. Just this afternoon she was content with her life and now part of it was being torn away from her. Within Gavin's eyes, Jillian could see the same sadness and destitution that she felt, for he too was losing a part of his sanctity.

As Cy rowed the short distance to the sandy beach Jillian watched her father standing at the railing of the ship, hands on his hips and long legs spread. The lantern light reflected off his copper hair that curled wildly around his head and shoulders, making him look like the devil himself. She remembered thinking this when first she saw him, but now he seemed so small, so gentle. Her heart ached at the thought of losing him.

Gavin's arms tightened protectively around Jillian, as if he sensed her thoughts and she leaned against him, cuddling in his warmth. Gavin held her, seeking her strength. He felt abandoned, discarded, yet he knew Terrance had made a wise decision and would be successful against his foe. It would finally be finished.

The small boat skidded upon the sand and Cy and Micah leapt into the water to tug the dinghy higher onto the shore. Gavin picked Jillian up and gave her to Cy, who carried her easily to dry land. When Jillian's feet touched the sand, her legs gave way beneath her, but before she crumbled to the ground, Cy caught her, supporting her slight weight.

"Ho, now, missy. Looks as though you're still on sea legs," he said, laughing.

"Goodness!" Jillian exclaimed. "I don't remember the sand being quite this hard before."

"Aye, it takes some time getting used to, the good old Mother Earth, it does."

Cy held Jillian until her legs supported her, then helped Micah and Gavin unload the remaining trunks from the dinghy. The three men, carrying what they could, and Jillian holding the lantern, made their way along a narrow path into the forest. The path led up a steep hillside which fell away at one point to the ocean. Jillian kept to the inside of the trail, avoiding looking down at the blackness that she knew was the ocean far below. Once at the top of the incline, the path continued deep into the forest. The lantern light illuminated the eerie depths of the foliage, casting long shadows that danced from surface to surface as they passed.

Jillian looked in wonder at the world around her. Never before had the trees seemed so colorful, the air so fragrant with the richness of earth. Even the sound of their feet upon the forest floor seemed loud with a crispness that she had never noticed before. A nighthawk shrieked overhead as it dove for an unsuspecting moth that hung in the lantern's light above them. All four ducked their heads in unison, and then laughed at their own antics.

As they walked deeper into the forest, Jillian could hear the babbling of a brook and soon their path followed the water upstream. After a short time, the forest opened to a clearing that surrounded a pond. The lantern's yellow flame shed light on the pond's smooth black surface which stretched beyond its reaches. In the distance, the roar of a waterfall could be heard, spilling cool water from an unknown source. Jillian imagined that the falls fed the pool, but because of the darkness of the cool night she couldn't be sure that it was so.

Gavin touched Jillian's back, urging her to proceed along the water's edge. Ahead of her, Jillian saw the remnants of a fire pit where someone had previously built a campfire. Cy and Micah circled the stones and then lowered the trunks. Gavin put his burden down, then lit another lamp that he carried and handed it to Cy.

"This is farewell, my friend," Gavin said, as Cy took the lantern.

"Aye, Gavin." Cy extended his hand to Gavin, who took it firmly within his own. "Take good care of our princess now, mate."

"You can rest assured my friend." Gavin said. "Take good care of the old man, Cy."

"Aye, I will indeed, Gavin," Cy reassured him.

Jillian put the lantern down on one of the trunks and turned to see Gavin saying farewell to their friends. She waited, giving them this time. The three laughed and hugged and slapped each other playfully on the back. The apprehension of saying goodbye hung delicately in the air with each man fighting the urge to lose control. When all was said, they stood silently, waiting for someone to call an end to their sadness.

Jillian came to Cy first, putting her arms around him. She held onto him tightly. He softened in her arms and she heard his whispered, choked farewell.

"Take care, my handsome pirate," she told him. "Come back to us."

She held his hands in hers for one brief moment, giving them a gentle squeeze as if to emphasize her words, then turned to Micah, who stood silently, waiting. Jillian took a deep breath to steady herself before taking him in her arms. The look in Micah's eyes told her that he too, was having a difficult time saying goodbye. She wanted more than anything to change what was happening, to change the wicked twist that was tearing her loved ones from her life.

Micah quaked with the sorrow that overtook him. He held Jillian tenderly at first and then hugged her fiercely to him, hearing the choked sob that escaped her. He swallowed hard, holding his own emotions in check. Leaving Jillian and Gavin was the most difficult thing he'd ever had to do. She was like the sister and friend that he had never had. Gavin was the older brother who had seen him safely through so many good and bad times.

Golden curls tickled Micah's cheek and he inhaled deeply, imbedding their fragrance in his mind. The firmness of her embrace, the sleek arms that bound him to her, the tiny waist that fit within his outstretched fingers, every curve, every sound, every movement, Micah memorized them all. He took with him every part of her that he could grasp. Her essence would be his salvation in the days to come; her essence would be his strength.

Jillian responded to his mind's plea. She knew that he was frightened and sorrow-filled. She willed her strength to sustain him in his time of need; she willed him to return to her safe. In the few moments that they clung to each other, Jillian gave Micah her all and he received her strength, feeling it entering his soul. When at last, they gazed into each other's eyes, Micah felt fortified by Jillian's spirit. She saw his strength refreshed, renewing her confidence in his return.

Micah was astounded by the feelings resonating within him. Jillian had given him much more than a farewell embrace. She gave him the strength and insight to know that he would survive the days ahead and return to her unharmed. Again, Jillian instilled in his heart a confidence that knew no bounds. He realized that she knew his need and answered it with an unknown energy that filled him with the belief that anything was possible.

"Farewell, my brother," Jillian said, cupping his cheek. "I shall miss my right arm," she finished, trying with much difficulty not to cry.

"And I shall miss you, sister dear," Micah said, again holding her to him.

Placing a hand reassuringly on Micah's shoulder, Cy squeezed it gently. "It is time young friend. We must return or our Captain will be leaving without us."

"Aye, I suppose it's time," Micah said, pulling away from Jillian.

No further words were spoken. Jillian and Gavin watched as the two disappeared into the darkness of the forest. The light from their lantern followed leaving them within the lit circle of their own lantern. To Jillian, it seemed as though the darkness beyond the lantern's light crept ever closer, chilling her to the bone. Seeing Jillian's chill, Gavin came to her, holding her close.

"It's always the hardest time, saying goodbye. We can only hope that they will return safely to us," he murmured against her neck.

"If only we could be certain, Gavin. If only there was a way to be sure."

"There are no guarantees, Jillian. The Captain, your Father, knows what he's doing. He will bring the Pegasus through the battle and back to us somehow."

"I pray you are right, Gavin. I don't know what I would do without them."

"You have me, you know. You're not alone." Gavin smiled suggestively.

"Yes, Gavin" she sighed. "It's just that I feel so empty, so helpless. I would give anything to be a man and be able to help fight the battle alongside them. Sometimes I think being a woman is a curse."

"Don't say that, Jillian. For if you were a man, I wouldn't be able to do this," he said, nibbling her ear. "Or this," he sighed, pulling her hips against his.

Breath held, Jillian absorbed the sensations that Gavin's actions evoked. She felt his heat pressed against her most sensitive places, making them throb, making her long to have his body even closer to their source. The passions of the moment and the longing that she felt drove her, mind and body, to one end—satisfaction. She wanted to feel it and to give it to Gavin. She wanted to hold him, caress him, claim him, and to never let go. Gavin was hers and she his. She wanted to lay claim to his passions and devote hers to him.

Gavin felt her need and answered in kind with his own. He never wanted to be left behind, but had resigned himself to the fact that he was not only a part of the Pegasus and her crew, but more importantly, Gavin was Jillian's husband, friend, and protector. He would give his life, if need be, in her defense, as would Terrance and the Pegasus crew. The danger of having her aboard the ship while fighting the warship was too great. Now, they were here and he was Jillian's only protector and companion. They would have to make the best of their situation while waiting for the Pegasus to return. Gavin had plenty of things in mind that they could do to pass the time until the ship's return.

A soft moan brought Gavin's mind back to the beautiful wanton that writhed against him. He groaned, wrapping her tightly in order to hold her sensuous body still while he gained his composure.

"Jillian, we cannot just yet," Gavin's voice pleaded.

Jillian leaned back, looking into Gavin's pain-filled eyes. "You started this, remember?"

"I know but there is something that we must do first."

"Perhaps take our clothes off, Gavin?" she grinned.

"Yes . . . I mean, no! Oh, just come with me," he said, pulling her behind him.

Holding the lantern high to light their way, Jillian protested as Gavin led her hastily through the forest, over the path leading to the lagoon. They stopped abruptly, coming to the place where the pathway descended the steep hillside. Below them, Jillian could hear the sound of waves breaking against the jagged rocks that lined the cliffs surrounding the lagoon. Her heart pounded from the hurried pace with which Gavin traveled the pathway, but also with the knowledge that with one misguided step, they could plunge to the rocks and water below. The mist from the surf billowed around them as they stood in the darkness.

Suddenly, the sound of a cannon blast rang over the ocean. Gavin held the lantern high, swinging it back and forth, answering the cannon's crack. Gavin pointed off to the left where the mouth of the lagoon merged with the ocean. Jillian watched as the Pegasus breached the cliffs and headed for the open sea passing directly in front of her and Gavin. Like a shadow on the water, the Pegasus silently made her way out to sea. Once more Gavin held the lantern high, swinging it back and forth. The ghostly ship answered his signal with another blast from her cannon. Then as swiftly as she had come into sight, the Pegasus disappeared, blending in with the blackness of the water.

"Father is a wise man, planning this when there is no moon," Jillian said, deep in thought.

"Yes, he is a wise and cunning man. He will need all his wits to defeat William."

Shocked at what Gavin said, Jillian froze, letting this knowledge sink in. William. Gavin had said, William. Certainly, he couldn't mean the same William, the man who claimed to be her father for all those years, the same William who had betrayed Terrance and her mother so many years ago, the warship Captain with whom Terrance meant to do battle and either destroy or be destroyed by him. Please God, she prayed. Don't let them be one and the same.

"Jillian, Jillian!" Gavin exclaimed, shaking her. "What is it?"

It took Jillian a moment to regain the use of her voice. When she did, the words strangled in her throat. She couldn't, she wouldn't believe that this was true. The two men in her life whom she called Father were destined to do battle against each other. One, she had once loved, the other, she had come to love. It was like making a choice between them. How could she honestly hope that Terrance would not be killed if it meant that William would? How could she hope that William, Siriann's father, would be saved if it meant that Terrance would perish?

Terrance's words suddenly took on much more meaning to her. "Let me win this one last battle for you, Jillian so that you may be safe," he had said.

"My God," she whispered, "I am the reason that the warship pursues the Pegasus relentlessly. I am the one to blame for the constant flight that the Pegasus and her crewmen have been forced to endure. It's all because of me." Jillian sank to her knees, her face in her hands.

"You didn't know?" Gavin asked, bewildered. "Terrance never told you that it is William who captains the warship?"

"No. He never told me, for if he had, I would not have left his side. He knew that, of course."

Kneeling beside Jillian, Gavin took her in his arms, cradling her against him. "I'm very sorry, Jillian. If I had known, I wouldn't have told you."

"But don't you see, Gavin," she said, looking out over the blackness. "He didn't want me to know until it was too late. He wanted me to be here with you for fear that he might not survive the battle. He wanted both of us to survive."

"I told you he was cunning, Jillian. It looks as though we both were taken in by his scheme," Gavin said, shaking his head. "Please Jillian; you can't blame yourself for the warship. It isn't the first time William has been in heavy pursuit of the Pegasus."

"It isn't? What do you mean Gavin? Tell me everything"

"Although I never realized it until the day we found you, I think that many times before, Terrance had tried to return to find your mother. Most of those times, a naval ship sailed in pursuit of us until we were forced to leave England's waters. A few times, one warship in particular would follow, staying with us longer than any other. That must have been William's ship."

"Oh, Gavin. What have I done? What have I done?" Jillian cried in desperation.

"There is one thing I know, Jillian. Terrance wouldn't trade one minute of the last three months with you for anything in the world. You have brought him more joy and happiness than he has ever had. Don't ever think that he has any regrets about bringing you aboard the Pegasus because he doesn't and neither do I. He loves you, as do I."

Until late that night, Jillian and Gavin sat at the cliff's edge, hoping and praying for the safe return of their companions, feeling safe in each other's arms, yet vulnerable to the unknown that lay ahead. There would be no turning back now. They had no alternative but to wait for the successful return of the Pegasus.

Chapter 28

The next morning Jillian awoke alone in a makeshift bed near the pond. She didn't remember coming back to the campsite where they had brought the supplies. She didn't remember undressing or making the bed upon which she was lying. She didn't remember much of anything about last night after the Pegasus had sailed out of sight. What she did remember was being left behind by Terrance, who sailed away to do battle with the man known to her as father for most of her life.

Thinking about William sent a shiver of dread through Jillian. She remembered the troubled childhood that she had endured; the beatings and degradation of her mother and herself. She remembered everything.

Trying to reason through the chaos in her mind, it seemed to Jillian that times of extreme emotion and stress triggered memories of times in her life that she had forgotten. The powerful feelings of loss and abandonment that she and Gavin suffered last night brought with them terrifying memories of her former life. As the memories flooded her mind, Jillian shuddered with their intensity. She fought to keep the horrors hidden where she wouldn't have to deal with their truths.

Bringing one of the blankets with her, Jillian rose from the bed, wrapping the blanket around her shoulders for warmth. The sun, not yet cresting the surrounding trees, rendered little heat to help chase the chill from her body. The splashing of the waterfall, becoming visible with the rising sun, sent a chill straight through her. The clearing was cold and damp, not nearly as warm as Jillian would have thought it would be. But then, she thought, never had her heart felt so cold and empty as it did now.

Gavin stopped at the edge of the clearing upon seeing Jillian, her back to him, standing near the edge of the water. His arms were loaded with wood that he had gathered for their morning fire. Disappointed, Gavin wanted to return with the wood before Jillian awoke so he could build a fire to warm her. The way she clutched the blanket around her,

Gavin could see her chill and knew that she was naked beneath it, for he'd undressed her himself the night before.

Hearing Gavin enter the clearing, Jillian turned to see him laying the wood down near the fire pit. She felt slightly warmer seeing him surrounded by the forest and the earth, realizing that this was the first time they would truly be alone since her arrival on the Pegasus. His strong arm muscles flexed as they released the wood, letting it fall to the ground. She watched his movement of strength beneath tanned flesh as he arranged the pile neatly, a safe distance from the pit. His black leggings stretched over his firm buttocks, then down the length of his legs, disappearing into the tops of his boots. He stood then, stretching his back, placing his hands on his hips. His hair now fell past his shoulders in pale splendor. Jillian thought to herself how much it had grown since she first saw this beautiful man.

Gavin sensed her attention on him but continued with the task of building the fire. The night had been long for both of them and Gavin wasn't certain how Jillian would handle their predicament this morning. She had cried and he had held her until late into the night, when she finally fell asleep in his arms on the cliff edge. It wasn't until almost daylight that Gavin had carried Jillian back to the clearing, undressed her, and placed her between the blankets for warmth. He hadn't been long in gathering the firewood, so he knew she hadn't slept much since he had left her there.

A thread of smoke filtered up through the dry grass beneath the kindling in the pit. Gavin blew gently; bringing forth flame, then put bigger pieces of wood over it so that the fire could lick their surface and catch. Once the fire was built, Gavin turned his attention to Jillian.

The morning sun was full upon her now, illuminating the golden depths of her translucent curls. He remembered her hair catching the sunlight this same way on their wedding day; the memory brought a broad smile to his face. Her eyes, full and bright with emotion, held him mesmerized. He watched as she took the softness of her bottom lip between her white teeth, held it, and then slowly released its pink fullness. A part of him felt those same brilliant teeth taking him in their grasp, holding him until their sensual grip threatened to bring him near the brink, then releasing him ever so slowly, leaving behind delightful traces of their throbbing possession.

Rolling his eyes closed, he groaned, seeking composure that he really didn't want to have. Jillian felt his frustration and answered it by opening the blanket. The cool rush of air sprinkled her flesh with goose bumps that heightened the sensation to her already sensitive state.

"Come to me, Gavin. I need you," she beckoned.

Gavin needed no more invitation and was instantly within the blanket holding her fiercely against him. His crushing warmth pressed sweetly against her naked flesh while caressing hands made quick work of ridding her skin of the goose bumps caused by the chill and replacing them with ones of passion.

Her need for him was great. Jillian quickly rid him of his clothes, dropping them casually from the confines of their wrapping as they made their way toward the makeshift bed. Walking was difficult, for their bodies were thoroughly entwined. Their lips devoured, their hands possessed, their minds claimed each other, heart and soul. Their bodies melded into one passion-filled being, striving for ultimate fulfillment. Neither noticed when the blanket fell away as they slowly lowered to the earth. The fury of their passion was fueled by a need seated within the depths of emotion that raged from the very heart of their souls.

Their lips never left each other and Jillian opened her body to Gavin's pressing need. His manhood found and entered her warmth in one swift thrust, sending flashes of radiance to her closed eyes as it touched the entrance to her womb. Gavin paused for a moment, taking quick breaths. Jillian also sought control, but was quick to urge him on.

"I cannot be gentle, love," he warned from between his teeth. "I am beyond that now."

"I want to feel the full power of your love, Gavin."

Gavin slowly rose above Jillian, locking his arms beneath her knees. His actions raised her hips off the blankets. This position gave Gavin power over Jillian's movements and also gave him better access to depths of pleasure still unknown to her. An instant of shock went through her but desire won out. Trusting him, she clung to his powerful arms, pulling him ever closer. Gavin withdrew slowly from her, until the tip of him caressed her womanhood, then thrust himself to the very hilt of his sex, sending Jillian's body into instant spasms of passion making her cry out.

Keeping control of his body, Gavin plunged deep, again and again. Slow tortuous withdrawals and hard driving thrusts sent Jillian beyond any pleasure she had ever dreamt possible. Her body shuddered again and again before Gavin showed signs of his own pleasure peaking. When he could hold out no more, Jillian was sated as she had never been before and to her amazement, saddened that it couldn't have lasted longer.

Exhausted, Gavin released her legs from his manacles and collapsed upon her, his labored breath warming the flesh beneath her ear. She lay quietly beneath him, listening while her own breath slowed to a more normal state. She could feel his love flesh, still locked within her, returning to a relaxed state.

"Are you alright?"

"Yes, I'm fine. I never knew."

Raising himself so that he could look into her eyes, Gavin saw her sated contentment. Beads of perspiration glistened on her forehead where tiny wisps of hair clung to the moistness. Swollen from the bruising of their lovemaking, Jillian's lips beckoned for more.

He did not disappoint her, kissing her thoroughly before answering. "You mean, my love, you never knew that your body could respond again and again to my lovemaking?"

"No, my sweet," she answered, gently stroking his cheek. "I never knew the strength of your love. It has filled me with such emotions, such need. I can't begin to describe the desire I felt come from within you. It had such . . . power over me."

"Aye, my love. Now you know what I have felt all these many months."

"It's more than desire we feel for each other. Our love is what gives this desire life. Without love, desire would be an empty thing."

"I love you Jillian, my sweet."

"And I love you," she answered, letting his mouth claim her fully.

After some time, Gavin rose, bringing Jillian with him to bathe in the pool. Using soap that they found in the supplies, they washed away the remnants of their lovemaking in the water of the cool splashing falls, letting it bathe new life into their bodies. They dove and swam, splashing and playing for a time before the water's chill drove them from it. Then, both climbed up on the large stone near the edge, letting the warm sun dry their bodies.

Fast asleep upon the stone is where Gavin left Jillian while he dressed and then headed for the beach to retrieve the remaining supplies left there the night before. It would take him a few trips to do this himself, but he knew that Jillian needed to rest after last night's events and this morning's lovemaking. It shouldn't take too long, he told himself, taking one last look at her sleeping form before leaving the clearing.

*   *   *   *   *

The scent of man was in the air, stronger than at any other time. The closer she came to the falls, the more intense the rancid odor became. She advanced with caution. The recent birth of her two cubs had kept the lioness down for only a few hours, and having no mate made it increasingly difficult for her to hunt and take care of her young. Food had been scarce throughout the summer, and now that the cubs were older it was impossible to keep their stomachs full. At this age they were no help to her, for they were more concerned with playing with the squirrels and mice that they pounced on than in killing them for food. When their stomachs cramped and their strength lessened, maybe then, they would hunt instead of play.

The splashing of the falls made the big cat's mouth water, for she had chased a stag a great distance before his cunning flight and the waning of her own strength allowed him to escape. Again, the scent of man invaded her nostrils, stinging them into alertness. She crept cautiously into the clearing near the waterfall.

Her yellow eyes explored, locating the campfire that burned low within a circle of stones. She knew better than to go close to the fire, having seen what fire could do to animals if they were to venture within its reach. At the side of the clearing were wooden containers of some kind. She slowly made her way to them, all the while keeping watch for the human's return. She sniffed the surface of one of the crates, sensing that food lay within. On the top of the next crate was a white length of something she had not seen before. She sniffed it once. It smelt sweet, like flowers. Her stomach growled. The lioness timidly licked the bar of soap, and then sprang back coughing and gagging on the bubbles that foamed in her mouth. The more she worked the substance with her tongue, the more it foamed and stung the inside of her mouth. The big cat leapt for the water of the pool, paying little attention to her surroundings, having only one thing in mind, which was to clean the putrid bubbles from her mouth.

On the rock above the cat, the breeze caught Jillian's hair, lifting it from the stone, then gently setting it back down. The movement caught the big cat's attention. She arched her back and sniffed the air for any sign of man, but all she could smell was the sweet, flowery scent of the soap. Inching forward, the lioness stretched her sleek body toward the stone. Still, nothing could penetrate the smell and taste of the soap that dulled her senses. She crouched back, deciding whether to investigate further or leave this place and its awful human traps.

Entering the clearing, Gavin stopped dead in his tracks, seeing the massive cat crouched at the base of the stone and ready to spring to the top where Jillian lay sleeping. The cat's attention was riveted upon Jillian's hair spread over the rock, the ends flipping in the breeze. Gavin knew it would only take a moment for the cat to rob him of Jillian. It would only take a moment for the big cat to take away the only person who mattered to him.

Suddenly the lioness turned, seeing Gavin. She arched her back, growling a warning. Gavin's heart stopped dead when Jillian, awakened by the yowling panther, rose from the stone behind the cat. The lioness's attention flitted to Jillian, then back to Gavin, as she became aware that she lay trapped between the pond, the stone, and these two humans.

With only one thought in mind, Gavin dropped the supplies and ran, yelling at the top of his lungs, toward the stone and Jillian. The big cat found an escape route, which she gladly took, for the crazed human frightened her. Jillian still numbed by slumber, stood bewildered on the rock's surface. Before she realized what Gavin intended to do, or could attempt to stop him, Gavin leapt through the air, catching her in his arms, plunging both into the water of the pond. Together they submerged into the frigid depths, the shock of the icy water making both frantic for the surface.

"What do you think you are doing?" Jillian yelled. "Are you trying to kill me?"

"Kill you?" Gavin coughed. "I was trying to save you from the panther."

"Save me? Gavin that poor animal was so frightened of you that she was long gone before you so rudely threw us both into the pond."

"Gone?" Gavin asked, searching the clearing. "But I thought she was going to attack you when she saw you on the rock."

"Oh, Gavin," Jillian said, wrapping her arms around his neck. "I don't think she will ever want to see this place again. I have never seen anything so frightened in all my life. When you ran toward the stone, she only wanted to get away, not attack."

Gavin hugged her to him. "I have never been so scared in all my life, Jillian. I couldn't bear to lose you."

"You are not going to lose me, Gavin. Thank you for scaring away that nasty panther."

"Jillian, how can you tease me now? This was serious. You could have been killed."

"Never, my love, for you will always be there to protect me from harm."

"And you will be the death of me some day."

Lifting her into his arms, Gavin made his way out of the water and to the blankets where he lowered Jillian, coming up fully on top of her. He made love to her then, cherishing her every gasp and sigh. Gavin made love to her as if to reclaim the moments lost to the panther and the threat of losing her. They spent the rest of the day making love near the edge of the pond.

Seeing and hearing no sign of the big cat, Gavin and Jillian enjoyed each other to the fullest in quiet seclusion. They spent the next several days exploring and gathering necessities from the forest that were not included in the supplies brought from the Pegasus. Roots, herbs and other plant life that her mother and Sue Ki had taught Jillian about were stored for use when they returned to the ship. Wild mushrooms and mint were dried in the sun, while turnips and other rooted plants were stored safely in dry sand to keep them fresh.

The days passed and with their passing came uneasiness. Gavin became increasingly aware that the time for Terrance's return had come and gone. Try as he may, Gavin couldn't conceal the fact that the Pegasus may not return and that he and Jillian would have to leave the cove. When making their plans, he and Terrence had discussed what they were to do if the Pegasus should not return. At that time, Gavin would not even entertain the thought that this plan would have to be used. Now, it seemed the worst had happened and Terrance would not be coming back.

In his heart, Gavin knew that he had made the right decision in bringing Jillian to the safety of the cove, but he worried for Terrance and the crew of the Pegasus. They would have no choice but to find a village where word of the battle might be. It was the only way to find out what had happened to his friends. He especially wanted to learn of Terrance's fate. He prayed that Terrance and the crew had survived. Gavin made up his mind that he and Jillian would leave at first light the next morning.

Gavin was not the only one worried about the Pegasus. Jillian had also become uneasy as the days passed. Without warning, feelings of dread surged through her. Today these warnings were stronger than ever, foretelling of a great tragedy that Jillian did not understand. The only thing she could do was wait and hope that by having this premonition she could prevent whatever was going to befall them.

Late into the night, a rustling sound woke Jillian. Listening for a moment, she suspected that a rodent bent on relieving them of some of the supplies had most likely made the noise. Rising slowly, Jillian saw a mouse skittering around the bottom of the wooden crates. She smiled with relief at its antics, for the mouse was no match for the stout wood of the crates.

Gavin slept soundly beside her. A little puff of air escaped his closed lips and gently brushed her shoulder. She smiled, remembering him doing this before and feeling content with this simple intimacy. The last ten days had been the happiest of Jillian's life. They had used this time to become more fully acquainted with each other's mind as well as body, and Jillian felt as if she knew Gavin even better than she knew herself. But also, they had lived with the fear of losing Terrance and the crew of the Pegasus to the warship's destruction. The two emotions, in extreme contradiction of one another, were what Jillian blamed for the foreboding feelings that she was experiencing. Soon it would be over, for they would leave in the morning to seek information of the Pegasus's whereabouts and the fate of her crew. The rustling sound again brought Jillian's attention to the crates, but this time she saw no rodent.

Stretching, Jillian decided to wash away her uneasiness with the cool water of the pond. Careful not to wake Gavin, Jillian left the warmth of the blankets. She put Gavin's white linen shirt on to cover her nakedness as she walked the short distance to the water. Black depths of the water reflected the full moon in the night sky, and when Jillian scooped the smooth surface with her hands, the disturbance made the moon's reflection dance away upon the ripples. The crispness of the icy water brought Jillian more fully awake and she shuddered as the water trickled down her chin, neck, and then between her breasts. She smoothed the coolness over her face and neck, enjoying the sensations it brought with it.

Without warning, the hair on the back of Jillian's neck suddenly stood on end. She straightened in alertness, listening, waiting for any sound of the danger she felt was close. The memory of the panther came back to her, making her even more uneasy. Seconds passed and the water of the pond calmed. The reflections of the moon returned, vividly clear on the pond surface, and still there was no sound of danger. Her mind eased slightly and she decided she was being silly. What could possibly be a threat to her and Gavin here? They were secluded and happy, finding sanctuary in each other's company.

Suddenly, a hand covered Jillian's mouth, and an arm bound her from behind. Her heart stopped, as instant recognition and memories flooded her mind. The putrid odor of his flesh, the way his arms held her imprisoned against his body. The intruder could be no other than Jason. The knowledge of who held her made Jillian tremble with fear. She remembered the evil within his soul. She remembered the promises he had made as the men threw him over the side of the Pegasus. Every word rushed to Jillian at once, overwhelming her with sickness. The man who held her was a monster.

"Aye, my little slut. I can tell you know it is I," he whispered. "You knew I would return for you, didn't you? You are destined to be mine, Jillian. All mine."

Jillian fought back tears of fear, gasping beneath his hand for life-giving breath. She tried to clear her mind of panic and think of a means of escaping this evil being. She thought of Gavin and grew even more frightened. If Gavin were to wake and see Jason taking her, he would surely fight to the death to protect her. This made Jillian panic even more, for the thought of losing Gavin was worse than suffering anything that Jason could ever do to her.

"She will never be yours, you swine," Gavin said from behind them.

Gavin's words turned Jason's attention to him. Jason turned, placing Jillian between them, putting a knife to her throat. Sword raised, Gavin stood his ground, becoming more angry and frightened than he'd ever been in his life. He couldn't believe that this man could use Jillian so. All he could think of was killing the evil coward, ridding their lives of him forever. But doing this, without putting Jillian in even greater danger, would take cunning.

"So we meet again, Gavin," Jason seethed. "But this time, the girl will be mine."

"She will never be yours, Jason. She is my wife."

"Aye, I will console Jillian after I rid her of you."

Jillian struggled. "Gavin, please no," she pleaded. "I could not bear to lose you."

"Don't be afraid, my love. This coward is no match for my talent," Gavin said arrogantly, tossing his blade from hand to hand, knowing that Jason would not resist his challenge.

"So, you think to confront my ego, do you?" Jason returned. "I accept your challenge only because I planned to kill you all along. Only when you have taken your last breath will I ever truly enjoy the taste of Jillian upon my lips."

He turned and slowly licked Jillian's cheek, all the while watching for Gavin's reaction. Jillian whimpered, gagging back the bile that rose from her stomach. Jason smiled with satisfaction, hearing Jillian's helplessness, and seeing rage overtake Gavin's senses. He shoved Jillian roughly aside, then drew his own sword, readying for the battle that was to come.

Feeling even more enraged, Gavin watched as Jillian collapsed to the ground. The man was a vile beast, a sick fiend. Gavin knew he could never let this monster touch Jillian again. He knew he had to keep his wits about him if he was going to defeat Jason. He must keep Jillian safe.

Swords drawn, Gavin and Jason circled each other as Jillian backed away from them; trembling with fear. Determination showed in their every movement and neither was going to let the other get an advantage. Both men wanted the same thing, Jillian, who watched as the battle started with Jason thrusting toward Gavin, who agilely diverted the sword by striking it with his own. Her heart leapt with each thrust, fearing the outcome.

Gavin was the first to draw blood, having struck Jason's upper arm with his sword. The crimson stain, black in the darkness of night, went from shoulder to elbow. Gavin's style was steady and sure, while Jason fought wildly and randomly, making him seem less skilled. Jillian hoped that the wound would be enough to weaken Jason. She huddled in silence, watching this endless struggle for dominance.

After what seemed to be an eternity, the strength of both men began to wane. They locked bodily together more often, yet neither gave in to the other. At long last, Gavin clearly had the advantage over Jason, having knocked the sword from his hand, then pinning him on the ground near the fire pit. He held him there, his chest heaving with exhaustion from the fight.

"It's over, Jason," Gavin hissed between breaths. "Concede, while you still can."

"Never!" Jason shouted, throwing a handful of ash from the pit into Gavin's eyes.

Jillian screamed, seeing the hot ash spray into Gavin's eyes. The ash blinded him, leaving him vulnerable against Jason's attack and he covered his face, trying to clear his eyes of the burning ash. This gave Jason the opportunity to strike Gavin with a rock from the fire pit, throw him off, and then find his sword nearby. Jillian watched in horror as Jason recovered his weapon, turned and ran Gavin through while he lay defenseless on the ground. Another scream came from her as she ran to Gavin. Jason withdrew the sword, readying for another thrust that would finish Gavin, but just before the sword struck, Jillian flung herself over him, stopping the blade from its destination.

"You fool!" Jason shouted. "Remove yourself or you will die along with him!"

Jillian didn't move from Gavin, who lay unconscious beneath her, but instead turned to face Jason, focusing her hate-filled eyes on him. She had to stop him from taking Gavin's life. She had to find a way to save Gavin.

"Don't kill him, I beg of you," she pleaded. "I'll go with you. If only you will spare his life."

"Oh, what honor the little slut does possess. Are you truly willing to give yourself to me in exchange for the life of this weakling?" Jason laughed.

"I'll do anything. Just don't kill him, please."

Jason stood over her, the tip of his sword under her determined chin. She looked so beautiful. Her amber eyes pleaded for mercy for the man beneath her.

"You will not fight me?"

"Nay, I won't, if you will let Gavin live." Jillian shuddered. The look in Jason's eyes filled her with terror.

"Give me your hands," Jason ordered. Jillian held them out in front of her, bowing her head in submission. "Behind your back. I want them behind your back."

She did what he said, turning to lay partially over Gavin in order to do so. Jason took a length of rope from beneath his shirt and bound Jillian's hands tightly. She felt the warmth of Gavin's blood seep through the front of his shirt and stain her breast, the sweet fragrance of his life slipping from him. He had to survive until Terrance returned to the cove. As Jason pulled the rope tighter, Jillian kissed his lips one last time.

"Farewell, my love. Do not forget," she sobbed, tears falling freely.

Jason jerked her roughly away from Gavin, pushing her to the ground at Gavin's side. He forced a filthy rag into her mouth then secured it with his kerchief, tying it so tight that it pulled Jillian's jaw painfully back. Jillian struggled but stilled with the feel of Jason's hand on her bottom. With sudden sickness, she remembered that she wore nothing but Gavin's shirt, which had been drawn high around her waist with her actions. There was nothing to protect her from his prying eyes and hands. She also knew that nothing would prepare her for what Jason had in store for her. He was evil, evil like she had never known.

"There now, that should keep you. Lie still while I look for supplies. We'll be needing them where we're going."

Jillian listened while Jason went through the crates, stuffing things into a sack that he found in one of them. Gavin lay unconscious, bleeding beside her. Blood flowed freely onto the ground from the wound that Jason had inflicted upon his side. It was so black and ugly, like a serpent winding its way from his chest to the earth, draining his life with every passing moment. She could barely see his chest rise and fall with shallow breaths.

"Thank you, God," she said, offering a silent prayer. "Let him live."

Jason wrenched Jillian to her feet, bringing her fully against him. He pressed her hips against his, smiling when she shut her eyes and swallowed hard. He was hard for her; he would take her in due time, but now they had to hurry. He had to put distance between them and this place. Everything that he could carry was stuffed into the sack. There was only one more thing to take care of.

A moan from Gavin brought Jillian's eyes to Jason's, only inches away. She saw amusement in them. He looked down at Gavin and then back to her. She read his thoughts and tried to stop him, struggling to knock him over, to kick him, to do anything to stop him from what he was about to do. His strength was much greater and with little effort, Jason forced her to the ground once more.

"I want you to watch, Jillian," he said, turning her face to Gavin. "I want you to see your man die."

She tried to rise, to turn her face away, but Jason pressed his boot on the back of her neck, making it impossible for her to do anything but watch. She did not want to keep her eyes open, but something inside made her watch. She saw Jason raise the blade then plunge it deeply into Gavin once more. Gavin opened his eyes, curling his body against the pain of the sword severing everything in its path. Their eyes met one last time before Gavin rolled over, collapsing to the ground.

Jillian screamed and screamed and screamed, the agonizing sound muffled by the gag in her mouth. Jason pulled the sword from Gavin's chest, wiping a droplet of blood from the edge with his fingertip. He examined it as if it were a precious jewel, then slowly sucked the life giving nectar from his finger. She wanted to die; she wanted to join Gavin in death. With Gavin gone, there was no reason for her to live.

The boot left her neck but Jillian did not move. Jason rolled her limp body onto her back, put a length of rope under her arm, and brought it back under the other, looping it through a slipknot in front. Jillian thought of the irony of being imprisoned by the very same knot that she had used to save Corky. Once the rope was secure, Jason lifted her to her feet, put the sack over his shoulder and without another word, led her from the clearing.

Jillian's eyes never left Gavin until she was out of the clearing and stumbled over a downed branch. She hit the earth hard, striking the side of her face against a stone. Before she could move, Jason jerked her roughly to her feet.

"You'd better be more careful from here on out, Jillian. I'll not have you delaying me by being so clumsy," he warned.

Jason struck her then with the back of his hand. Her head reeled; she staggered, but did not fall again. "Aye, that's more like it. You'll get more of the same each time you delay me." he laughed. "We'll see if you try it again, won't we?"

The perfume of blood was thick in the air. The lioness bristled with the hunger pains the scent evoked. Hunting was sparse these last few days and it had taken some time to get her sense of taste back after licking the vile foam in the human camp. The cubs were no help to her, only hunting small rodents that were tasteless after being played with. The aroma hit her again, coming in on the night breeze. It was the fragrance of human blood. The big cat knew the smell, remembering it well from the battlefields that she and others like her had scavenged.

Giving in to her hunger, the lioness leapt from the rocks, making her way steadily down the cliff next to the falls. She crept carefully into the clearing, lifting her nose to the air. There was no movement within the camp. She pressed on, seeking the source of the bloodletting, her nostrils and stomach urging her forward in the darkness.

The human lay sprawled upon the ground in a pool of blood that seeped into the earth. She sniffed his feet, springing back cautiously, then sniffed again, continuing toward the source of the blood. There were two wounds, now thick with dark, coagulated crimson. The panther's mouth watered as she began to slowly lick the sticky mass from the human's body.

*   *   *   *   *

Sue Ki ran, trying to keep up with Terrance. The trail was steeper and longer than he remembered and it seemed as though it was taking them forever to reach the top. The Pegasus returned to the cove after days of not being able to find the warship at sea. Both, Sue Ki and Terrance had sensed that something was terribly wrong and had wanted to return to Gavin and Jillian as quickly as possible. The winds were not in their favor and the trip took much longer than they expected. Carrying no lantern made the climb to the falls even more treacherous, but because of the circumstances, Terrance felt that he couldn't take any chances by carrying light that could be seen from the ocean. At last, they were at the top of the rise and heading for the clearing. Terrance slowed in front of Ki, silencing his question by putting his finger to his lips.

"I don't want to startle them by storming in, only to find that our alarm is for not," he told Ki, and then walked slowly toward the clearing.

The cat licked the wounds clean and sniffed the fresh blood that ran from one of the holes in the human's chest. She didn't hear the approach of the others until one of them ran toward her in the darkness, waving his arms and screaming at the top of his lungs. She was frightened and wasn't going to stay around to find out what this apparition wanted. In an instant, the lioness was gone from the clearing, leaving behind, for good, the crazy humans and her dinner.

Terrance followed Sue Ki into the clearing, feeling relieved that the big cat had fled. He found a lamp on one of the crates and quickly lit it, looking to Ki who leaned over the body. His heart sank and his legs felt weak, but he made his way to where Sue Ki rocked back and forth, singing something in his native tongue. Holding the lantern high, Terrance saw that it was Gavin.

Crying out, Terrance sank to his knees beside Gavin's lifeless body. He called to him but Gavin was gone. His face, so pale in the lantern light, looked serene, at peace, and Terrance knew that he had found his way beyond this world. Beside Gavin's lifeless body lay the locket Terrance had given him not so long ago. Terrance held it to his lips.

Terrance wept at Gavin's side, remembering the young boy whom he'd rescued from an abusive father. Terrance thought back to the day when he and some of the crew had ridden so swiftly down the narrow London streets and seen the small lad come flying out of a doorway and onto the cobbled road, directly in front of their horses, that reared and almost trampled the boy beneath their hooves. From a cottage lumbered a fat, filthy man. He jerked the boy up then slammed his fist into the youngster's jaw. Before he could hit the child again, Terrance was off his mount and on the man, hitting him squarely in the chin. The man tumbled back, sprawling on the ground like a lump of blubber. The boy watched as the huge red-headed man laid his father out with one quick punch. He clenched his teeth waiting for his father to get up and give the man the same but his father never moved. Terrance came toward him and the boy backed away shielding his head with his arms to protect himself from another blow. Terrance cringed, seeing the boy's fear so clearly. He was in a pitiful state, his mouth bruised, his eye blackened, blood from a cut under his chin, down his neck and onto his filthy and torn shirt.

"I won't hurt you" Terrance told him. "What is your name, son?"

The boy looked up at Terrance. In his eyes, Terrance could see hope. Terrance held out his hand to the child, helping him to his feet. One of the crew picked up a bucket from near the open door and threw the contents over the boy's father, waking him.

"What, what's going on here?" he spat. "Why'd yea go and hit me for?"

"You were about to strike this poor child a second time."

"Aye. His ma and sister ran off just this last night. I was just teaching this mouthy imp a lesson."

"That, I can see, but you won't do it again, will you?" Terrance threatened.

"Now, can't say that I won't. The boy is as snippy as a young pup. He needs a good lesson now and then."

"But you won't hit him again, will you?"

"Well that'll just depend now, won't it?" the man said thoughtfully. "As long as I'm the one paying for the brat's food, he'll get what's coming," he said, pulling his hulk from the road.

"Maybe you won't be the one paying."

"You mean you want to keep him?"

The man's eyes lit up when Terrance pulled out a money pouch. "How much will it take not to strike the boy again?" he asked. "Never again. How much?"

The man weighed his son's worth and the wealth of this stranger. "One hundred pounds."

"Is that all? One hundred pounds will make you stop hitting him?"

"Aye, unless you want to give me more, of course."

"Of course," Terrance said, handing the money to the boy. "If your father hits you again, you are to use this money to get as far away from him as you can. Do you understand, son?"

The boy didn't say anything, just nodded and took the money. Terrance turned back to the man, giving him a final warning. "Don't hit him again, you hear? This should be enough to buy you a good meal and clean you up."

He handed the man another pouch of coins, then gathered the reins and mounted his horse. The boy looked up at Terrance high on the gelding. He looked like a god up there, so strong and sure. Terrance gave the lad a smile, then turned his mount back down the cobbled road, heading for the ship that was waiting for them.

Not far down the street, Terrance glanced back just in time to see the man slam his fist into the boy's stomach, sending him flying along with the coins that Terrance had just given him. Anger flared in Terrance as he turned his horse, spurring him into a gallop toward the man. The man was so busy picking up the coins that he didn't even glance up when Terrance stopped his horse just short of the youth who lay unconscious in the street.

Terrance checked the lad over, making sure that he caught his breath. He patted the boy's cheek and smoothed back the blond curls that waved wildly around his face. His eyes slowly opened and Terrance could tell by his expression that the boy was glad that he had returned.

"How old are you, boy?" Terrance asked.

"Almost thirteen years, sir," the boy answered, wincing.

"Have you ever been on a ship?" Terrance asked. The boy shook his head no. "Would you like to come on my ship with me?"

The boy's eyes lit with excitement. Terrance didn't wait to hear his answer but helped him up and led him to his horse. They passed the boy's father, still crouched, picking up the coins scattered on the street. Once he was on the horse, Terrance held out his hand to the boy, who gladly took it, coming up behind the huge man.

"My name's Gavin," he said from behind Terrance. "Just Gavin." He turned, watching his father. "Just Gavin," he said again, holding onto Terrance tightly. Terrance patted the small hands that clung around his stomach and then turned the horse back toward the dock and the Pegasus.

That same innocent lad now lay before Terrance and Sue Ki. His lifeless form glowed pale in the lamplight, making him look even younger than the first time Terrance had seen him.

A voice from behind brought Terrance out of his grief.

"So, my friend. We meet again."

Turning, Terrance saw that they were surrounded by at least twenty men from the warship, all with swords raised and pointing toward

Terrance's chest. There was no chance of escape for him or Sue Ki. The commander of the group was his former friend, William.

Hatred between the two men was thick in the air as silence held its own. They sized each other up, measuring the changes that time and hardship had taken on them both. Terrance observed little change in William, other than some weight gain and a softening of his body. It was obvious that William had lived an easy life compared to the one to which Terrance had been condemned.

William stood tall in an attempt to hold himself more upright than usual. Terrance still towered over William, both in stature and in honor. He knew that he would never be the man that Terrance was, then or now. He hadn't taken Terrance's place in the Admiral's mind or in Sybil's heart. No, things hadn't worked out as William would have wanted. Nevertheless, that didn't change the fact that he could now destroy Terrance. He was a fugitive and William had every right to take him prisoner or kill him on sight.

"Where's Jillian?" Terrance demanded, not acknowledging any of the men surrounding them. "What have you done with my daughter?"

Instantly, William remembered the girl that Jason had told him about on the Pegasus, the girl that Jason asked to have once the ship was taken. Jason had said her name was Jillian, but William had no reason to believe they were one and the same. Now he made the connection, reveled in the fact, and finally understood why Jason had escaped. He wanted to have the girl, and this girl was Jillian, Terrance's bastard, and his daughter!

William felt like laughing. This was all too good to be true. He knew that Jason had Jillian, but Terrance did not. Terrance thought that William had killed this man and had taken Jillian away. It was all too perfect.

"It does not matter where Jillian is now, does it?" William said, coming toward Terrance. "What matters is that she led us right to you and now you are mine. This time, you will not escape. This time you will suffer as no man has ever suffered. Jillian hates you. Didn't you know? She never wants to see you again."

"It's not true!" Terrance yelled. "She doesn't hate me! I am her father. I love her."

"Jillian had you all fooled. She always was a gifted liar. She said that you killed her lover that you made her come with you against her will, and that you subjected her to humiliation at the hands of this man," he said, pointing to Gavin's body.

"This man is her husband and my son," Terrance gulped. "Gavin loved her beyond all else in life. He would never harm her. She knows that."

"Is that why she told us where you were, because she loved you?" William smiled, thinking how easily he read Terrance. "Why did you kill her husband? Is it because you wanted to have her just as much as he did?"

"You lie!" Terrance shouted, lunging toward William.

William was caught off guard. Terrance clutched William's neck between his hands with all his strength, wanting nothing more than to squeeze the very life from him and stop his lies forever. Before he could accomplish his goal, William's men were upon him, trying to pull him away from William, but they were no match for the strength of Terrance's hatred. They couldn't release William from his grasp. Suddenly the hilt of a sword came down on Terrance's head, sending him into darkness. He fell forward, on top of William who gasped beneath him.

"Get him off me. Get him off me!" William ordered.

The men hurried to remove Terrance from William and help the wheezing man to his feet. Clutching his neck, William sucked air back into his lungs, coughing and sputtering as it burned its way down his swollen throat.

"He tried to kill me. You all saw him," William said. "The man's deranged."

"Sir, who is the girl, Jillian?" his first officer asked. "Should we go and look for her? After all, the fiend is on the loose."

"Nay. We have no time. We have a much more valuable prisoner now," he said, straightening. "This man is a pirate and a traitor. We'll gain much by bringing him in."

Remembering the oriental man who had been by Terrance's side. William turned to where the body lay. The little man was gone and so was the body of Terrance's son. He quickly scanned the clearing, seeing no trace of either.

"Where is the oriental? Where is the dead man?" he asked.

The first mate and the rest of the men, who had been distracted by the scuffle between Terrance and William, quickly searched the immediate area, finding nothing. They were ready to fan out and search further, but

William stopped them, giving orders for them to carry Terrance back to the ship. The oriental man and the dead body were of no concern to William. He had what he wanted and that was Terrance, the pirate that he had pursued for so long, the Captain of the Pegasus.

Never in her life had Jillian been in so much pain. It took every ounce of strength she had just to put one foot in front of the other. Her feet and legs bled from cuts made by sharp stones and thorny branches. She had lost track of time and didn't know how long they had been walking, or how far they had traveled from Gavin. Gavin, her beautiful Gavin, was dead; murdered by the horrible man that led her to a fate filled with pain.

The sun rose hours ago, bringing with it the stark reality of her situation. She gasped from behind the rag, still stuffed in her mouth, when she noticed the front of her shirt. It was covered with Gavin's blood, with Gavin's life. It stained her skin beneath, as if to brand her with the knowledge that he was gone. She sobbed with the realization. Her mind fought to keep some portion of reality with her, for it was easier for her to slip into that darkened place, a place where things didn't reach her, a place where pain couldn't touch her soul.

They trudged on through the thick woods, stopping for only short periods. Jason rested during this time, for he knew that Jillian wouldn't last much longer and that he would have to carry her if they were going to put enough ground between them and the cove today. She looked as though she was ready to drop at any minute, but each time he tugged on the rope, Jillian pressed forward. He had to admire her for this. She had more strength than he had given her credit. But that strength would die soon enough; he would make certain of it.

By the time night fell, Jason was indeed carrying Jillian slung over his shoulder. She had collapsed unconscious only moments ago and he couldn't bother to beat her for it again. She had tried to keep up with him for the last few hours, but her body gave out long before her spirit. He smiled, thinking of the way she tried to fight him when he put her over his shoulder. Even in her half conscious state, Jillian was not ready to willingly submit to Jason's touch. He liked that.

He pressed on for as long as he could, finally giving in to his own body's cry for rest, then lowered Jillian to the ground, laying her carefully on her side. Seeing that she was still unconscious, Jason left to hide their trail. He figured they had put miles between them and the cove, but wasn't going to take the chance of William and his henchmen catching up to them. No he had to hide the trail, then make camp and plan his next move.

Jillian lay there in the dark for quite some time before she was sure that Jason wasn't coming right back to her. She didn't know where he'd gone but she wasn't going to stay around to find out. The rag in her mouth, moistened by her own spit, gagged her with its pungent taste. There was no time to rid herself of it, for the handkerchief was still tied very securely. It oozed filth into her mouth and Jillian fought to keep her stomach from emptying, for fear that she would choke to death if she were to vomit with the gag in place. She had to get out of here and away from Jason.

She struggled to her feet using a tree to wedge herself against. It scraped and cut her skin but she didn't care. She had to walk even though her feet ached with pain from the deep cuts on them. Wincing as the pain shot up her legs, Jillian closed her eyes and fought against it as she stumbled away. She walked, and then ran, once she got the pain under control. She forced her mind to block the pain and willed her whole body to feel completely numb. She took advantage of this relief, pressing herself to quickly get away from Jason.

It seemed that she'd gone a long way when she heard the laughing. Evil echoed through the forest like the wail of a ghost come to haunt an ancient castle. Chills crept up Jillian's spine when she realized that he hunted her. He was after her; she was hunted by a beast who only wanted to play with its prey. It was a game to him and she was his toy to torture and humiliate. But he would have to find her first.

She ducked into some bushes that, even in the darkness, she could tell were thick enough to hide her. The branches scratched her face and legs as she crawled on her knees deeper into them. When she could go no further, Jillian sat down, curling into a ball, making herself as small as possible, hoping to become so small that she could disappear. She waited, listening for Jason's approach, listening for the evil laugh, listening to the pounding of her heart and wondering if he could hear it too. A twig snapped somewhere behind her and she held her breath, becoming stone still within the thicket.

"Do you think it is that easy to escape me, Jillian? Do you think you can ever escape me?" She wanted to scream, to run, to flee him, but terror held her where she was. Maybe he didn't see her. Maybe, he would leave to look elsewhere and she could get away. "I can smell your fear, Jillian," his voice whispered, closer. "Did you know that I crave that fear? It makes the game so much more enjoyable, don't you think?"

Suddenly, Jillian was dragged from the bushes by her hair. Kicking and screaming, she fought him with all her might. He forced her back to the ground coming over top of her, pinning her beneath him. "Aye, she is a feisty one now, isn't she? How long will the little bugger fight? Aye."

With that he pinched Jillian's nose, blocking off what air she was able to gasp. For a few seconds, Jillian held her breath, not wanting to give him the satisfaction of seeing her panic but then, she needed air. He didn't let go of her nose. She didn't panic or fight. She just looked him straight in the eye as she blacked out.

"I'll be," Jason said, bringing himself off her. "She has more spirit than I thought."

*   *   *   *   *

Terrance's head ached. He had to relieve himself. He was hungry. Still, no one had come to untie his hands so that he could take care of his needs. Was this how it was all going to end, him being stuck again in the hull of a ship, taken prisoner by the same foe who had destroyed his life before? Even if he were to get free, his life was ruined. Gavin was dead, the Pegasus was captured, and Jillian hated him.

"What could possibly be worse than living life knowing that you had destroyed everyone for nothing more than a bit of revenge?" he asked himself out loud.

"Yes, what could possibly be worse?" William agreed from the doorway. "Talking to yourself now, aye?" He moved further into the room, but stopped a safe distance from Terrance. "I've spoke to Jillian and she told me that you forced her to marry that scoundrel, Gavin. Then you left her with him to fend for herself at his hands."

"That's a lie and you know it. Just let me talk to Jillian and we'll get this all straightened out," Terrance pleaded. "I don't know why she is saying all this, but I'll wager that she isn't doing it of her own accord."

"She doesn't want to see you or talk to you. You only remind her of the horrible things that happened to her while you held her prisoner." William sat down, making himself comfortable. "My question is, why did you kill the lad who you claim to love as a son?"

"I told you before, I didn't kill him. We found him in the clearing. He was already dead." Choking with the memory of Gavin's still form, he murmured, "You can ask Sue Ki, the oriental with me."

"Aye, the dragon man. He's of no help," William smiled. "He won't tell us anything. Just keeps babbling in that tongue of his. Can't understand a word he says." Terrance pondered why Sue Ki wouldn't speak English to William or his men. Ki knew the language; why wouldn't he talk to them and tell them what happened? "No matter. If you didn't kill the man, Jillian did." Terrance's head snapped up. "It would be one neat little package, having you and her rot in prison for the rest of your lives."

"No, you can't do that, William. Please, let me talk to her," Terrance pleaded. "If only for a moment. Let me find out what happened to Gavin."

William knew he had Terrance where he wanted him. All he had to do was give him the final hook and he would confess to anything that William wanted. It had all worked out so nicely. Terrance believed that Jillian had betrayed him. He believed that the warship had captured the Pegasus once the crew knew they had their Captain. He believed it all. Now he was going to pay for the rest of his life.

"Let's compromise, Terrance. You know that I have your ship, and that all on board will be executed once we reach London." He waited, letting his words sink in. "You know, that Jillian despises you and what you did to her so much that she killed the man you forced her to marry. And finally, you know that you will be hanged as a traitor, regardless of whether Jillian is the one who killed the man or not. Therefore, if you will confess to the killing of this man, relieving Jillian of the guilt, confess to kidnapping her and forcing her to marry against her will, then I will set the Pegasus and your men free."

"You can't be serious."

"I give you this opportunity in all seriousness," William reassured. "I will release your ship and all on board if you will confess to these crimes. Why not save Jillian from the torture of having to testify to the fact that she was the one who ran a man through because of what you did to her? It will be hard on her. I'll make certain of it."

"I'm sure you will," Terrance said in disgust. "Whatever made you hate me so much? Even back then you detested me. You were supposed to be my friend, William. What did I do to deserve such hatred?"

"Sybil loved you!" William yelled. "Even before she met you, she loved you. It was Admiral Chandler. He put fantasies into her head about you. Then, when she saw you that first time, she fell for you. I couldn't compete with that. I couldn't compete with a legend. I loved her more than life itself, but I couldn't compete with you."

Terrance watched William crumble. He truly believed that Terrance was to blame for the love that Sybil felt for him. All of this had happened because William couldn't accept that Sybil loved Terrance. He'd taken his revenge on Terrance and reaped the rewards of that revenge—emptiness. Terrance couldn't conceal the fact that if it were not for William, he may have had a happy life with Sybil and Jillian. They could have had a normal existence. All this was lost to him because of the greed and jealousy of someone he used to call friend.

"No, you could never have competed with me William, because you are weak and hateful. You are as spineless as they come, taking advantage of your friend's love to gain your station in life. And what has it gotten you, but grief? For you and everyone you have touched. Especially Jillian. The things you did to her while she was growing up are beyond words. Sybil could never love you the way that she loves me because our love is true. Truer than anything that you could ever imagine. She is all that kept me alive through the years. The thought of having her, of seeing her again kept me from death. When I found out that there was a child, a girl, I vowed to take her and Sybil away and start a new life for the three of us. But Sybil wouldn't come because she has more honor than both of us."

There was silence in the cramped little room. Terrance waited for William to take in all that he had said before continuing.

"I confess." William raised his head, questioning Terrance's words. "Yes, you heard me. I confess to kidnapping Jillian and forcing her to marry Gavin, if that is what you want. I confess to killing him, if it will keep Jillian out of prison and take away some of the pain that I have caused her. I confess."

*　　*　　*　　*　　*

Waves lapped against the safe rock, lulling Jillian to sleep with their soothing, rhythmic sound. The sun was warm against her skin as she sat perched on top of the smooth surface. Back and forth she rocked in peaceful meditation, feeling safe, warm, and protected. She moved with the motion of the ocean's waves that splashed against the stone, their spray moistening her heated skin.

Jillian opened her eyes to the vast ocean, scanning the water for a ship sailing to an unknown destination. She saw one there, gliding on the horizon just like the gulls glide on invisible waves of air, high in the afternoon sky. The ship seemed to have wings that lifted her above the water and it soared over the surface of the sea.

Suddenly, that same ship took on a different shape, the hull taking on the shape of a horse, the sails becoming wings that carried it toward shore, toward Jillian. She stood on the rock, holding out her arms to the approaching entity, recognizing it, remembering it, The Pegasus, the winged horse, like the one on the pendant around her neck. It was coming for her, to take her away upon its strong wings.

Just as suddenly as the ship had come into view, the sky grew dark enveloping Jillian, surrounding her with dread and fear. The Pegasus came near but could not reach her before the blackness hid her within it. She heard the Pegasus bray, screaming a warning to her that echoed within her mind.

"Come back," she called. "Don't leave me, please. Come back." But the great horse didn't hear her words. It was too late. He was gone from sight.

Jillian woke when she felt a hand gently smooth the hair from the side of her face. The night was dark, making it hard for Jillian to see who it was that held her so gently. "Gavin?" Could it be him?

"There, there little one," he said. "You are safe."

A sudden chill ran through Jillian, making her whole body shudder. It wasn't Gavin who held her at all, it was Jason! How could she have mistaken his touch for the sweet caress of her beloved? She thought about the dream and the blackness that surrounded her, hiding her from the Pegasus and her rescue. The Pegasus, she thought, was now her only rescue with Gavin gone. They had to come for her. Her father wouldn't give up until she was safe with him again. Jillian prayed that her prayers would be answered and that her father would come for her soon. If only she could outwit Jason that long. If only she could stay alive.

It had been two days now since leaving the cove. Jillian's hopes for rescue were dimming with each passing mile. When she couldn't walk any longer, Jason had carried her. She fell, weak and unconscious more often now, the effects of dehydration taking their toll. Jason hadn't released the ropes that bound her hands behind her back or taken the gag from her mouth since binding her that night while she lay and watched Gavin's life drain from his tortured body. She was hungry and thirsty and exhausted from the long hours of walking that she had endured. He didn't stop, not even to let her take care of her needs and she knew that her body could not tolerate much more. Nevertheless, one consolation was that Jason also hadn't stopped their flight to take advantage of her. She wondered how much longer that would last.

"I see you are finally awake," he said. "There is a cabin, not far from here, that will do well for us to take shelter in for a time."

He said nothing more; lifting Jillian to her feet and then holding her steady while she strengthened her legs beneath her. They walked on in the dark before morning, making good time. Once the sun rose, Jason became more cautious, stopping now and then to listen to the sounds of the forest. Jillian heard nothing, but knew by his actions that they must be close to civilization. She prayed that they were. She prayed that someone, anyone would see them and come to her rescue.

It was mid afternoon when they came upon a cabin nestled serenely in a hidden canyon. She thought if circumstances were different, how this place would be peaceful and perfect. Jillian could hear the babble of a brook not far from where the cabin stood. Instinctively, she turned toward the sound, giving in to the thirst that drove her unsteady legs. Jason released the rope that bound her to him, letting her make her way to the water alone, while he investigated inside the cabin.

Jillian went quickly to the water, falling to her knees beside it. The coolness beckoned but Jillian quickly realized that she was helpless. Her hands were still bound and her mouth still stuffed with the rancid cloth now dried by the lack of her own saliva. She couldn't drink or soothe her parched throat. She was dependent upon the mercy of a merciless man whose cruelty was ever more apparent. Even in this, Jillian realized why he had let her approach the stream without him; he knew that she was helpless until he was ready to release her. Lying down beside the stream, Jillian stared hungrily at the water, its promise so far away.

The cabin was empty except for a bed of straw that lay scattered in one corner. On the same wall, a single pot was suspended over an empty fireplace, blackened by years of use. Jason knew that the cabin had been abandoned years ago; the occupants of the cottage had moved on and not returned to this secluded place. Jason was glad, for this place would do very well for what he had in mind.

Leaving the cabin, Jason made his way toward the stream and Jillian. He had no doubt that she would be there waiting for him to remove her bindings so that she could drink from the brook. She lay on the ground beside the stream with her back to him, her hands still bound. Jason noticed the blood on her wrists where the ropes had chafed her tender skin when she had tried to get free from them. The torn and filthy white shirt that she wore was pulled up around her hips, fully exposing her slender legs and rounded buttocks. Jason saw the swollen purple flesh of a bruise that covered the entire length of her leg, from hip to mid thigh. It must have happened during one of the many times she fell during their journey. After the fourth fall, Jason quit hitting her, feeling that she was no longer trying to delay him but struggling to keep up. His eyes wandered the length of her body, coming to rest on her feet. He cringed, seeing the deep, bloody gouges that crisscrossed their bottoms. They were swollen and festering and he wondered how she had been able to make it this far, knowing that she must be in terrible pain.

He felt regret at having been so hard on Jillian and even wondered why he hadn't just killed her as he had planned. But, Jason wanted revenge and Jillian was his means of getting it. With Gavin dead, Jason could do as he wished with Jillian. The thought brought him sudden need of her.

Tugging roughly on the ropes, Jason freed her hands, then released the handkerchief and removed the putrid rag from her mouth. She didn't move, couldn't move, for a moment. Weak from lack of nourishment and petrified by the fear that Jason brought with his closeness, Jillian lay unmoving, waiting for him to allow her to drink the cool water. Jason realized he had her then, had complete control over even her body's cry of thirst, complete control over her every need. This knowledge brought him great satisfaction. Yes, this would be sweet revenge indeed, he thought.

When he gave her permission to drink, Jillian did, taking in huge gulps of the liquid splendor that eased the burning of her parched throat and stomach. She splashed water on her face, bathing away the tears of grief that had gathered dust during their passage through the forest. Then, she drank more of the soothing liquid, filling the void in her stomach but not the void in her heart.

"That's enough, Jillian," Jason commanded. "You'll be sick if you drink too much."

However, Jillian was beyond hearing what Jason said, letting her thirst drive her hands again into the water for another swallow of its coolness. Grabbing her by the waist, Jason pulled her away from the stream. Kicking and screaming, Jillian fought him, but was no match for his strength. Before she realized it, Jason had again bound her hands, this time in front of her and was picking up the rag that he had taken from her mouth.

"No, please," she pleaded, her voice raspy from the dryness of the last few days. "Please, don't put that thing back in my mouth."

He paid no attention to her pleas, and digging his fingers between her clenched teeth, he stuffed the foul rag between them, bruising her pale cheeks. After securing the gag with his handkerchief, Jason led Jillian to a nearby tree, throwing the length of rope that bound her hands over a branch above their heads. He pulled the rope up tight, causing Jillian's arms to stretch painfully above her head.

"That will keep you while I hunt for food," he said, caressing her bruised hip. "And when I return, I'll taste more of what you have to offer before taking your life."

With that, Jason was gone. Jillian hung from the branch of a tree like an animal left to cure after the hunt like some trophy, a prize that he won in his quest for revenge against both, Terrance and Gavin. Nevertheless, the torture would soon end, she thought. Jason had said that he would return and take her life. It would be over and she could join Gavin in sweet death.

Jillian sensed his presence even before she saw him approach. She knew that he had returned to the cabin with some animal that he'd killed. He came to her, blood still fresh on his hands, smiling that same evil grin that he had after killing Gavin. Jillian closed her eyes to his approach, praying that it would all be over soon. She felt him appraise her with his eyes, his gaze searing its way over her length. He moved behind her, and her heart jumped when his hands rested on her hips.

"You are a fine woman, Jillian. Do you know that?" he asked, bringing his hands up under her shirt to cup her breasts softly. Jillian sucked in her breath, waiting for his next move, astounded by the gentleness that he displayed. "I have wanted you since the first moment I saw you on the beach. The wisps of hair around your sweet face, your skirt tucked up so provocatively at your waist." His hands moved downward, pulling her back against him. "I couldn't let the Captain or Gavin have you. You were destined to be mine and now you are."

Jason kissed her shoulder, hugging her firmly to him. Jillian waited, trying to anticipate his next move. She struggled to calm the pounding of her heart, all the while wondering from where this gentle side of Jason had come. Confusion overcame her, feeling the gentle hands that caressed her breasts. Could this be the same man who had slain Gavin so mercilessly? The one who had threatened his revenge upon her and her father?

"I want to hear you say it, Jillian. I want to hear that you love me," he told her, while untying the handkerchief. "I will spare your torture if I know that you love me."

Still dangling from the branch, Jason easily swung Jillian around to face him. His eyes searched for any sign that she would do as he bid and say that she loved him.

Jillian couldn't believe that Jason would ask such a thing from her. How could he possibly think that she held any feelings for him, other than hatred? He had murdered her beloved Gavin before her very eyes, even after she said that she would do anything to save his life. Now, he wanted her to declare her love for him? He was mad.

Gathering courage, Jillian spat in Jason's face. "You pig!" she screamed at him. Backing away in disbelief, Jason wiped her saliva from his cheek. "I'll never love you. I loathe you. I despise you. I hate everything that you are. You are evil beyond evilness. I would die before I would declare anything but hatred for you."

Rage filled Jason. Jillian made her feelings very clear, and for that, he vowed she would suffer. "If you will not speak the words that I want to hear, then I will hear no words from you at all." he threatened, coming toward her, the gag held in both hands.

Jillian kicked out at him, losing her balance, making her arms take all of her weight. She screamed with the pain that shot through them but kept kicking, fighting his advance. She held him off for only moments before he subdued her protests, stuffing the rag back into her mouth and securing it. He left her there to dangle while he retrieved the second length of rope that had bound her hands, holding it out for her to see.

"I'm going to teach you a lesson, Jillian," he said, slapping the rope against his thigh. "You will do as I bid or you will be taught to do so."

A spasm of pain engulfed every muscle in Jillian's body when the first lash from the rope touched her skin. Every ounce of her strength drained by the time she had counted the fifth stroke and she allowed her mind to take her from the pain. The blackness was a welcome relief from the whipping Jason inflicted upon her. His strokes were fierce and well placed, cutting the tender flesh of her back with ease. How long the punishment lasted, how many strokes Jillian's flesh had endured were lost to her, for she was safe within her mind, a place where even Jason was unable to touch her. A place that, so long ago, Sophie had taught her to hide from William. A safe place, away from pain and heartache and the tortures of despair.

The trial was short. Terrance didn't testify in his own defense, for the evidence and his signed confession was all the magistrate needed to determine his guilt. Neither Jillian nor Sybil came to the trial, his daughter being too distraught to attend, William had explained to the court. Then again, there wasn't any need for them to come, for Terrance's fate had been decided long before the trial took place. With haste, he was convicted of kidnapping and murder. Although Terrance pleaded for a quick death, the magistrate, in his twisted sense of punishment, sentenced him to spend the rest of his life in prison.

Finishing the last line on the parchment, Terrance signed his name at the bottom then set it aside so that the ink could dry before folding it. Thoughts of Gavin and Jillian and the love that they had shared during their brief time together on the Pegasus, brought memories of their happiness to mind. Terrance clung to the memories. It was hard to believe that all was lost in one brief instant.

Even now, it puzzled Terrance that Jillian could have turned on Gavin, inflicting a mortal wound. Terrance could think of no explanation for Gavin's loss. Who else was there besides Gavin and Jillian? Who else could have killed him? Terrance knew that he would never find the answers that would bring him some sense of peace. He and he alone bore the burden of Gavin's fate by taking that responsibility from Jillian with his confession. If it made up for the wrong done her, then he didn't regret having made that decision. He hoped that she had found peace and told her so in his letter to Sybil.

Now, if only he could convince Douglass, the guard, to deliver the letter to Sybil. They had befriended each other in the days since the trial. Terrance came to like Douglass very much and looked forward to hearing his steps approaching the cell. Douglass knew all there was to know about Terrance and the trial, as relayed to him by the guards who had transported Terrance to prison. Regardless, Douglass accepted Terrance for the man he had come to know, not the man they had told him he was. Terrance was grateful for this, for the guards beat him mercilessly during their travel to the prison and warned Douglass to continue the misuse if he knew what was good for him. Terrance knew William was behind his mistreatment but never protested or fought back, having no fight left in him.

He thought of Sue Ki, the little dragon man who had defended him against the pirates that fateful day; that day becoming his salvation from the clutches of the British prison that held him for so many long years. Where were Ki and the Pegasus crew? Had William truly released them? Terrance felt fairly sure that he had, for he was certain that if the ship was brought in the men would have been tried and convicted with him. He pictured the Pegasus sailing on the high seas far away from England and this prison, away from the danger of being captured.

He knew Sue Ki would take Gavin far out to sea for burial. It would have been what Gavin wanted, having loved the sea as he did. His heart ached, remembering raising Gavin from that scared thirteen year old boy into the handsome man who loved and married his only daughter. How much Terrance had hoped that the two of them would go on to love a lifetime.

The steady clop of Douglass's boots on the stone floor brought Terrance's thoughts back to the letter that he had written to Sybil. Carefully folding it in half, Terrance wrote her name on it. He took the pendant from its hiding place under the straw as he heard the key rattle in the door; the hinges squeaking as it slowly opened.

"How are you today, my friend?" Douglass greeted him, as he entered the cell carrying a wooden bowl filled with gruel, the steady diet within the prison.

"I've been better," Terrance answered, as the light from the corridor lit his cell more fully.

Setting the bowl near Terrance's feet, Douglass noticed the parchment. "I see that you have taken my counsel and have written to that woman you've been pining for."

"Aye, I've written telling her to forget me and asking for her forgiveness." Terrance stood, handing the letter to Douglass. "So you are willing to take this letter directly to Sybil for me?"

"Aye," Douglass smiled. "Won't do any good for me to tell yea to set her free if she never gets the letter now, will it?"

"You're a good man, Douglass McKibben, that you are. I thank you for this. I only wish that there was some way of repaying your kindness."

"No need, my friend. There is little I can do to ease the pain that many suffer within these walls. This is something I can do to ease yours, if only for a short time." He grinned sadly, taking the letter from Terrance, then turned to leave.

"A moment, Douglass, I want to give you something," Terrance said, taking off his boots. "I want you to have these. They won't do me any good wasting away in this prison. Please take them. They're all I have to give you."

Douglass took the boots gladly from Terrance. He'd admired them since the first day Terrance arrived at the prison. The boots had very few traces of wear on the slick, black leather. On each side, a silver Pegasus looked ready for flight, giving the boots a mysterious appeal. Douglass was speechless, knowing the sacrifice that Terrance was making. The prison was damp and cold; the prisoners having little to keep the chill from their bodies. Terrance would most likely catch his death with no boots to keep his feet from freezing. With that thought, knowing that Terrance wouldn't take no for an answer, Douglass removed his own worn boots and handed them to him.

"I wouldn't want you to catch your death on my account, friend."

"No, I wouldn't want my death on your conscious, Douglass" Terrance answered, taking the worn boots willingly from him.

"I'll be off then. It will take me two days to reach the village. I hope that all will be well while I am gone."

"What does it matter now? My life is in order. Once you deliver this message to Sybil, I can leave this world to meet my maker. Only then can I truly know the reasoning behind the death of my son."

"Don't speak of such things, Terrance. You and I have become close friends. I know that you have many questions still needing answers. I would be honored to be of help in finding those answers for you. Give me time. Give me a chance to help you."

"Aye, there are still some questions and all I have is time, my friend. I'm certain that I will live long enough for you to return," Terrance promised. "There is one other thing you must take with you." He handed his pendant to Douglass. "Give this to Sybil. Only when she receives this will she know the truth that is written in my letter."

Douglass took the pendant, tucking it safely in his pocket along with the letter that Terrance had written. He smiled, trying to reassure the prisoner of the letter's safety. Douglass knew the consequences of helping the men in this godforsaken prison.

*   *   *   *   *

Two days later, Douglass walked into the small, seaside village where Terrance told him Sybil lived. He stopped at the town's only tavern to ask for directions to her cottage. The tavern was crowded with patrons and it took awhile before Douglass was able to get the barmaid's attention. He ordered a tankard of ale, then asked the girl if she knew where Sybil's home was.

"Aye, that uppity up. Aye, we all know where her high and mighty lives," she answered loudly. "Me own hubby is up there. Goes up when hers ain't around. She pays him a pretty price for what he gives her. Better her than me, if you know what I mean, deary," she said, winking at him.

"Just tell me where she lives," Douglass said angrily.

The barmaid gave him directions, along with the tankard of ale for which she charged him double, stuffing the difference down between her breasts. What did he know anyway, he being new to the village? He wouldn't guess that she had taken him for double, with him none the wiser for it. Another feather in her cap she thought, serving ale to some rowdy men at the table next to the stranger's. Richard, her husband, would never know that she was hiding money from him and the tavern owner. Someday, she thought, I'll have me enough to leave this miserable place and Richard behind.

Meanwhile, at the cottage, Sybil leaned with all her might against the door, keeping Richard Dinkin outside her home. She hadn't thought to lock the door that afternoon after coming home from another day of staring out over the ocean. Sybil waited for a signal, any sign that Terrance and Jillian would return to her, but each day there was no sign and Sybil came back to her empty home alone. Richard Dinkin had become an unwelcome intruder into that emptiness, coming to "comfort" her he explained. Sybil grew weary of his intrusions but was unable to thwart his efforts. Despite the many times she had chased him off, he just kept coming back.

"Please Richard, go away. Go back to the tavern, to your wife," she pleaded.

"Ah, come now, Sybil. It's been months since your man was around" his voice slurred from the ale consumed earlier. "Bout time you had yourself a real man."

He shoved with all his might against the door, knocking Sybil forcefully to the floor. Half dazed by the fall, Sybil stared up at Richard in disbelief. She thought that he was about to leave when he suddenly shoved the door inward, catching her off guard and making her lose her balance. Before she could recover, Richard pinned her to the floor with his body. He held her arms above her head, bringing his mouth forcefully down, bruising her lips beneath his. Sybil struggled under him but was unable to budge his heavy bulk. Her struggles aroused Richard even more but Sybil would not concede. A voice from above them brought Richard's mouth away from hers.

"I don't believe the lady wants your attention, man," Douglass spoke firmly. "If I were you, I'd remove myself before someone did it for me."

"Is that a threat, stranger?" Richard asked, turning to see who it was that interrupted his fun.

Douglass towered over them, his blue eyes flashing and ready for a fight. From shoulder to shoulder the man took up the entire width of the doorway, making his very presence a threat. His jet black hair was shoulder length, the blackness continuing in the full beard that he sported. It covered his mouth and when he spoke again to the bewildered Richard, no movement could be seen making it look as though the voice came from out of nowhere. He was a frightening but welcome sight to Sybil.

"It's time for you to leave," Douglass commanded, hauling Richard off Sybil by the back of his britches.

Richard landed on his face on the walk outside the door of the cottage. Getting to his feet quickly, he didn't wait to see if the giant man was behind him, and scurried away from the cottage, like the weasel that he was, in the direction of the village and the tavern. Douglass watched him go, laughing at the plump man's antics.

Sybil dared not move from the floor where Richard had pinned her, feeling suddenly leery of this man. He had saved her from Richard's unwanted advances, but for what? Why was he here? What did he want with her? Sybil's eyes widened as he turned toward her, coming closer.

"Now there, wee lass," he said, holding out his hand to her. "Allow me to help you up." Sybil stared at his offered hand, then back to his face that softened with a smile, barely detectable beneath the massive beard. "I have not come to harm you. I bring a message from a man who pines for you night and day."

"And just who would this man be?" Sybil asked, still not taking his offered hand.

"Why Terrance McCarthy be his name, lass."

Douglass watched the woman's eyes roll as she fell backward onto the floor unconscious. "I'll be," he said, reaching down to gently lift the fragile lady from the floor. "If she be this weakened by the mere mention of his name, just imagine what her reaction will be when I tell her of his fate."

Sometime later, Sybil's eyes fluttered open, a moist cloth bringing her gradually awake. She flinched, seeing the giant man so near. Douglass ignored her movement, continuing to pass the wet cloth across her forehead until she could look at him without crossing her emerald green eyes. He could see how Terrance could love this woman, for she was beautiful.

"Who are you?" she asked, taking the cloth from his hand.

"My name is Douglass McKibben, milady," he answered, moving slowly away from her. "Can yea sit?"

"Yes, I'm fine," Sybil answered, refusing the help that he offered, and propping herself against the headboard of her bed where Douglass placed her. "Why did he send you instead of coming himself?"

"Aye, just as I thought. You have no knowledge of what has happened to Terrance and your daughter, Jillian, have you?"

"Nay, I haven't heard a word since the day that Terrance came for us both and I refused to go with him." Her face saddened, showing lines from hours of worry.

Douglass wondered if these lines had just recently appeared due to the time that she spoke of. Not knowing what had happened to her child, countless hours anticipating the arrival of some stranger who would bring her whole world crashing down on her, was sure to bring lines of worry. He regretted being the man who would do the deed, but knew that he was her only link to Terrance, the only one who could tell her both stories of the tragic end of the people she loved. However, one thing struck him. She said that she'd had no word of either Terrance or her daughter since seeing them that last day. How could this be? Jillian was supposed to be here with her mother, recuperating from the tragedy that had befallen her. Where was Jillian?

His suspicions were correct. Douglass had felt all along that Terrance had been duped and that Jillian had not betrayed him. Only now, he had proof that things were not as Terrance was told. Things were not as the magistrate was told. William had lied to the courts, making up much of his story in order to convict Terrance of a crime that he did not commit. The only hope Douglass had in finding the truth lay with Sybil and Jillian. Somehow, he had to bring the two of them back together for Terrance's sake.

Sybil listened to his words but her mind was numb. She couldn't believe the tale that he wove. She wouldn't believe it. If the things that he said were true, then Terrance was lost to her forever; imprisoned for the rest of his life for a crime that he didn't commit. If it all were true, then where was Jillian? Did she kill the man she married while on the Pegasus? Sybil found it all too hard to believe; her child would never hurt anyone. Jillian wasn't capable of acting out with enough hatred to take someone's life. At least, the Jillian she had known would not have been able to. Sybil remembered Jillian retreating to her dream world whenever something bad happened.

If Douglass spoke the truth, then William was behind the entire tragedy. William had betrayed Jillian and Terrance, destroying what happiness they may have found together. Sybil would never forgive William; he had gone too far.

Douglass finished what he had to say but wasn't sure if Sybil heard any of it. He handed her the letter that Terrance had written then left her alone to read it. He busied himself making some tea, finding the ingredients in Sybil's well-organized pantry, feeling sure that she would need some once she finished the letter.

After a time, the tea was ready. Douglass cautiously entered the bedroom to find Sybil curled into a ball, sobbing upon the bed. Out of instinct, Douglass cradled the sobbing woman in his arms. His own heart went out to her and Terrance because of the terrible injustice that befell them. If there was one thing that Douglass was sure of, it was that he would do everything in his power to help set things straight for his newly found friends.

"I don't know what to do," Sybil sobbed. "How can I help him? How can I get him back?"

"Are you willing to take risks for Terrance? Are you strong enough to give him the will to live?"

"Yes, I am strong enough," she answered. "But of what kind of risks are you speaking?"

"The kind that would mean saving Terrance's life," he said, pausing to shift her position so that she looked him in the eye before finishing, "or the loss of your own."

Sybil pushed away from Douglass, walking to her dressing table. She looked at her reflection in the mirror for quite some time before speaking. Who was she to think that she could do anything to help? Nevertheless, if ever there was a time to be strong, it was now. She searched the face staring back at her. Where was that daring young girl who rode so swiftly through the woods, the woman who stuck the point of a knife against the ribs of the man she was to marry? Where was the strength that had helped her endure losing her beloved Terrance? Was it there? All these years, William told her that she was weak and worthless. Now Sybil could see that it was how he controlled her strength. The threats to the children and herself were effective in making her forget how very strong she once was. The time had come to reclaim that person, for Terrance's sake and her own.

Sybil turned back to Douglass. "Do you have a plan?"

Douglass smiled, seeing the determination in Sybil's face. "Aye, I have a plan," he said, rising from the bed, "and we can start by taking your clothes off."

Beyond the darkness, Jillian heard the sound of voices speaking quietly somewhere close by. She felt the warmth of a soft bed beneath her aching body and knew that she must be dreaming. She thought of how long it had been since she had felt something so wonderful against her skin and realized that she couldn't remember much of anything that had happened to her in the past few weeks. She moved her hand over the surface of the linen sheet that she lay on, wincing at the pain that shot through her arm with the movement.

"Are yea awake, me deary?" a hoarse, yet feminine voice came from Jillian's side.

Too afraid to speak, Jillian lay stone still, not giving any indication that she heard. She kept her eyes closed and her breathing steady, although her heart leaped with the fear of discovery. For an instant, Jillian wondered why she should feel so frightened, then realized that this entire situation frightened her. Where was she and how did she get here?

Just then, another voice thundered into the room. Jillian shuddered. "Isn't that little whore awake yet? It's been three days," Jason bellowed from the doorway. "I can't make any money off her if all she does is sleep."

"Your wife is a very sick woman," the woman explained. "She needs some time to heal before the auction or you won't be making any money off her at all."

"She has four days, no more," he growled. "If she isn't fit by that time, I'll make use of her lying on her back. That's the way most men like it anyway."

"I'll have her up for yea, that is, if you'll just be leaving her alone long enough for her to heal," the woman said, dismissing Jason.

"Four days!" he grunted, leaving the room.

Jillian felt a gentle hand on her forehead. "Four days, indeed. It'll be a miracle if you survive at all after what that monster has put you through. I can't imagine the pain you must have endured at the hands of a man who could make these kinds of marks upon the delicate skin of such a beauty."

The blanket covering Jillian slowly lowered, making her realize that she was completely naked beneath it. She felt the color rising in her cheeks as the blanket slid down her legs coming to rest at the foot of the bed. She was on display for the entire world to see and her only defense was to cover herself with her hands, for all the good that would do. However, the movement of doing so brought so much pain that Jillian's arms dropped helplessly to her sides. Tears slipped from the corners of her closed eyes upon realizing how vulnerable she was.

"Just as I thought, me deary, you are awake," the woman whispered close to Jillian's ear. "But don't you be worrying,. He'll not be coming around you again. I've made sure of it."

A soft cloth dabbed the tears from Jillian's eyes with gentle precision and then the woman began to bathe her with soothing strokes. Jillian slowly opened her eyes. The woman smiled at her, showing several teeth missing, yet it was still a warm and friendly smile. Jillian was glad to see a kind face.

"How's me girl, this fine morning?" she asked. "Me name's Cora." Jillian tried to speak but only made a hissing sound. She closed her eyes and tried again but the same thing happened; no sound came from Jillian's throat. With frustration, Jillian clenched her fists tightly at her sides.

"Don't let it worry you none, dear. My very own grandmother lost her voice one night after fighting with me grandfather. Never did come back until after the old geezer died. I suppose it was once she was happy again."

Happy, Jillian thought. Was I ever happy or not frightened? I cannot remember. Jillian realized that she could not even remember her name or the names of anyone that she might know. Frantically, she looked around the room for something she might recognize, but found nothing the least bit familiar.

"Are yea wondering who it was that I be talking to?" Cora asked. "Well, I find that talking to meself is lots more satisfying than talking to most the people in these whereabouts. Most of them don't have a brain in their heads. No sense in wasting my time on the ungifted. But you, me dear, now you are a different sort," she said, finishing the bath and pulling the blanket back over Jillian. "I can see that you do have a brain in your head even if you don't have the voice to go along with it."

Cora put the cloth in the basin of water and cleared away several other rags that lay beside it. Before she took them away, Jillian saw that they were covered in blood and realized that it must have been her own. She tried to move her aching body, but again the pain it caused made her gasp and lay still.

"I'll bring you something for the pain as soon as you drink a little brew," Cora said, sitting Jillian up, and gently supporting her back with strong arms. "You'll be needing all your strength for the days to come."

The salty broth went down her throat with ease. Jillian's stomach growled even though she drank a good portion of the mug. It must have been some time since she had eaten, Jillian thought. Again, she realized that she couldn't remember anything beyond waking up in this room. Cora eased her back down to the bed, then promised to return with something for the pain. Jillian smiled with gratitude, hoping that Cora saw sincerity in her smile.

With great difficulty, Jillian raised her hands from beneath the blankets, wincing in pain but fighting it to be able to see the damage she could feel around her wrists. It was worse than she thought. The pain she felt came from open wounds that encircled her wrists, which could only have come from one source—ropes. Someone had bound her.

Cora hurried into the room. "Aye, I see that you do have some strength left." Jillian let her arms drop. "It ain't the half of it, you know? The rest of you looks the same or worse. You will need this for a few days. It'll make you sleep but that will be best," she said raising Jillian so she could drink. "It's laudanum, me dear. It'll help you rest while your body heals."

Jillian drank the foul liquid, grimacing as she swallowed it. Cora lowered her to the bed then corked the brown bottle and put it between the mattress and the blankets of Jillian's bed.

"I have to hide it from the cook, me dear. He has a liking for the stuff." Cora rose from the bed. "Now don't you worry your pretty little head, I'll protect you from that husband of yours until you're fit," she reassured Jillian, then left the room.

Husband, Jillian thought, I don't remember being married to anyone.

It wasn't long before the laudanum took hold and Jillian drifted to sleep, still trying to remember a life forgotten and a husband she didn't know.

For three days, Jillian drifted in and out of consciousness, the laudanum keeping the pain at bay while her body healed. When she was lucid, Cora told her all about herself and her "good for nothing" husband. It cheered Jillian up to hear the tales that the woman wove, but as soon as Cora left the room, Jillian became frightened; each sound from somewhere below brought fear and dread to Jillian. She realized that she must be above a tavern or joy house because every night, rowdy voices bellowed from beneath her. Sometimes there were fights and sometimes the patrons would sing cheerfully in deep baritone voices.

Today was the fourth day. Jillian awoke early. Cora had cut the portion of laudanum the night before, explaining to Jillian that she would need to be herself tomorrow. Indeed, Jillian did feel better.

Through the window, Jillian could see the sun breaking the horizon. She sat up slowly testing her muscles for strength, fighting the ache that the movement brought. The sunrise was inviting and Jillian was determined to view it to its fullest. Cautiously, she swung her legs off the edge of the bed, resting her feet on the floor. The blankets slipped from her body and Jillian gasped at seeing the scars on her skin. Suddenly, her head spun and she was forced to lie back on the bed in order not to lose her balance and fall to the floor.

"Well, me dear. You're awake bright and early," Cora said from the doorway. "It's all for the best now mind you," she said, entering the room holding a tray of steaming food. "We've only got one day to get you ready. The auction is tonight."

Cora turned away guiltily. She had bathed and nurtured this poor young girl for the past seven days and she knew the girl still needed more. However, her husband was impatient to get rid of her. His only care was that he could make a profit off her at the sale tonight. Cora had kept him away from her for the past several days, claiming that she wasn't up to fulfilling her wifely duties, and if he wanted to get a return from her, he would have to allow her to heal. One of the barmaids helped out by serving him ale laced with laudanum, which kept him away for most of the day and docile during the night before he passed out. This man was dangerous. Cora could tell by the threats that he had made when bringing his wife in. She was thankful that the girl hadn't died but was fearful for her fate. But Cora felt that being sold at an auction to any man would be better than living with a monster like Jillian's husband.

Cora fed Jillian a hearty breakfast of eggs and biscuits and loads of gravy left over from the hams that had been served in the tavern the night before. The innkeeper wouldn't spare any of the ham for Jillian, saying that he had put out enough on such a wisp of a girl. Cora knew that he would be well paid for his effort by the night's end, for he would receive a portion of her price in payment for her stay at the tavern.

After breakfast, Cora had a tub and plenty of hot water brought up from the kitchen so that Jillian could take a long, soothing bath. The trek across the room made her head spin and muscles burn. With help from Cora, Jillian lowered into the wonderful warm water. For one brief instant, Jillian thought about another tub. Flashes of black flitted in her mind but just as quickly vanished. The image puzzled Jillian.

"Now, don't be telling me that you never had a bath before, me dear," Cora said, seeing the puzzled look on Jillian's face. "Or maybe it's just been a while?"

Without further comment, Cora went to work scrubbing Jillian with gentle hands. She washed her hair, using one of the buckets to dump water over Jillian's head to rinse it. Jillian puffed as the water flowed over her face, spraying Cora. They smiled and laughed, having a glorious time, and for the first time since awakening, Jillian felt happy.

Once the bath was finished, Cora dressed Jillian in a sheer chemise. Jillian's eyes questioned the revealing garment. "It will bring the price up, me dear," Cora told her turning away from Jillian's questioning eyes.

The girl didn't know what was to befall her with the coming of night and maybe it was better that way. She left Jillian after tucking her back into bed. Cora wouldn't be able to come up again until it was time to fetch the girl for the auction. It would take all day to help the cook and barmaid prepare for the feast that would lure the wealthy buyers in. Cora had seen this many times before, but never was there a child so beautiful brought in for such a common sale. Still, Cora's heart was gladdened by the fact that once the sale was complete, the girl's marriage was over. One of the provisions of the contract of sale meant that she would be free of the monster who had brought her to the auction.

* * * * *

The carriage slowed to a stop in front of an old inn on the outskirts of Cambridge. Marcus Eyre stretched his long legs, using the seat opposite him as a footstool. The trip to Ely had been laboriously long and uneventful. Other than his cousin Ada's marriage to a fine nobleman from Westchester there was little about the journey that pleased him. The wedding was a fine undertaking, lifting a burden from Marcus's shoulders that he thought he would never be rid of.

Marcus was Lord of Havenwood Manor, an estate held by his family for generations. Ada Upham was a distant cousin who, at a very young age, had lost her parents and was entrusted to the Eyre family to raise. Upon the death of his own parents, Marcus assumed the responsibility of the young girl. He had watched her grow into an unnaturally tall and big-boned girl by the time she was of a marriageable age. Marcus thought that he would never find a man suitable for the girl. But Jonathan Thompson had arrived one day at Havenwood and Ada had fallen head over heels for the gangly young Lord. To Marcus's amazement, Jonathan was just as infatuated with her and soon asked Ada to marry him. He was the younger son of a Duke and he assured Marcus that, although he wasn't destined to inherit his father's fortune, he would be well provided for upon his father's death.

This knowledge wasn't the factor that Marcus needed to consent to Ada's marriage; it was the look in her eyes whenever Jonathan was near that made him give the union his blessing. He remembered well the pleasure of having someone to love, although, it had been a very long time since Marcus had experienced those kinds of feelings himself. He was pleased for his young cousin, knowing that he wouldn't have to worry about her happiness now that she was married.

He stretched his legs once more while waiting for Henry, Havenwood's footman, to secure the carriage. Even more than that, Henry was a valued friend and confidante of the Eyre family. Henry had been with his family since Marcus was a child and had been like a father to him throughout his life. Wherever Marcus went, Henry went. So it was that they were together in Ely to witness Ada's marriage.

Marcus thought to himself how glad he was that Henry was there as his companion instead of Isabel who had once again refused to leave the estate. For more than ten years, his only sister had chosen to remain firmly grounded to Havenwood, refusing any and all invitations from the outside world. Over the years, Marcus became glad of it, for Isabel was a shrew of the worst kind to anyone who came to Havenwood for a visit. Even the servants at the estate avoided her whenever possible; for no one knew when her fits of temper would flare and an awful scene would occur.

His thoughts were interrupted by a rather loud, rowdy bunch of men who passed the carriage on their way inside the inn. The smoke-filled tavern came into view before the door slammed shut. Marcus sighed, thinking of how he disliked crowds of drunken men, but also remembering that he hadn't eaten anything since the night before at the wedding feast. His stomach growled, reminding him of the fact as he stepped out of the carriage.

"You go on in and find a suitable table, my Lord," Henry said formally, trying to once again become the hired footman and not the friend and companion to Marcus.

Thinking that Henry could never pass for one of those formal butler types; Marcus did as Henry bid and entered the tavern smiling to himself at his friend's determination to keep his station in front of others.

Marcus was astonished at the number of men the tavern held. He had to push his way through them in order to find a place at one of the tables near the entrance to what must have been the kitchen. It was the last available place to sit and Marcus soon realized why. A plump little woman rushed through the swinging door just as Marcus was seating himself, holding a tray of soup bowls above her head. Cursing at the top of her lungs, she spun away from him just in time to catch herself from dumping hot soup on his head. The men in the immediate area laughed and jeered at her antics. She returned their comments with a few choice words of her own and they hushed rather than receive her wrath. Marcus watched her skillfully move through the tavern, delivering the meals without spilling a drop. He assumed that she had been doing this for quite some time and was used to the boisterous patrons.

The main door of the tavern opened and Henry stepped into view. Marcus stood, getting his attention as Henry came closer, and catching the eye of the woman who now emptied her tray. Marcus seated himself once more, watching as Henry moved through the crowd and arrived at the table at about the same time as the woman.

"Are yea here for the sale, my lord?" she asked.

"Sale? No, certainly not," Marcus answered, knowing nothing about what she had asked. "We are only here to have a hot meal."

"Oh," she said, surprised. "'Tis a shame, it is. She is a fine one."

Again, Marcus had no idea what the woman was talking about. He impatiently ordered their food and drink and dismissed the woman with no further thought to what she had said. Cora shook her head, feeling saddened by his response. Surely, he would make a fine master for the girl. She could tell that he had the riches to buy her. In his eyes a kindness shone through even when he became irritated by her questions and tried to dismiss her. He doesn't quite have it in him to be mean, she thought. Yes, he would be kind to the girl. Cora wondered how she could detain him long enough so that he would be present for the sale. It was half past ten now and the auction wasn't to start until midnight. Just maybe, he could be kept here for that long.

The night dragged slowly on, the men became increasingly drunk and loud. The smoke from their pipes hung thickly in the air until Marcus could not see clearly across the tavern. His head ached from the lack of fresh air and his patience wore thinner by the minute. The woman who brought their drinks seemed to be purposely avoiding their table and the kitchen, where Marcus knew their food waited, getting cold. Finally, Marcus caught the woman's eye, giving her a look that let her know that his patience was thinning.

Cora plopped a dish down in front of Marcus, chastising herself for not being more creative in keeping the man here longer. She scanned the tavern for the girl's husband, who had spent the better part of the night at the bar, boasting of the "talents" the girl had for pleasing a man in bed. Cora knew that he was lying in order to get the girl's value up, which only made her feel more uncomfortable when she couldn't locate him among the patrons. It was after eleven o'clock, and less than an hour before the auction.

Marcus and Henry finished the meal of ham and boiled red potatoes. It was a surprisingly tasty meal served at such a meager tavern, Marcus thought. He laid coin on the table, not willing to wait again for the woman serving them. The meal was fine but the service was the poorest that Marcus had ever seen. He was anxious to be away from the rowdy crowd that grew louder by the moment. They made their way toward the main door, but stopped short when silence fell upon the tavern and all eyes raised to the top of the stairway.

The smoke seemed to part so that the object of the men's gaze appeared as if straight out of the heavens. Standing with her hands braced on the railing directly above Marcus and Henry's heads, her eyes wild with indecision, her chest heaving from exertion or excitement Marcus could only guess which, was the most exquisite sight Marcus had ever seen. Her hair, the color of spun gold with streaks of copper beneath, curled wildly around her face and shoulders, cascading the length of her body, right down to her knees. She wore nothing but a revealing chemise that left nothing to the imagination. Marcus felt his body immediately respond to the sight of her.

When his eyes met hers, Marcus felt a pang of guilt for having such a response, for in her eyes he saw how terrified she was. Her eyes softened pleadingly when she looked at him, telling him that she was in danger and that she needed his help, not his lust. Her deep amber eyes reminded him of a doe, one who was frightened by the hunt and prepared for flight from the hunter.

After a moment, her composure began to waver. The crowd, sensing her panic, began to shout lewd jeers at the girl, frightening her even more. She lifted her hand toward them, toward Marcus, as if to plead for assistance then dropped it to her side as if in defeat. Although the throng of men shouting at her to show them her wares hindered Marcus, he slowly eased toward the staircase.

Suddenly, from one of the rooms above, a man roared a command for the girl to stop. She spun around just as the man was upon her. His face was covered with blood from a deep gash across his forehead. The girl gasped as the man seized her by the shoulders, holding her in place.

"I'll teach you!" he yelled, striking the girl across the face so hard that she spun and fell to the floor at the top of the stairs.

She recovered enough to make her way unsteadily down the stairs using the wall for support. She never turned her back to the man who followed her menacingly, one stair at a time. His heavy footsteps echoed through the tavern that fell silent with anticipation. The girl backed slowly down the last stair, then into the crowd, who parted for her, surrounding her. Feeling even more threatened, the girl turned from one man to the other, searching for the one who might help her. Again, her eyes caught Marcus's beyond the circle of men and he was filled with guilt and rage at what he was witnessing.

The dark haired man's voice, raised to a frightening pitch, broke the silence. "She needs a teaching, boys," the man spat. "Hold her. There, against the wall," he said, motioning to the men.

In an instant, they were upon her, fighting for the privilege of being the one to hold her while the lesson was learned. Those who lost the struggle gained satisfaction by grabbing and squeezing her delicate body as she passed. The sight sickened Marcus, who felt so stunned that he was unable to move from where he was. The girl fought as hard as she could but soon weakened from the exertion. The men held her arms high above her head, stretching them painfully against the wall.

The dark man ripped the thin chemise from the girl, leaving her body exposed to the tavern. For an instant, Marcus felt glad that her back faced the throng for the sake of the girl, but quickly felt wretched when he recognized the mark of previous "lessons" on the girl's delicate back and legs. This whole night had become barbaric beyond reason. Marcus's blood boiled.

"This whore has tried to kill me," the dark man yelled, pointing to the open gash on his forehead and holding a leather strap high. "For that, I'll teach her a lesson."

The strap came down on the girl's back with a deafening crack. Her body wrenched in taut silent pain with the blow. Before Marcus could move, another crack pierced the tavern. From somewhere behind him, Marcus heard the serving wench cry out for the madness to stop before the girl was killed. With strength that he never knew he possessed, Marcus pushed through the men toward the girl. A third and then a fourth crack of the lash sounded before he was able to reach his destination.

Jason was shocked when the strap stopped in mid air, wrenching his arm. He turned on his attacker, ready to get on with the lesson that Jillian needed, but stopping short upon seeing the richness of the man's clothes.

"You have no right to stop me. I'm her husband," he yelled. "Unless you pay for the privilege, of course," he said, smiling.

"One thousand pounds," Marcus stated flatly. "No man will top that bid." He turned threateningly to the crowd. "No man."

"For a thousand pounds the privilege is all yours," Jason said, handing the strap to Marcus.

Marcus took the strap from Jason in disgust, throwing it away from him. He took a pouch from his breast pocket and handed it to Jason, who grinned wickedly. "There is more than a thousand in there. That is for your promise to never lay eyes on this girl again," Marcus demanded.

"It will be my pleasure," Jason quipped, bowing to Marcus.

Rushing to her, as she was still held against the wall, Marcus removed his cape, wrapping it around the now unconscious girl. When the men released her, she collapsed into his arms and Marcus immediately carried her toward the tavern door where Henry stood, holding it open. Without so much as a glance backward, Marcus swiftly made his exit into the cool night carrying Jillian, now his possession, in his capable arms.

They wasted no time retrieving the carriage from the stable. Marcus wanted to be as far away as possible from the tavern and the evil man when the young girl awakened. He couldn't be sure, but he felt that this girl did not belong with that terrifying creature. Marcus knew that he was now responsible for her safety.

The light from a full moon flashed intermittently across the unconscious girl's face as the carriage made its way through the small, sleeping village. The bluish illumination gave her pale features an even deeper deathly hue. Marcus knew that the best thing for the young woman was to remain unconscious, for if she awoke, the pain from the strokes across her back would be excruciating. Air hissed between his teeth when he thought of the brilliant red streaks that cut across her delicate skin, the same flesh that he now held in his arms. The thought made him feel even guiltier about the way he held her and he couldn't help but think that his handling of her would cause unbearable pain if she were conscious. She would survive this ordeal; she would survive and he would come to know who she was during her recovery.

Marcus felt the girl's slight stir and the grimace of pain that followed her movement. The moonlight, blinking between the buildings they passed, gave her face moments of illumination. The distress that flashed across her face as she began to feel the pain of every lash that she had endured tore at Marcus. He regretted not being able to reach her before the first stroke had damaged her flesh. He regretted the moment of lust that held him spellbound, like all the others, until it was too late to help her. He was ashamed of the way his body responded to hers even after he realized that she was in danger.

Soon the carriage left the main road and onto an open lane that led toward a thick forest and magnificent home. Marcus gazed out the open window toward the blackness of the trees that marked the boundary of his vast estate. She would be safe there.

Again, the fragile girl stirred in his arms, moving his attention from the window and back to her face, now illuminated fully by the moon's light. Her eyes held his as she studied the man who held her so gently. She recognized him as one of the men in the crowd at the tavern, but felt no threat from him, for in his eyes she saw a man of integrity and regret. She knew that he had no part in the terrible fate that Jason had planned for her, but was simply an innocent bystander to the travesty of her predicament. Jillian felt she must release him from the guilt that was so apparent on his face, guilt that he was forced to share with all the others present at the auction.

Emotions played across the lovely features of the young girl's face. Pain, fear, and terror all registered as he watched. Her eyes changed from deep amber to a lighter gold color and he knew that she recognized him as one of the throng of men who had abused her. Just as suddenly, that look of recognition changed to one of compassion and Marcus felt himself hope for forgiveness from her, rather than hatred.

"I'm so sorry," he offered, tears welling in his blue eyes.

"Thank you," she mouthed, no sound escaping her pale lips. "Thank you."

Her eyes closed, her body relaxed, and Marcus knew that she was again unconscious. Then a sudden realization hit him. She had not spoken to him, only mouthed the words. He suddenly realized that he had never heard a sound from her, not even when the strap had assaulted her tender flesh. No sound. The girl was mute.

Chapter 34

Sybil held the papers in her hand, the papers that, at long last, would grant her precious moments with her love. It had been a trying time gaining the trust of the prison guards, most of whom would sooner slit her throat than grant her access to the prisoners. Nevertheless, with the help of Douglass, the plan had been perfected.

Soon, my love, she thought, soon we will be together. Sybil hoped that he didn't notice her hands trembling as she handed the papers to the guard. If he did, she was sure that he would also see that the black nun's habit she wore was also shaking with the fear that her body couldn't seem to control. What if he didn't allow her to pass today? It was her first chance to see Terrance since this began. She prayed that nothing would go wrong as the young man, who looked not much older than Jillian, quickly read through the papers.

He looked her square in the eye, thinking to himself that she was much too comely for a nun. For a moment, her emerald eyes mesmerized him, holding him. The nun smiled demurely at the boy and his resolve melted. She had a wonderful smile, like an angel, he thought. He handed the papers back to her, holding onto them as she took them in her grasp. Just for the briefest time, there was silence between them.

"Be careful today," he warned. "The prisoner you soothe is a murderer and a traitor to his country. He doesn't deserve to have his conscience eased."

"Everyone deserves to meet God with a cleansed spirit, my son." Sybil covered his hand with hers. "Even the most evil person's soul can be saved."

His hand grew warm with her touch. His body answered in kind. He took his eyes from hers so that she couldn't see the lust that pulsed through him. Ashamed of his reaction to this holy woman, the boy couldn't raise his eyes again. He ushered her on without a word, hoping that she wouldn't know his disgrace.

"Thank you, kind sir," she told him, taking a step past him, only to stop. "May I ask your name?"

"Gregory, mum," he squeaked. "Gregory."

Sybil smiled her most chaste smile. "Well then Gregory, I am sure that we will become fast friends."

"Yes, mum," he answered, relieved that the nun was finally walking through the opened gate.

She walked the short distance to the next checkpoint with her head held high. If only he knew that her legs felt as if they would collapse from beneath her at any moment, she thought, he would not be quite so embarrassed.

*   *   *   *   *

Marcus woke from a fitful sleep to find himself, for the second morning, at Jillian's bedside. He rose slowly from his chair, stretching his weary muscles, to feel her forehead. The fever was finally gone. He thanked God, letting out the breath that he hadn't realized he was holding. For two long nights, Marcus had kept watch by her bedside cooling her face with moist cloths, bathing her whenever the fever would not be controlled by any other means. For two long nights, he came to know Jillian more intimately than he had known anyone else in his life. Not even his wife, now deceased, had allowed him the knowledge of her body that he had with this fragile stranger.

"Thank God for Constance," he thought. If it had not been for her, he most assuredly would have floundered in his endeavors to care for Jillian. Constance was his strength, supporting his every whim.

When the carriage had arrived so late that first night, Constance took over ushering the unnecessary staff back to their rooms. It was Constance who stood up for Marcus when his sister, Isabelle, ranted and raved about him bringing his whores into the house. It was Constance who helped him bathe the girl and care for her wounds that seemed too many for such young delicate skin to endure. Marcus wished that there was some way to repay Constance for the many years that she had spent at his disposal.

At that very moment, Constance entered the room. She carried a tray filled with biscuits, still steaming hot from the oven, jam made from the raspberries she grew herself in the garden, and piping hot tea, served in a fine china teapot.

"Has she woke yet this morning, your Lordship?" Constance asked, putting the tray on the bedside table. She watched his expression and knew without his saying that the child hadn't awakened. "I begin to worry that she may never wake."

"Yes, I too am very concerned about her state. Is there anything else we can do to bring her out of this Constance? Anything we may have overlooked?"

"Nay, your Lordship, we have done everything there is to do. The rest will be up to her." She handed him a cup of tea and their fingers brushed. "You look so very tired, Marcus. Will you go to your room and rest? Just for a little while? I'll keep an eye on the little one."

He smiled to himself hearing her slip of tongue. She rarely called him by his first name unless she was concerned for his well-being. It was a close relationship they shared and she knew his every thought.

"Yes, Constance. You are right. I am weary this morning. Perhaps a bath and a short rest in my own bed would benefit these sore muscles," he said, stretching his neck and shoulders. "Are you certain that you can stay with her for a short while?"

"Now, don't worry yourself, your Lordship. I've finished all my morning duties and the house staff have their daily tasks. All will be fine until the noon hour, I'm sure."

Marcus felt Jillian's forehead one last time, finding no fever had returned, then gave Constance's shoulder a gentle squeeze before leaving the room. He was bone-tired; he was weary. However most of all, he was angry, angry with himself for being so frozen with lust that he allowed such a fragile child to be so mistreated. Even now, he could do nothing but watch as her life seemed to fade away. Feeling completely inadequate, Marcus walked slowly down the hallway, stopping to open his bedchamber door.

"So, the slut still lives?" Isabelle's hateful voice caught Marcus off-guard. He spun around, coming face-to-face with his older sister.

"Yes, she still lives. No thanks to you!" he shouted. "Don't you have anything better to do than skulk around the halls like some black cat searching for prey?"

"And don't you have anything better to do, dear brother, than to bring your whores into our household? Mother and Father would be so ashamed at the disgrace that you have brought on us."

"Mother and Father, God rest their souls, would never want for anyone to suffer as she has suffered. Not even you, dear sister."

"What did you do to her, brother?" Isabelle asked, circling Marcus with her fingers curled like claws. "Did you have carnal knowledge of her to the extent of wounding her well used flesh? Did you pound your man's flesh into her so hard that she will never be serviceable again?"

Filled with rage, Marcus clasped both of Isabelle's hands in his steel grip, jerking her body so close to his that she could feel the inferno that burned within his eyes. Fighting for control of his anger and his hatred for his only sister, Marcus spat his next words at her. "Enough! If you weren't such a piggish shrew, maybe you would have had the chance to know the joy shared between two people making love. But, alas dear sister, there is nothing left for you but a spinster's life filled with hate and regret."

"The only thing I regret, dear brother, is that you never died like the rest of your mother's spawn," Isabelle growled, tearing her hands from his grasp to run down the hallway, disappearing into the darkness at its end.

Shivers ran up his spine as he watched his sister's flight. Marcus knew her hatred; had witnessed it countless times, but this time seemed more venomous than ever before. If only he could understand why she was so filled with hatred, maybe he could help her overcome it. Help her, he thought, I can't even help myself, let alone help someone as obviously sick as Isabelle.

Shaking his head to clear the vision of his sister, Marcus shoved his bedroom door open to find a steaming hot tub prepared for him. Constance. What would he ever do without her?

* * * * *

The corridor to the worst of the prison cells was dark, damp and rat infested. Sybil chose her steps carefully. At one point, something slithered across her path, barely visible in the dim light of the torches burning infrequently down the narrow passage. Keeping to the opposite side from where the slimy creature had slipped beneath the stone floor, Sybil held her breath until she was safely past. Her arm felt wet through the habit she wore, but Sybil didn't attempt to brush whatever it was away. She had learned, over the period of time that she visited the prison, that many indescribably putrid substances hung from these walls. Better to let it dry on her clothes than to deal with it in this darkness.

Ahead in the dimness, a guard stood awaiting her arrival. He held the torch high, lighting her way. Sybil felt a flood of relief when she saw him. His face was shadowed by the torchlight, but Sybil knew by the sheer size of him that it was Douglass McKibben.

"Ye must hurry, lass." He motioned her to pass him by. "We're a wee bit late this morn."

"I know," Sybil whispered, hurrying past him. "At every check point I came to, it seemed that the guard had to read through every page."

Douglass laughed. "My dear woman, there's not a guard at Newgate that can read a lick. It's just that they are so taken with the beauty of our fine nun that they all want a few minutes to enjoy her presence."

Stopping so suddenly that Douglass, with his huge bulk, almost smashed her against the slimy wall, Sybil stood fast, chagrined by what he had just said. "You mean to say that not one of those men can read?"

"It's the truth of it, Sybil. Word is that they cannot wait to be on duty to see your sweet face."

Fear swept through Sybil like the cold, forbidding cells that surrounded them. Not for one moment had Sybil thought that the men paid her that much attention. Only Gregory, just this morning, had seemed to notice her for the first time.

"What if they recognize me when I enter again this evening? What then, Douglass? All will be for not if we don't succeed."

"Don't yea be thinking like that, Sybil. We're too close to get frightened away. Terrance is depending on us."

Terrance? Oh God, how could she have forgotten? Sybil's heart quickened at the sound of his name. He was here, maybe within hearing distance, and all she could think about was her fear of being caught. The one thing that had helped Sybil through the last two months was the fact that one day, the time would be right to approach Terrance with their plan. That day was today. No more delays, no more praying with the other prisoners, holding their hands, watching them die. Today, Sybil would be with Terrance and he would rejoice in her efforts to free him.

"How could I be so selfish, Douglass? How could I forget that he needs us?"

"Ouch, now. Don't be blaming yourself for a moment of weakness, me girl. You are one of the bravest lasses I've ever come across. Not too much longer and this will all be over." Douglass gave her shoulder a pat then motioned her further down the passageway.

They came to a stop at the very last cell, the wood of the door blackened by mildew hanging in gentle sweeps across its surface. The dank smell of human waste stung Sybil's eyes. It wasn't the first time she had suffered the noxious odor, but this time it seemed to be the strongest ever. Maybe it was because she knew that someone she loved so very dearly was behind the rankness of the prison walls. Maybe it was the smell of her own fear that brought Sybil close to tears, for just beyond this blackened door was Terrance, her love.

The fear of not knowing what to expect hung heavy in the corridor. Douglass understood her fear, but also knew that she had to face what lay beyond. Terrance was counting on her, even if he didn't realize it himself. He needed Sybil to bring him back from the grave and give him the strength to live. Douglass had opened many doors in Newgate prison to this strong and beautiful woman. She comforted and forgave many souls before they left these walls for good. Now it was time to give one soul the will to fight for life, the will to become strong, and the will to love her for the rest of their lives.

"Please be patient with him Sybil. Remember, he doesn't know that we're coming."

She said nothing, just took a deep breath and nodded her head signaling Douglass that she was as ready as she would ever be for the fight of her life.

*   *   *   *   *

Jillian awoke to a weight on her chest. Her eyes snapped open to see just what it was. It took several blinks to focus, and when they did, she was startled to find a pair of mischievous, blue eyes staring back at her.

"Who are you?" his precocious little voice inquired. "Are you the new cook?"

Jillian watched the very small boy, with tightly curled brown hair, ease off her chest and sit next to her on the edge of the bed. He examined the play sword that he brandished back and forth in the air, testing its weight and its edge for sharpness. He wore a white blouse, buttoned tightly to his neck, and finished off with a most proper bow, tied at the collar with a blue ribbon. His short legs, covered by matching blue knickers, swung back and forth on the edge of the bed.

"If you're not the cook, then maybe you're my new mother?" he asked innocently, turning to inspect Jillian more closely.

His face was as round as a cherub's. Finely arched brows rose at perfect angles above his sparkling blue eyes giving his face an angelic essence. Below a perky little nose, his lips, the color of pink roses, pursed with the anticipation of her answer. He waited, his face questioning her silence.

"So then, you're not my new mother. Maybe, you're my new playmate. I could be a knight and protect you from fire breathing dragons."

With that, the boy stood on the bed, ready to do battle with the devil himself. Jillian watched the boy parry this way and that, ridding the room of all sort of vermin, a look of pure joy on his face as he displayed his many talents for her. Ignoring the pain that it caused, Jillian propped herself up, just a little bit higher, as to give him even more room to slay his aggressors. Both Jillian and the boy were so caught up in his fantasy that neither saw Isabelle enter the room.

Without warning, the boy was caught in midair by the back of Isabelle's hand, sending him off the side of the bed and onto the hardwood floor. Jillian tried to scream but no sound came. She bit the back of her hand in frustration. Focusing on the boy, Isabelle walked around the end of the bed to tower over him, a wicked smirk on her face.

"Ian, how many times have I told you not to come out of your room? You never mind, do you?" she screeched. "I just have to teach you, again and again and again." She raised her arm to strike the child once more.

Before Jillian knew what had come over her, she was off the bed, knocking a tray off the bedside table, and grasping the woman's arm so that she couldn't strike Ian again. Startled by Jillian's agility, Isabelle struggled with her, trying to break her hold. However, Jillian's strength was greater and she held Isabelle until Ian had safely slipped beneath the bed. The strength that Jillian had soon began to wane and Isabelle was able to knock her off balance landing Jillian on the floor amongst the glass shards of the broken china teapot from the tray.

Isabelle took advantage of the moment, bringing her hand down across Jillian's cheek. "That will teach you to raise a hand to someone above your station. Why you're no better than the gutter rats that scurry at the back of the taverns in the square."

Jillian clasped her hand over her stinging cheek. Tears welled in her eyes as she stared at the woman, who looked more devil than human. Her eyes were aglow with mischief and venom, and Jillian wondered what made this woman hate her so much. At that moment, Ian scampered from beneath the bed, coming up behind Isabelle, who was raising her hand to strike Jillian again. He swatted Isabelle on the behind as hard as he could, breaking his wooden sword in half. Isabelle turned her wrath on Ian, who backed slowly away.

"You dare to strike me, you little bastard? I'll show you just as I showed the rest of those bastards. I'll stick a needle into your brain making you as crazy as a loon. Even your dear father won't have anything to do with you after that."

"No!" Ian cried, diving beneath the bed once more. "You're bad, Aunt Issy."

"You're the one who's bad, you nasty little boy. All men are bad from the day they are born. Even your dear father. He's the worst!" Isabelle yelled, swatting at Ian with one of the broken halves of his sword.

"What's going on here?" Marcus bellowed over the top of Isabelle's ranting. "Isabelle, what are you doing? Who is under the bed?" he asked coming around to the side where he saw Jillian curled in fear.

"Oh, dear God!" Constance screamed from the doorway. "Stop her Marcus before she kills herself."

Marcus, thinking that Constance meant Jillian, hurriedly picked her up from the floor. Her gown was soaked with blood, and her face was even more bruised than it had been the first night he'd brought her to Havenwood. Her eyes met his and in them he saw such panic that Marcus wasn't sure of whom she was more frightened—him or his lunatic sister. However, the panic focused on something or someone else, for as soon as Marcus put Jillian upon the bed, she leapt for the side, searching wildly underneath it. It was then that Marcus saw Constance struggling with Isabelle. In her hand was half of Ian's toy sword and Isabelle was slicing with all her strength at her own wrist. It was a sickening feeling that Marcus had, not knowing whether he wanted to stop her or not. Constance made that decision for him finally freeing the sword from his sister's grasp. Once free, Isabelle bolted from the room, screeching insanities all the way to her bedroom.

Jillian slowly pulled a sobbing Ian from beneath the bed. She held him close against her breast, soothing his cries. Her eyes moved to Marcus for help, knowing that she could offer no words of comfort to the small lad. Jillian placed the boy within his father's gentle embrace and Marcus cooed to him softly, calming his son.

"There now, Ian. You are safe."

Jillian felt an odd sense of familiarity with his words. Had he once said those very same words to her? Or was it someone else?

"I was just playing with my new friend, Father. I wasn't being bad," Ian cried. "Aunt Issy is the one who's bad."

"Come now, Ian. Let Constance take you to get cleaned up. Then, you may come back and meet our new friend in a proper manner."

"Alright, Father," Ian said, reaching for Constance. "But only if I am the one to protect her from the dragons."

"Yes, Ian," Marcus chuckled. "You may protect Jillian from the dragons."

The door to his cell creaked slowly open, the sound echoing against the cold stone walls of his confinement. Terrance made no effort to acknowledge the intruder, thinking that the guard must be coming back for more entertainment. The fight was gone from Terrance and he knew all that was left for him was death. He wished for it at times. Death, sweet death.

Time had no meaning for Terrance. He wasn't certain how long he'd been at Newgate prison. It didn't matter. Nothing mattered to him anymore. Once death came to claim him there would be no more pain and that would be a godsend. He awaited the Grim Reaper with open arms.

Hearing a muffled cry, Terrance opened his eyes to see the Reaper himself standing in the open doorway. He was shrouded in black from head to toe, made even more evident by the torchlight illuminating the passageway behind him. Terrance smiled to himself, thinking that this Grim Reaper fellow was short for such a frightening entity. It moved toward him slowly, seeming to float on the thick air of his cell. It stopped before him in silence.

"You're short for your station in life. Or is it in death that I should be referring?" Terrance chuckled. "No matter your stature, I am more than ready to go with you."

"Are you truly?" the Reaper asked, in a voice that sounded surprisingly feminine. "I was hoping that you would be."

Thinking that he was surely hearing things, Terrance squinted to see the Reaper more clearly. It was then that Douglass, holding a torch, appeared beside the entity, illuminating its face.

"Sybil," Terrance whispered, the sound barely escaping his cracked lips. "I must be dead and gone to heaven."

"No Terrance, you're not in heaven. It is I," Sybil breathed, holding back tears. "Douglass and I have come to help you."

"Help me? There is no help for me. Only in death can I be freed."

"No Terrance. There is a way. You have to get out of here."

"Foolish woman. I have no reason to want freedom. All is lost, don't you see," he said turning away from her gaze. "Leave me."

Anger rose in Sybil's chest. He couldn't desert her now; he had to live. Terrance was her only link to what had happened to Jillian. He was her only chance to find her daughter and to have a life filled with pure love. Sybil remembered the way that he loved her; she remembered the way that he held her, caressed her and made love to her. She needed him and he needed her; she would not let him give up now.

"If that is how you feel about it, I will go find Jillian on my own."

Douglass piped in. "Sybil no, you can't do it on your own. I will come with you. I will be your companion."

Douglass knew Terrance would not stand for him to become so close to Sybil. He motioned for her to leave, but before they could, Terrance leapt upon Douglass with the speed of a great cat, sending the torch flying through the air. It landed in the corner, catching some straw on fire. The two continued to struggle as Sybil retrieved the torch and put out the small fire by stomping it. She turned to find Terrance and Douglass rolling as if in an embrace on the floor, like two small boys fighting over a favorite toy. Something about the whole situation amused Sybil and she began to laugh. It might have been the easing of the tension that she felt, but whatever it was, she could not stop.

The two men stopped their half-hearted brawl to stare at Sybil in disbelief. Under the circumstances, Terrance found nothing amusing, but Douglass joined in, laughing with all his might.

"What is so amusing?" Terrance demanded.

Gaining some control of herself, Sybil answered, "We were so worried about how to get you riled, and how to bring back the fight in you and this is all it took."

She pointed to the two men, still in each other's arms, on the floor. The two looked at each other, Douglass with a wide grin and Terrance with his brow furrowed in anger. Within an instant, Terrance too saw the humor in the scene and burst into laughter. Douglass rose, offering his hand to Terrance, who took it gladly, then dusted off the dirt from his clothing. Terrance made no attempt, for his eyes at this moment were fixated on Sybil, who had stopped laughing and was staring back at him.

"I can see that you two have many things to discuss. I will leave you to it." Douglass said as he rose and left the cell. However, neither paid him any notice.

The cell walls closed in around them, making the isolation of Terrance's imprisonment ever clearer to them both. Not even the light from the torch, which Douglass had placed in the sconce next to the door, could bring warmth to this dreary room. Nevertheless, Sybil felt the trickle of perspiration between her breasts and down her back. Her body felt as if it were on fire, ignited by the sight of the man she had secretly loved all these years. Though she could see that the months of being in this terrible place had taken their toll on Terrance, he was still the most magnificent man she had ever seen.

"I've wanted so much to see you again, Terrance," Sybil spoke breathlessly. "Douglass and I have a plan to get you out of here. We've worked very hard to make all the arrangements. I've . . . um . . . I've been masquerading as a nun just so I would have access to the prisoners, you see," Sybil stammered. "And the time has come to . . ."

Her words drifted away as Terrance slowly reached out to stroke her cheek with his palm. Her eyes closed with his touch. Her breast rose with the intake of much needed air. Sybil turned her face and kissed his palm, nestling her lips against it. She had longed many nights for his touch, dreaming of being locked in his embrace, feeling him deep inside her heart, in a place no other man reached. Then, waking to calm her rapid breathing and heartbeat, lying there for what seemed like hours, afraid to go back to sleep and find him waiting for her. At times like those, Sybil struggled to get Terrance out of her mind if only to keep her sanity for a while longer.

Terrance's blood boiled within his veins, surging through the silence so mightily that he could hear only the pounding of his own heart within the tight confines of his chest. He couldn't resist touching her, stopping her words. He dreamt each night of holding her and making love to her. And each night he had known that this was all he would ever have of Sybil, just dreams. But she was here now, and by some miracle he would have this time, if never again, just to touch her, taste her, and soothe the worried look on her sweet face. He would hold the memory of these few brief moments with her forever.

Pulling Sybil to him, Terrance wrapped her in his arms and she responded in kind. They stood locked in each other's embrace in the center of the dank and dirty cell. Becoming acutely aware of every sensation, Terrance breathed in the fragrance of her desire, and he felt the heat of her curves, even through the layers of the habit she wore. He touched, caressed and stroked Sybil until he thought he would go mad with the intense desire that burned within him. Then, needing to taste her sweetness, Terrance took her face in his hands and kissed her with such tenderness that even he was shocked that he could be so gentle. His reward was sweet ecstasy, for she tasted succulent and ripe, and his for the picking.

"God, help me. Give me strength that I don't take you here and now."

"You must pray for me also, Terrance," Sybil whispered. "For I want you as well. This is not the time and I have very little of it, my darling. Please I need to tell you everything."

A short time later, Sybil emerged from the cell and was greeted with a wink from Douglass, who had given them some time to get reacquainted. Carrying the torch to light their way out of the depths of Newgate, Douglass spoke not a word until they reached the sunlight in the main yard.

"Are we prepared to go then, lass?" he asked quietly.

"Yes, we are. But I didn't tell him everything, Douglass," she confided as they made their way to the prison gates.

"God help us, lass, when he finds out."

"I'm sure God will help us all, my son," Sybil said loudly, as a guard approached and passed them by. "God will bless us this fine day."

Terrance, on the other hand, was not so sure about the plan which Sybil had spoken. However, he was sure about one thing; Sybil loved him and had come for him. He had tried to talk her out of the scheme that she and Douglass had devised to free him from this hell, but she would hear nothing of it. She could not be swayed to forget this foolishness and return to her safe world back at the cottage.

Sybil had become angry at his request, and once she told Terrance about Jillian disappearing, Terrance too felt rage like never before. All this time, Terrance thought that Jillian was safe with Sybil. Terrance began to see that they both were lied to and kept from the truth of Jillian's whereabouts. This gave Terrance the determination that he needed to go along with Sybil's plan to escape Newgate, so that he could find Jillian and discover what had happened to Gavin that night at the cove.

The thought of seeing Gavin's body lying so still in the darkness gave Terrance shivers and a deep sense of loss that chilled him to the core. He suspected that something horrible had happened to Jillian, but was duped by William into thinking that she was in some way responsible for Gavin's death. How could he be so very blind? Many things were making sense to him now. William must have been there even before he and Sue Ki found Gavin. Had William killed Gavin and then made up the whole story about Jillian? Or had there been someone else Terrance wasn't aware of, who had come upon the couple in their sleep?

The biggest mystery of all, where was Jillian? Had she been there, hiding in the forest or maybe being detained by some of William's men? William had said that she was on the ship and didn't want to speak to Terrance, but was she really there? Terrance doubted even more the story that William had told him and the court at the trial. It didn't make any sense. Something or someone was missing and Terrance had to find out. One thing was for certain, he couldn't do it from this prison cell. Sybil was right, he had to escape and help her search for their daughter. All he could do now was wait for the signal from Sybil. It would not happen in the next few days, but after a week or so, Terrance would make his daring escape and be free of his bonds. Or so he hoped.

Meanwhile, Sybil made her way back to the village where she and Douglass shared a cottage. She stopped about halfway, taking a trail off the road and into a ravine, where she quickly removed the nun's habit and dressed in her own clothes for the rest of her trek to the village. She carefully wrapped the habit within a shawl and tucked it up under her dress making her waistline bulge as if she were with child. The disguise had worked for the three months that she and Douglass had been acting out their plot to free Terrance. But, Sybil knew that the time was approaching when she could no longer claim to be pregnant and she would have to think of some other way to hide the habit for the remainder of her journey. There was also the explanation of her baby that would have to satisfy the nosey villagers who lived near Douglass's home.

Douglass was a godsend. At a time when Sybil thought there was no hope, Douglass found her and gave her hope. At a time when she was ready to give up, Douglass would lift her spirits and quickly set her back on the path to freeing Terrance. If not for Douglass, Sybil would not have had the few moments with Terrance today that had renewed his will to live. Through it all, Douglass asked for nothing more than to come with them when they escaped. It was an easy wish to grant after all that he had risked in freeing Terrance. Although Sybil was not sure where they would be going, Douglass was very welcome to come with them.

The day had grown extremely warm for a late fall day, or maybe it was the anxiety and excitement of tonight's events that made Sybil's face flush and her back drip with perspiration. Whatever it was, Sybil would feel much better once she reached the cottage and could remove the added burden of the habit from beneath her heavy skirts. She made her way steadily along the road, entering the village near the market so that she could purchase a few items for the evening meal. Douglass wouldn't be coming home this evening, for he worked extra hours now and then in order to acquire some much needed money for the time after they set Terrance free. It also worked right into the plan to free Terrance. Douglass would need to be at the prison when the time came, and it would have to be done in darkness, so working the extra hours had become an advantage.

The market was bustling with vendors. Patrons scurried from stand to stand making their purchases. Sybil spotted Morgan James, a most comely young woman with whom she had made a recent acquaintance. Morgan lived not far from the cottage where she and Douglass lived and as a coincidence, Morgan was within days of giving birth to her second child. She wore her blonde hair in two braids that started at her temples and met at the nape of her neck. There, she tied them together with a wide white ribbon, making a rather large bow that gave the effect of girlish poise. Her skin was fair, but on the rosy side, given the heat of the day and her delicate condition. Her best asset was her amazing big blue eyes, which looked as though they would pool with tears at anytime. It could be happy or sad tears, but tears all the same. Morgan seemed to always be on the verge of an emotional outbreak and sought Sybil's companionship and calming ways. She felt as though they had so much in common, being they were both expecting a child. Seeing Sybil from a distance, Morgan slowly made her way toward her through the market so that they might walk the rest of the way to their homes together.

"Good day to you, Sybil," Morgan called above the chaos of the crowd. "Will ye be heading home soon?"

"A few more vegetables to purchase and I'll be going that way," Sybil replied.

"I'll wait for ye then," Morgan said, coming to stand beside Sybil in front of a wonderful display of vegetables that one of the local farmers was selling.

He looked them both over, grinning to himself at their condition. "Would you care for a ripe juicy apple? It's good for what ails ye."

"What ails us is this blasted heat, sir," Morgan snapped. "No apple is going to cure this," she said, turning sideways so that her swollen belly looked even larger.

Taken off guard by her crudeness, the farmer turned to Sybil for help. "We'll take six apples thank you," she told him with a smile. "You'll have to forgive my young friend. She is getting close to her time."

Sybil paid the farmer for the apples and some fresh green beans that were wilting quickly in the heat. They made their way out of the market place and down a shaded lane toward home.

Morgan suddenly stopped short. "Oh! There it is again," she said, clutching her swollen stomach. "This baby is going to come out kicking and grinning. You can wager that."

"If he's anything like his mother, I imagine he will," Sybil replied and moved on down the road.

"Why did you buy the apples, Sybil?"

"Because he was trying to be kind to two very irritable women. I felt sorry for him when you showed him your huge belly. I thought he was going to have a fit of apoplexy," Sybil laughed.

Morgan giggled behind her hand but could not contain herself as Sybil laughed even louder and harder at the poor, old farmer.

"It was very funny how his eyes bulged out with the immenseness of my girth."

Suddenly Sybil felt her bundle slip from her waist. With all the purchases in her hands, she almost didn't catch its descent before it was plain that a baby didn't reside there. Morgan saw her sudden movement and the clutching of her stomach and mistook Sybil actions for the same feeling that she had experienced just a few moments before.

Covering her actions as best she could, Sybil exclaimed, "Oh my! I think the little one is trying to tell me something. Maybe we should both go home and get some rest."

"Are you certain that you'll be alright, Sybil? Looks to me that the baby may be dropping a wee bit," Morgan said, as she tried to help Sybil gain control of her bundle of purchases.

"I'll be fine," Sybil reassured her. "I just need some rest and a privy. Thank goodness we are here," she said, pointing to her cottage that they were indeed standing in front of.

"Ouch, I'll be off then. Take care of yourself. See you on the morrow," Morgan called as she continued down the lane to her own cottage.

"That was too close," Sybil scolded herself after shutting the cottage door. "I'll have to remember to take something with me next time to secure the habit in place," she muttered.

Placing the green beans and apples on the table, Sybil let the bundle drop from beneath her skirt and then placed it next to her purchases. The sudden rush of cool air from the lessening of her burden made Sybil somewhat lightheaded, so she sat down to take a few minutes to collect her thoughts and plan the rest of the night's events.

It would take her at least an hour to make the trip back to Newgate after dark. Then, she would have to stay there with Douglass until just before dawn. Yes, they had planned it all very well and everything seemed to be going fine. Soon, it would be time to liberate Terrance from the bonds of Newgate.

Today had been such a shock for Sybil, but she never let on to Terrance just how stunned she was. Terrance's condition was beyond anything that Sybil had ever imagined. His face was bruised from the beatings inflicted by the guards and gaunt from the lack of nourishment in his steady diet of gruel. The smell of death was all around him; it overpowered her at one point and she had struggled to keep her senses about her. Then he had touched her and there was nothing and no one else but her and Terrance. They had shared a brief moment of passion, taking in every detail of each other. When Terrance had embraced Sybil it was as if he absorbed a part of her; she felt herself being taken there, to the very heart of him. In that journey, she had also felt his soul emanate something that became a part of her, something that would bind them together forever. She hadn't felt that sensation in a very long time. In all honesty, it had been since they were separated, almost seventeen years before. Realizing this, Sybil knew that what she was feeling was the discovery of her soul mate, someone who was committed to her by emotions so deep that the tie would never be broken. Even after all the years of separation, Sybil knew that in Terrance's arms was where she was destined to be.

A knock at the door brought Sybil quickly out of her thoughts. Her chair tipped over with her sudden action. "Just a minute!" Sybil exclaimed, quickly putting the bundle under her dress again. "I'm coming."

Upon opening the door, Sybil came face-to-face with a very frightened Morgan. "I believe my time has come."

"Oh dear," Sybil said, with concern for Morgan. "Where is Johnny? Is he at home?"

"He's still at the pub. Sybil, what am I going to do?" Morgan asked, doubling over in pain.

"Now, don't you worry about anything. I'll fetch the midwife and all will be well."

Sybil settled Morgan into her and Douglass's bed, then put a pot of water on the stove to boil. "Where is little Ben this afternoon?"

"He's with me mum. Mum thought that my time was near and said that I should get all the rest that I could. She's bringing him back on Sunday."

"That was kind of her. How unfortunate that she couldn't stay for the blessed event herself." Sybil surprised herself with the sarcasm of her statement.

"It's very hard for her to get away, what with all me brothers and sisters. There are eight in all, four boys and four girls. Ben will have plenty to keep him busy while he's there." Another pain gripped her. "Oh hurry, Sybil. Please!"

Sybil ran from the cottage and down the lane, clutching her stomach to keep the bundle from falling out. At the end of the lane, an unoccupied carriage blocked her view of the street. The cabby had pulled the horses up short, seeing the very pregnant woman running toward the street as if she were about to give birth.

"Hold there," he told the horses that pranced because of Sybil's abrupt arrival. "Are ye needing any help this fine day, lass? You look as though you do."

"I need help, Sir. But it's not for me," Sybil explained, winded by her run down the street. "My friend is back at my cottage and is in labor. I must get the midwife, Sarah Tilford. Do you know of her?"

He thought for a moment. "The one on the corner near the market?" he asked.

"Yes, she's the one. Could you please go and fetch her so that I may go back and tend to my friend? I would be forever grateful, sir."

He nodded his head and without further ado snapped the reins, lurching the carriage forward down the street toward the market and the midwife. Sybil sighed with relief for not having to run all the way to the market, for if anyone were to see her running that fast they would surely question how she could do it in her condition.

She headed back down the lane to her cottage, noting that no one seemed to have noticed her flight just a few minutes ago. Wiping her brow, Sybil opened the door and was stunned by what she found inside.

For Jillian, the days were filled with her every whim being catered to by either Marcus or Constance. Even little Ian tried his best to do things for Jillian that made her life easier. Discovering that she couldn't speak, Jillian was thankful for the education she apparently had, for writing on a tablet became her only source of communication. Isabelle had not made an appearance since the day that Jillian woke from her sleep and struggled with her to protect Ian from her wrath. For this, Jillian was very grateful but she knew that Isabelle was not a person to stay away forever. Jillian was sure that she would make another attempt to rid the house of what she thought was vermin. What troubled Jillian most was the fear that Ian and Marcus were the targets of Isabelle's madness.

There were many things that Jillian couldn't piece together. She had discovered very quickly that she didn't have any memory of her life before opening her eyes to Ian's chubby little face that morning a few months ago. Marcus had been very kind to fill in details for Jillian and she began to realize what a kind and gentle soul he was. He explained that she had taken a terrible fall from one of Havenwood's prized mares, hit her head and was unconscious for days before she woke. That explained the bruises and scrapes that Jillian found on her person but still she felt that there was much more to the story than he was telling her. She felt it from some of the staff, who gave her questioning glances whenever they were near, but most of the time Marcus or Constance were her companions and told her not to fret over what she couldn't remember and to just enjoy her leisure life. When she felt better, Marcus had promised to give her some duties that would make her feel useful.

It was hard for Jillian to stay in bed during the day, so she asked if she could go out and get some much needed sun. Marcus arranged for a chaise to be put out at the gazebo in the gardens off the south side of the mansion. It was near the kitchen, where Constance could easily see Jillian in case she needed anything or anyone. Marcus had some business to take care of in the village and wouldn't be able to join her, however all the preparations were made and Jillian was more than ready for the fresh air.

Constance helped Jillian dress in a yellow gown that made her long even more for the sunlight. Having no clothes of her own, Jillian was given several gowns that had belonged to Marcus's mother. Constance took them in where necessary to fit Jillian perfectly, and even though some of the styles were outdated Marcus swore that he had never seen Jillian look so lovely.

When Jillian was ready, Constance helped her make the trek from her room to the gardens. Jillian's legs were still weakened by her ordeal but she felt that she was gaining strength every day. She was determined to walk to the gardens without help; Marcus had been her legs for far too long. He had insisted on carrying her everywhere she needed to be for the first few weeks after the accident. It took both Jillian and Constance to convince him that she was ready to walk on her own. Since then, Jillian practiced daily to regain the strength in her legs and to be self-sufficient.

It was a glorious day. The gardens were groomed immaculately and the pathways were swept clean, making the cobblestone surface looked polished from the years of keeping them spotless. They passed roses of every size and color. There were delphiniums and bellflowers with brilliant blues and purples, bordered by pansies with little faces that turned toward the bright sunlight. The fragrance of the gardens was seductive.

It gave Jillian a heady feeling that was somehow reminiscent of another time and place. She wished she could remember that time, and lately there had been a few instances when things seemed so familiar to Jillian, yet she could never quite place why they were. It caused her many hours of frustration not knowing what had happened before, however Marcus and Constance both seemed unconcerned by her memory loss and were very helpful in explaining who people were or why something seemed recognizable.

"There you are, missy," Constance said, settling Jillian in the chaise. "Here is a wrap, if you need it."

She handed the shawl to Jillian who set it aside. Jillian mouthed "thank you" to Constance who reassured her that she could see her from the house and would come straight away if Jillian so much as waved to her. Jillian again thanked Constance, who then returned to the mansion and the business of preparing the evening meal.

"I'll have Andrew bring you out some lemonade in a little while," she called, before entering the kitchen.

Jillian waved her thanks, then settled in for a rest on the chaise. The journey from the mansion was more difficult than Jillian had anticipated, but she held her own until Constance was gone. If Marcus found out how weakened she had been by the walk, he would not allow her to come out again for days. She didn't want to be cooped up in her room for another day, and a little rest would renew her strength. It wasn't long before Jillian drifted to sleep, nestled on the chaise in the shade of the gazebo.

At the mansion, Ian ran full force into the skirts of his Aunt Isabelle, who grabbed him by the shoulders and shook him before he realized who had blocked his path.

"You little imbecile," she said hatefully. "Watch where you're going or you may have another accident." Struggling to free himself, Ian yelled for her to let him go and then kicked her in the shin with all his might. Isabelle had no choice but to let go of him in order to keep her balance while hopping on one foot and holding her wounded shin. "I'll get you for that, you little brat," she warned.

The warning fell on deaf ears, for Ian was on his way to the gardens to spend some time with Jillian. Ian was madly in love with his newfound friend and he told her so every chance he got. He visited her in her room, romping on the bed with her until his father allowed Jillian to escape from her bedroom. He sat with her in the library, where they shared pictures from the many books that were dusty from being unused for so long.

One night, Marcus found them curled up together fast asleep after thumbing through a volume about animals from the wild. He picked Ian up, careful not to wake Jillian, and put him to bed. When he returned for Jillian, she was still asleep and Marcus sat for the longest time just studying her peaceful face, so divine in slumber.

Constance heard Ian long before he came careening into the kitchen. She poised herself to catch him by the collar so that he wouldn't get by her and out into the gardens to disturb Jillian's peace.

"Please, let me go see Jillian. She needs me," he protested, as Constance shuffled him into a chair at the table.

"You just sit there, young man, and help me snap these beans," she insisted.

*   *   *   *   *

Andrew had only been employed at Havenwood for a few weeks and this was the first time he was able to see the mystery woman whom all the servants talked about. She was indeed as beautiful as they said, but to him she was even more than beautiful; she was what he had been looking for so long. Now, if only he could have a few words with her alone, he was sure that he could convince her to come with him.

Andrew stood above Jillian for a few moments, studying her delicate features. She was fast asleep and he wasn't sure if he should wake her. The lemonade on the tray would be getting too warm to drink if she didn't wake soon.

"And what are you gawking at, boy?" Isabelle's voice broke the silence. "Give me that tray and be off with you," she ordered, taking the lemonade from him.

With all due haste, Andrew fled the gazebo and Isabelle's hateful voice. He would have to wait for another opportunity to speak with Jillian, but for now, getting far away from Havenwood's witch was all Andrew wanted to do.

The splash of cold lemonade in Jillian's face brought her up out of her peaceful slumber. She choked back the tears that threatened, trying to focus on the nemesis that towered over her. Recognizing Isabelle, Jillian cowered in the chaise, trying to put some distance between them, being terribly frightened of her. After the things she had seen Isabelle do, and from what Jillian was told by Constance and Marcus himself, she had good reason to be. The woman was mad; that was a fact. She was someone with whom nobody wanted to be alone, especially Jillian.

"I see that you are finally awake, you lazy sot," she said, circling the chaise. "I can see that my brother's whore is well kept. Did you know how much you cost him?" Isabelle leaned even closer to Jillian, who backed away, putting her hands up to protect her face. "One thousand pounds. Yes, I can see you didn't know that," she said triumphantly, observing the shock on Jillian's face. "So he hasn't told you the truth has he? He hasn't told you that you were sold to him by your own husband." Isabelle took a parchment out of her skirt pocket. "Yes. Now, what was his name? Oh, here it is. Gavin. What an odd name."

Jillian grabbed the paper from Isabelle's hand and quickly read it. This couldn't be true yet there it was in writing and it was even signed by someone named Gavin. Jillian shook her head. No, it was a lie. She was making it all up. Her world started to spin. Jillian felt as if she couldn't breathe. She stood, clasping the gazebo railing, trying to sort through what Isabelle had just told her. She wanted to scream; sparks of light danced before her eyes and she felt as if she might faint. She had to get out of there, as far away as she possibly could. In her mind she screamed, "No! No!"

In the kitchen, Constance heard what she thought was a child in the gardens who was hurt. When she got to the doorway, she saw Jillian and Isabelle struggling on the gazebo. Isabelle threw Jillian to the ground, then followed her retreat, kicking with all her might. The spiteful things she was yelling at Jillian made Constance cringe; she had to save her from Isabelle's wrath.

Calling for Andrew, the houseboy, and any other staff that could hear her, Constance ran from the kitchen to the gardens heading straight for the gazebo. She hoped that she wasn't too late.

Focused on the scene before her, Constance was unaware that Ian had also seen the fracas in the garden. Being that he was still small enough to fit between the shrubberies, Ian had taken a short cut and arrived at the gazebo before Constance. He lunged at Isabelle with all his might, landing squarely on her back. Isabelle yelped in pain as Ian's tiny fists pummeled the side of her neck and face. A quick move from Isabelle threw Ian over her shoulder and onto the ground in front of her. She then turned on Ian, who had no defense from the blows from her sharp shoes.

It took a moment for Jillian to realize that the beating had stopped, and when she saw that the beating was now been directed at Ian, she became so enraged that she lost all control.

"No!" she screamed, flying at Isabelle.

They tumbled to the ground away from Ian. Jillian fought with everything she had. She felt as if she had a demon within her; all she could think of was killing Isabelle. Getting the best of the older woman, Jillian hauled herself over Isabelle and began to choke the life out of her.

Constance and Andrew both arrived at that moment. Constance went straight to Ian while ordering Andrew to stop the fight. Andrew tried to pry Jillian's hands from Isabelle's throat but found it very difficult, for Jillian was indeed possessed with so great a strength that Andrew couldn't break her hold. Finally, he tried appealing to her senses, begging her not to kill Isabelle.

"She isn't worth it, Jillian."

Hearing his words, Jillian looked into his eyes and saw someone there she thought she recognized. The realization brought her to her senses and she let go of Isabelle's throat and stood clasping his hands in hers. Jillian didn't break the stare, but studied his features, puzzled by the sensation of knowing this man before.

No one noticed Isabelle rise from the ground and scurry off into the garden, clutching her swollen throat.

"Do I know you?" Jillian asked him. "Have we met before?"

"I feel as if I know you very well, but no, we haven't met. I'm Andrew."

"Dear God child! Are you alright?" Constance interrupted. "Oh my, Jillian. You can speak."

"I . . . oh, I can speak," Jillian whispered. "I can talk."

"She can talk! She can talk!" Ian cried out hugging Jillian with all his might.

Constance joined in the hug, wrapping her arms around Jillian and Ian. Andrew slowly backed away from the three and left the garden. There would come another time to talk with Jillian. For now, she should enjoy the return of her voice. It was a joyous occasion and he wanted more than anything for Jillian to have some happiness because he knew just how short-lived happiness could be.

Later that evening, Marcus returned from his business in town. Jillian and Ian were in Jillian's room when he arrived. Constance stopped Marcus before he went in search for them and asked him to join her in the study. Once there, she related the details of the afternoon. She told him all that she heard Isabelle say to Jillian and assured him there was more, taking the parchment from her pocket.

"Isabelle showed Jillian this."

"How did she find it? I hid it so that no one would ever know."

"I don't know about that, but the lass is very upset about this and is waiting for you to explain it all to her. Can you tell her the truth, Marcus?"

Shaking her head, Sybil stepped into the cool shadows of the cottage. Morgan sat at the table, eating one of the apples that Sybil had purchased at the market. She looked up when Sybil arrived, a sheepish grin on her face.

"I suppose it was just gas," Morgan said, taking another bite.

"Tell that to the midwife when she gets here. I don't think she will find this very amusing after coming all the way down here to deliver a babe only to find that it's nothing more than a bubble. I'll go up to the corner to meet her so that she doesn't come all the way. Maybe, that will ease her anger."

Rising slowly from the chair, bringing her bulging stomach gradually up with her, Morgan apologized to Sybil for the inconvenience and thanked her for the apple then left the cottage without further ado.

Sybil grinned to herself at Morgan's antics, but was relieved to see her go, for she had much to do in preparation for tonight's plan. Douglass would be waiting for her and she could not be late. If all went well tonight, this would be something she did many more times before Terrance would escape. Everything was planned and timed right down to the last detail. She prayed that nothing would go wrong.

Later that night, Sybil made her way back up the lane to Newgate. She wasn't the only woman to make the journey so late at night. Several other women, all gaily dressed in their finest clothes, walked the few miles between the village and the prison, hoping to make a few quid by selling their bodies to the prison guards and sometimes the prisoners themselves. This was the night she and Douglass had been waiting for. The plan was to get Sybil into the prison, twice in one day; masquerading as a nun in the day, and a lady of the night in the evening. Tonight would be the first time that they carried out this part of the plan and Sybil was more nervous than she had ever been in her life.

Not since the night when she had first met Douglass had she ever been so frightened. She remembered how he had saved her from Richard that night so many months before, and how he had told her to take off her clothes. At first Sybil was ready to throw him out of her home, but once he explained that they would travel as a priest and a nun, Sybil was convinced that Douglass did indeed know what he was doing.

The masquerade had continued from that day on, until they arrived at the village as man and wife. Douglass told the neighbors that his brother had passed away in a terrible riding accident, and that he had taken his brother's wife, who was heavy with child, as his own. Questions were asked and Douglass always had an answer. Sybil learned very quickly to let him do the explaining and to listen very carefully just in case she was asked some of the same questions.

He talked to her at length about carrying out the plan and also about her hopes and fears for a future with Terrance. Sybil found herself telling Douglass things that she had never even admitted to herself. Somehow he understood the love she had for Terrance better than she did herself, and was determined to see Sybil and Terrance reunited.

A sudden wind blew beneath Sybil's skirts, making them billow and swirl around her legs. She clutched her shawl more closely, covering her bare shoulders, regretting that she wore such a revealing dress. But, it was all part of the plan.

The gates of Newgate, tall and dark, opened before the women. Beyond the gates, several guards gathered in the mist of the yard, waiting to choose a companion for the night. Sybil searched their faces, panic rising in her throat. What if he doesn't come? The only thing for Sybil to do would be to choose one of the men and carry through with the plan, or turn and run as hard as she could, never to return to the gate at night. There was no choice, Sybil had to stay and see this through, for Terrance and for herself. Staying to the back of the group, Sybil prayed that Douglass would come and take her before one of the other men did. Where could he be?

Several women were chosen and left with their fares for the night. Just two remained beside Sybil. Gregory, the young boy who had so shyly checked Sybil's papers only this morning, appeared before them. The hunger in his eyes was the same hunger that Sybil had seen when he had looked at her that morning, only this time; there was no embarrassment or shyness. This time Sybil saw the raw need for a woman, a need that would take some skill to squelch. He passed the others by and stopped directly in front of Sybil.

"You're new to the gate." Gregory said questioningly.

"Yes, milord." Sybil said, with a cockney accent.

"Let us see what you have to offer," he said, lifting the shawl from her shoulders.

Sybil kept her head down, praying that he would not recognize her. Her painted face may hide the virginal nun, but she knew her eyes would be a giveaway if he were to look into them. His hand traced the line of her milky white shoulder, continuing downward. Sybil's breast rose with every bated breath. Fear was all she could feel at this moment, fear of lying with this young man with only one end in mind, freeing Terrance.

From a distance, a familiar voice thundered in the darkness. Sybil was never so glad in her life to hear it.

"Hold there. Hold I say!" Douglass roared, as he grew nearer. "Why is there no one on the tower?" he bellowed to Gregory, who flew to attention.

"We were just having a bit of sport, sir."

"A bit of sport, you say," he said menacingly. "Aye, you can have your sport tonight by guarding in the tower until dawn."

"But sir, I've had a full day and am on duty come morning."

"Don't bother me with your prattle. Get you up to the tower posthaste."

"Yes, sir." Gregory saluted, then left Douglass and Sybil alone.

"You were very hard on the boy," Sybil whispered.

"Not as hard as it would have been on you had I not arrived when I did. The boy is insatiable, I hear."

"Why, Douglass. That cannot be true. He's just a child."

"He's more of a man than you care to concede, milady. Now, if you would accompany me for the night, I would be very grateful. If you know my meaning," Douglass declared, loud enough for the guards and the other woman to hear.

"Of course, sir. That is what I am here for, is it not?"

*   *   *   *   *

Marcus contemplated what he could tell Jillian to mask the shame that he felt by deceiving her. In his heart, he knew that adding more lies would only make matters worse, but how could he tell Jillian the truth? He had hoped that Jillian would eventually either remember her ordeal or find out the truth from someone else. Why did that person have to be Isabelle? She was so vicious in her joy of destroying other people's lives and relished the anguish that she created.

"Jillian has to know the truth," Marcus told Constance. "I can't take the chance that she'll remember on her own and not understand why I did what I did."

"That may be true, milord," Constance said, "but there is something else that you must consider."

"And what is that, Constance? What else could possibly be more important than telling Jillian how her husband, this Gavin character," he spat, "sold her to the highest bidder after displaying her to the crowd like some prized mare. I've seen horses treated better than he treated her. You saw the marks. The man was an animal!"

"Yes, the man was an animal, but he is still her husband."

"Still her husband? Are you out of your mind? I bought her from him. He has no claim to her now."

"He may not have a claim to Jillian, Marcus," Constance contemplated before going on, "but what about his claim to his child?"

Marcus was taken aback. Child? He'd never thought about the possibility. It was hard to fathom.

"I don't believe that Jillian is pregnant. After what she has been through, how could she possibly be?"

"It isn't just a possibility, milord. Jillian is with child. Have you not noticed?"

"Noticed? No, I haven't seen any signs. She has put on a few pounds but that is only because she is recovering from near starvation, not because she is pregnant."

Coming closer to Marcus, Constance put her hand gently on his shoulder. "Marcus, she has not had her womanly flow since she arrived at Havenwood months ago. She's put on enough weight through the middle that I had the seamstress take out the waist in all her dresses. Oddly enough, Jillian hasn't mentioned that she suspects a thing."

"Of course she doesn't suspect anything of the sort. Up until today, she thought she was a pampered guest of the household. Up until today, she had no reason to think that she was a woman who has lain with a man. Now, thanks to my demented sister, she knows part of the story and I am left to tell her the rest. I don't even know anything about her before that night in the tavern. What do I tell her about how she came to be there and how she was sold to the highest bidder?"

"Marcus, you saved her life, that's what you did. If it were not for you, some nasty bloke may have purchased her and abused her worse than her husband ever did. You saved her."

"Now, Constance, what do I do? If she's with child, I have an obligation to them both. How do I redeem myself?"

"Oh, you'll think of something, milord. You always do. But for now, just tell her what you know and leave it at that. She'll have to deal with it all sooner or later. You are the only one who can explain why you did what you did. Jillian will understand."

Later that night, Jillian and Marcus sat in the study in silence. Marcus told the story of how he came to know her, about the scene in the tavern, and everything he knew about her cruel husband. He tried not to leave anything out, including the feelings of lust that had held him witless while he watched the torture of a defenseless girl.

Now there was only stillness between them. Marcus sat facing Jillian, his hands clasped together on his knees, his eyes focused on the expensive Persian covering on the highly waxed wooden floor. His guilt kept his eyes from seeking her reaction. He knew he was a coward and felt even more paralyzed at this very moment than he had when watching the lash of Gavin's whip strip Jillian's flesh of its purity. His only thought was of self-condemnation for his deeds. He could only hope for her forgiveness; he did not want her pity.

Jillian sat immersed in her own thoughts. For just a brief moment she thought this scene was being played over and over in her life, a source of déjà vu to which she couldn't connect. She chuckled at her thoughts; somehow she knew that this wasn't the first time that horrible things had been revealed to her, but she couldn't remember when or where this had previously happened. What a contradiction this was, to know or have a feeling about the happenings of a time that couldn't be remembered, and to know that scenes were being played out once again, without knowing the outcome of the first. Jillian thought it comical at the very least.

Marcus glanced up, hearing Jillian's mirth, and wondered about her thoughts. He expected her to scream at him and call him a liar, but instead she sat in amused silence and let him finish his explanation of the bill of sale she was shown this afternoon. She understood and believed his incredible story. Perhaps she remembered some of it. The thought made Marcus wince and his own guilt hit him in the chest once more, cutting like a saber through his heart.

"I am so sorry, Jillian. I wish with all my heart that it wasn't so, but it is the truth and is all I know about you. One thing I do know is that you have a pure soul and whatever brought you to that tavern, at that exact moment, was meant to be. I was meant to find you there and bring you here to us."

Jillian pondered his words. Was Marcus right? She didn't question that he was telling the truth but she did question whether it was right for her to be here with his family. She thought of Ian and his sweet heroic ways and how he had fought his own aunt to save her, not just once but twice, without thought or fright. She thought about the kindness of the staff, especially Constance. She had been so comforting while Jillian was ill when she first awoke. Jillian felt that she was like a mother to her. This realization jolted Jillian from her thoughts. Surely, she must have a mother herself, but where? Only Marcus knew anything about her, and his knowledge was limited to the last few weeks. Jillian suddenly came to realize that if she had a family somewhere, she had to find them.

"Marcus, is that all there is? Is there anyone else who would know anything about me? Perhaps the innkeeper or the barmaid?"

Startled by her question, Marcus straightened himself to answer. "Why, I'm not certain. We left the tavern so quickly. I was terribly frightened that your . . . husband would change his mind about the sale, that all I could think of was getting you out of there. I sent my scribe back for the official papers. I didn't want him to know where you were."

"Might your man have asked some questions when he retrieved the papers?"

"That he may. At the time, my greatest concern was that you lived. I didn't ask him anything other than to ascertain that he was not followed."

"I understand." Jillian hesitated, then timidly continued, "Will you help me once again, Marcus? Will you help me find out who I am?"

Marcus had realized that Jillian would someday want to know who she was and where she came from but he was not yet ready to commit to helping her find what destiny was out there for her. She had to know everything he knew before she made the decision to seek the unknown. She had to know that there was someone else to consider before she took the chance of encountering a past that could prove to be even crueler than the husband who had sold her to the highest bidder.

"Jillian, there is something else you need to know."

"Something else? What else is there to know? I already know that you own me." Frustrated, Jillian waited for her words to seep in. "I already know that I have no right to be in this house and living off your generosity."

"Don't think like that, Jillian. I have an obligation to take care of you after what I did," he said, his guilt showing clearly in his strained features.

Jillian's tone softened. She knew that she was taking out her anger and frustration on Marcus; a man who had only showed her kindness.

"Oh, Marcus. Kind, gentle, Marcus," Jillian murmured, cupping his cheek in her palm. "What you did was save me from that wicked man. From what you have told me, I would be dead if it were not for you."

"I should have stopped him sooner," he said, taking her hand in his.

"You stopped him soon enough and I am alive, thanks to you."

"I would give anything for things to be different, Jillian," Marcus said, gathering his strength for his next words. He pulled Jillian down to sit, and knelt in front of her, holding both her delicate hands in his own. "I would give anything not to have to tell you this, but you will recognize that fact soon enough."

"What is it, Marcus? Tell me the rest."

"Jillian, I . . ." he paused. "Jillian, dear Jillian. Will you marry me?"

Sybil smiled at the cherubic face blanketed safely in her arms. The babe sucked on his lower lip in contemplation of his first suckling yet to come. A low moan from the bed where Morgan lay sleeping brought a sigh of disappointment, for Sybil's own breast ached to nourish the babe in her arms. She smiled to herself, thinking that it was odd how a woman's body never forgets the need to nurture. She remembered another babe held in her arms and the love so deep in her being that she felt as if she would burst with the joy of it.

But then she remembered William's eyes and the way he had carelessly held Jillian as if he didn't care if he dropped her at any moment. He had laughed at her in her desperation to take the baby back to her breast. But when Father or Sophie were near he would act like the doting father and gloat over Jillian as if she were a prized bull.

When Sybil gave birth to Siriann, William was so much more of a father to her and cast Jillian aside like someone's garbage. He spoiled and coddled Siriann to the point of absurdity. After Siriann's birth William never again held or comforted Jillian but became even more hardened to her.

Sybil's tears never comforted her as she recalled William's mistreatment of Jillian. Tears were wasted on him and were of no help to Jillian now. She dried her misted eyes and again focused on the babe and his increasing need for nourishment. Sybil rose to wake Morgan so that the babe could be fed.

Reluctantly, Morgan roused herself from slumber and took the babe to her breast, giving thanks to Sybil for all her assistance during the birth of her child. It had not been long after Sybil sent the midwife home that Morgan's pain had begun in earnest. Sybil was not inclined to run after the midwife for another false alarm after the midwife had voiced her displeasure about coming all this way for nothing. However, Morgan's pains were real this time and the babe came so fast that Sybil didn't have time to call for help. Sybil delivered the boy on her own, as if she were born to the task.

Letting the two become better acquainted, Sybil left the cottage. She squinted in the darkness of the street, trying to catch sight of a passerby to send to the pub for Morgan's husband, but no one was in sight. That no good husband of Morgan's was never around, Sybil thought, least of all when you needed him. How Morgan had ended up with him was a quandary.

From a distance Sybil heard the sound of hooves on the cobblestones of the street above and focused on the horizon of the dimly lit street that swooped over the hill toward her. This crest was the barrier between their class and the upper class of London. If Morgan and some of the other occupants of the neighborhood knew that Sybil was not part of their distinction they would not be so trusting of her. She was sure that they would run her out if they knew that her father was an admiral and that she was married to a ship's captain.

The roles that she was playing were treacherous. If anyone found out what she was doing it would be her demise. Living as the pregnant wife of a prison guard, all the while making visits to the prison as a nun during the day and a whore in the evenings, was about as bizarre as life could get, but she would do it all over again if it meant getting Terrance out of the hellhole he was in.

Her thoughts turned to Terrance for the thousandth time today, making Sybil's womb quiver with need of conception. Memories of Terrance grew stronger with every passing day. From the first moment she saw him galloping so freely through the woods to attend dinner, to the last time she looked back at him in his prison cell as the door slammed shut, blocking his sweet eyes from view, she remembered everything.

For so many years, she tried to forget him and the way he awakened her mind and body. He was taken from her so suddenly and returned to her the same. He had turned her world upside down, yet Sybil knew no regrets in loving Terrance. Her only regret was not being strong enough to resist the pressure from her father to save her name and his, by marrying William. How different things would have been in her and Jillian's life had she not married William.

"It's not safe to be out here alone," Douglass whispered to Sybil from behind.

Startled, Sybil lurched away from him, but Douglass caught her arm and pulled her back to him.

"Douglass, you scared the devil out of me."

"Ye were deep in thought, lassie. I stood by for a few minutes, waiting for you to notice me there," he said, pointing to the crest of the hill. "Jenkins was kind enough to give me a lift on his way to get Lord Mosley."

"That was very kind of him," Sybil said, flushing. "I was just thinking."

"Aye, I could see that, and I could also see who you were thinking about. Your face lights like a lighthouse on a stormy night when ye think of me," he winked. Motioning to a passerby, he pulled Sybil into his arms and, to Sybil's chagrin, kissed her lips ever so lightly. The young man gave a satisfied whoop as he walked on by.

"That was nice," Douglass murmured softly. "Of course, it was for his benefit," he said, still holding Sybil close and watching as the man rounded the corner out of sight.

"Of course," Sybil agreed, recovering from the sudden gentleness of this giant man. Remembering the occupant of their tiny cottage, Sybil pulled Douglass toward the door. "I've got a surprise for you."

"Now, sweetling, it wasn't that good of a kiss, was it?" Douglass teased.

"No. I mean yes. No," she said again. "Douglass, please be serious. Morgan has given birth and I need you to find her husband."

The door to the cottage opened, revealing the mother and babe cuddled together on Sybil and Douglass's bed. Shaking his head, Douglass sighed. "And all I wanted was my bed tonight."

"That will have to wait, for right now, Morgan needs her husband and her own bed. You go and find him and I'll make us all a late sup before he takes them both home," she said, swooshing him back out the doorway.

"Ouch, woman, you'll be the death of me," he joked. "I'll return with the youngster by the scruff before you can think of another chore for me this eve."

"You do that," Sybil laughed, waving him off, then shivering at his words. The death of him, she thought, praying that his words would not come back to haunt them both.

Sometime later, Sybil lay beside Douglass, listening to his even breaths, signaling to her that he was deep in slumber. Since the day that they had taken up residency in the village, they had shared this bed. Never once had

Douglass touched Sybil in any way other than friendship, until tonight. When Douglass had kissed Sybil so unexpectedly, it had startled her. Being so indulged by this gentle man and he asking nothing in return, Sybil hadn't questioned his intentions or their mission to free Terrance. Now she lay awake wondering if she was being fair to Douglass. His feelings were not something she had considered before, but were the focus of her thoughts now.

Was he falling in love with her? Did she have feelings for him as well? Of course she cared for Douglass. He had been so helpful to her and to Terrance. Sybil knew that the only reason Terrance was still alive was because of Douglass's care at the prison. Before Douglass came to Sybil, he had helped Terrance, bringing him extra bits of food that he smuggled from his own plate, and making sure that he had more straw for his bed so that Terrance might be a bit warmer in the bowels of his confines. These may seem like meaningless gestures to people who had plenty, but to Terrance they meant life itself. Only when Terrance had lost all hope and had given up had Douglass sought the one thing he knew would give Terrance the will to live and escape his prison. Sybil.

Douglass watched Sybil from beneath his half-closed eyelids. He knew where her thoughts had taken her and felt a sudden pang of guilt for having slipped this evening. His loyalties were to his friends and to their quest for Terrance's freedom, but he could not help the feelings that he had for Sybil. He knew he loved her before he had ever met her, for the picture that Terrance had painted of Sybil with the stories of his love for her and their daughter had captured his heart many long nights ago. It took every ounce of strength Douglass had to resist pulling her into his arms and showing her just how much he did indeed love her. Douglass knew that his loyalty to Terrance was the one thing that would save him from death at Newgate prison and that he couldn't break his vow to his dear friend or the woman that they both loved.

"Are ye alright, Sybil?" he asked. "Ye seem troubled."

"Oh, I thought you were sleeping, Douglass. Did I wake you?"

"Nay, I woke with my own thoughts. After all, tomorrow is an important day for us all."

Sybil shuddered. "Yes, tomorrow is worrisome. Are you certain that our plan is set?"

"As set as it will be, I suppose. I smuggled in what Terrance will need this evening before I left for home. He hid it in the straw so no one will notice. Not that anyone ever comes around to mind him none. He should be safe enough until I give him the signal."

"I hope he never finds out my roll in this, Douglass," Sybil said, her voice giving away her fear. "I'm not sure he would want to come with us if he knew."

"Aye, he would be angry but would be free. That will count for something," Douglass said pulling her toward him and fitting her bottom neatly against him.

His actions and the warmth that emanated from his body, so close to hers, alarmed Sybil. "Douglass, I have something to ask you."

"Nay, Sybil. We need our rest, for tomorrow will be a long, trying day and we need all our wits about us. Go to sleep," he commanded, patting her on the hip. "It will all be over tomorrow."

Although his actions troubled Sybil, his body snuggled so close did indeed comfort her and she found herself drifting to sleep with thoughts of Terrance and Jillian and their future life together.

Douglass pulled her even closer, vowing chastity for the coming hours. He could not lose his resolve to rescue his friend and give him back his life. If it was the last thing Douglass ever did, he would complete this quest and reunite Sybil with Terrance.

The next morning, Sybil bid Douglass farewell as he left for another day at Newgate prison. Sleep had eluded them both throughout the night as they lay together for warmth and comfort, contemplating the day ahead. Although Douglass sustained an air of confidence, Sybil knew that he was weary from the strain of devising and carrying out such a complex scheme to rescue Terrance from prison. They had gone over and over the plan that morning while breaking the fast, discussing every step in detail to ensure that both were very much aware so that if anything unexpected were to happen, they would know what to do.

Sybil slipped back into bed, hoping for a few moments of sleep before her part in the plan started. She prayed silently to herself for the strength and courage she needed to succeed in this endeavor. Terrance depended on them both, even though he was not aware of the true danger of the plan for his escape.

It was nigh on noon when Sybil approached the prison gates dressed as the simple nun who gave comfort to the dregs of the prison. Today, she would see Terrance for the second time and hoped that he was ready to make his way out of this horrible place. She had to keep her wits about her in order for the plan to succeed. It would be very difficult to master this if Terrance overly questioned her. Sybil found it hard to lie to him.

Gregory watched the bewitching nun make her way up the lane in the midday sun. He could have sworn that the sunlight spun a halo over her head. He feared and adored her all the same and wondered many times why she had turned to a life of celibacy when clearly she could have had any man of her choosing. He felt himself harden with his thoughts and cursed again the effect that this mere woman had upon him. As he had many times before, he stalked away angrily to avoid the green eyes that saw through his cool demeanor and knew his lust for her.

Sybil was relieved to see that Gregory was not at his post once more. She hadn't dealt with him for some time now and was happy for it. The other guards treated her with disregard, but not Gregory; his interest in her was evident by the bulging of his uniform. At first, Sybil was flattered by his interest, but as time wore on and she was at the prison more and more, Sybil knew his recognition of her was a danger to Terrance. She had to tread lightly and not attract any more attention than was necessary to gain entry to the prison. The attention was better spent on her evening visits when she needed all eyes on her.

The guard bid her entry without question and she recognized his irritation in having to take over when Gregory suddenly vanished from his post. As she entered the prison building, aided by an awaiting Douglass, she could hear Gregory's return and the whooping of the guards who hassled him over his incessant need to relieve himself every time the nun approached the gate.

The chilly air in the bowels of the prison crept deep into Sybil's garments, making her shiver as she remembered the first time she had made this journey to Terrance's cell. The smell and feel of the slime that clung to the stone of the corridor seemed even more pungent than before. Sybil's knees quaked beneath her, making her footsteps even more treacherous.

Once again, Douglass led the way to Terrance. Sybil felt a pang of déjà vu and wondered if Terrance had heard them coming and knew that today was the day of his escape. Of course, Douglass had spoken with him many times about his part in the plan, and had more than likely told him that it would be soon. Douglass had also been slipping more and more food to Terrance so that he would have the strength to make his way from the prison walls. Sybil prayed that he was fully nourished and ready.

The door gave a mourning groan as it slowly swung on rusted hinges into the darkness of Terrence's cell. As he stepped into the light, Sybil's heart wrenched with relief at his apparent good health. He looked much improved compared to the first time she had seen him some five weeks earlier. His face was aglow with health and nourishment and his eyes had lost their dullness, which had been replaced by hope and renewed spirit. His smile lit the cell and Sybil flung herself into his waiting arms, softly murmuring his name.

"God, you smell so good," Terrance cooed. "I sensed you long before I heard the many passage doors being unlocked and locked behind you. There it was, that fragrance, the one that haunts my every waking hour and comes to me in my sleep until I'm not sure which is which." He gently disengaged her arms from his neck, putting her at arm's length to examine her face more clearly. "But I'm not dreaming this time."

"No, Terrance. You are not dreaming. The day has come for your escape," Douglass said from the cell door. "Ye must hurry if we are to carry this out. Come now and prepare to leave."

They made their way carefully from the cell through the many passages that led to Douglass's private office. Terrance stumbled once but regained his footing, finding it difficult to walk after so many months of being afforded only two or three steps within the confines of his cell. His head spun from the effort and he silently chastised himself for his weakness. Terrance negotiated the slick hallways with an awkwardness that he didn't need at the moment.

Douglass let out a sigh of relief as he opened the office door and ushered the two within. After a quick glance down the corridor, Douglass shut and locked the door behind them. Both Sybil and Terrance also let out breaths that they didn't realize they had been holding but relief was short-lived because there was much to be done to ready Terrance. Douglass retrieved a chest from beneath a small bed in the corner of the office. The bed being there struck Terrance as odd; his eyes questioned Douglass.

"Ouch man, a man needs his rest now and then," Douglass muttered, shrugging off any further mention of the bed. "Now let us see how we can make our man look a little more like a nun."

He handed Terrance the razor and strap, motioning to the washbasin on a small table that Douglass also used as a desk, then slipped from the room into the quiet hallway.

Terrance removed his tattered shirt, leaving on only his pants. Sybil picked up the razor and went to work on Terrance's wild mane, cutting away the snarls and creatures that made their home in it. She held back her disgust at the condition of his scalp, knowing that he had not been afforded an opportunity to cleanse himself.

When she finished cutting his hair, Terrance went to work sharpening the razor for the next task. He carefully shaved away his red, matted beard until all that was left was thick stubble. Again, he sharpened the razor, stroking the strap with careful motion. His hand quivered as he lifted the razor to his chin. Seeing this, Sybil stopped his hand, grasping it and the razor.

"Let me," she said, taking the razor from Terrance.

His eyes shone bright with relief as he let go of the razor and tilted his head back against her breast so that she could finish shaving him which she did with great precision. When she was finished, Terrance filled the basin with cool water and began bathing away the months of scum that clung to his festering skin. Douglass had provided a bar of lie soap that stung his flesh as it stripped away the filth and decay. Terrance could not have believed anything could feel so good, but with every sting, life came back to him.

He felt renewed, alive, for the first time in a long time and he stripped off the rest of the rags that he wore for clothes, until he was stark naked. Terrance bathed every inch of his flesh, refilling the basin several times with fresh, clean water. He enjoyed the bath to its fullest, ignoring the chill that prodded him into life even more.

Sybil stood in awe, watching the delight of Terrance's ministrations. Even in his current state, Terrance was a gorgeous man. His lean, strong muscles rippled beneath his pale skin as he wrung out the cloth he used to bathe. He was lost in the joy of feeling alive and clean again; Sybil was lost in the joy of watching him.

She recalled Terrance under the oaks of her father's estate, reading her poetry and singing to her as he had so long ago. His face had been bronzed by the sun and his hair streaked with light from the many days out at sea. He was the most handsome man she had ever seen, and she loved him so much. That was the day she had realized that she was pregnant with his child. That was the day the soldiers had come and taken him from her, before she had a chance to tell him.

Terrance stroked her chin with his thumb, waking her from her thoughts. "Where were you just now?"

"Under an oak," she said, laughing. "Oh dear," Sybil muttered, realizing how close he was to her and how gloriously nude he was. "You must get into the nun's garment. Douglass will return shortly and I have to be leaving soon."

"Not just yet," he said pulling her to him. "Have I told you that I love you? There has never been another for me," he cooed, tilting her face to his. "There never will be."

He kissed her then, softly at first, just a whisper of a caress against her anxious lips. Again, he kissed her; still gentle but urgent, nibbling on her bottom lip. She sighed sweet warm breath against his lips as he kissed her once more. Her breath seared at his resolve and he took her lips with urgent need, melding them together with his own. Sybil moaned in his embrace, her hands stroking his flesh, driven by desire. He lifted Sybil into his arms, finding strength from his need of her, to place her gently on the makeshift bed.

After so many years of yearning, Terrance found it most difficult to hold back the passion that raged through his body. He wanted to make their rejoining an expression of that longing, a glorious climax to the long days and nights of being alone.

Sybil was so beautiful. The years apart, however difficult, had not destroyed her magnificence. She was supple and generous, inviting Terrance to remove her clothing, helping him when his hands shook with the power of this moment. He carefully relieved her of the last of her undergarments, then gaining control over his own need, took a moment to gaze down at her splendor. Light from the only window, rendered a warm flush to Sybil's creamy skin. Terrance slowly knelt next to the bed, never taking his eyes off hers.

"You are the most beautiful of God's creatures." He reached out to gently caress her cheek. She began to say something, but Terrance stayed her words by laying a finger against her lips. "Do not speak. Only let me love you the way I have dreamt these many years."

Sybil sighed, closing her eyes with anticipation of that love, for she too had dreamt of this time and all the magic that it would bring.

When she felt his lips upon hers, Sybil met them with all the yearning and desire that had lay hidden for so long. She welcomed his exploration of her mouth and greeted his tongue with her own. Her arms intertwined around his neck as she clung to him with wanton passion while their tongues danced the dance of forbidden ecstasy.

Terrance explored the depths of her soul with every flaming lick of his adoration. His massive, yet kind hands, began the awakening of each fiber and nerve that lay hidden beneath the surface of Sybil's longing. He explored the softness of her neck and shoulders, the gentle swell of voluptuous breasts, their crescent peaks alive with nipples erect and sensitive. They were wonders of majestic beauty, ready for his awakening. His mouth followed this journey, joining his hands caress, to bring Sybil close to bursting with each touch, and every taste savored by him. Sybil could barely suppress the arousal of her own flesh, moaning between baited breaths in sheer ecstasy for Terrance, who fought for control of his own wanting.

"Do not hold yourself, sweet Sybil. We have waited too long for this moment. I want to hear your cries of pleasure," Terrance whispered, while continuing his descent toward the core of Sybil's love.

His fingers reached her first, parting the protective folds, teasing the hard nub of her womanhood. Sybil gasped and arched against his hand, longing for something deeper, hidden somewhere within the depths of her unknown. She had never been made love to like this, had never been awakened to her own sensuality. She moaned with the rhythm of her womb, which tightened and throbbed with each tender stoke of his finger. When Terrance's mouth found her there, her body arched, jolting with the intense surging of power coming from between her parted thighs. She softly cried out his name, feeling an immense urgency, pleading for the promise of things yet to come.

It took more strength than Terrance had ever had to summon to hold off his own pleasure until Sybil reached the point of no return. Bringing them together, to bond their ecstasy as one, would take his utmost resolve. For now, this was his mission. Concentrating on the delight at hand, Terrance dipped the tip of his tongue into Sybil's pleasure center, rendering her further down the path of fulfillment. She entangled her fingers in his shortened hair, pulling and pushing him closer to his goal of erotic peak for both of them. He held her hips steady, so as not to lose this moment with wanton clumsiness, as he manipulated the sensitive flesh of her woman's mound with his tongue.

It was not enough. Sybil wanted, no, she needed more, and she made an attempt to guide him upwards so that he could enter her, but Terrance only let go of her hips to use his hands for other purposes, inserting the tip of his finger just enough to initiate the first clenching spasm of Sybil's climax. Tiny moans, turning into whimpers of bliss, escaped Sybil's passion swollen lips as Terrance swept her inhibitions away, one by one. But soon, the momentum toward ultimate joy reverberated from her, and the echo of Sybil's screams of delight rewarded Terrance as she reached the pivotal point when it was time for so much more.

Easing himself upon her, Terrance held his breath, pleading for strength to last long enough for both of them. In her need to have him inside her, Sybil clutched his lean hips, begging him to enter her.

"Steady, Sybil," Terrance breathed. "Give me a moment. I promise it will be worth your wait."

"Oh, please Terrance. I cannot wait. I want you inside of me."

He entered her then, just a slight invasion at first, testing her, as to not cause her pain. But Sybil was no virgin and knew what he had to give her. When he would have pulled back to ease their joining, Sybil urged him toward her with all the strength she could muster, forcing the length of him to the very entrance of her womb. There was nothing more that Terrance could do to hold himself in check, and he matched her guidance with the fierce plunging of his hips, feeling the very core of her existence.

Sybil could restrain herself no more, burying her face in a pillow, wailing into it with every stroke of Terrance's penetration. With that, Terrance lost the struggle for control, his body quaking, spilling his seed deep within the woman he loved.

*   *   *   *   *

Sometime later, when Douglass reentered the room, he sensed the wholeness of the two people who awaited his return. They smiled at each other from beneath guarded lids, with bashful, embarrassed gazes that said more than any words could. He felt pangs of loss and satisfaction at the same time, squelching his own feelings to find joy in theirs. He felt suddenly glad that he hadn't been able to return as soon as he had planned. He wouldn't have wanted to interrupt the reunion of such deserving souls.

"We must hurry, Sybil," Douglass said, uncoiling the rope he hid under his cloak. "The changing of the guard is upon us. Are you ready?"

"Yes," Sybil said, looking away from Terrance's questioning gaze. "Are you sure they won't see me?"

"Not if you make your way straight for the forest," he said, pointing out the window toward the west. "The sun is close to the treetops and the guards will be blinded for just a few minutes if we time it right."

Shrugging to get the nun's garment off, Sybil was glad that she had remembered to put her underclothes back on after she and Terrance had made love. Terrance grasped Sybil's arm, holding her close to him and away from the window.

"What are you doing?" he questioned, looking from Sybil to Douglass. "You can't mean to go out the window?"

"It's the only way, Terrance. You can't fit through the window. I can."

"By all that is holy, you'll kill yourself Sybil!" He was frantic. "I can try. Here . . ." he said, making his way toward the window.

But Douglass caught Terrance before he could pull himself up. "No my friend. We've planned this from the beginning. Sybil knows what to do. We've even made sure that she can fit through the porthole. She's the only one of us small enough." Looking Terrance square in the eye, Douglass dropped his next statement into the silence of the room like a shattering glass. "You, my friend, are going out the front gate."

They stood in awkward silence, each contemplating the other. It was Sybil, standing in front of Terrance with strength and dignity, who made the final decision to proceed.

"Kiss me now, one last time as a hostage of Newgate prison. When we are free, kiss me then as the man with whom I intend to spend the rest of my life."

Terrance swallowed hard, then plunged his mouth fiercely onto Sybil's swollen lips, exploring her intensely, then easing up with all the gentleness and passion that he possessed. The kiss consumed them, sealing their fates to join them together beyond the walls where they now stood.

It was with immense difficulty that Terrance pulled his lips from hers, realizing that if the plan were to succeed, there could be no more delay. He couldn't wait one more day to have Sybil as his own. He watched helplessly as Sybil shimmied her small frame through the tiny opening in the prison wall. To her, it seemed as though her hips were wider than they had been weeks ago when she and Douglass had made sure she could fit. A sudden rush filled her as she thought that maybe her hips were wider after making love for the first time in a very long time. Her lips were still swollen and sensitive from the thorough kissing Terrance had given her during their lovemaking, but nothing compared to the goodbye kiss they shared before she climbed up to the window for her escape. Feeling their bruised fullness brought blushes to Sybil's cheeks and an ache to her loins. She smiled, thinking how comical it must be to think of such things while hanging some sixty feet above the ground; held only by what now seemed to be a very short rope.

Douglass and Terrance lowered her slowly toward the ground below, each taking pains to not let go or lower her too quickly. She was weightless at the end of the rope. Terrance let Douglass hold the end until he could see just how far she had to go to be safely on the ground. The rope was at least twenty feet short of setting her down.

"Pull her back up. It's too short."

"It's the longest that I could find. I hope the hangman doesn't need it soon."

Terrance's look of horror squelched anything that Douglass was about to say. He motioned out the window to Sybil, letting her know that they were bringing her back up. She shook her head violently, silently telling him to drop her to the ground. He shook his head and began to tug her upward.

Quickly, Sybil untied the knot and dropped the remaining feet to the sloping ground below. She plunged to the ground, landing hard on her side. It seemed to her that she bounced and landed again, this time on her back. Although she wanted to lay there and scream in agony, Sybil wasted little time before she was on her feet running to the safety of the forest. Dead silence followed her.

Douglass listened for the alarm from the guards but heard nothing. He sighed in relief. Before he knew what hit him, Douglass was laying flat on the floor of his office, Terrance towering over him, fist readied for another blow.

"I hope you got that out of your system," Douglass said, rubbing his throbbing chin.

"Damn you, Douglass. She could have been killed," Terrance yelled, clenched fist raised and ready for another blow.

"We may all be killed before this is over, friend. The worst is yet to come"

Terrance hesitated then put out his hand to help Douglass to his feet. "That scared the hell out of me. I don't know what I would do if she were hurt."

"I don't know either," Douglass said, pulling the rope back through the window. "Now is not the time to lose your resolve. We have to get you out next."

Sybil made sure the trees hid her before she broke down, falling to her knees in pain on the forest floor. Her side throbbed and she knew that she must have broken some ribs in her fall. The side of her face and shoulder were scuffed and bruised, oozing droplets of blood, which she wiped away with a piece of cloth that she tore from the hem of her skirt.

She was in a great deal of pain but knew that her part in this was only just beginning. She forced herself to get up and make her way down to the stream, to the bundle of clothes waiting for her to dress in for the evening. She prayed that Terrance and Douglass were making ready for the next part of their plan.

Defining Preparation   _Chapter 39_

Jillian stretched dreamily beneath the feather comforter that enclosed her in glorious warmth. The fall weather had turned to winter quite suddenly, making her morning personals even more forbidding than ever. A few more minutes under the covers wouldn't matter.

It was only a matter of days before she and Marcus were to be wed. At first Jillian did not agree to marry Marcus, but after some coaxing from him and Constance, Jillian relented. Especially after she realized that what they had told her was true; she was with child.

It didn't seem to matter to Jillian that she had no recollection of the baby's father; it didn't matter to Marcus that he wasn't the father. All that mattered was that she somehow knew that this baby would bring her happiness. She knew deep down inside that a new life would come into this world and all would be well for her and the babe.

So much had happened in such a short time. Jillian woke every morning pinching herself to make sure that she wasn't dreaming. So many things had changed for her in the month since she came to Havenwood. It was hard to believe that she could be so lucky as to have been rescued by Marcus and to have him love her as he had professed the night he asked her to marry him.

The thought of his rescuing her brought a flicker of doubt to Jillian. Try as she might, she couldn't remember anything prior to waking up and finding herself at Havenwood. There were brief moments when she felt that something was familiar but then it would fade. Jillian hoped that she wouldn't suddenly remember something that would destroy the contentment she had come to savor. In her heart, Jillian knew that with time, she would come to love Marcus for more than just her rescuer. She wanted desperately to love him, as he deserved, as her husband.

The preparations for the wedding were well underway. Constance had taken on all the planning as if she were planning her own wedding. Jillian was overjoyed to let her, for she had impeccable taste and knew Marcus and his finances better than anyone. There were no worries for her in regard to the wedding being one that the community would never forget. Constance made sure that all the finest ladies and gents were invited and that no gossip would ruin the affair.

At first, Constance had seemed distant and forlorn about the wedding. Jillian thought that she resented her for being the one, who Marcus asked to marry, but Constance assured her that there was no ill will; she was happy for Marcus and Jillian. Still, there seemed to be an underlying sadness that followed Constance these days. Even with all the preparations, and as thorough as Constance was, joy was not in her.

Smoothing the silk nightgown down over her healing body, Jillian felt the increasing swell of her breasts, the evidence of her pregnancy growing more evident with each day. She felt the slight elevation of her lower abdomen, the roundness filled with new life, so tiny, yet so important. Smiling to herself, she wondered whether she carried a boy or a girl. Secretly, she hoped that it was a boy, for the males of this world had far fewer problems than the females. Either way, this baby would make her and Marcus's life whole; so much rested on this new life and her new life with Marcus.

Just then, in a flurry of skirts, Constance rushed into the room, immediately opening the drapes to the bright sunlight of morning. Squinting, Jillian shielded her eyes form the piercing light, while bidding Constance good morning.

"And good morning to you, milady," Constance said, ushering in the handmaids with fresh warm water for Jillian's bath. "It's getting late, milady, and there's plenty to be done this fine day. Ye must be getting those lazy bones out of bed."

"Oh, but it feels so good and warm," Jillian teased, stretching lazily under the covers. "I could stay here all day."

"Could you now? Will we be bringing the preacher up here to say your vows in bed then?"

"Yes, that will be just fine. Don't forget Marcus. He'll want to be here, too."

"I'm sure he'll have something to say about that."

Jillian thought for a moment that Constance didn't sound so cheerful anymore and thought better of keeping up the fun at Constance's expense.

"I guess you're right, Constance. There is work to be done and I haven't been that much help, have I?"

"Now, don't be worrying your pretty little head none. Everything is being done as if it were me o—" she hesitated briefly, "well, as if it were me own wedding, you know."

"Yes, Constance, I do understand and I love you all the more for it," Jillian said, seeing sadness return to her friend's face.

Before she could say anything else, Constance coaxed Jillian out of bed with a tray of freshly baked muffins, laced with finely ground brown sugar, and steaming hot tea to wash them down. Her belly growling loudly, Jillian eased from beneath the warm covers, slipping her feet into her slippers before standing on the cold stones of her bedroom floor. An apple muffin melted like butter in her mouth and she closed her eyes, enjoying the flavor.

One of the handmaids built up the fire in the fireplace and it began to emit warmth throughout the cool room. Steam from the tub, now filled with hot water for her bath, reminded Jillian of just how cold it was in the mornings here at Havenwood. This was something that she would have to get used to, for she knew that she would be here for a long time after she and Marcus wed.

Life had certainly changed for Jillian, or at least she thought it had, beings she didn't know what kind of life she had before coming to Havenwood. What she did know, was that she loved it here, and loved Marcus for bringing her here. He was so thoughtful and kind and never showed any signs of anger with her or with Ian.

Jillian had fallen in love with Ian the first moment she had opened her eyes and gazed into his cherubic face. He was a delight to be around. Every moment, filled with his inquisitiveness about the smallest things, made Jillian thoroughly enjoy her time with him. He constantly asked questions about everything he happened across. When he wasn't asking continuous questions, he was dallying with a dragon or a monster in his make-believe kingdom, where Jillian usually played the damsel in distress. His antics brought happiness and life to each day. Smiling to herself, Jillian remembered how he had defended her even from his own Aunt Isabelle, who loathed him for no apparent reason.

Isabelle was another matter altogether. For reasons unknown to Jillian and most of the household, Isabelle detested her brother and his child. She detested anyone who made her brother happy, and that included Jillian and Constance. Fortunately for all of them, Marcus had sent her away after the attack on Jillian in the gardens. As far as Jillian knew, she was somewhere where she could no longer inflict pain or vile words on anyone close to Marcus. For that, Jillian was very grateful. Isabelle was the most evil person Jillian had ever known. She couldn't imagine anyone more vile.

Someone else was also gone from Havenwood. The servant, Andrew, had disappeared as fast as he'd come. Jillian hadn't been able to get to know him very well, for he'd only been employed for a few weeks when he just up and left, just after Marcus proposed. Havenwood needed all the employees it had and Andrew was nowhere to be found. Andrew seemed somehow familiar and sought Jillian's attention when she was alone, but they never got a chance to speak before he left. Jillian was sorry for that, for she felt he had something to say and never got the chance to say it.

Even with all the changes, the plans for the wedding had progressed very nicely and now it was only days away. Jillian felt excited about the wedding, her new life as Marcus's wife and Ian's mother. But hidden deep inside Jillian, was a sense of impending doom, like a blanket of darkness waiting to fall over her make-believe happiness. It wasn't a new sensation; Jillian felt it often, but what would one expect when she couldn't remember anything of her life before Marcus and Havenwood.

Being an understanding man, Marcus was patient with her, calming her worst fears with reassurances of his protection. He accepted Jillian for who she was, finding long periods of time to talk to her so that he may know in his heart who she was. Nothing that came before could dissuade Marcus from rectifying his deeds by marrying Jillian. It mattered little to him that he didn't know from where she came. He had proof that she was free to marry him on the bill of sale.

Gavin's signature was all he needed to verify to the priest that Jillian was free to be his wife. Despite talk in the village, Marcus was steadfast in his mission to go through with this marriage. He hadn't regarded the gossip's validation in the past and wouldn't do so now. The wedding would proceed as planned and there was no one who could stop it. Two more days were all that stood between them and their nuptials.

* * * * *

Sybil struggled with the stays of the corset; her swollen ribs ached a steady beat with every tug on the tightening strings. It was taking her longer than expected to dress for the evening's activities. She prayed that Terrance and Douglass would not panic with worry and spoil the plan by coming to find her. If they weren't careful, they might be discovered and all of them imprisoned within the walls of Newgate.

Tying the final bow, Sybil sucked in a painful breath, feeling lightheaded from the exertion of doing so. She applied powder to her swollen cheek, hoping to cover the redness of the scratches that had stopped seeping only a short time ago. Without a looking glass, she couldn't be sure that they were completely indistinguishable and hoped that her entry into the prison would be brief.

Gathering all the courage and strength she could muster, Sybil made her way up from the creek toward the main road to Newgate, careful not to attract attention from the vendors going back to the city after a day of supplying the prison with their wares. Sybil wondered if the men and women imprisoned at Newgate got the privilege of sampling some of the fresh vegetables and bread that the vendors supplied. After seeing the conditions to which Terrance was subjected, she doubted very much that any of the unfortunate prisoners were treated to the delicacies paid for them from the prison coffers. Knowing that one less soul would have to suffer another night in the hellhole that was Newgate gave Sybil renewed strength to carry on with the evening's plan.

The sun was well below the horizon when Sybil reached the gates. She stood for a brief moment, looking up at the tower beside the main entrance. There was no sign of Gregory, and for this, she was grateful. If there was any one guard she feared would recognize her, it was Gregory. He had fallen very hard for the nun who frequented the halls of Newgate. Sybil was very careful not to let the woman of little virtue she portrayed at night be subjected to the same demise. Taking a deep breath, Sybil bid the guards to grant her entry, then waited for the signal from Douglass that the time was upon them to free Terrance.

Losing his patience with Terrance, Douglass explained for the third time, the plan for his escape. It wasn't that Terrance was daft, but rather that he couldn't believe that Douglass and Sybil could come up with such a harebrained idea to start with. How they could think that he would go through with it was beyond him.

"Are you insane, man?" Terrance asked, shaking his head in disbelief. "It is more dangerous than Sybil going out the window. I'll find a way out of the gates instead. If I make it, then I make it. But this, this is beyond comprehension."

"It must go as planned, Terrance, or we may all be caught. The guards are used to seeing Sybil leave as a nun. There must be a distraction when they see a nun leaving who resembles a large bull."

Trying hard to add some humor, Douglass still guarded himself, anticipating another blow from Terrance's massive fist. None came and Douglass was relieved for that. Still, he knew that all their fates rested on the successful completion of the plan. Terrance must not deviate from it in any way or they may be discovered.

"Will you put us all at risk this late in the day? Will you put Sybil and your future together at risk?"

"Of course not, Douglass. But mayhap, if I had known the plan before coming this far, I would have had a better idea."

"You might have indeed. Still we are where we are and Sybil should be at the gate, as we speak. Please do not reveal yourself no matter what happens. Once you are out of the gate, wait for Sybil by the creek to the north. She may be a few hours. Take that time to rest for your journey to safety. She will need you to be strong."

When Douglass emerged into the courtyard, a scene of utter chaos greeted him. Two of the night guards rolled in the mud at the entrance. Douglass sought Sybil among the fracas. He briefly caught a glimpse of her before she disappeared into the throng of faces surrounding the fighting guards. He kept his eyes focused on the place where he'd seen her while running toward the crowd. Whatever had caused the disturbance only added to the difficulties that he and Sybil would face tonight. Douglass forgot all about Terrance, who had followed him into the courtyard.

"Stop this!" Douglass roared above the goading of the horde. "Stop it this instant!'

"But sir, he started it," the guard defended himself, pointing to the other guard who was face down in the mud. "He wanted to keep her all to himself, he did. I told him we could share her but he wasn't hearing none of it."

The guard on the ground spit and sputtered, clearing his eyes and mouth of wet earth with his equally muddy hands. "She wanted to come with me. Isn't that right, sweetling?" he asked, now searching the faces surrounding them.

With that, Sybil stepped forward, "Now ain't you the cocky one, Gregory? First, you accuse me of being someone else and you then want to have your way with me." Sybil kicked him in the stomach as hard as she could then clutched Douglass by the arm, pulling him toward the tower door. "Come on, me fine hunk of man. I feel the urge to ride tonight."

Sybil glanced back at the open mouths of the bystanders as she opened the door to safety for her and Douglass. Beyond the crowd, standing at least a head taller than all of them stood Terrance, his mouth,—hanging open in disbelief. His knowing eyes pierced Sybil's heart. In that instant, Sybil silently pleaded with him to make his escape while the guards were distracted. She watched as he slowly turned and walked through the gates to freedom.

As the tower door shut, Sybil's knees gave way, and she was immediately lifted into Douglass's waiting embrace. Wrapping her arms around his sturdy frame, Sybil buried her face into his massive chest, crying with the relief of having their plan succeed. Douglass returned her hold but was alarmed by a cry of pain from Sybil. Douglass carefully carried her up the many stairs to his private quarters.

Once they were safely behind closed doors, Douglass laid Sybil on the bed, where only hours ago she and Terrance had made love, then began to strip off the strumpet's clothes she wore, wanting to see what had caused her to cry out so. When it came to the corset, he carefully untied the many bows holding the front of it together. With each binding release, Sybil gasped for breath behind closed lids. Douglass lifted her shift to see what was causing Sybil such discomfort.

"Jesus, Mary and Joseph!" Douglass cried out. "Who did this to you? Was it one of my guards? By all that is holy. I will have him flogged within an inch of his life."

"Douglass, no. Please, stop shouting. You'll have all the guards in here with us if you don't stop."

"Which one, Sybil? I demand that you tell me."

Seeing the anger in his face Sybil realized at that moment how very much Douglass cared for her. She'd known it all along but hoped it wasn't so. She cared for him also, but loved Terrance with all of her heart. The memory of Douglass kissing her saddened Sybil, for there would never be a relationship between them that was deserving of him.

"Nay, Douglass. It wasn't one of the guards, but I who injured myself when I untied the rope," she said, as she motioned to the window. "That is when I bruised my face and ribs."

Gentle fingers turned Sybil's face to the side so that he could examine the partially hidden scratches. In his zeal to remove Sybil from the danger in the courtyard, Douglass hadn't noticed the redness of her left cheek. He sighed in consolation that somehow they had come through it without being caught. However, his thoughts brought him back to the state of their plans. He remembered seeing Terrance walk through the open gates just before the tower door had closed. There hadn't been any alarm bells ringing since then. He had to assume that everything was going as scheduled and that Terrance now awaited Sybil near the brook as planned.

"We did it, Sybil. Terrance is a free man," he said, pulling her gently into his arms where she sobbed in relief of all the tension of the past months of secrecy, needed in carrying out their elaborate scheme.

The magnitude of what they'd accomplished hung in the room. Terrance was safely out of prison but Sybil and Douglass were now locked inside, at least until the time was right for them to leave as they normally did when Sybil came in at night. It would be good for them to rest during this period of waiting to gather their wits about them before walking out the front gates of the prison.

Once out of the prison gates Terrance dared not look back to see if his companions had been discovered. Hearing no alarm bells confirmed to him that the guards were unaware that the rather large nun was actually a prisoner escaping their walls. It was all he could do not to turn around and make sure that Sybil was no worse for wear. Though doing that, he knew he ran the risk of exposing them all to the danger of being caught and imprisoned within the Newgate walls. He couldn't take that chance, not after everything that Sybil and Douglass had risked to free him. Carrying out the plan successfully was the only way to ensure that he and Sybil could be together once more. All he could do was wait by the stream as instructed by Douglass.

Making his way in the dark to the creek bed with skirts tangled around his long legs was no easy task. It would be a joy to remove the habit and bask naked in the moonlight until his ladylove arrived. Thought of this brought new vigor to his step and soon he found the place Douglass had described. A huge oak tree stood at the center of the stream parting the rippling waters. Tall willows on both sides secluded the area, lending welcomed privacy to Terrance, who began to strip away the habit from his chilled body. Still tender from the thorough cleansing earlier that afternoon, the autumn air caressed his skin, arousing his desire to feel its briskness. September had come with gentle winds this year, and Terrance was thankful for their freshness.

He sat at the stream's edge, reminiscing about the encounter with Sybil only a few short hours ago. Smiling to himself, he remembered every whimper and moan from her parted lips. Though they were together so many years ago, it was at a time when lovemaking was new to both of them; nothing then compared with what they had experienced this day. Terrance began to make plans for future rendezvous with his ladylove. The awakening of her body today was just the beginning of promised pleasures of the future. The years of dreaming of what it would be like to hold Sybil in his arms once more, did not compare to the true experience. Terrance felt himself harden with his thoughts.

So many needless years of pain and longing were now behind them. There was only potential for goodness and a long life of loving each other. Taking Sybil far away from here was the only answer to their dilemma. William would never rest until he hunted Terrance down. Sybil being with him would only serve to make William even more determined to find and kill Terrance. How could he accomplish freeing Sybil and himself from William's relentless pursuit?

Wondering how much time had passed, Terrance decided to ready himself for flight once Sybil and Douglass arrived. He searched the banks of the stream seeking the bundle that Sybil had left. Douglass had said that there would be clothing and nourishment for Terrance in a satchel hidden in the willows along the shore.

The beating of horse hooves brought Terrance's attention away from his task. It sounded as though many horsemen were approaching Newgate at a very fast pace. He clamored up the gully walls to have a closer look at the cause of the commotion, hunkering down in the grass along the narrow road.

It was hard to see in the dark of night, a half moon lending very little to his cause, but as they passed Terrance did spot a familiar figure at the head of the brigade approaching the gates of the prison. It was William.

His head reeling and heart sinking, Terrance watched as the gates opened, welcoming the English soldiers to Newgate prison. With no thought of his own safety, Terrance leapt to his feet and began running toward the entrance, but before he got even a few feet, the prison gates slammed behind the soldiers with a thundering crash. It was as though the sound reverberated to the very depths of his soul. Terrance fell to his knees, hitting the ground in desperation. Why? How could William possibly know that Sybil was here at the prison? Surely he was here to prevent their plans from succeeding.

"I must do something," he muttered to himself, frantically. "I have to warn Sybil and Douglass."

He got to his feet and hurried back to find his clothes near the stream all the while forming a plan in his mind to rescue Sybil from a fate worse than death—discovery by William.

Inside the courtyard of Newgate, calamity broke out as the younger guards on duty scurried to accommodate the soldiers' demands. Gregory ran to fetch Douglass, who he remembered, was in his chambers with his trollop. Suddenly, he was giddy at the thought of interrupting the tryst that he himself had wanted that night. Skidding to a stop at Douglass's door, Gregory burst in without so much as a knock to warn the two inside.

He wasn't disappointed at what he saw when the door opened. Upon a makeshift bed in the corner of the small chamber, Gregory could see Douglass on top of the trollop, pounding his loins forcefully into her spread legs, her feet bobbing above his hips. The whore's moans of pleasure echoed through the room.

"What is all this?" Douglass demanded, bringing Gregory out of his stupor. "Can't you see I'm occupied?"

Now staring at the chamber floor, Gregory could feel the scarlet burn of embarrassment rise up in his face.

"My apologies, Douglass. There is an English officer here to see the prisoner down in the dregs."

"An English officer, you say?" Douglass asked, raising himself from Sybil and handing her the blankets to cover herself. "Who might this officer be?"

"I am Sir William Crighton," came a voice from the hallway.

Sybil's eyes widened in horror. "It's my husband," she mouthed to Douglass, then hid her face beneath the blanket before William gained entrance to the room.

Douglass pulled his pants up from his ankles with all the dignity he could muster. "May I be of service to you, sir?"

"Are you the man in charge?" William spouted indignantly, looking from Douglass to the trollop skulking beneath the covers of the bed. "And do you often take guests when you should be on duty?"

"Oh, no milord," Douglass apologized, dipping into a bow before him. "Tis only an occasional fucking I get these days. Me own wife is fat with child." Sybil, surprised by what Douglass said, couldn't help but let out an indignant yelp. It went unnoticed by the soldiers who laughed with Douglass, slapping one another on the back. "So you're wanting to see the traitor?"

"Yes," William admitted. "I believe he knows more than he's told us before the trial and his ship has been seen in British waters more than once in the last few weeks. They may be planning to break him out as we speak. I've come to take him to a more secure place."

"Well then, we'd better get to it," Douglass said, making his way toward the door. "Get yourself up and see yourself out, the same as before," he called to Sybil, as the door shut behind them.

She felt as if her heart would jump right out of her chest, it was beating so fast and hard. Thank God Douglass had such keen hearing and had anticipated that they may be discovered. Her clothes were already off for his examination of the damage from her earlier fall. He had just begun to apply some bandages to her swollen ribs when he heard the sound of footsteps running toward the chamber door. Before Sybil could ask what the matter was, Douglass had pulled down his trousers and leapt upon her, whispering to her to follow his lead. There was no time to ask what he thought he was doing or to push him off, and the next thing Sybil heard was Gregory inside the room. That was when Sybil had begun to moan and writhe beneath Douglass with all the wanton that befit the part she had to play.

Replaying it in her mind did not comfort her in the least. They were in great peril and she knew that there wasn't time for modesty. William could return at any moment and discover who she was. Douglass was a man of many mysteries, but even he would be hard pressed to escape William if it were discovered that he played a part in Terrance's escape. The only thing Sybil could think to do, was to find Terrance, and together they would figure out what to do next.

Once dressed, Sybil headed to the chamber door, silently easing it open just enough to peek down the hallway outside. Gregory stood at the end of the corridor and it occurred to Sybil that he was waiting for her to emerge from the chamber. Shutting the door just as silently, Sybil leaned her back against it, contemplating her next move. It was then that she remembered what Douglass had said to her. *Get yourself up and see yourself out, the same as before.*

He hadn't meant for her to go out the front gate, but to escape as she had earlier this afternoon. Only this time, there would be no one to lower her to the ground. She would have to climb down the rope herself and hope that she didn't break her neck this time. Her ribs suddenly made their presence known by throbbing harder than ever before with every beat of her heart. She felt the bandages that Douglass had managed to secure, prior to Gregory's entrance, to reassure herself that all had been done properly and that nothing would slip while she descended the rope to freedom. Thinking about how she would manage the twenty feet was something that Sybil didn't want to do at this moment. She would decide what to do when she came to the end of her rope.

Before she could make her escape, Sybil had to make sure that Gregory wouldn't discover her and turn her over to William for punishment. As quietly as possible, she moved the table in front of the chamber door and wedged it up against the handle, then pushed the bed up to it, hoping to add extra protection from the door being opened easily.

Once the door was secured, Sybil found the hangman's rope in the chest where Douglass had hidden it. While standing on the chest for height, Sybil tied one end to the bars and began the process of feeding the rope out the window. After that was accomplished, Sybil painstakingly pulled herself up to the window ledge, all the while trying to ignore the pain that shot through her ribs with every movement.

Just as she managed to wiggle herself through the window and was preparing to climb down the rope, there was a knock at the door. Sybil pondered whether to answer the inquiry. Surely it was Gregory, who had most likely tired of waiting for her to emerge from the chamber. Maybe she could gain a few more minutes.

"Yes," Sybil called, from outside the window.

"May I be of some assistance?" he asked.

"Nay," Sybil replied. "Just wait a few moments and I will be dressed."

"No need to dress on my behalf. I would be willing to double whatever Douglass was paying you, if you will grant me a moment of your time."

"Just a moment," she called, beginning to lower herself as quickly as possible.

She could hear the thumping of Gregory's body against the door as he forced his way into the chamber yelling for the guards once he gained entrance. At this point, Sybil was just halfway down when she glanced up to see Gregory's head pop out of the window. Their eyes met. He wasted no time in calling for the guards once more, then was gone from the window. Sybil knew it wouldn't be long before the guards emerged from the gates and captured her.

She desperately tried to hurry her descent and began letting the rope slip through her hands, ignoring the tearing of her palms as the hemp scourged them. She used the prison wall to repel her way toward the ground safely, but painfully miscalculated the length of the rope, feeling the end of it slip from her hands. As if in slow motion, Sybil waited for the feel of the hard ground to rise up and splatter against her spine. Instead, she landed in the arms of someone unknown and was lowered gently to the earth.

"That is the second time today that you could have been killed," Terrance said, standing on unsteady legs. "Hopefully, it will be the last."

He clutched her to him and she swooned against his chest, relieved that she had made it to safety and into the very arms that began this entire journey. Remembering Douglass, Sybil began to tell Terrance what happened inside the prison, and that their friend was in great danger, when the sound of the alarm bells rang out in the autumn night.

Terrance ran, carrying Sybil in his arms, toward the forest edge and shelter from their impending capture. Once under cover of the thick trees, Terrance set Sybil down, crouching beside her to watch for approaching guards. The forest was quiet except for the sound of the Newgate bells. A wisp of smoke filtered through the thick trees, smelling of fireplaces used for warmth and cooking by the villagers on the outskirts of London.

Soon, riders on horseback flew from the gates at breakneck speed. Terrance and Sybil anticipated that they would turn to come toward them, but were surprised when they continued straight toward the city instead. One last rider emerged behind the others; it was William who followed the entourage.

At that point the alarm bells stopped. However, in the distance, the bells of London rang out over the city. From where Terrance and Sybil were, the prison walls and the crest of the hill on which Newgate stood obscured their view.

"Let's see what has saved our hides this fine September night," Terrance said, holding Sybil's hand and guiding her to the far side of the walls to get a better look at London.

As they approached the crest of the hill, a glow lit the night sky. When they reached the horizon, they could see that a section of London was burning, fueled by winds from the sea toward the interior of the city. It wasn't large yet, but you could see that it had consumed several buildings in the Pudding Lane area and was just beginning to spread to Fish Street Hill near St. Margaret's church.

"Oh, my God, Terrance. It's heading toward our home," she yelled, turning to run back to the prison to find Douglass.

Grabbing her arm and turning her back to face him, Terrance asked, "Whose home do you speak of?"

"Mine and Douglass's, of course. There is no time to explain now. We have to save Morgan and the babe." Terrance had no choice but to follow Sybil to the roadway where they were lucky enough to find Douglass among the hoards of people coming from the prison.

Many were on their way to their own homes to rescue loved ones and salvage anything they could before their houses were consumed by the fire. The homes in the city were made of dry wood, with straw carpet and thatched roofs, and were highly flammable. Fire in London had destroyed most of the city before, and with very little organized prevention, this fire would be no different.

Chaos broke out within the city as the flames licked their way through homes at such breakneck speed that no one was able to salvage much of anything. Looting and fighting broke out on every corner, with most of the Londoner's making their way to the higher grounds of the countryside to wait and watch.

Douglass, Sybil and Terrance fought their way through the masses, combatting the onslaught of panicked families fleeing in terror. The flames hadn't reached the market place where, just days ago, Sybil had bought fresh fruit and vegetables. However, the winds were picking up and the stench of burning homes wafted toward them as they finally came to the cottage that Douglass and Sybil shared as man and wife.

Douglass burst through the door but found no one in sight. Sybil called out to Morgan, lighting a lantern on the table with a wick from the smoldering fire, but heard no answer. She carried the lantern in the direction of the bedroom door, holding it high to light her way. Just then

Morgan burst out of the doorway, baby in one arm and a knife in her outstretched hand.

"Oh, it's you," she yelped, putting the knife down by her side. "I thought you were me no good husband. That bloke came and beat the living Christ out of me for not having his sup ready. Then he headed out the door. Said he was going to pray for forgiveness at St. Margaret's church."

Sybil gasped, seeing Morgan's blackened eye. "St. Margaret's church?"

"Aye, if you ask me, I'd wager he was down on Fish Street at the pub again. Been gone a long while."

"Morgan, I can't explain right now, but you must come with us," Sybil demanded.

"Hey!" Morgan shouted. "Last time I saw ye, ye were with child and ye weren't no doxy either. And who's this mighty fellow anyway?" she asked, pointing to Terrance.

"As I said Morgan, I can't explain now but you must come with us. The city is on fire and it's spreading fast. This house will be gone come morning. Please get what you can and let us all go now," Sybil said, grabbing what she could and shoving the items in a gunnysack.

They hadn't made much progress in packing when there was a knock at the door. The four fell quiet for just a moment, each questioning who it might be since most of the neighbors had already left their homes for the safety of outlying areas.

"Must be me bloke of a husband come back to take another poke at me," Morgan said approaching the door. "It'll be me making the only poke tonight."

Before he could stop her, Morgan threw open the door. Terrance ducked behind it before whomever was on the other side caught sight of him. It wasn't Morgan's husband, but it was someone that Douglass and Sybil knew. Gregory stood grinning at the young woman who stood before him, then looked past her to meet Sybil's eyes.

"You're a hard one to catch up with milady," he said, bowing sarcastically. "When I saw the three of you meet up outside the prison walls, I knew I was onto your game. Is she a sister or a doxy?" he asked, stepping inside, directing his question at Douglass, yet never taking his eyes off Sybil.

He didn't see it coming. Terrance hit him in the neck with the side of his hand in a swift, chopping motion. Gregory fell unconscious on the cottage floor, while Morgan let out a scream and dashed behind Sybil, her eyes as wide as saucers.

"Don't be afraid of him, Morgan." Sybil comforted her.

"It's not him that frightens me, Sybil. Look!" She pointed toward the open door where flames were licking at the houses on the opposite side of the lane.

"Douglass, bring him. Morgan, you're coming with us now!" Sybil shouted.

Heaving Gregory onto his shoulders, Douglass led the way out of the cottage and down the lane, away from the fire. Sybil followed him, dragging Morgan, the babe clutched in her arms. Terrance carried the gunnysacks and kept a keen eye out for any other persons who might be inclined to follow them.

Soon the five were on the outskirts of the city, along with thousands more who fled for their lives to safety. Hopelessness and desperation were thick in the air as people watched the blaze engulf their homes and shops; their livelihood eaten up by the unfeeling inferno. The group didn't stop their flight, but continued on, with Terrance taking the lead.

"Where will we go?" Sybil asked, catching up to him.

"I know a place where my men will come, sooner rather than later. With any luck, we won't have much of a wait before they arrive."

"But Terrance, how do they know you will be there?"

"They don't. That is a chance we'll have to take. We can't stay here and when our young friend wakes up," he pointed to Gregory who was still unconscious and slung over Douglass's shoulder, "we don't want to be around someone who will listen to what he has to say about all this."

"You're right about that, Terrance," Douglass said, slightly short of breath. "He could get us all caught once he realizes that we have a prisoner from Newgate with us."

"Oh, my Lord!" Morgan exclaimed. "We'll all end up there if we're caught."

Sybil stopped, turning to Morgan, who almost slammed into her back. "You don't have to be a part of this, Morgan. We can get you to safety somewhere."

"Not be a part of this? Blimey Sybil, if you ain't the most peculiar sort of woman. From what I can see here, ye have two men who seemed to be husband-like and one who's wanting to be," Morgan said, pointing to Gregory. "I wouldn't want to miss this for all the tea in China."

Giggling, Morgan walked past Sybil, who stood open-mouthed in astonishment. Douglass and Terrance, giving Sybil sideways looks, followed her in silence. It was Sybil who didn't seem to understand the implications here.

"I will be needing to fetch up the rest of me brood from me mum, you know," Morgan called back to the group. "She doesn't live far from here and we can get food and water for the trip. How far did yea say this place was?"

The Revelation  Chapter 40

Jillian and Marcus's wedding day had arrived; September 5th turned out to be a glorious day. A bit of haze hovered in the gardens in the early morning but a slight breeze cleared it away as the sun rose above the treetops. Marcus sat at the dining table enjoying a fresh cup of piping hot coffee that Constance had brewed for him. The stillness of the house grated on his nerves this morning as he reflected on his decision to wed the lovely Jillian. Had he made the right choice? It seemed to him that there wasn't any other. Making amends for his behavior was one thing Marcus felt the need to do.

The plans for the wedding had taken a turn for the worse when news spread about the great fire raging in London. Most of the guests had fled the city to wait out the fire and would not be able to make the trip to Ely for the wedding. The countryside was in chaos, with homeless people fleeing the city to find a relative willing to take them in. By the look of things, the wedding was going to be a private affair with very few guests, most of them being the staff from the household.

Marcus didn't find these changes the least bit stressful, for the grand affair that had been originally planned was quite overwhelming for him. Constance had made all the preparations with ease and diligence, putting a loving touch into every detail, but Marcus was ill prepared for the influx of nosey bigots who relished the thought of gaining insight into the reason for the immediacy of this marriage. After all, he was a very private person and didn't want his affairs up for public ridicule.

Perhaps his irritation was caused by something else. Maybe it was the fact that although marrying Jillian seemed to be the right thing to do, second thoughts had begun to haunt him ever since he had talked her into it. And he had talked her into it, after all. Jillian was not a willing partner at first, but after Marcus explained that the child she carried would need a father or be considered a bastard under the law, Jillian had acquiesced, agreeing that it was for the best. So why was he taunted by regrets? He would have a beautiful wife, a mother for his son, and a new babe on the way.

Just then, Constance entered the dining room.

"Oh, Marcus, milord. I didn't expect to see you still here with everything that needs to be done before you leave for the ceremony and all."

"I was just thinking about things."

"Just thinking? What about?"

"About, whether or not this is the right thing to do, Connie."

"Now's a good time to be thinking those kinds of thoughts."

"I know, it sounds crazy, but I'm not sure. I just feel like something isn't right about it, that's all."

"Marcus. Jillian is a lovely girl. Ian loves her. She'll be a good mum for him. She will be very grateful to have you for a husband."

"I don't want her gratitude, I want her love. I don't have it. I feel her withdrawal every time I try to hold her."

"Give her time, Marcus. She'll come to love you as much as I do." Constance blurted out. "Oh, I mean as an employer, of course."

"Of course." Marcus said angrily, catching her off guard. "She'll love me as an employer." With that he stormed out of the dining room and out the front door of Havenwood.

Constance stood, eyes transfixed on the door. She'd never seen Marcus so angry and unhappy. Realizing that his outburst distressed her greatly, Constance didn't understand why he'd lashed out at her that way. How long had she devoted her heart to him, knowing that there would never be a chance for any relationship between them besides employer and employee? She served him and his family well, seeing him through the worst of times, when the babes had died and then his lovely wife had followed them to heaven. She cared for Marcus and Ian, making sure that their needs were met and nursing them back to health in times of sickness, all the while hiding the love that she felt in her heart for him. Even now, she did everything in her power to make this wedding happy for him, and yet it wasn't enough. How could he still be unhappy?

The only thing left to do was to get Jillian, Ian and Marcus to the cathedral in Ely for the ceremony. Surely everything would be fine once the vows were spoken and things settled down. If only her heart didn't ache so much to be the one taking the vows with Marcus.

*   *   *   *   *

The cathedral was empty except for a few guests who had weathered the trip to Ely through crowded roads filled with people fleeing the Great Fire of London. It had burned for three days through homes and businesses, sweeping the narrow streets clean of garbage, rats and run-down makeshift homes where, just a year ago, thousands had perished from the plague.

Jillian fretted over her dress, catching Constance and her handmaid off guard. It was uncharacteristic of her to be in such a state. Constance thought it must be the excitement of the day catching up to everyone.

When the organ began to play, Jillian's signal for the ceremony to start, there was a moment of panic. Doubts that had plagued her the last few days rose up once more to make her question what she was doing. Somehow she just didn't feel right about marrying Marcus. There were so many unanswered questions. Was she doing the best thing?

Jillian thought about the things that Marcus told her, about how he had purchased her from an evil man. He was truthful with her. For that, she was grateful but there was something missing in this union. Love. She could come to love Marcus in time; he was a kind and gentle man. Jillian already loved Ian, the little boy who called her mother; he was her greatest joy. But, in her heart, Jillian felt that her devotion was for someone else, someone from a past that she didn't remember. Surely, it wasn't the man named Gavin who had treated her so horribly?

The organ music resounded in the waiting chamber; it was time for the ceremony to begin. Jillian started to say something to Constance but stopped when she opened the doors, spilling sunlight into the darkened room. Constance ushered Jillian from the room to the cathedral entrance, positioning her in the center of the long isle leading the way to the altar where Marcus and Ian stood waiting for her, their faces beaming with anticipation.

Jillian gazed at the man she was about to marry. Marcus looked so young and dapper in his blue waistcoat and leggings. His sable brown hair gleamed in the light from the stained glass windows that sent beams of every color down upon the altar below. The brown of Marcus's eyes deepened as he caught Jillian's gaze, seeking to assure her that they would be good together.

Maybe it was the brightness of the sunbeams that made his eyes seem so dark but suddenly Jillian could see eyes so black and void of emotion that she felt the need to flee. Panicked, Jillian looked away, trying to clear this vision from her mind. Fighting for control, she took deep and steady breaths, forcing herself to look at Marcus once more. When she did, all that she saw were the eyes of a sweet and gentle man. The darkness that she had seen before was gone. Still, there was an odd sense of impending doom about the cathedral this day.

Timidly, Jillian stepped forward, following Constance, who was her only witness. The music of the wedding march echoed throughout the cathedral but Jillian could not hear it for the ringing in her ears. She concentrated on keeping in step with Constance by watching her feet as they made progress toward the altar and Marcus. As she got closer, the ringing became louder, becoming almost unbearable, making her head ache and spin. She blinked her eyes several times attempting to clear her vision, searching for something steady to focus on.

It was Marcus who saw her distress, reaching out to her, supporting her by taking her hands in his. She looked into his eyes, finding some comfort and strength.

All at once, chaos broke out in the foyer outside the cathedral. Marcus pulled Jillian to him protectively as the doors opened with a resounding bang. Light streamed in, illuminating the barren pews. Jillian and Marcus swung around to face the intruders; neither knowing who or what they would encounter. The unwanted guests' faces were in shadow.

"Jillian!" one of them shouted.

"Stop the ceremony!" another cried out, advancing toward the altar, "She is already wed."

Beyond the advancing men, Jillian focused on one figure, a man who leaned upon a shorter person whose braided hair swung to the side. When the two stepped forward, where their faces could be seen, Jillian gasped in recognition.

"Gavin?" Jillian whispered.

"Gavin?" Marcus yelled. "He is not Gavin."

"Aye, but I am," the man exclaimed. "I am Gavin. I am Jillian's husband."

A collective gasp rang throughout the cathedral. The few guests present began to whisper, the noise buzzing in Jillian's ears. She didn't take her eyes off the approaching men, watching in bewilderment as the one who claimed to be Gavin leaned upon the shorter man while they made their way to her and Marcus.

As he drew nearer, Jillian suddenly became frightened by his expression of deep sadness and by memories that blasted into her consciousness. Scenes of lovemaking, of pirate ships, hurricanes and death, memories of joy and hate, of cruelty and lust bludgeoned her mind. She felt agony and relief flood her heart. She felt Marcus clutching her tightly and Ian wrapping his arms around her legs as if to never let go. Jillian's heart pounded a wrenching rhythm within her chest, every beat screaming for relief from the pain that invaded her very soul.

Gavin and Sue Ki stopped within an arm's reach of Jillian, while others, Cy and Micah, stood at their sides in anticipation. Jillian looked Gavin over, her eyes drawing to the places where she had witnessed the sword's entrance, his handsome face ashen from the many months of recovering from the wounds inflicted by a deadly sword. A force that she didn't understand pulled her hands toward him, stopping where bandages covered wounds, still healing. Gavin watched her gentle hands move over him, feeling a warm glow each time they stopped. When her fingers came close to touching him, Gavin flinched in anticipation.

Their eyes met once more, hers questioning, his reaching out for her love. Jillian brought her hand up to caress Gavin's cheek. The instant she touched him, pain so intense that she almost collapsed, bore through her. She remembered everything all at once, the fight between Gavin and Jason, the sword plunging into Gavin's heart, taking his life from hers. Her hand jerked back from him with that realization. He died that night, or at least she thought he had. She touched the place where the sword had drained his blood onto the ground, pooling before her eyes.

The moment her hand touched his chest, it was as if a lightning bolt seared through her body. Gavin felt its power, fearfully grabbing her hand to push it away, but was only held more firmly by an unknown force emanating through Jillian and into him. He experienced heat of great intensity attacking his wounds, barely healed after months of Sue Ki's ministrations. Gavin looked at Jillian, seeing that she was lost in a deep trance, her pale skin glowing blue with celestial light, her eyes closed, her face calm with an angelic smile. It comforted him, giving him peace from the nagging pain of not being able to save her from Jason's evil clutches, freeing him from the guilt and pain he had carried these many months.

He clung to her hand, feeling life return to his desperate soul, knowing that she was healing him from the inside out. This transfer of strength took only seconds, and when Jillian opened her eyes, she realized what was happening and what she was giving to Gavin. Smiling knowingly, Jillian mouthed, "I love you", then collapsed against Gavin's chest in exhaustion.

Sweeping Jillian into his arms, Gavin asked the priest, who hadn't seem to see this miracle, if there was any place he could take her to recover. After a puzzled look at the two, the priest pointed to the waiting chamber beyond the foyer where Jillian had prepared for the ceremony. Everyone in the cathedral watched as the once weak and wounded man carried Jillian away as if she were weightless in his arms. They hadn't seen the healing exchange and knew not what had transpired between the two.

Hours later, Jillian awoke to the sweet smile of Ian's little face watching for signs that she would return to them. Not saying a word, Ian winked at her and ran from the room, yelling at the top of his lungs for his father.

Still dazed, Jillian lay there reflecting on what had happened. She was stunned to discover that she remembered everything. Times that were once blanks in her memory were very clear to her now. She remembered times from her childhood that were once a source of great pain, but now seemed comforting to know, just to have the knowledge that they did happen and were part of who she was. The secrets of all those years, once lost to her, were now part of her and Jillian felt a great sense of peace come over her.

There was something else she remembered. It was something, that when she was a child, she thought she had dreamt, but now she knew it was not a dream. It explained everything to her, all the years of feeling like she wasn't part of her family or her surroundings, the many years of longing to be somewhere else but never knowing where she might go. It all made sense to her now, but how she would find what she knew was her destiny, she did not know. It was a journey that she would have to make.

Voices from the foyer broke into her silent contemplation. She remembered Gavin's loving arms wrapped protectively around her after her collapse. She remembered those same arms wrapping her in his warm embrace as they made love on the sandy beach at the cove, in the waters of the pond beneath the falls, and when he carried her from the white cliff base to the ship that she made her home.

Her thoughts turned to her father and the men of the Pegasus. Cy, Micah, and Sue Ki had journeyed here with Gavin to find her and return her to the people she knew as her family. But where was her father now? Why hadn't he come with them to take her back to where she belonged?

Gavin entered the chamber, crossing over to the chaise where Jillian lay. Behind him were Marcus, Constance and Ian, their faces pale with worry.

"How are you feeling, my love?" Gavin asked, taking her hand in his.

"How are you feeling?" she asked, bringing his hands to her lips to kiss them.

"I am fine now that I have you back, Jillian."

"I, too, am fine now," she reassured him. "Now that I know."

"Know what, Jillian?"

"Now is not the time, my love. There are things I need to do before we leave."

"You can't leave me!" Ian cried, flinging himself into Jillian's arms.

"Ah, but I must, my sweet. I am not who you thought I was." Looking up at Marcus, Jillian explained, "I have many secrets that I cannot share with you now, but someday we will meet again and I will tell you tales that will make your head spin."

"But I don't want you to go!" Ian cried.

"I know, but I must. For now, I wish to speak to your father and Constance. Can you guard the door while we talk?" she asked, messing up his hair.

"Yes," Ian said, disappointed to be sent from the room. "Can I kill the dragons?"

"Oh, yes! Please do," Jillian pleaded.

They all watched as Ian, holding his chin high, strutted from the room to slay an unsuspecting dragon.

"I will miss him dearly," Jillian sighed.

"You can't mean to go?" Constance asked.

"Yes, I am going back to where I belong, Constance. Marcus, I am so sorry for everything and grateful that you were the one to come to my rescue. If it were not for you I would still be lost in the fog of my mind."

"I was glad to do it, Jillian," he said, grasping her outstretched hand.

"There is one more thing I would ask of you before I go."

"Anything, Jillian," Marcus replied. "What can I do?"

"Please, marry Constance."

The motion of the horse beneath Jillian gave new meaning to the word sore. With every step of this powerful steed, the chafing of her raw thighs grew in intensity. They had ridden for many hours, putting as much distance between Ely and themselves as they could. The ship would meet them at the cove on the night of the seventh and they had waited an extra day to leave.

It seemed only proper to stay for a time after the marriage of Constance and Marcus. It was a small ceremony with only the few guests who were originally there to witness Jillian's marriage to Marcus staying to see what would happen next. They were more than happy to celebrate the nuptials of Constance and Marcus once Jillian convinced them how much they loved each other.

It was obvious that Constance was a better match for Marcus. Constance was more than willing to marry once Marcus looked into her eyes and declared that he had always loved her. Jillian knew in her heart that the two were meant to be together, feeling that all the warning signs she had experienced before her own ceremony, were a clear sign that these two were the ones who should be getting married. Or, could it have been that she knew Gavin was approaching the cathedral? Whatever the reason, it had all worked out for the best.

Gavin shifted behind her, pulling her against him to take some of the pressure off her thighs. Her breath hissed through her teeth, for there was no comfortable position for her at this point, her skin not being used to such abrasion.

"Does it hurt much?" Gavin asked.

"Yes, I'm afraid I'm not used to riding astride in these types of garments," she laughed, remembering Constance's gasp when she saw the britches that Jillian donned for the ride to the cove. Thank goodness Cy had decided to bring them along, just in case. But regardless of what she wore, her tender skin was just not up to the punishing pace that they maintained for such a long time.

"We are almost there. I'll send the men ahead to see if the cove is unoccupied. I think we will spend the night near the stream leading to the falls," he whispered, his breath warming Jillian's neck beneath her ear. "We need some time alone."

Gavin stopped the stallion, allowing Cy and Micah to pass, telling them to go on ahead and that he and Jillian would meet them in the morning at the pond. Each one gave the two a knowing look of envy. Jillian smiled back at them, winking at Micah who she recognized as Andrew the hired man at the estate. Once news of the wedding was announced, Micah had left to alert the ship's crew that Gavin would have to wait to heal any further. Jillian's rescue had to happen before the wedding. If not for Micah following Jason's trail, Jillian would not have been reunited with Gavin. She was thankful to him for that. Sue Ki stopped his horse before going with the others.

"You be fine, missy?"

"Yes, Sue Ki. I'll be all right. Gavin is with me now."

"Yes. You be velly good fo each other."

"Yes," Gavin said. "Velly good."

Sue Ki smiled at the two, tipping his straw hat as he kicked his mount into a trot to catch up with Cy and Micah.

"How does he manage it?"

"Manage what?"

"Staying on his horse while bouncing about like that."

They laughed as they watched Sue Ki balance between his horse and the ground, making his way up the trail to join the others.

Gavin turned the stallion away from the trail, toward the cover of the forest, where he hoped to find a place for he and Jillian to stay for the night. The sun was just beginning to set but there was still enough light to help them make their way to the stream. It wasn't far before they found a brook and a good place to make camp. Gavin swung himself down from the back of the mighty steed, being careful not to offset Jillian, who shifted uncomfortably in the saddle. Stress from the hasty trip showed in her features. He knew that she hadn't slept since the journey began last evening and was likely still exhausted from the events at the church.

Touching his side, where once there had been a mortal wound, Gavin thought about what had happened and how grateful he was that he had found Jillian when he did. Marcus took great pains explaining to Gavin his reason for marrying his wife. Jason had signed Gavin's name on the papers that gave Marcus possession of his greatest love. One part of Gavin wanted to throttle Marcus for it, but the other wanted to thank him. His greatest fear was to never find Jillian, living the rest of his life knowing that she was in the hands of an evil so depraved that even God could not save her from it.

"You're thinking about him, aren't you?" Jillian asked. "I can see it in your eyes."

"Yes, I was. But now, I am thinking about you. Can you see a difference?"

"I suppose there is a difference, but it's not in your eyes," she joked, looking at his groin where a bulge began to grow. "Do you know how much I love you, Gavin?"

"Yes, I believe I do. Enough to heal me and then torture my existence by making me sit through hours at a wedding celebration and then torment me by riding before me on a horse who undoubtedly knows the scent of my rutting heart."

"Get me down, Gavin. I cannot do it myself. I have to touch you now."

Her demand was met with his own urgency. It had been too long since they made love next to the pond. It had been too long since they held each other in their arms, joining their lives together. Gavin reached up to gently lift Jillian from the saddle, the movement causing her much pain, which she tried with all her heart to ignore. When her feet touched the ground, her legs collapsed beneath her, but Gavin caught her to him, lifting her into his arms.

"We'll have time for that later. First, I must see to your legs."

Gavin took her to the stream's bank and set her down upon a stone before retrieving her bags from the stallion. She watched Gavin unfold a blanket, spreading it out for her to lie upon, then search the bags for a nightgown for her to wear and some soft cloths to wash her wounds with. He moved with purpose and strength and a gentleness that warmed her heart. Jillian's palm splayed protectively across her taunt abdomen. When fitting into the trousers, they stretched to the brink of tearing but eased after a time, giving Jillian a sense of security that the babe would not be harmed by the hard ride to the cove. Thinking of the tiny life growing inside her made Jillian all the more aware that Gavin may not be the father. How would she tell him? Would he send her away from him?

"What troubles you, Jillian?"

"There is much that I must tell you, Gavin," she said, looking deep into his eyes. "I have remembered all of it, the time with Jason and the time before. I remember all of it. But, there is more that I remember. Things that happened when I was a child."

"You must tell me all of it Jillian. Once you share yourself fully with me, I will help you bear the burden of it." He gently lifted her, placing her on the blanket. "First, I must see to your wounds as you saw to mine."

He began to undress her, removing the leather shoes given to her by Marcus for the ride. They were finely made, part of his wife's wardrobe, left behind by her family after her death. The britches that she wore were snuggly fit. Removing them without hurting her was nearly impossible but Jillian didn't flinch, even though Gavin knew she was in pain. He winced when he saw the raw chafing of her inner thighs, the welts threatening to burst the swollen skin. Gavin dipped the soft cloth he'd found in the stream, bringing it to cool her wounds. Jillian's breath hissed through her teeth when the cloth touched her.

"I am sorry for your torture," Gavin apologized. "We should have rested more along the way. I pray that the babe is well within your belly."

Jillian's look of surprise took Gavin off guard, for surely she was aware that he knew her state.

"How did you know? Is it because of my girth?" she asked.

"How could I not? For you hadn't had your woman's flow long before we went to the cove." He smiled at her disbelief. "I wanted to speak with you about it then, but you were so worried about your father. I couldn't burden you with more to fret about."

Wringing out the cloth yet another time, Gavin placed it on her again, looking squarely into her eyes. "I was so frightened that you might lose the babe when Jason took you. I didn't protect you, as I should have. I didn't die but something inside me did when I lost you. And then, Micah made contact with the ship. He'd found you and you were well, but did not remember him. I thought that it was a good thing. I only hoped that once I came to you that you would remember me."

"Oh, Gavin. You are my salvation. Somewhere deep inside of me during that time you were with me, guarding me from harm, promising to come for me. I saw you suffering in my dreams. It was more than I could bear. So the coward that I am fled to that place inside where there is nothing but peace. When I awoke, I nearly killed Jason trying to flee, but he captured me yet again. That is when Marcus bought me before Jason could kill me. I blocked it all out. It was easier to forget than to deal with the pain of losing you. I thought that you died. And a part of me died with you that night. Until I saw you in the chapel, I had little reason to live in that world."

Jillian flung her arms around Gavin, clutching him tightly, sobbing into his strong chest. He held her against him as she cried out the pain of her ordeal, his own tears joining with hers. It was some time later before either of them spoke. It was Jillian who broke the silence.

"I need you, Gavin."

"I will never leave you again, Jillian."

"No, I mean that I need you now, Gavin, deep inside me. I want you to claim me once more. Claim me from the evil that has come between us."

Saying not another word, Gavin removed the rest of Jillian's clothes, baring her naked body before him. Jillian watched as he stood to remove his own clothes, undoing the laces of his high boots.

"Let me," Jillian said, moving his hands away so that she could undress him.

She was on her knees in front of him, gloriously nude, her pale skin radiating in the falling darkness of night. Jillian slipped each boot from his strong legs, feeling his calf muscles tighten with each movement. Her eyes were even with the laces of his belted pants, his erection vivid beneath the leather layer. Her fingers trembled, becoming inadequate at the task of relieving him of his trousers.

Gavin's own hands shook as he helped her unfasten the belt and untie the bindings at his waist. Again she pushed his hands away, following the descent of leather with her gentle touch. Once the pants were at his feet, he stepped out of them, being careful not to trip and fall.

Her hands were on him again and he groaned, aching, giving way to the pleasure that her touch gave his body. He didn't wait for her to rise and remove his blouse, for if he waited there was no telling what would happen. He flung it from him, not caring where it landed.

Jillian felt his urgency, but wanted more of him. She wanted to taste and tease him into life. Hugging him around the waist, she could feel the tautness of his buttocks under her grasp, his manhood caressing the side of her neck. She began to kiss him then, there, where a trail of fine golden hair drew a map to the treasure of him. They were soft kisses, licking kisses that drove Gavin wild with pleasure, his fingers entangled in her hair, his head thrown back in ecstasy. Soon her mouth found the length of him, his smoothness fascinating her tongue as she drew his measure with each savory taste. It was more than his undoing. Gavin fell to his knees, holding her at arm's length.

"Nay, Jillian. I can stand no more," he murmured, his breath catching in his lungs.

Gavin kissed her then, and his flavor fresh upon her lips gave him even more cause to lose control. His tongue probed her lips, beckoning them to part for his exploration. Jillian conceded, meeting his tongue with her own. They circled each other in a dance of love that grew more intense with each nip and lick, their breaths becoming gasps as the seconds passed. Their hands explored, finding scars and marks of times now seeming so far in the past. It was a cleansing of some sort, a joining of two beings who had never really been apart.

Their bodies fell together, lying upon the blanket in the moonlit night, intertwined in a fusion of souls seemingly lost but now found. Gavin rolled Jillian beneath him, careful not to injure her. He felt the length of her under him, her breasts full and round against him, his member nestled between her tender thighs. Gavin raised himself to gaze into Jillian's eyes. They were brilliant with light and filled with tears.

"Have I hurt you?"

"Aye, it hurts to be this close to you, to want you so deep inside me that you can never depart. It pains me to have just one moment when you are not with me."

"But, I am here with you now, Jillian. I will ease your pain and give you great pleasure at the same time."

His knee nudged her legs apart with little resistance. Jillian was ready for him to fill her again, to feel him against the womb where his child lay. But, he did not yet enter her.

"Gavin, please."

"Your pleasure first, my love."

Just then she felt his hand slip between their bodies, his gentle fingers sliding inside the folds of her womanhood. Gavin caught her gasp with his lips as they claimed her, challenging her resistance, but there was none. She matched his adoration with her own, driving him further toward the climax of their love. His fingers moved with a rhythm of their own, bringing her nearer and nearer to the brink of despair with the wanting she felt. His other hand molded her nipples to ripe peaks, each tightening to a painful intensity that beckoned to be healed. It was his mouth that answered, as he suckled each with such great heat that Jillian almost exploded with it, her fingers digging into the muscles of his shoulders.

Gavin could bear it no more and knew that Jillian felt the same. He eased his body upward finding the entrance that called for him. Jillian wrapped her legs around his strong hips, meeting his thrust with her own, setting the rhythm that drove them together to the edge, the sound of their love echoing throughout the forest. They came together, each climaxing in a spasm of pure pleasure, Gavin's breath hissing through his teeth, Jillian gasping for air.

Lying together in a tangle of blankets, clothes, and Jillian's long tresses, their breathing calmed enough for them to gain awareness once more. It was night, pitch black, yet they could see each other more clearly than ever before. Jillian marveled at the beauty of her man. Gavin admired the strength of his lovely wife. The night grew cold and they were weary. Gavin wrapped the blanket around them, enveloping their bodies within. As Jillian started to speak, Gavin put his finger to her love swollen lips.

"Nay, we are both tired and you need to rest, for the babe. We will talk in the morning while waiting for the Pegasus to arrive. Tonight, we will sleep and dream of our future. I love you, Jillian."

"And I love you, Gavin. Sleep well," she said, sighing against his neck.

"Sleep well, my love," Gavin said, drifting into slumber with Jillian safe in his embrace.

Deep into the night Jillian awoke with a start. Had she heard something? She listened to the night, motionless beside Gavin, his breathing serene and steady. She listened for a long while before deciding that she had heard nothing but the silence of the night forest. With little effort, Jillian slept once more, nuzzling closer to Gavin.

Sometime later, Jillian awoke again, this time having to relieve herself. Easing quietly from beneath Gavin's arm, Jillian crept a short distance away to take care of her needs. While returning, she stepped on something; it was Gavin's blouse, thrown to the side earlier in unbridled haste. She pulled it over her head, finding the sleeves with her hands before bringing it down.

It was then that she saw him; a scream caught in her throat. He was just inches from her, a knife pressed against her temple. Jillian glanced over to where Gavin lay. He was asleep, oblivious to what was happening. She shook her head; this could not be happening again.

"Back up, into the forest," Jason commanded, but Jillian did not move. The knife came down to Jillian's belly where her unborn child rested within the safety of her womb. "Do it now or I will slit your whore's belly open and devour the babe before your eyes."

Believing that Jason would do it, Jillian began to walk backward, not taking her eyes from his. Once they were away from the camp, Jason turned Jillian around, grasping her by the waist; the knife pressed more firmly to her breast.

"I have dreamt of this night. I knew you would return to find the Pegasus. Those dimwits are more predictable than the seasons. And now, I have you."

"You will never have me, Jason. I know your secret. I know who you really are."

"Don't taunt me, Jillian, else I may not wait to take you far enough away that poor Gavin can't hear your screams for mercy."

"You won't go far." Gavin said, from behind them.

"Gavin!" Jillian cried out, whirling around to see him.

"Don't come any closer," Jason commanded. "I will kill her and my child."

"It is not your child." Jillian screamed.

"What did he tell you, my sweet? That it is his?" he sneered, his breath hot against her cheek, as he pulled her further away from Gavin. "Of course, he would tell you that. But you bled the first week that I took you and none after that."

"You lie!" Gavin raged, matching each step.

"Why would I lie? What would I have to gain?"

His steps quickened, pulling Jillian deeper into the forest. She struggled for balance but he held her tightly. When she would have fallen, he dragged her backward even faster than before. Jillian pried at his arms to no avail; he had much greater strength than she.

Gavin watched each excruciating step taking Jillian further from him. He would not let this happen again; this time would have a different outcome. This time Jason would die.

Ducking behind a tree, Gavin crouched down, watching every step that Jason took. He looked for something, anything that he could use for a weapon, having nothing with him but his wits. When they were just out of sight, Gavin circled to the side, hoping to come up behind them in the cover of darkness.

"You see, your brave man has given up on saving you," Jason sneered into Jillian's ear. "He's left you to fend for yourself."

Jason continued to force Jillian to come with him, all the while watching the forest around them for Gavin's attack. He knew Gavin would not let him take Jillian. It fit his plan perfectly, to goad Gavin into another fight, finishing him off this time. He hated Gavin with all that he was. Terrance had favored the boy ever since he'd found him in the road being beaten by his father. Who was Gavin anyway, but a beggar's son with no means to make his way in the world? If Terrance hadn't come along that day and rescued Gavin, Jason would be the first mate of the Pegasus and first in line to captain her after Terrance was taken to prison. Where was that beggar's son now, Jason wondered.

Jillian calculated how she would free herself from Jason's grasp. If it weren't for the knife that he held at her breast, she could easily escape. In an instant, Jillian remembered something that Sophie had taught her as a child. Sophie had assured her that if she concentrated hard enough, she could move things with her mind. Feeling powerful with the memory of taking a ball from a neighboring bully with nothing but her mind, Jillian stiffened her body, concentrating on the knife flying from Jason's hand and into the forest. But, nothing happened.

"What are you doing, whore?" Jason seethed. "Why do you stiffen?"

"You are going to die this night. Do you know that Jason?" Jillian laughed. "You will die by your own making."

"It will not be I who does the dying, whore. Your lover, Gavin, is the one who will die, right before your eyes."

"No!" Jillian screamed.

She felt it then, the power. Thinking of the knife once more, Jillian saw it fly from Jason's hand, burying its tip deeply into a tree some twenty paces away. His surprise was her release and she flung herself away from him, running full force into the forest. His footsteps were close behind her, but she didn't turn to look, only ran faster away from his clutches. The forest tore at the bare skin of her legs, striking her, leaving scratches that encouraged her to go on, for they were minor compared to what she knew Jason was capable of doing.

She was a fool for running, but now that he had dropped his only weapon, Jason could only catch her and use her as a weapon against Gavin. He knew Gavin followed them, for he could hear him not far behind. Getting to Jillian before Gavin caught up was his only salvation.

The knife was hot in Gavin's hand. He'd been crouched down behind a tree just off to the side of Jason and Jillian, when suddenly the knife had come toward him, just barely missing his head. It had taken some strength to pull it out of the tree before following. Although he'd hidden well, Jason must have seen him and thrown the knife, hoping to end his life. Gavin was catching up to him. It wouldn't be long now before he would kill Jason.

Jillian stopped suddenly. She had run straight into the wall of a cliff, the slick stone barring her flight. Her chest was heaving and her side ached from the pace of her escape. She was against a stone wall with nowhere to hide. It was then that she saw the yellow eyes staring down at her from the ledge above. Jillian backed away slowly, making no abrupt moves to startle the cat further. Then, there was a growl behind her. Jillian turned slowly to see another cat, not quite as large but just as threatening, lying on the low branch of a nearby tree. Two, she thought, but that was not the last one to enter the scene. From out of the shadows came a giant panther, her sleek black fur glistening in the moonlight. The cat walked slowly toward Jillian, whose heart raced loudly in her ears. The yellow eyes scanned Jillian then she backed away into the shadow, staring at the area from which Jillian had come.

It was then that Jason caught up to Jillian, bursting forth with fierce determination, bellowing as he lunged for her. She was faster than he had anticipated and avoided his grasp, leaving him to fall to the earth at her feet.

Before Jillian could take a step, Jason grabbed her ankle, propelling her to the ground. As he rose above her in the night, Jillian heard the scream of the mighty cat, raising the hair on her arms and head. She knew this was the end of them both and braced herself for the attack.

Jason had little time to see the cat before she flew through the air, taking him to the ground with her. In that very instant, the other two panthers were upon him, attacking their prey from all sides. Jillian felt herself being dragged backward by strong arms. She didn't look to see who had come to her aid, knowing that it was Gavin. Jillian couldn't take her eyes off Jason and the cats.

He put up a mighty fight, Gavin would have to give him that, but he was no match for the three cats. Gavin tried to take Jillian away so that she would not have to witness Jason's demise but Jillian would have none of it. At one point she turned to Gavin, her eyes pleading him to help Jason, but she said nothing, turning back to watch death come to him. It wasn't long before the big female had Jason by the throat, her mighty jowls clamped tightly around his neck, smothering the last breath from him. The two smaller cats, obviously her cubs of last spring, held some part of him in their mouths, mimicking their mother's kill.

With Gavin at her side, Jillian moved a little closer, not sure what she wanted to see but knowing that she must. It was then that their eyes met, Jillian's meeting Jason's. Gavin saw Jason smile as his eyes closed for the last time. Jillian saw it too and looked away quickly, covering her mouth to squelch a sob.

"It's over, Jillian. He's gone," Gavin said taking her into his arms. "Let us leave this place."

It was then Gavin saw the glow of light on the trees behind them as they walked. He felt Jillian go rigid in his arms, stopping abruptly and turning to see where the light came from.

The cats yowled and hissed, then jumped away from the dead form lying splayed against the ground. Jillian stepped closer as the cats leaped into the night. She felt Gavin pulling her away, back from the apparition that grew from Jason body, away from the light that grew ever so brightly. It called to her, beckoning her to come closer. When she did, the glow turned from white to red and Jillian felt impending danger and fear. The glow called to her, Jillian tried to resist, but when she did, the light grew even fiercer. She watched it rise from Jason's body and float in the air toward her. Gavin cried out and placed himself between Jillian and the entity that threatened them, holding the knife high as if to slice the being from the air. It hovered there, waiting for what, they didn't know.

Suddenly, Gavin heard Jillian's voice from behind him. She was speaking in a tongue foreign to him. It sounded like some kind of chant that she repeated over and over. Gavin didn't take his eyes from what must be Jason's soul, only listened to Jillian chant softly to it. Another voice joined Jillian's. He didn't recognize this woman's voice and turned to see who had come out of the forest.

Sybil walked slowly and steadily toward Jillian and Gavin, her chanting becoming a familiar song to Gavin. From behind Sybil, he could see Terrance and others watching what was happening, their faces shocked and filled with awe. Sybil now stood beside her daughter, and they began to sway to the chanting song, closing their eyes to the apparition of Jason's soul. Gavin watched the color drain from the air. The red mist dissipated toward the ground as if giving up the fight. He didn't understand everything that had happened this night, but knew that with time, he would come to know the powers of the women he loved so dearly.

The song faded with the red glow of Jason's soul. Jillian felt faint and weak, knowing that it was finally over. It was then she realized that her mother stood beside her. She cried out and flung herself into Sybil's arms.

"There, there, Jillian. Nana Sophie would be so proud of you," she cooed.

"I don't understand, Mama."

"I didn't understand until now but after what I just witnessed, I think there is much more that your Nana Sophie may have to teach and tell us."

*   *   *   *   *

Jillian felt the babe stir within her womb. It had been three months since they returned to the Pegasus, and her time for birthing was drawing near. She smiled to herself, feeling that she had never been quite as happy as she was this day. She cupped her rounded belly in her hands feeling the growing bulge heavy against her thighs. Sitting at the helm of the Pegasus was where she felt the safest. Gavin was beside her, enjoying the day just as much as she. They watched Terrance and Sybil stroll hand in hand along the deck, speaking with the crew as they passed. Jillian couldn't remember seeing her mother so happy.

"Can I get you some water?" Gavin asked.

"Yes, that would be wonderful."

He gave her a quick kiss on the cheek and left to fetch the water. Jillian watched him go; his long strides tightening the muscles of his legs. Feeling this happy had to be a fluke, she thought, remembering the night that Jason left this earth.

They had left his body for the cats to claim and made their way to the pond where Terrance and Sybil were camped waiting for the return of the Pegasus. Sybil told Gavin and Jillian how they had rescued Terrance from the prison the very night that the great fire had started. She explained who each of the people were and why they were with them. The one named Gregory didn't seem very happy to be along, but the woman, Morgan, kept him close at hand along with her children. She saw Douglass looking often toward her mother and father with a longing that was palpable. Jillian wasn't quite sure where he stood in all this, other than if it weren't for him, Terrance would still be in Newgate prison.

Jillian found herself amazed by the story; she had never thought of her mother as an adventurous person, but she was wrong. She saw great strength in her mother now and wondered why she hadn't seen it all along. The other things that only she and Sybil talked about, when no one else was around, frightened Jillian but soon they would be at her grandfather's estate and all would be told. At least that is what Sybil had promised.

The baby kicked against her ribs, bringing Jillian back to the present. She stood, massaging the swollen bulk, coming to stand at the railing of the ship. The wind whipped through her tresses and Jillian closed her eyes, savoring the cool mist from the waves lapping against the hull of the Pegasus. It was a glorious feeling, to be here in this moment.

"Where were you just now?" Terrance whispered in Sybil's ear, his breath caressing her lobe.

"Under an oak," she giggled. "Look at our daughter up there so deliriously happy."

"Yes, she has the look about her," Terrance said, bringing Sybil into his arms.

"What look?"

"You know, the look a woman gets when she is with child. That warm glow about her," he chided. "Like the look you get sometimes."

"How did you know?" Sybil asked without turning.

"I'm the Captain. I know everything," Terrance said, holding Sybil tightly against him.

Just then Gavin strolled happily past them, a goblet of water splashing in his hands.

"Here you are, love." Gavin said, giving the goblet to Jillian who drank down the entire contents.

"Thank you, Gavin. I was more parched than I thought."

Gavin moved behind her, embracing her and the babe. Jillian stroked his cheek and then rested her arms over his. They watched the sun dipping lower on the horizon, its crimson glow filling the ocean with fire. The breeze was warm for a December evening, but a storm brewed on the horizon and Jillian knew it was going to be a long voyage to a safe location.

The journey back to her grandfather's estate would not be without peril, but Jillian knew that her destiny lay in the hands of her Nana Sophie. Only she knew the secrets of who Jillian was and what powers lay hidden in the darkness giving her comfort in the worst of times.

Even Sybil was surprised and shocked that a simple lullaby had such great powers. She also wanted answers, and was willing at the risk of capture, to journey back to the estate of her birth to find them.

For now, Jillian was content to embrace Gavin, the man she loved, and the new life that grew inside her heart. For now, at this very moment, all was right in her world.

And so the end began.

Jillian's adventure continues. Victoria James is currently working on her next novel, "The Pegasus Passion, The Soul Seekers".

Prologue to:

The Pegasus Passion—The Soul Seekers

Darkness of night shields a shadowy figure moving like a ghost toward the grand estate. Bundled in a woolen scarf a babe sleeps soundly clutched against the breast of the intruder. The fragrance of freshly sown earth wafts in the wind that catches the black cape shrouding the identity of one on a mission-a mission to change the destiny of a family doomed by years of burden, years of secrecy, years of silence. This night would mark the end of an era filled with longing, and bring forth the beginning of one of promise.

Lanterns, set low for the night, leant little help to the failing eyes of the figure who tripped on the hem of the cape while attempting to enter soundlessly through the servant's entrance, just off the kitchen. Catching balance was made more difficult by the weight of the bundled child, who was not awakened by the jolt. The potion administered to the mother earlier had passed to the child through rich breast milk, making her sleep deeply.

The figure skirted the kitchen, barely breathing, listening for shouts of alarm from the household staff who may have heard the clumsy entrance. No such alert came. The figure quietly made its way to the second floor by way of the servants' stairway, listening and ducking at every creak from the aging mansion.

At the top of the stairway an open door was clearly that of the Master's bedroom. The grandness of the room revealed the status of the owner, who fortunately was not in residence this night.

Once on the second floor, women's voices whispered from behind closed doors. The figure stopped to listen. From the conversation, the intruder determined that one of the people in the room was a nurse maid and the other from the kitchen staff. They were worried about the babe who would not suckle the sweet teat that was being forced into its mouth.

"What more are we to do? The Mistress will not nurse the babe and the babe does not suckle the teat." a young woman fussed.

"There's naught that we can do, Emma. Let nature take its course is all."

Later, the women left the room. The babe lay asleep in the cradle. Out of the shadows crept the figure entering the room with another sleeping babe. Destiny followed with every step.

About the Author

Victoria James and her family live in Fallon, Nevada. She has four children and four grand children who are her inspirations. She is currently working on an Associate degree and practices Reiki and Kinesiology. The Pegasus Passion is her first novel.